CHILD *of* AWARENESS

ABIGAIL SILVER

THE REDEEMING GRACE TRILOGY

BOOK ONE

ISBN-13: 978-1-7373558-1-6

Cover art and design by: Abigail Silver

Edited by: Harlow Kelly

Cover and typesetting by: Lee Davis

Printed in the United States of America

DEDICATION

This book is for my parents and brother -
Christine, Jerry, and Karl

Thank you for teaching me what love and family really look like.

CONTENT ADVISORY

This is a work of fiction intended for mature audiences.

This novel contains mature language and adult situations including sexuality, violence, self-harm, and child neglect that may be disturbing to some readers.

Reader discretion is advised.

CONTENTS

PRELUDE

Who is Gabriel Usuriel?

That's the question I've been asking all my life.

Countless people have asked it. There are dozens of books, news articles, holo-specials, and every other type of media hype swirling around his story. And, of course, no two can agree on anything but the most basic facts.

Some say he's a hero of the people, a shining dark-haired knight who piloted our generation ship, the Inspiration, to a new world. Others say he's a demi-god, an immortal soul who cast off worldly pleasures to save his sanity in a universe of ephemeral mortal beauty. Still others cast him as a narcissistic womanizer who slept his way through every organization he's ever been in. By far the darkest take on Gabriel's character is the rumor that he and the infamous Sorrow might just be one and the same.

For most people, playing the guessing game is an amusing sideshow to the dreary humdrum of life. They turn on their holo-projectors and watch a program while they eat, escaping into the fantasy that is the hunt for Gabriel Usuriel's true past.

It's not a game for me. You see, Gabriel Usuriel is my father.

CHAPTER 1

MY FIRST HEARTBREAK

The first time I met my father I didn't know anything about his history. In fact, I didn't know he existed until I was old enough to read.

As a young child, I knew little outside of the yellowing paint and peeling wallpaper of my mother's apartment. Occasionally Mother and I traveled to an outdoor park. She'd push me on the swings, a smile on her gaunt face and her dyed blonde hair up in a messy bun. That was rare. More often, my mother slept during the day and didn't have the energy to take me places in the daylight. Thus, those stained walls contained most of my world.

Not to say that my mother was unloving. Each day she brushed my hair, tutting at how my wavy red strands tangled.

"My hair was just like this when I was a little girl," she'd say, running her fingers through its silky length. "And so was my nose—covered in freckles, just like yours!" The warm pad of her thumb would wiggle the tip of my nose and I'd giggle. Her smile lit up my whole world. "Ah well, at least you got your father's eyes."

"What was my father like?"

A dreamy look would come into her lined face and she'd pull me into her lap. "He's very handsome. And powerful.

I think you'll like him." Her arms squeezed me tight. "One day I'll take you to meet him."

That day never came.

Like all small children, the rest of my early years have been reduced to a few bright flashes of color and the smell of old tobacco smoke. The last memory I have of my mother, however, has not faded or blurred with age.

I was about five at the time and home alone in our apartment, playing with a stack of chipped wooden blocks. After a time, I rummaged up a bowl of rice crackers from our pantry. I nibbled the edge of one. Stale, but still edible. Standing on tiptoe, I ran the tap into a battered plex drinking cup we kept near the sink. Bringing my prizes with me to the living room, I grinned at my growing block metropolis on the stained rug.

Voices in the hall. My head shot up.

"Stay quiet and..." my mother had said as she walked out the door, waiting as always for me to fill in the end of the phrase.

"Don't open the door," I'd intoned dutifully.

With a smile and a kiss on my brow, she'd left in a cloud of perfume and fake fur.

Her instructions had never been tested before. No one ever knocked. The only time the door slid open was at my mother's palm. To say I was startled at the loud, sudden rapping from the entrance hall is an understatement.

A spooked rabbit, I scurried toward the relative safety of the bedroom. One scuffed shoe caught the edge of my block tower and it fell in a loud jumble behind me.

"Hello?" called a muffled voice through the door.

Clapping both hands over my mouth, I backed up as silently as I could. Fetching up against the bed, I wriggled beneath it in a flurry of pale, awkward limbs. My vision was a narrow tunnel of red curls, abandoned shoes, and clumps of dust. My heart throbbed in my fingertips.

The off-key chime of the palm reader split the tense silence. I sucked in musty air through clenched teeth. The

lock clicked and the squeaky ball bearings gave their protest as the door slid open. I heard several footsteps and a
familiar voice.

"Hello? Anyone 'ome?" It was the fat man who swept the
halls and yelled at the little boys two doors down for running in the lobby. I didn't know his name, but I recognized
his lazy drawl.

A long pause, then a second voice. This one I didn't
know.

"Hello? Miss Blackmon?" The voice softened. "What was
the little girl's name? Gracie?"

"Yeah, just her and Amaya. They the only ones livin' here.
I ne'er see anyone else comin' or goin'."

"Well, I heard something when you knocked. Let's take
a look around. She might know we have a warrant for her.
They could be hiding or have slipped out a back way."

The building man chuckled. "No back way out of here.
Not 'less you wanna fall four stories outta window."

My breath caught in my throat. I was trapped. I clamped
my sweat-slimy hands over my mouth again.

"What the hell? Who are you? Gracie? Where's Gracie?
Where's my little girl?" My mother's voice was light in a
dark room. Tears streamed down my cheeks as I fought my
way out from under the bed.

"Momma!" I shrieked, rushing into her arms. She knelt
and wrapped me up tightly against her. Cigarettes and
stale perfume enveloped me. I breathed them in, my heart
still racing, but the churning in my stomach settling a bit
with her familiar scent.

"What is the meaning of this?" My mother demanded,
her voice cracking. I snuggled deeper into her breast.

The unfamiliar man cleared his throat. I could just see him over the edge of my mother's arm. He was wearing a uniform, the pale gray cloth of his starched collar smooth and the silver of his buttons gleaming in the wan light.

"Is there somewhere we could speak in private?"

My mother's arms tightened around my shoulders. "Whatever you have to say to me, you can say it right here."

The strange man reached into his coat and pulled out a battered memory pad. I can still remember the way the cracked screen flickered in his hand.

My mother looked at the pad as if it were made of Death's Head spores. Then, slowly, she took the device in one pale hand and scrolled through the document on its screen. I immediately felt her begin to shake.

"No." Her voice was barely above a whisper. "You can't. You have no proof."

"I'm sorry, madame, but there's a judge's signature at the bottom. That means I have to enforce it."

"No!" My mother cried again, a shrill exclamation in my ear. She wrapped both arms around me, lifting me into her arms. With slow, shaking steps she backed away from the man. Her grip was deathly tight. I buried my face in her shoulder, the hot damp of her tears mingling with my own. I clung to her neck with all the strength in my tiny body.

"Please," my mother whimpered. "Please don't do this. Please. She's all I have. You can't! I'm begging you!"

A hand closed around my shoulder and I shrieked, cold sweat rushing over me.

"No!" Momma's fingernails clawed at my shoulders. "It'll never happen again! I'll find someone to keep her! I'll get a real job! I swear! I'll never go out on the street again! Never! Never! Stop it! Please! I swear!"

I was screaming along with her, the sound of her pleading punctuated with my own shrill cries.

It was to no avail.

"No! Gracie! Please! Give me back my baby! My baby!"

That's the last image I have of my mother: eyes wide and fingers grasping at thin air. Her wispy curls fell into her puffy face as she fought the broad shouldered men whose arms wrapped around her waist. The dingy doorway of our apartment framed her, then all that was left were her echoing screams.

In the back seat of the hover car, I buried my face in my knees and cried.

That's how I ended up in a child's version of hell. They didn't think the word orphanage was forward thinking enough, I guess, but that's what it was. A huge, rickety, bare wooden floored house full to the brim with children but completely empty of hope. It echoed with our tears and our heartbreak—a place where tiny lives came crashing to the ground before they'd even begun.

CHAPTER 2

THE GROUP HOME

The kind staff at the group home spent hours asking me questions, trying to get some kind of information out of me that might lead to a better placement. And they were nice, if disheartened and overwhelmed by the task of looking after all of us wayward waifs.

"Have you ever met your daddy?"

"No."

"Did your mom ever say his name? Or where he came from?"

Mute head shake.

"Do you ever go visit your grandparents?"

"Who?"

"Granny? Nana? Grandma or grandpa?"

Empty, confused gaze.

The gentle social worker eventually sighed and patted me on top of my coppery hair.

"I guess you'll just have to stay at the group home for now."

The stay was supposed to be temporary, until they found a foster home to take me in.

"You're such a cute, quiet little thing," the same social worker said in that first interview. She had mousy brown hair and soft, hazel eyes. I remember thinking she was plain.

I later learned her name was Clara. "Don't worry, we'll find a family for you in no time."

That was before they found out how much I like fire—or rather, how fire likes me.

On the first day, Clara gave me a stuffed dog and I clung to it like it would somehow teleport me back to my mother's safe, cluttered apartment. It didn't. Instead, it was warm and soft and it soaked up my tears when I couldn't hold them in anymore. I guess it was just what I needed.

There were three other girls who shared the long hall-like dormitory, but they were several years older. Their eyes were cold and they acted as if I wasn't even there. One of them hissed an angry word at me when I sat down on what was apparently her bed. I moved to another bed and they went back to pretending I didn't exist. Rejected and alone, I crawled under the covers and buried my head against Doggie Dog's comforting stuffed warmth.

Clara came in to check on us. She made us brush our teeth and get into our pajamas. Since I didn't have anything except the clothes on my back, she took me to a little closet down the hall and pulled out a yellow and pink nightgown. It was worn and itchy and so long it dragged the floor. It smelled like a stranger's laundry and I wrinkled my nose at it. Still, it was warm, and that was all that mattered to the social worker.

Clara bundled me back to the bedroom and into the skinny bed with the thin sheets. She patted my head and told me to sleep well. Then she said goodnight to the other girls, turned out the lights and left.

In the dark, clinging to Doggie Dog, I found out how echoingly empty the world can be when you're small and alone.

My mother's work meant I was alone a lot at night, but I'd always known she would come back. Late, late at night, she would come home rumpled and smelling of the flowery perfume she kept on the dresser. Her eyes would be sad and she'd wrap herself around me in bed. I'd cuddle deeply into her arms and fall back to sleep.

Here in this sterile group home, I didn't have the promise of my mother's loving arms to comfort me. Instead, the whispered giggles of the unfriendly girls across the room isolated me further. I burrowed into the scratchy sheets, trying to ignore the harsh, unfamiliar scent of the oversized nightgown. A thin whimper escaped my lips and hot tears rushed up to wet the pillow.

"Shut up, baby," one of the girls hissed. She was at least three years older than me with frizzy blonde hair and a salting of freckles. "I don't want to listen to you cry all night." The foot of my bed bounced as she threw something at me. The mystery object was hard because it clattered to the floor.

Now frightened as well as heartbroken, I buried my face in between the pillow and Doggie Dog. I couldn't stop the tears or the wracking sobs, but I could close my mouth and try to muffle them in the covers. It must have worked because no more airborne toiletries came my way. After several miserable hours, I finally managed to exhaust myself and fall into a restless sleep.

The only other scene I remember clearly from that first week was when the social workers realized what a problem child I would turn out to be.

I sat in the kitchen, its black and white checkered tile stretching for what seemed like a mile under my Velcro-sneakered feet. They dangled from where I perched atop a four-legged stool. The massive butcher's block table was solid and thick edged; too thick for me to wrap my pudgy hands around. Instead, I leaned against it, Doggie Dog clutched to my chest while I chewed on my finger. It was a nervous habit I didn't break until I was much older.

Across the kitchen was a huge old hearth, stained and charred from decades of heating the center of this sprawling manse. There was a wrought-iron screen in front of the gaping arch but I could see the warm flicker of flames licking the underside of the grayed stone.

My mother might have been a careless parent in some regards, but she'd never had an open flame bigger than a candlewick around me. I knew what fire was, but I'd never seen such a large example. I stared at it, unable to look away from its moving light.

One of the caregivers, a portly, middle-aged woman with dark hair, bustled at the counter to my right. It was tricky to wriggle my way down from the high stool without knocking my head on the butcher's block, but I managed it. Doggie Dog's soft bulk made it twice as hard, but with the grim determination of a five-year-old, I refused to put him down while I slowly slid to the floor. I hit the tile harder than I thought I would, but the pain in my feet wasn't enough to bring tears. When I'd recovered from the shock, I redoubled my grip on Doggie Dog's neck and walked towards the fireplace.

The metal grate was taller than me by a few centimeters. Its heat warmed my face now that I was on the floor. Through diamond shaped holes, the flash of yellow and orange flames licked at several blackening logs. I found myself hypnotized by their rapid dance, completely drawn to their liquid beauty. My stuffed toy slipped to the floor, thoughtlessly abandoned in my complete fascination with the flames.

I didn't notice the heat's intensity growing. I don't remember walking forward, but suddenly I was standing next to the grille, both hands outstretched to its entrancing contents. The licking, devouring tongues rose towards me, blowing my hair back from my face like a warm caress. With a dull roar the flames reached for me from behind their iron prison.

"Gracie!" The social worker snatched me into her arms just before the rumbling flames exploded outwards, enveloping the spot I'd been standing. A huge plume of fire and smoke billowed up from the hearth, wrapping up and over the marble lintel.

I looked up into the woman's wide, frightened eyes. It was that more than the close call that made my tears well up.

"Shhh, there now. You mustn't get close to the fire or you'll get burned!" She glanced back at the still-grumbling fireplace. The flames had already receded, but the smoke was taking a few moments to dissipate. "Well, I'd say finding your relatives will be easier. I don't think your mother is from the Family, so I'm guessing your father must have a touch of Awareness. There's only so many with that gift in Skykyle City."

CHAPTER 3

CHILD OF AWARENESS

At the time, I had no idea what the social worker meant by Awareness or the Family. Odd to think that the first time I heard those words were from the lips of a mortal whose name I can't even recall. I did, however, spend days turning them over and over in my mind—as if I knew the shape of my future lay within them if only I could puzzle out its edges.

As weeks went on, however, finding my father continued to prove an impossible task. That is, I assume the social workers kept looking for him. They didn't mention him again for a long while, instead focusing on finding me a foster home. I suppose they didn't want to get my hopes up.

Still, my father was the dream I clung to, especially when the foster families turned cold the instant they learned about my little fire incident.

"We really don't have the experience to care for a child of Awareness," one prim, blonde woman said, giving me a pitying glance out of faded blue eyes. I tried my best to sink into the couch. Trying to ignore my itchy tights, I focused on my black buckle shoes. They were a size too small and pinched my feet, but they looked nice. They were certainly the nicest shoes I'd ever owned, even if they weren't new.

"Her mother has been declared unfit and we haven't been able to track down any record of a father. No one claimed her on the birth certificate," Clara said. The brown haired social worker put a comforting hand on my thin shoulder. "If she doesn't find a foster home soon she'll have to go into lessons here. You know how hard it is to switch them around once they've started school. I was really hoping she could start somewhere with a new family."

The blonde woman eyed me. She was deciding if I would be too much trouble. It was a look I was becoming familiar with. It made me feel like a dog at the pound. Maybe she'd take me with her if I promised not to pee on the rug.

"I am sorry," she sighed and spread bony, white hands. They fluttered about her knees like birds about to land on her expensive gray slacks. I suddenly hated everything about this perfect woman, from her clumped eyeliner to the precise creases in her silk shirt. I stared at the hem of those elegant, tightly woven trousers. My anger crystallized into a burning heat and I experienced a tremble of satisfaction as the smallest spark flickered along the bottom edge of Miss Perfect's pant leg.

A sharp pinch brought me out of myself. I lost concentration and the tiny flicker of flame died. I glanced guiltily up at Clara. She gave me a look that told me I'd be in trouble later. She got to her feet and held out a hand to my prospective foster mother.

"Well, thank you for coming anyway. We do appreciate it," she said. I squirmed, hoping the social worker would let me change out of my itchy tights once the lady left.

After the woman in gray took her leave, Clara rounded on me.

"That was completely unacceptable, Gracie." Her hazel eyes flashed with anger and disappointment. I hugged myself tightly, wishing I had Doggie Dog to bury my face in. "Look at me when I'm speaking to you, child! Playing with fire is dangerous. You could have hurt someone. Even worse, you'll never find a new home if you keep this up. Don't you want to have a nice place to call home? Don't you want new parents?"

I sniffed. Despite the hurt of being rejected again, I didn't want to disappoint the social worker. She was the only person who had been nice to me since my mother. I mutely nodded and gave her huge, sad eyes.

"Promise me you won't do that again, okay?" she coaxed, bending down to be eye level with me.

"I promise," I whispered. She held out her arms and I squirmed off the couch to give her a hug. It was the first time I'd gotten a real hug here. I clung to her warm, slim body and pressed my face to her frizzy hair. "Will you promise to find my daddy?"

Her arms tightened around me. "I can't promise that, Gracie, but I will try. Okay?"

Sensing it was the best I was going to get, I nodded and allowed her to pull away. She took my hand and I followed her back to the girls' dormitory to change out of my dress clothes.

There weren't many more prospective parents after that. The few I did meet all ended up the same way. Once they found out about my Awareness, I was suddenly too much trouble.

Days turned into weeks and weeks into months. I began lessons at the group home. They weren't hard. I learned my letters and numbers easily, unlike a few of the young boys who struggled through their first books with painstaking slowness. I sped through all five books the little classroom had on the beginner reading level and began to work my way through the intermediate. Books gave me an escape, a way to avoid the cold reality that was thin sheets and rude older girls.

Between being quiet and getting my work done well on my own, I was mostly ignored by the tutor who came to give our lessons. She'd set me to working, then move over to help the other children. Occasionally she'd look up, correct a mistake or two on my paper, then turn back to the antics of my unruly classmates.

Life fell into a quiet, washed out rhythm. Breakfast, lessons, lunch, crafts—we kept an unwavering routine. In the afternoons we had outdoor time, and after dinner there was a holo-set that the boys always claimed for their sports programming. The older girls read gossipy articles on one of the ancient memory pads and did each other's hair. That left me to my own devices. Usually, I borrowed a book or memory pad from the tutor and spent what little time I had to myself reading.

On Landing Day, I stood on the doorstep watching the other children set off tiny, sparking fireworks on the cracked pavement in front of the manse. Our tutor, an elderly woman with dull, brown skin and bright eyes, came to stand at my side.

"Would you like to set off a cracker?" she asked, offering me a tiny white packet of powder. The boys were chasing each other with handfuls of the stuff, causing loud, harmless explosions and tiny flashes of light at their feet. I shook my head.

Her warm hand found my shoulder and I glanced up, slightly startled. "You still miss your mother, don't you," she said softly. Her weathered features swam as hot tears rushed up. A horrible emptiness twisted my chest and I glanced fearfully at the other girls, lest they see me cry.

"Come on," the elderly tutor murmured, "let's go inside. There's something I want to give you."

I followed her wordlessly into the house, down into the little school room with its dusty shelves of cracked memory pads and faded books. There she opened a drawer in her desk and pulled out two items. One was a box of crayons, the other a large sketch pad with gleaming, metal wire binding one edge. Unlike the other supplies we'd always been given, these were crisp and clean. Each crayon still had its factory-made, squared off point and the box didn't bear a single childish scribble on its cardboard surface. The sketch pad was bright white and sharp-edged, not crumpled or stained like the paper we practiced our letters on. Her large, wrinkled hands put them in my small, pudgy ones and the bottom of my vision began to waver again.

"I've been saving these for you," her ancient voice quivered, moisture clinging to her lashes as well. "Happy Landing Day, Gracie."

After that, the crayons and drawing pad were never far from my hand. I spent countless hours doodling and giving my childish efforts to Clara. She hung them up over my bed and in the little room that she used as an office. Thus, a year of my young life passed and slowly I began to hate my lot just a little bit less.

CHAPTER 4

MOTHER

One night, I had a dream. I was in a dark place. The walls were bare cinder block, stained with some kind of seeping moisture. The rest of the details swam in the half-formed mist of dreaming, blurring and twisting into a general impression of hopelessness.

My mother's face rose before me. She didn't look much like the last time I'd seen her. Her cheekbones stood out sharply in a too-thin face and her eyes were sunken into deep bruises of skin. Still, she seemed at peace. She smiled at me, reaching out to touch my face.

"Goodbye, Gracie," she whispered, her blue-green eyes full of pain and love. With a swish of her white dress, she turned away from me and walked out the door.

A sharp pain stabbed my chest. I tried to cry out but I was frozen, held motionless in the paralysis of sleep. I couldn't move; I couldn't breathe. It felt as if a giant were squeezing my ribs. I clawed at my prison, swimming up through layers of unconsciousness until I sat bolt upright in bed.

"Momma!" I shrieked, my body covered in sweat. My hands were balled into fists in the covers and my heart slammed against my ribs. It took me a moment to realize that I was still in the girls' dormitory at the group home.

One of the older girls rolled over with a groan at my outcry, but the rest had slept through it completely. Breathing hard, I lay back down and cuddled up to Doggie Dog. I laid awake for a long time thinking of my mother.

I woke up the next day to an empty and echoing life. My usual escapes seemed hollow and pointless. I tried to read, but the words bled together. I picked up my crayons, but the drawings felt meaningless. Finally, I gave up and stared out the windows of the group home with an empty gaze. I couldn't focus on my lessons and got a scolding from the tutor. Even gentle Clara took a sharper tone with me when I didn't come to the table for dinner promptly.

"What's wrong with you, Gracie?" she asked, her hazel eyes concerned. I didn't answer. I felt too miserable. Though at the time I was too young to understand or put it into words, looking back I knew my mother was gone. All the hope of seeing her again had been erased in that terrifying moment when the pain woke me from my sleep. My hope for a foster home died many months ago. I think the only reason I got out of bed that morning was because I still clung to the idea that they might find my father. It was a fading hope, but it kept me from completely falling into the abyss.

For two long weeks, it rained. Storms like I'd never seen before raged over the old, creaky house. A shutter blew loose and slammed against the wall, making a frightening counterpoint to the wind's high-pitched howl. The rain was a dull, slapping roar against the tall windows and solar paneled roof. The other children and I huddled inside with mugs of hot chocolate and went slowly stir crazy. Our caregivers amused the others with games and educational holo-programs on a variety of topics. They tried to include me, but the weather merely gave me an excuse to completely withdraw. I took it.

I sat in the corner and stared out the window. I pretended to read one of the books my tutor had lent me so that Clara and the others would leave me alone. The slim chapter book had fallen closed in my lap and I didn't care. I stared at the water pouring down from the sky, as if it were grieving along with me.

Then, slowly, the clouds parted and the sun began to shine down on the wet world in front of the group home. We were in the old part of the city, so the cracked concrete of the paved walk held puddles deep enough to soak me up to my ankle. I watched the clouds reflect golden light into their rippling surfaces.

That was when I saw him.

His dark hair was pulled back in a ponytail and his clean-shaven face had crisp, finely chiseled features. His limbs were slim but his shoulders were strong. A white button down showed off the slim taper of his waist without being overly tight above his black slacks and black leather shoes. When he glanced up at the sign above the group home's door, I could see that his eyes were an incredibly saturated shade of blue. That wasn't the most remarkable thing about him, however. What I noticed most was the way he moved. It was different from the—admittedly few—men I was familiar with. It was not a slouch nor was it a heavy plodding. Instead, this man walked with a complete economy of motion, no energy wasted, in a smooth, effortless glide. It gave the impression that he was in complete control of every muscle, every movement, and that there was a vast amount of strength hidden in his slim form. When he took the stairs up to the door, he flowed upwards so easily I nearly didn't see him touch the cement steps.

Trailing in this surreal man's wake was a woman with bright, copper curls. Her face held the same fine, chiseled lines as the man's. The brown skirt suit she wore showed off a slim, strong figure with bold, tailored lines. Her movements were also oddly elegant though not quite as smooth as his. I wondered if they were brother and sister.

For the first time since the dream, I was interested in something. Forget interested, I was captivated by this pair. I hadn't been this intrigued by anything since I'd discovered the fireplace. My book and my melancholy forgotten, I leaped up from the window seat. I heard the bell ring even as I raced to the door.

When I got to the foyer, I saw that the dark haired social worker had gotten to it first. Her thick figure blocked most of my view from where I lurked in the hallway. I was curious about this man, but I was frightened, too. I hadn't seen many men since the ones who came to take me away from my mother and I was cautious. I tucked my slender body behind the corner of the doorway into the foyer and watched with wide eyes. The hinges creaked as the social worker opened the door.

"Hello." His voice was not deep but also not reedy. It was a strong, solid voice, just like its owner. "I am here to collect my daughter."

CHAPTER 5

GABRIEL

Hope squeezed my lungs at the stranger's words. I tried briefly to convince myself he was probably speaking about one of the other girls but my heart knew exactly what I wanted. With every ounce of my tiny body, I wanted this to be my father. I wanted this strange, beautiful man to be the one I'd dreamed of for so long.

Still, I had been rejected and turned away so many times. I didn't know if my fragile spirit could take such a huge disappointment. So rather than approach him, I watched with a mixture of trepidation and euphoria, frozen between hope and fear.

"I'm sorry, sir, I haven't been informed of paperwork going through on any of the children." The social worker sounded nervous. Knowing what I do now, I'm sure she was terrified. The fact that she stood up to him at all says something for her devotion to her charges. At the time, however, I just wanted her to ask who his daughter was. I wanted—no, I needed—to know if he was talking about me.

"I believe I have the paperwork you are referring to," he replied evenly, pulling a bundle of papers from the thin air to his left. He offered them to the social worker. I couldn't be sure, but I thought I saw him stifle a small smirk at her startled expression.

All I could feel was an incredible amount of excitement. Of course! I should have known his smooth, flowing gait was an indication of Awareness. I was the only child in the house with any sign of the gift. He had to be my father!

It was just as my young mind reasoned this out that he looked past the social worker for the first time. His intense blue gaze went directly to my own. He smiled.

"I...I'm sorry Mr. Usuriel. This is highly irregular. I have to make sure this has gone through the proper channels..."

Mr. Usuriel's gaze snapped to the social worker's, his face suddenly hard. "The judge signed it this morning. My mother was witness. You can see her signature right there." He tapped the document and gave the woman a stern glare. If he'd turned that look on me, I would have cowered. "Are you calling Gloria Usuriel a liar?"

The social worker shrank back a step. She'd turned a touch so that I could see her face in profile. Her eyes were wide and she licked her lips nervously. Mr. Usuriel wasn't overly tall for a man, but he knew how to use every inch of what he had. With a lean and half a step forward, he towered over the portly caregiver.

"No, no of course not," she quivered, her hands smoothing over the papers. They made a wrinkling sound in her hand.

Just as quickly as his temper had sprung to life, it slid smoothly under the surface again. With a gesture of one hand, he indicated that the social worker should lead the way into the house.

"Well then, why don't you take me to meet my daughter?" he suggested with a slight smile.

"Ummm…" the social worker turned and saw me hovering in the doorway. With a sigh, she held out a hand to me. "I should have known you'd recognize him. Come here, child. Come meet your father."

My heart, already wedged in my throat, began to flutter frantically. This was it. This was the moment I'd been dreaming about for over a year. Feeling as if I were in a holo-program, I slipped from behind the wall. I took a step forward and Mr. Usuriel dropped to one knee to be on my level.

"Hello, Gracie," he murmured, his voice gentle. "My name's Gabriel. It's a pleasure to meet you."

He held out a hand to me. It was long fingered and graceful. I stared at it for a long moment. Then, my nervous eyes found his again and he gave me that same reassuring smile. It was gentle yet confident, handsome yet approachable. He was everything I'd ever hoped for. I dashed right past his hand and wrapped my arms firmly around his neck.

His arms came up around me and I could feel his strength as he held me tight. He smelled of tobacco and mint. For a long moment he let me cling to him. I remember feeling as if I was safe and wanted for the first time in a year and a half.

"Let me look at you," he said, stroking my hair with one hand. Reluctantly, I allowed him to peel me away from his shoulders. His expression was gentle as he gazed at my face. "You have your mother's hair," he murmured, "but I'd recognize those eyes anywhere. I'd say you're officially mine."

I glowed with his words. "Are you going to take me home?" I asked. "Can I take Doggie Dog with me?"

Gabriel looked up at the social worker questioningly. She gave a rueful shrug. "It's her stuffed toy. She takes it everywhere." She turned to me. "Of course, sweetheart, Doggie Dog is yours. You can take him with you when it's time to go."

My father stood up and took my hand. "Well, let's get your things packed, then. I have a room already waiting for you."

I could barely contain my excitement. This was more perfect than a dream. Any moment I should wake up in my tiny little thin-sheeted bed. Instead, I tugged on my father's hand and practically dragged him up the stairs to the girls' bedroom.

"Come on! You can see my drawings! Do you have paper and crayons at your house? I love to draw. What about books? Do you have lots of books? Does my new room have bookshelves? I want lots and lots of bookshelves!"

It was more than I'd spoken in months all crammed into one long run on sentence. Gabriel laughed and allowed me to lead him to my bed where I started piling all of my treasured possessions. There weren't many of them. Doggie Dog was first, then my pad of paper and the worn box of crayons. Two books with torn covers that my tutor had let me keep completed the pile.

"Excuse me," Clara's voice from the doorway sent me into a thrilled frenzy.

"Look! Look! My father's come for me! Did you see?" I ran to her and had I been a more gregarious child I would have hugged her. Instead, I pranced in front of her with a huge grin on my face.

Clara didn't smile or encourage my outburst. "I see him, Gracie," she said, putting a hand on my head. "I need to talk to your father a moment. Why don't you draw him a picture?"

That sounded like a perfectly reasonable suggestion to my child mind, so I raced over to the bed where I'd placed my paper and crayons. I threw myself down on top of Doggie Dog and instantly began a serious rendering of the moment I'd met my father. It was the most wonderful thing that had ever happened to me, so of course it needed to be immortalized in crayon immediately.

Gabriel and Clara didn't go far. I could hear their muffled voices right outside the door. They didn't sound happy, but right now nothing could ruin my mood so I focused completely on my crayons.

I was adding in the social worker's dress when my father's voice got very loud. I glanced up from my drawing just as he slammed open the door.

"I've seen quite enough of this place," he snarled as he stormed into the room. "I know it's the best you can do, but I am not leaving my daughter here another night. I don't care what rules or regulations have to say about it. I'm taking her to Angelus Quietum right now. If you want to call the city watch, you can tell them exactly where to find me."

He gestured sharply with one hand and snatched a small, blue suitcase from the formerly empty air next to his left hip. "Come on, Gracie. Where are your clothes? Put all of your things in here." With swift, efficient movements, he set the suitcase on the bed and opened the latch. The case was lined with blue, silk cloth. I'd never seen something so nice just for carrying other things before. I stared at it for a moment before holding up my crayon masterpiece.

"I drew this for you," I said, holding it out to him.

His expression softened and he took it delicately from me. "Thank you, sweetheart," he said. "It's lovely. We'll put it on the wall when we get home. For now, let's pack it with your other things, okay?"

"Okay," I replied and slid off the bed to go get the few shirts and pairs of pants I'd been given.

"Really, Mr. Usuriel, I realize your family is… different, but… regulations must be applied…." Clara followed my father into the room, her face troubled. Gabriel cut her off.

"Yes, we are different. Perhaps it would be wise of you to remember that," he snapped, putting my books into the suitcase.

Clara blinked at his tone, her expression carefully blank. "Are you threatening me?"

I didn't completely understand what Clara was talking about. Gabriel hadn't done anything threatening other than speaking loudly, at least that I could tell. The adversarial tone of their conversation had put a cold lump in my stomach, however, and I watched them both carefully as I handed my father my folded shirts and pants. He took them from me and put them neatly into the case. I could see his jaw working as if he was trying very hard not to say something angry. I didn't completely recognize the expression at the time, but I did know enough to realize that I didn't want to set him off. Instead, I very quietly began gathering my crayons and putting them into their box.

With a long sigh, the tension went out of my father's shoulders. He closed his eyes for a moment before turning to face Clara.

"No. I would not harm someone for doing their job," his voice was even and calm despite his earlier outburst. "However, there really is nothing you can do to stop me from taking Gracie. I promise you, I am clean and quite sober which means I can teleport myself and a child her size with very little effort. So, for Gracie's sake, let's keep this as pleasant and normal as possible, shall we?"

I watched Clara think about it. Her hazel eyes looked down at me as if trying to decide what would be the least of two bad options. Finally, her eyebrows went up in a look of happy helplessness.

"I suppose, if the board decides to come after my job..." she trailed off, tilting her head at my father.

"Tell them I was a raging terror," he offered quickly, blue eyes earnest. "Tell them you were afraid for your life. I will take all the blame."

Clara shook her head, an amused smile threatening at the corners of her mouth. "Aren't you afraid the Overwatch will come and arrest you?"

Gabriel glanced down into the suitcase. "You're sure this is everything?" he asked me. I nodded solemnly. With a nod of his own, he closed the case, latched it and picked it up by the handle. He held out a hand to me and I eagerly took it.

With a graceful turn, he faced Clara again. "I have yet to meet the jail cell I couldn't get out of," he said with a smile that was both proud and a little sad, "nor the constable with enough courage to try to put me there."

"I can see how you've gotten your reputation, Mr. Usuriel."

"I aim to please," he replied, giving her as elegant a half-bow as he could with a suitcase in one hand and me clinging to the other. Then his expression turned serious and he met Clara's eye. "Thank you for taking good care of my Gracie. I won't forget it."

With those parting words, Gabriel turned to me. "Ready?" I nodded. Then, I felt the pull of his power for the first time—a warm wind that sang through every part of my body. I closed my eyes and clung to his hand.

When I opened them again, we stood in front of a quaint log cabin overlooking a lake.

Finally, I was home.

CHAPTER 6

ANGELUS QUIETUM

Angelus Quietum was my home for twelve years. I can close my eyes now and recite every detail of the place as if I were standing there. Thick, red-brown logs stacked with precision into the long, single-story house. My eyes squinted into the burning brightness of the roof's solar-energy glare. The smell of pines and kyoss trees permeated the frigid morning air, their thick sap congealing in translucent yellow globes. The mist rose from the lake, obscuring the mountains' reflections as the sun came up over them in a thousand golden colors.

Nothing I say, however, can do justice to the contentedness I found there. The first ten years I spent in that little cabin by the lake were the happiest of my life. If I'd known what lay ahead for me, I'm not sure I ever would have left.

When we arrived from the group home, my father had my room all ready and waiting. It wasn't a large house. A main living room with a fireplace, a dining area that ran into the kitchen, and a wooden porch that looked over the lake completed the public areas. A small hallway led from the living room to the three bedrooms. There were two doors on the left side of the hall and one on the right. The two on the left led to my bedroom and the guest room. At the end of the hall was my father's master suite and on the right a second bathroom. That was it; simple, clean and rustic.

Still, there were signs of old wealth if you knew where to look. Every surface was in pristine condition. There was not a leak in the roof or a smudge on the mantle. The floor-boards were so even a marble would have nowhere to roll. The building materials and upholstery were of the finest quality. Paintings of starscapes and distinguished individuals in colonization-era ship suits adorned the walls.

I only knew that it had an air of elegance. It seemed to fit my proud father. How well I understood him even then. His taste reflected in the clean lines and simple furnishings as clearly as in his white button-down and black leather shoes.

My room was the same way. A single bed sat under a high window with white lace curtains. The bedspread was a simple white. The only nod to decadence was the mound of sumptuous pillows on top. To the right of the bed, a small bedside table bore a little reading lamp. A white dresser sat next to the closet door with a long mirror hanging on its back.

"I know it's a bit impersonal right now," my father said as he easily lifted the suitcase onto the bed, "but we'll fix that soon enough. What do you think?"

"It's perfect!" I cried, flinging my arms around his waist. This interrupted his methodical opening of my suitcase on the bed, but his low sigh of a laugh told me he didn't mind. His hand tangled in my hair and I thought I might explode from happiness.

"Come on, let's put your things away," my father suggested. With graceful fingers, he sorted through the contents of my case. Out came Doggie Dog, looking a little rumpled from his ride. I set him lovingly on the pillows while Dad put away the few clothes I owned into the chest of drawers. Next, my books, crayons, and drawing pad were placed carefully on the little shelf of the night stand.

Gabriel shook his head when everything was put away. "Not even a toothbrush," he muttered more to himself than to me. I was too busy admiring how wonderful the bedroom looked with Doggie Dog in it to care.

"What happened to that drawing you did?" Dad asked, regarding the room with his hands on his slim hips. "We can put it up on your cork board."

We'd had a cork board at the group home but it had been for everyone's artwork, along with announcements and schedules. I was surprised to see a pristine new one hanging on the wall opposite the closet door. Not only did I have my own room, my own closet, my own bathroom, but I had an entire cork board all to myself. The enormity of how much my life had just changed slammed into me and hot tears welled in my eyes.

"Gracie, what's wrong?" Gabriel looked startled. Quickly, he dropped to one knee and peered up into my watery gaze. His eyes were so gentle and so blue. I could hardly look at him for fear he might up and disappear.

When he saw that I wasn't going to be able to give him an answer, Gabriel picked me up and sat on the bed. There, sitting on his lap, my head buried in his broad shoulder, I cried out all the fear and helplessness I'd felt for so long. It all came pouring out as I balled my hands into the crisp cloth of his white shirt. He let me exhaust myself, rocking and murmuring the gentle things a parent says to a crying child. It reminded me of my mother and a fresh wave of tears wet my cheeks. Finally, when my sobs had turned into little hiccupy gasps, he kissed my forehead and set me on my feet.

"Come on, there's someone I want you to meet."

CHAPTER 7

STELLA

With one hand, my father reached up to the back, right side of his neck and tapped it. A tiny light the size of my smallest fingernail glowed pink under his skin. I stared at the spot in wonder. Then, something shimmered to life behind him and my eyes went wide.

She was beautiful. A slim, femininely curved figure covered by a skin-tight silver garment. It began at her neck and covered all four graceful limbs. Her silver hair pulled back into a tight bun. Her large, silver eyes looked out of a smooth, high cheek boned face.

As I marveled at her ethereal beauty, I began to realize that I could see the dresser and doorway through her torso. This woman was semi-transparent, like a hologram. Yet her eyes focused on me as if aware of my presence, unlike the holo characters I was familiar with. I blinked at her in complete wonder, all my tears forgotten.

"Stella," Gabriel said, standing and turning his body slightly toward the gently flickering figure, "this is my daughter, Gracie. "

The woman's head turned slightly and I was struck by the way she moved. Even as a child, I could easily tell she wasn't human just by that small movement. Amazing how sensitive we are to such things.

"Hello, Gracie." Her voice was smooth and even, just like her silver gaze. She didn't blink or let her eyes slide from mine the way a real person would.

"Stella is an AI," my father explained. "Do you know what that means?"

I shook my head, still staring up at the impossibly beautiful projection.

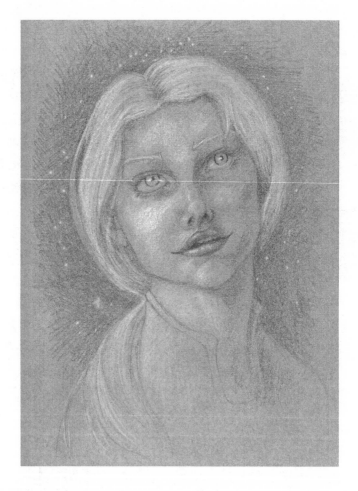

"It means I am an artificial intelligence," Stella purred. She tilted her head at me, much the way a dog will when they are curious about something. "How old is she, Gabriel? Why have I not seen her before?"

"Her mother didn't tell me about her until recently," was his reply, "and she'll be seven in five weeks. Isn't that right, Gracie?"

"Yes," I agreed absently. The AI interested me far more than how close my birthday was. Mom had never made a big deal about birthdays and the group home had absolutely ignored mine last year. "What is an artificial intelligence?"

"She's a computer. Kind of like the memory pad you use to read books, just a lot smarter," my father told me.

Fascinated, I took a step forward. Stella didn't move except to follow me with that steady, unblinking gaze. With one hand, I reached out and touched her arm. Rather, I tried to touch her arm. My hand passed through her faintly flickering sleeve as if it were thin air.

I glanced up at Stella and my father to see if they were upset at my forwardness. Instead, both of them seemed faintly amused.

"What you're seeing is a hologram, just like the holo-projector. Stella doesn't have to stay in one place, however. We have a system built into the house so that she can move anywhere in it," he explained. "She has access to the Inspiration Landing University library along with almost every database on Cybele. She'll be giving you lessons from here on out."

"You have a library?" I'd only ever been to a library once, with the group home's tutor. It had been amazing. There were so many books and memory pads I hardly knew where to start.

"I do not own a library, Gracie," Stella corrected. "I am one."

"Just ask her for any book you want," Gabriel said, pulling a memory pad from thin air in that casual way he had. "She'll send it to your screen."

"What if I don't know what book I want?"

"I make excellent recommendations." Stella's smooth voice sounded a touch smug.

"She also runs the house's electronics, so if you need anything just ask her." My father ruffled my hair. "But now I think it's time to eat. Stella, will you preheat the oven please?"

I followed my father into the living area where light was streaming from the huge bay window. It fell across the leather furniture in golden bars. The lake outside gleamed in the setting sun; the ragged mountain range behind it reflecting as if in a shimmering mirror.

"Why don't you go outside and get some fresh air while I make dinner?" Gabriel suggested, laying a kiss on the top of my head before gesturing to the back door. "There are some trees by the lake that would be excellent for climbing."

I'd always been a quiet child, first because my mother rarely had the energy to deal with me and later because the hopelessness of my situation weighed like a constant burden on my small shoulders. Now, however, I felt as light as air and I wanted to shout my joy to the world. The thought of climbing trees and doing handstands suddenly seemed incredibly appealing.

With a grin and a quick nod, I followed my father's advice and dashed outside to explore.

CHAPTER 8

A HAUNTING

After playing for about an hour outside, with the wind in my hair and tree bark under my nails, Gabriel called me in for supper. We had a simple meal before he pulled up a book on my memory pad and spent a good hour reading aloud while I cuddled up beside him on the couch. Then he told me it was shower time, gave me a towel, toothbrush, and night dress and sent me into the bathroom. I came back out clean and ready for bed.

Gabriel knew exactly what a little girl fears when she spends her first night in a new place. First, he turned on a night-light by the door, its soft glow painting the room in shades of pink and yellow. Then he tucked me in tightly next to Doggie Dog before making a show of checking the closet and under the bed for monsters. Declaring the room safe for occupancy, he laid a last kiss on my forehead and wished me sweet dreams.

I lay in bed a long while after he turned off the overhead light and left, memorizing the outline of my new room. The dresser cast a long shadow on the wall next to the door. I ran my eyes over the angles of it, watching how they slid into the door frame of the closet. The full-length mirror reflected the soft glow of the night-light with a gentle reassurance.

As I was gazing at the mirror I caught a bit of movement out of the corner of my eye. I turned my head quickly, my grip on Doggie Dog white knuckled.

"Stella? Is that you?" I whispered.

With a shimmer, the AI projection appeared at the foot of my bed. "How can I help you, Gracie?"

I blinked up at her silvery presence. Her face was calm and perfect, just as she had been earlier. The light she cast was a soft blue and I knew for certain that I hadn't seen that particular color of light in the mirror until now. Whatever I'd glimpsed earlier, it wasn't the AI.

"Was there someone else here?" I asked. "A minute ago?"

She paused. It only took a second or two but the freeze was so complete that it felt longer. Unlike a real person, she didn't breathe or shift at all while she was thinking.

"No, there have been no other life signs in this room since Gabriel left ten minutes, twenty seconds ago."

My eyes darted around the darkened room. It appeared empty except for myself and the AI's flickering presence.

"Okay. Thank you."

"Goodnight, Gracie." The AI faded gently away, the blue light of her projection fading with her along with the feeling of calm I'd been trying for.

If you've never been a six-year-old alone, in bed, in a strange place, I'm not sure I can explain the anxious knot that took up residence in the base of my spine. Even though all of the recent changes had been good, there had been far too many of them in such a short amount of time for me to feel settled. Despite the AI's assertion that there was nothing else in my bedroom, my eyes continued to dart about the long shadows.

As I gazed into the darkened mirror, the barest flicker dashed across my peripheral vision. Just as before, my head darted towards the source of this movement, but this time I knew it wasn't the AI and didn't call out for Stella. Instead, I stared silently into the far, right corner of the room.

This time there was no doubt that something else was in the room. In fact, it wasn't a something but a someone. She stood in the corner, brilliant copper curls glowing faintly as if lit from within. Her green eyes were staring straight into mine.

I opened my mouth to scream but I couldn't get a breath. For one terrified moment I froze and it was in that brief hesitation that the woman shook her head gently and put a slender, white finger to her lips.

My mouth snapped shut, my heart hammering in my chest. My mind raced frantically. Who was this woman? Why couldn't Stella tell she was here? Why didn't she want me to call my father and what might she do if I did? I clung to Doggie Dog and shrank down into the blankets until they covered me all the way up to the bridge of my nose. Blood rushed in my ears and my mind shrieked with panic.

Long moments dragged on and the woman simply stood there in the corner, making no threatening movements. I blinked at her slowly and began to take in the details of her appearance.

She was average height for a woman, though her thin frame made her look taller. Her hair was cut short around a sharp-featured face. Her red curls caressed her cheek as if tumbled by an invisible wind that didn't touch the drawing pinned to the corkboard beside her. The edges of her brown skirt suit fluttered as well, catching the ethereal breeze. I frowned at her green eyes and felt as though she reminded me of someone familiar.

Then it hit me. I'd seen this woman earlier today. She'd been with my father when he came to the group home. I'd glimpsed her out the window. I didn't remember seeing her once the social worker opened the door. A chill went up my spine as I realized why her features looked so familiar. Aside from hair and eye color, she was a female version of my father.

"Who are you?" I whispered into Doggie Dog's comforting fur. The woman frowned and tilted her head at me. I tried again. "What do you want?"

The mysterious figure shook her head and faded gently away.

It took me a very long time to fall asleep that night.

CHAPTER 9

PYROKINESIS

When I woke up in the morning, I decided it must have been a vivid dream. I wasn't comfortable enough with Gabriel yet to confide such strange things, anyway. What if he thought I was crazy and sent me away? My problem was solved, however, when she failed to appear the next night. What was the point of bringing up a ghost who was no longer haunting me? So, without bothering my father about this strange detail of my arrival, I settled into life at Angelus Quietum.

The first unspoken rule I learned about living with my father was this: if it happened before I was born, I wasn't allowed to ask about it.

He would never have stated such an ultimatum aloud, but I was an intelligent child. Conversations on any topic remotely personal began and ended like this:

"Daddy, how did you meet my mother?"

"It's a long, boring story."

"But I really want to know."

"Gracie, I'm not going into it right now. Go get out your lesson for the day."

That is not to say that my father was unloving or impersonal. His concern for my happiness and well-being were always apparent. If he rarely answered questions about his own past, it was a passing oddity that I didn't remark upon until I was much older.

Of my mother, he did offer some explanation.

I was sitting in the living room for this conversation, my pad of paper spread out with an impressive pile of crayons. He'd presented me with a huge new box the day after I arrived and I'd been busily breaking it in all week. In fact, I'd gotten into my first bit of trouble by decorating one of my achingly blank bedroom walls when I ran out of paper. I swiftly found out I didn't like Gabriel's time outs.

Thus, a brand new notepad had been the next gift. The original drawing I'd done in the group home was now joined on the corkboard by half a dozen more. Most of them were of me, Gabriel, or Stella and I was slowly getting better at drawing our long hair. I loved the fact that my father's hair was long and wavy like mine, even if it was black while mine was red.

Like most evenings, Gabriel relaxed in his leather armchair. His eyes were distant, gazing out the huge bay window overlooking the lake. He'd watch the broad-winged birds as they swooped down to pluck fish from the sparkling water for hours as if it were the best entertainment in the world.

I observed him from my spot on the rug as the sun set in golden rays, casting his sharp features in stark relief. I think this was the first time I noticed the sadness in his eyes. How I could have missed it before baffles me, since it was such a part of his essence. Yet, I distinctly remember wondering what could make someone so beautiful look so sad. His melancholy reminded me of someone else very important to me.

"Dad," I ventured, still enjoying the way his head turned when I called him that.

"Yes, Gracie?" he raised an eyebrow in my direction.

"When will I see Mom again?"

His sigh was so reluctantly resigned. I've never forgotten it. I could always tell when he was about to give me bad news because that ominous sound preceded it.

"Come here, Gracie." He patted his knee. Obediently, I set down my crayon and climbed into his lap.

After resettling me more comfortably on his knee, he looked me in the eye. "Do you know why you were taken away from your mother's home?"

I shook my head, though I had a sneaking idea it might have to do with why she always came home so late.

"Okay," he said, running a hand through his dark hair. He wore it loose that day and it fell in gentle waves about his broad shoulders. "Well, sweetheart, your mother was sick."

I blinked at him, my finger creeping to my mouth. I still sucked on it nervously when I was lost in thought. "Like a cold?" I asked. I'd never been sick before, but the other children at the group home came down with the occasional sniffles.

"No, this is a little different," he shook his head, clearly having trouble explaining it to me. I frowned. I hated that look on adults' faces when they thought I wasn't old enough or smart enough to understand. I think he knew it because when he caught sight of my expression he cleared his throat. "Your mother was sick that way, too, but mostly she was sick here," he tapped my head, "and here." The second time he put a long fingertip to my chest.

"I don't understand."

"Hmmm," he glanced around the room as if looking for a way to make things simple for me. "Have you ever felt like things were so bad and you were so sad, you thought you might never be happy again?"

I thought about the two weeks it rained at the group home. I nodded.

"That's the kind of sick I'm talking about," he explained, "Imagine you were sad like that for months, even years. Just like your body, if your heart gets sick long enough it can be dangerous."

"That's why I couldn't live with her anymore?"

"Pretty much." He stroked a long, red curl out of my eyes.

"Is that why she died?"

Gabriel gave me a long, blank look. If I'd been older, I might have read the smallest hints of shock and fear on his face.

"What makes you say she died?" he asked cautiously, his eyes narrowing at me.

"She did, didn't she?" I said. It was more of a statement than a question. "I dreamed it."

My father licked his lips and leaned forward, a sudden tautness riding his shoulders. "What exactly did you dream, Gracie? Tell me every detail."

There wasn't much to tell, but what I could remember I told him. By the end, the tension had mostly left his body and he nodded at my words more calmly.

"Do your dreams often come true?" he asked when I'd finished.

"I don't remember most dreams," I murmured, still gnawing on my forefinger. "But I remembered that one."

"I can understand that," he replied. Then he paused for a long moment, seemingly lost in thought. I watched his face carefully, unsure what he would say next. "You're right," he admitted finally. "Your mother did die three weeks ago. That was how I found out about you."

Instantly riveted, I gave him wide blue eyes. Seeing that I wasn't going to respond, he went on. "Just before she died, Amaya left me a message. She told me what happened and where to find you. I spent the two weeks after that getting ready for you and making sure I got all the paperwork put through. My parents helped a bit, pulled some strings. They have a lot of connections."

I wasn't sure what he meant by connections, but I did understand what he was saying about my mother. For a moment, I could almost feel her loving presence and tears pricked my eyes again. Though she couldn't come for me herself, my mother had done the only thing she could to protect me from the cold neglect of the group home. She'd sent my father.

"I'm sorry, Gracie," he continued, apparently seeing the tears hovering on the edge of my lashes. "If I'd known about you I would have come for you much sooner. Your mother did try everything she could to get you back before she came to me. She loved you very, very much."

I nodded quickly and brushed the tears away from my cheek with a rough hand. Though I'd let him comfort me before, somehow these tears felt too personal to let him witness. I think he sensed my mood because he was silent for a long moment.

"Gracie, did you hear me?" he asked, his eyes peering up at my face from behind an errant lock of dark hair.

"I know my mom loved me," I murmured, shying away from his gaze.

He tilted his head at me and frowned. "I mean, in your head. You didn't hear me say anything up here?" He tapped my forehead gently.

Confused and quite neatly distracted from my melancholy, I shook my head. "No. People can do that? Talk in each other's heads?"

"Yes." Gabriel's voice sounded startled. "It's called telepathy and most of our family has it. The group home said you have Awareness, too."

I bit my finger a little harder than I meant to. My stomach knotted. "I don't hear voices in my head."

"Perhaps there is something else different about you?" my father suggested, raising an eyebrow.

I was a little shocked they hadn't told him. Of course, we hadn't dallied long at the group home. He'd swept me out of there so fast, Clara probably hadn't had a chance. Remembering how quickly the other foster parents had found an excuse to reject me after learning of my otherness, I hesitated.

My father frowned as if he could sense my reluctance. "What is it, Gracie? Come now, whatever it is, I won't be upset. You can tell me."

I hesitated, trying to come up with the words to explain my gift. None came to me. Instead, my Awareness tugged at my mind like an undertow. Now that I'd thought of them, I could feel the flames licking at the back of my mind, eager for me to release them. Well, showing was better than explaining, right?

Slowly, I took the hand out of my mouth and held it out between us, palm up. Gabriel watched me with a solemn expression on his face. I glanced back down at my hand and willed the flames to curl into my palm.

Last time I reached for the fire, it took a considerable amount of effort to bring them forth. Now, however, they leaped from my mind so swiftly I found myself holding them back before they consumed my whole body.

Gabriel took a sharp breath as a brilliantly orange column of fire roared to life in my hand. With a rush of hot wind the flames took, blowing back our hair and illuminating our faces in yellow light.

"I see!" My father's voice was surprised. I looked at him warily, uncertain of what his response would be. Instead of fear or anger, however, he gave me a wry smile. "No wonder you couldn't find a foster family. How much can you do with the flames?" he asked, turning his gaze back to my burning hand.

Though the fire surrounded my hand, it didn't hurt. I tilted my head at it. "I don't know. Clara didn't want me to play with it. She said it was dangerous." With that statement, I banished the fire. The sudden darkness made strange dots float in front of my eyes.

"It is," my father agreed, "but it is equally dangerous for you to ignore this ability as it grows. No, Stella will give you lessons on history, math, language and science. This, however, is my area of specialty. You will take lessons on Awareness from me."

"I thought you had tell apathy, not fire," I said, confused.

"Telepathy," Gabriel corrected. "And just because you have one gift doesn't mean you can't have another. See?" He mirrored my gesture, placing his right hand between us, palm up. The flames that licked up from his palm were blue and quieter, more controlled, than mine. However, there was no denying their gently glowing tongues as they surrounded his flesh without consuming it.

"Does fire have a special name, like talking inside of heads?" I asked, watching the blue flames lick over his pale skin.

"Pyrokinesis."

"Pyro what?"

"Pie-Roe-Kin-Knee-Sis," Gabriel sounded it out for me slowly and I repeated it a few times carefully. For the first time, I had a name for my gift. It somehow felt satisfying and safe. I wasn't a strange, dangerous child anymore. I was a little girl in a gifted family and I had pyrokinesis, just like my dad.

CHAPTER 10

ARIEL

Life began to settle into a steady routine at Angelus Quietum.

Each day, my father would wake me up and make us breakfast. He was a good, utilitarian cook. We had a few chickens on the grounds and we always had fresh scrambled eggs along with some rice or toast.

Once I'd cleared the breakfast dishes into the ancient dishwasher, I would sit at the solid old kitchen table and have my lesson with Stella. The AI stood directly in the center of the table, unperturbed by its wooden length cutting through her waist, while she pulled up dozens of floating screens above my head. I tapped my answers to her problems into the memory pad in my hands or simply stated them directly to Stella herself.

At the risk of sounding smug, I must say I was quite smart. Stella remarked on it to my father repeatedly, especially when I began doing reading comprehension and creative writing. I was quite proud of myself when she recommended skipping me three grades ahead in language arts. My father shrugged and told Stella to teach me at whatever level I was ready for.

"After all, you don't have any other students to worry about this time," he said offhandedly as he shrugged on a fleece lined coat. He often went outside to split wood or feed the livestock while I was at lessons.

After lunch, my father would insist I have some time to myself to play outside. I soon discovered the joys of chasing chickens, climbing trees, and skipping rocks on the lake. This was what he called "being a kid."

After an hour or two of fresh air, Gabriel would come outside and sit with me. These were the moments I truly treasured. We'd talk about everything and anything, from the names of the trees and mountains around us to the best way to catch a fish. Within a few weeks, Gabriel was more than my father. He was my best friend.

This was also when he began to explain the way our Awareness worked. Slowly he began to give me challenges and exercises to practice. They weren't all about my pyrokinesis, either. Some involved controlling the flames or how to enhance them, but more of these lessons were about strengthening my mind and body. We rode horses, practiced three different types of martial arts, and even touched on various meditation strategies.

Though he praised my progress, and my skill at pyrokinesis advanced rapidly, my father was disconcerted by the fact that he could never hear my mind.

"You're past head blind, Gracie," he'd sigh. "You're shielded so tight it's like you're not even there."

Even so, I found our lessons both fun and satisfying. I kept getting stronger, physically and mentally, and I was proud of it.

Once the evening shadows lengthened, we'd head into the house for dinner. This was a more formal affair, with true place settings and absolutely no technology at the table. Even Stella wasn't allowed to disturb us during our evening meal. I set the table while my father cooked. Then, after dinner, we would clean up together before settling in the living room to watch holo-programs or read a book.

My favorite evenings were when Gabriel would stack some logs in the fireplace and nod his head at me. I'd flash him a mischievous grin before summoning a torrent of flame with a wave of one hand. My father would laugh proudly at my display and settle on the couch to read. He was fond of reading aloud and I never tired of hearing his animated voice as he mimicked each character's personality.

It was during one of these evenings that I saw the woman with the copper curls again.

Gabriel had sprawled his full length along the leather couch with a blanket across his lap. I was tucked next to him, my head resting on his shoulder. He held the memory pad casually in one hand while the other arm wrapped around my shoulders. The rumble of his voice was low and reassuring as I read along with him on the memory pad.

A little flash of movement in the corner caught my attention. The woman stood by the fireplace this time. Her hair and clothing were the same, blowing gently in the intangible wind that followed her.

I was not afraid. Safely tucked into my father's arms with the soft glow of the fireplace illuminating the room, this lovely young woman simply didn't seem threatening. In fact, her gaze was soft, almost loving, as she looked down at us on the couch. I opened my mouth to say something to my father, but she raised a finger to her lips and shook her head gently just as she had before. Obediently I closed it again, tucking my chin against Gabriel's breast. Still, I watched her gently glowing form as she stood next to the mantel.

Apparently she noticed that my eyes hadn't left her because she gave me a small smile. I returned it and for the first time I noticed that she was holding a small, blue book in her hand. Her smile deepened into something almost amused and she pointed over my head.

With a frown, I looked up towards the back of the couch where the woman indicated. Had I not been curled up in the safest, warmest place I could imagine, I probably would have jumped out of my skin. Instead, I gazed sleepily up at another woman who sat gracefully perched atop the sofa back.

Where my father's sharp features were echoed clearly in the first glowing woman, this one seemed unrelated with a soft, rounded, mortal face. Her large eyes were green and her hair was the same copper color as the woman by the fireplace. The long, wavy strands fell about her petite shoulders in a shimmering curtain. Her clothing was blue and cut in an old-fashioned way with elastic at the cuffs of her sleeves. Unlike the other woman, she did not so much as glance at me. It was instantly clear that she only had eyes for my father. She gazed at him with a sad tenderness as she reached out a delicate hand to stroke his dark hair.

Gabriel didn't react to her touch. Instead, he continued reading aloud, scrolling down the page of the book even though I'd long since stopped paying attention. He'd be annoyed with me later when he wanted to discuss the plot, but I felt a complete relaxed fascination with these two women. I've wondered since if I was in some state of hypnosis or if I simply picked up on the gentle energy of these two apparitions. Whatever the case, I felt no fear despite the fact that I could clearly see the hallway door through the woman's faintly glowing head. Her hand reached out to touch my father's face and her shapely fingertips passed right through his skin.

Gabriel gave a shiver and tucked me closer to his body. "I'm sorry, Gracie," he gasped. I glanced up at him. His face looked rather pale. "I'm…" he hesitated, eyes dark with some kind of pain. I wasn't sure if it was physical or emotional, but I suspected it had to do with the woman's touch. He glanced down at me. "I'm not feeling very well. Would you mind if I finished this chapter tomorrow?"

"No, I don't mind, Daddy," I replied. I glanced up at the woman on the sofa back. Her hands folded back into her lap but she still gazed at my father with a look of hopeless longing.

"Thanks, kiddo," he said, tussling my hair affectionately, "Go get your shower. I'll be in to kiss you goodnight in a few minutes."

"Okay," I replied, leaning up to kiss his cheek as he slowly levered himself to a sitting position. Normally he moved so smoothly, but at this moment he almost seemed old. He gave me a weak smile and I felt a bit of worry squirm in my stomach. After all, I'd already lost one parent.

The thought was too horrible to contemplate, so I pushed it away and scampered off to the bathroom.

A few minutes later, damp but clean, I climbed into bed and waited eagerly for Gabriel to come and kiss me goodnight. It didn't take long before he did, looking thin and pale. He dutifully kissed my forehead and smoothed back my hair. His eyes seemed strangely sunken, almost bruised.

"Sleep well, sweetheart," he murmured. Then, after adjusting my blanket to make sure it covered the bed properly, he left the room.

It didn't take long for the woman with the brown skirt suit to show up again. This time, though, I'd suspected she might make another appearance and I wasn't afraid when she melted into the room. Instead, I watched with interest as she slowly materialized as if from thin air. Once again, I noticed the little blue book she was holding close to one breast.

My attempts to talk to her before had been futile, so I didn't make a sound. Instead, the two of us spent a long moment staring at each other. Finally, realizing that she wasn't making a move, I decided I had nothing to lose by trying again.

"I saw you in the living room," I said. I figured it was a little less direct than my first few questions. Perhaps this simple statement wouldn't chase her away.

The woman frowned at me and I thought I saw frustration on her face. Then, with a movement so sudden I nearly dove under my blankets again, she darted towards the closet door. Her body didn't cast a reflection in the mirror, nor did the door appear to offer any resistance. Instead, she poured right through the barrier as if it were nonexistent, disappearing completely into the closet.

It was my turn to frown. This was the most movement I'd seen from either apparition so far. I might have been a quiet, mostly obedient child for the last six years, but now that I was well-fed and wanted, I discovered a new aspect of my personality. I was insanely curious. So, instead of huddling in my bed like a nice, normal child, I decided to go take a peek in the closet.

For a moment I paused to inspect my reflection. This wasn't something I did on a frequent basis. After all, I'd just left a group home with a half dozen older girls who all claimed priority in the girl's room mirror. I never cared enough to muscle my way in front of the looking glass.

My father hadn't lied about my eyes. They were just like his: pits of midnight blue flame. They looked out of a face that was a little too strongly featured to be the typical cute six-year-old girl. The pale oval of my face was framed by a wild mane of wavy red hair. I was so thin, the curls seemed to envelop me completely as they tangled their way to my waist. My new pink nightdress fell to the floor, hiding my skinny legs and bare feet.

I reached for the door knob. My hand felt strangely detached from myself as I watched it in the mirror. Then I swung the door open and the mirror was no longer in my line of sight.

To my slight disappointment, the closet seemed empty. Several clean outfits hung from a long rail over my head and the small blue suitcase sat tucked up against one wall.

A few low shelves, perhaps intended for shoes, lined the right hand side.

A bit sad that the woman had completely disappeared again, I began to close the closet door. Then, just as the shadow fell across the low shelves, a little corner of something snagged my interest. I tilted my head at it and, wondering if I was seeing strange shadows, leaned in the door to get a better look at the object.

Thick dust clung to my fingers as I pulled the little blue book from the corner of the closet. I brushed it off on my nightdress and cringed at the gray fingerprints I left on the pale, pink fabric. I hoped Dad wouldn't be cross with me when he discovered it in the wash.

A soft, red light filled the little closet and I looked up directly into the glowing woman's gaze. Startled, I stumbled back a step. The woman made no move to reach for me, however. Instead, she held up the little blue book in her hand, then pointed to the one in mine.

I opened the cover of the book. I nearly choked on the amount of dust in the pages, which were so old and fragile they nearly crumbled in my hand. I could feel the spine cracking in my palms as I opened it. Fortunately, I was a gentle child and I handled the book with care. On the first page, I could see a lovely flowing script. It read:

"This journal belongs to Ariel Usuriel"

I glanced up at the apparition. "Is that your name? Ariel?"

The woman nodded, a smile lighting her face. She let her book fall open to the first page. Out of one pocket, she pulled a pen and wrote in the book. Eagerly, I turned to the first page in my book. It was blank. Then letters began to form as if the woman's pen was moving across the page in front of me.

"Hello, Gracie," the gently curved script read. "Yes, my name is Ariel. It is a pleasure to meet you."

"How did you know my name?" I asked, my head snapping over to Ariel's faintly glowing face. She smiled down at me, then she looked back at the book in her hands and began to write again. I quickly read along with her moving script.

"I heard what Father called you."

"Gabriel's your dad too?" I felt a bit confused. This woman looked old enough to be my mother. Gabriel hardly looked old enough to be my father, let alone father to a grown woman. Make that a grown ghost. I might be young, but I wasn't stupid. Ghosts were the only thing these women could be... right?

I wasn't sure, but I suspected from the expression on my new friend's face and the way her shoulders shook that she was giving me some silent laughter. When she recovered, she wrote another line.

"Yes, Gabriel Usuriel is my father."

"He looks younger than you," I told her bluntly.

Glancing down at the book for her responses was becoming natural. "That's because he has never, and will never, age a day past twenty-five."

I blinked at that information. "Really? Are all gifted people like that? Will I grow up and never get old either?"

Ariel shook her head, glowing curls tossing about her head. Her answer was much longer this time and I found myself impatiently waiting for each word to resolve on the page. "No, not all gifted people are like that. It will take a longer time, but eventually you will probably get old just like other humans. The Family members left who don't age are Vanessa, Lillian, Gabriel, and his parents, D'nay and Gloria."

I considered this for a moment then narrowed my eyes at her. "Left? You mean there used to be more of them? What happened to the other ones?"

"Just because you don't age doesn't mean you can't die," she wrote.

"All of them died?" I asked quickly. This was just the kind of conversation I'd been eager to have with my father, but he never seemed willing to broach the subject of his own Awareness. I'd stumbled across a gold mine!

"Do you always ask this many questions?"

"No." I tried for defensive but a yawn snuck into my mouth by surprise. Ariel did a little, silent ghost laugh again and began to fade into the darkness of the closet. Alarmed, I reached out for her. My hand slid right through her arm with no effect. "Wait!"

It was no use. My sister had completely vanished, leaving a well of shadows in her place. I glanced down at the book. One final line materialized in her neat, curved handwriting.

"Goodnight, Gracie."

Chapter 11

The Usuriel Homestead

Of course, we didn't stay at Angelus Quietum every second of every day. Though the property was far removed from most civilization, my father's gifts made transportation an inconsequential problem. A wink and a nod and we could be anywhere, from the top of a mountain to the heart of Skykyle City.

For routine things like groceries, Gabriel would leave me with our neighbor, Carol, while he went alone. Other times, such as clothes shopping, he'd check the weather with Stella before telling me how to dress. Then he'd take my hand and suddenly Angelus Quietum would bleed away in ribbons of liquid color while a new location faded into focus. We shopped in Skykyle City's upscale district on a fairly regular basis. For my seventh birthday, we went to four different shops and bought enough clothes to nearly fill my walk-in closet.

Very occasionally, Gabriel would tell me to pack for the night. The first time I looked at him blankly until he pulled out the blue suitcase himself and showed me how to pack an overnight bag. Oh, the simple things our parents teach us. I don't know that we ever really appreciate it at the time. I can still hear his voice in my head when I pack for a trip.

"Don't forget an extra pair of socks and underwear. You never know when you're going to need them."

Our first trip was a visit to my grandparent's house. They lived to the south in a small, richly-green valley nestled in the foothills of the Galloway Mountains. If you climbed the nearest rise, Lake Angelus spread out below you like a blue looking glass.

Chronurea Valley was a small collection of houses and other buildings in the middle of a wooded meadow. My father teleported us right in front of the largest of these: a huge, white country estate that overlooked the rest of the small yet scenic community.

We didn't stand there more than a moment before a young, blonde woman came running out of the front door.

"Gabriel!" Her voice was melodious and her smile infectious.

My father laughed and dropped my suitcase on the dirt path so that he could catch her with one arm. She wrapped herself around his neck in a flurry of long, golden hair. I realized how short she was when he lifted her fully off of her feet.

"Oh my! You must be Gracie!" She beamed down at me as she slid gracefully away from my father. "Oh, Gabe, she's beautiful," she said, turning to my grinning parent. "She looks just like Ariel, doesn't she?"

Gabriel's smile dimmed a touch before he shrugged ruefully and picked up the suitcase. "You don't have to tell me," he sighed, glancing down at me. "Gracie, this is your Grandma Gloria."

I stared up at the youthful, sparkling-eyed woman. Her eyes were a brighter blue than my father's—so clear they were almost like cut crystal. I'd never had grandparents, but I'd always imagined them with gray hair and wrinkles.

"Hello," I said, trying to sound polite despite my surprise.

"Gabe!" A man's voice called from the house and I glanced over Gloria's shoulder. For a moment I thought I was going crazy. I knew I was holding my father's hand, but the man walking towards us looked so much like him I truly mistook him for Gabriel. As he got nearer, however, I noticed subtle differences. When he stood next to my father, he was perhaps two inches taller and his dark hair, while also worn long, was perfectly straight. He shook Dad's hand affectionately and his skin was a shade or two paler than Gabriel's as well. Aside from that, they were as identical as twins.

This new man turned his intense, blue gaze in my direction and I met his eyes with open curiosity. When I didn't shrink back, he smiled and put a hand out to Gloria. She took it and wrapped his arm around her shoulders as she tucked her own about his waist. Clearly they were a couple.

"Gracie, this is your grandfather, D'nay," Gloria explained. I should have guessed. He couldn't look any more like his son if he tried.

"Nice to meet you, Gracie." D'nay's voice was a touch deeper than Gabriel's but not by much. He offered me a smile that showed very straight, sharp teeth. "Come on, I was just baking some banana nut muffins. I know they're your favorite," he said to my dad.

Gabriel groaned but couldn't suppress a pleased smile. "Trying to win her over with muffins already."

D'nay's laugh was exactly like my father's. It echoed over his shoulder as he and Gloria turned smoothly towards the door. Gabriel and I dutifully followed their lead into the house.

My grandparent's house was simple and elegant. Like Angelus Quietum, the building materials were all of the highest quality. The furniture's curves offered both grace and functionality. There was little clutter, though photographs and paintings hung on almost every wall. Quite a number of them featured my father.

As we walked into the sunlit living room, the aroma of baking muffins filled the air. I leaned into the irresistible scent, trying to peer around the corner of the dining room to catch a glimpse of the kitchen.

D'nay chuckled at my expression and held out a hand. "Why don't you let your dad get your things settled upstairs? I think those muffins are just about ready to eat."

I dared a glance up at my father. He nodded gently and let go of my hand. "Save me one or two, Miss Bottomless Pit," he teased, shooing me towards the kitchen.

It didn't take more encouragement than that. With a delighted giggle, I swapped one tall, dark Usuriel man for the other and began dragging my amused grandfather towards the kitchen.

"You're a fiery little thing, aren't you?" D'nay laughed as we burst into the kitchen. The smell of freshly baked muffins became overwhelming and my mouth watered.

The kitchen was a clean, classic affair with a smooth-topped stove and tall, white cabinets. A center island with a gold-shot marble top squatted in the middle of the room. Racks of cooling muffins sat steaming on the island.

"Can I have one? Can I? Can I please?" I begged, jumping up and down. D'nay looked so much like my father it was easy for me to feel comfortable around him.

"Of course," he said, snagging a wooden stool from the small mudroom next to the kitchen and setting it at the island. I settled onto it as he turned back to grab another one for himself. "I baked them for you and Gabe."

I didn't reply because my mouth was too full of delicious muffin. I could see why these were Dad's favorite. They were moist, rich, and fresh out of the oven—heaven in bran form.

D'nay watched me stuff my face with a rather satisfied expression. He poured me a glass of milk from the refrigerator, then leaned an elbow on the table to watch me, his long, dark hair falling into his eyes. "Well, any good?" he asked.

"Mmmm-hmmm!" I exclaimed through a mouthful of bananay goodness. My grandfather smiled.

"Glad you like it," he said, his blue eyes twinkling. "So, how's living with your dad? Do you like it at Angelus Quietum?"

I swallowed quickly and nodded hard at the same time. D'nay patted my back as I nearly choked.

"Sorry, I shouldn't ask when your mouth is full," he apologized. He waited for me to finish chewing before asking his next question. "You just had a birthday, didn't you? How old are you now?"

"Seven," I said proudly, giving him a crumb-filled smile. "Daddy bought me this dress."

D'nay tilted his head to get a better look at the dress. It was a lovely, green plaid that went well over my long sleeved blouse.

"The color suits you," my grandfather said politely, motioning to my red hair.

Gloria's voice floated in from the other room. "I just want to make sure you're taking it easy. I haven't seen you that sick since the *Inspiration*."

"Really, Mom, I'm fine," my father responded. His tone sounded petulant. Believe me, a seven year old knows something about petulance. "I'm even starting to gain some weight back."

"You still look a bit pale," Gloria sighed as they walked into view of the doorway. She was looking up at her son with concern, a small frown on her delicate face.

"Yeah, well, I haven't exactly been kind to myself the last few decades," he admitted with a self-deprecating smile. "Even Usuriels show wear and tear if you abuse us enough."

"That I do know." Her expression softened then, patting his shoulder before gliding over to D'nay's side. "Which is why I worry about you over there all by yourself. Doesn't it get lonely on the other side of the lake?"

Gabriel mirrored his father, bending over to lean an elbow on the island next to me while he snagged a muffin. He gave me a wink as he lazily chewed. "I'm not alone," he muttered through a mouthful of muffin. Swallowing the rest, he reached out a hand and stroked my hair affectionately. "I've got Gracie and Stella to keep me company."

A loud knock at the front door made all three adults snap to attention. Their heads swiveled towards the door and they froze in a look of rapt concentration. I found myself strangely proud of how fiercely protective they looked.

"I've told that pesky reporter to find something else to write about four times in the last two months," Gloria grumbled, her face relaxing from sharp alertness to re-signed annoyance. She ran a possessive hand down D'nay's back before pushing off the island towards the front door.

"You want me to give him a good scare?" Gabe offered, popping the rest of the muffin into his mouth.

"Don't you dare," his mother hissed, shaking a slim finger in his direction. "You've caused enough trouble as it is. Don't give him any more to report on."

My father held up his hands in a gesture of helplessness. Gloria rolled her eyes and stalked in the direction of the front door. Gabriel watched her leave, then turned back to D'nay. His father was glaring daggers at him from about six inches away. I sat very still, hoping my suddenly predatory grandfather wouldn't notice me.

"Be very glad your daughter is here. Otherwise I'd have some choice words for you, kid," D'nay growled.

Gabriel ran a nervous hand through his long, dark hair. "Come on, Dad, we've had this conversation already."

"That was before this investigative... jerk... started sniffing around." D'nay grimaced as he caught himself. "I'm not sure you know how much trouble this guy could be."

My father tried to keep the cavalier look on his face, but it fell a bit flat. Underneath I thought I saw something else cross his features. I wasn't sure what emotion it was, but I did know it made my confident, quick-witted father look more vulnerable than I'd ever seen him. I swallowed down a hard lump in my throat.

"No, I will not reconsider an interview and that's final," Gloria's voice sounded loud and angry. The whole house shook as she slammed the door.

The Usuriel men shared a quick glance that communicated far more than any words. Then Gloria stormed back into the room and the silent standoff was broken.

"I swear this is harassment," she grumbled, taking a muffin from one of the cooling racks. "If he comes to the door again I'm calling the watch."

"You would have every right to, love," D'nay agreed, finally snagging a muffin for himself.

There was silence while my grandparents ate their treat. They seemed unwilling to talk through their full mouths the way Gabriel and I had done. In fact, all three adults seemed lost in their own worlds. They stared off into space as if completely occupied with their own quiet thoughts. I joined them, wondering what exactly that reporter wanted to talk to my grandparents about. Given how willing my father was to talk about things he deemed 'adult matters,' I didn't bother asking aloud.

Once she finished chewing, Gloria gave a deep sigh and glanced around at the rest of us. "Well, that's that I suppose. What do you boys say we break out the old singles cards? I'll bet Gracie will be a real shark at that game."

Gabriel gave a quick smile that didn't quite reach his eyes. "Sure. That sounds like fun. What do you think, Gracie? Want to learn a new card game?"

"Okay," I agreed and slid off my stool. I took my father's hand and let him lead me into the dining room.

The rest of the evening was pleasant enough. Gloria beat us soundly in the first round. Then I won a hand or two before D'nay had to go start dinner. Gloria called an end to the card game and had Gabriel and I set the table while she helped her husband in the kitchen.

Dinner was a roast duck. I'd never tasted duck before. It was a bit chewier than the fat chickens my father kept out back, but it was savory in the sweet lemon sauce D'nay had let it simmer in.

"After my morning appointments, I ate lunch down at the University yesterday," Gloria said between bites of mashed potatoes.

I glanced between her and Dad for a moment, feeling a bit lost. I knew about Landing University because Stella had access to their archives, but I wasn't sure what Gloria was talking about when she said 'appointments.'

"Your grandmother is a healer at the Landing University Hospital," Gabriel explained to my questioning expression.

"Oh," I poked at a lump in my potatoes. "Is healing your Awareness gift, then?"

Gloria chuckled. "It's not the only one but yes, it's probably the psi I use most these days. Anyway, as I was saying," she cleared her throat and leaned towards my father. "I saw Lillian in the cafeteria. She's still teaching, if you can believe it. I really don't think she's aging at all. She might just be a half like you, Gabe."

My father swallowed hard, his face carefully blank. He gave my grandmother a long blink before looking back down at his plate with an intense interest.

D'nay cleared his throat and gave me a small smile. I smiled back and took another bite, trying to ignore the awkward silence.

"Do you like the potatoes, Gracie?" my grandfather asked.

"Yes, sir," I replied. "Dad doesn't make them with cheese."

"That's the good part," D'nay protested, giving Gabriel a playful glare.

Gabriel shrugged. "Carol's been out of cheese the last two times I've been down to the farm."

"You can always come up to Landing for supplies," Gloria suggested.

"You can do the celebrity thing if you feel like it," my father sighed. I thought he looked rather tired. "I'll pass, thanks."

"You know, if you went down there on a regular basis, people wouldn't stare so badly. I mean, they hardly even blink when your father and I go in for our groceries."

Gabriel shrugged and glanced at my plate. I'd pushed the peas around a bit, but otherwise the plate was clean. I liked my grandfather's cooking.

"Finished, Grace?" he asked. That might have been the first time he left off the 'ee' sound at the end of my name. It made me sound more grown up. I liked it.

"Yes, I'm full," I said, setting down my knife and fork.

"I put your things in the guest room upstairs. Why don't you go read for a bit?"

I knew when I was being dismissed and I wasn't sure I liked it. I'd been about to ask to be excused to do exactly as he'd suggested, but if they didn't want me in ear shot they were about to talk about something interesting. I hesitated, glancing at my grandparents. D'nay's face was carefully blank, but my grandmother gave me a gentle smile.

"Go on, sweetheart. I'll come up and show you some stills in a little bit."

Slightly mollified by the idea of getting Gloria's undivided attention, I dutifully cleared my place into the kitchen sink and went upstairs.

Chapter 12

Olivia

The upstairs of my grandparent's house was very much like the living area. I admired the clean and homey landing, its large windows letting in the buttery yellow light of the setting sun. The carpet was thick and plush, its buff color giving a sense of light to the flower-patterned wallpaper. Above a plush chair hung a large still life done in rich, saturated colors. Next to the painting a tall doorway led to a hallway lined with more framed artwork. These were not of fruit or flowers, however, but people.

I paused at the entrance to the hallway. A small part of me was interested in the paintings, but the other, larger part was straining my ears to see if I could catch any of the adults' conversation downstairs. To my great disappointment, there was complete silence from the dining room. So instead, I allowed my eyes to wander over the portraits hung in the hallway.

The first was clearly Gloria and D'nay. They were dressed in the same oddly cut blue uniforms I'd seen on the glowing woman at Angelus Quietum. Gloria's hair was shorter and cut to frame the sharp angles of her cheekbones. Her husband wore his hair back in a tight ponytail. Gloria sat in a sleek metal chair, her back straight and her head set at an almost arrogant angle. D'nay stood behind and slightly to one side of her, one graceful hand resting possessively on his wife's shoulder.

I moved on to the next painting. This one was a soft-edged scene of mother and child. Gloria's hair was still short. In fact, that was the only way I recognized her from one painting to the other. The artist had captured the curve of her neck and breast but neglected to include much of her face. The child was thin for a baby, but cute in the way that infants usually are. The child had huge, wide eyes and reached up towards Gloria's face. A blue sweep of blanket, wrapped around the baby's waist, hid their gender. I wasn't sure if my father had any brothers or sisters. If so, he'd never mentioned any.

The last painting was clearly a wedding portrait. I knew for sure that my father was front and center of this piece. His broad shoulders filled out a cleanly-cut formal suit. The tie and lapels were not modern but classically elegant anyway. On his arm stood a woman with wavy copper hair, green eyes, and a smattering of freckles. She was dressed in the formal white and blue gown of a bride, lace spilling from every available surface. A band of silver held the hair out of her beaming face. I had a sneaking suspicion she was the unnamed glowing woman I'd seen at Angelus Quietum. The two of them were framed by an elaborate stained glass window depicting a starship amidst swirling constellations.

My eyes were drawn back to my father. Something was different about him but I couldn't put my finger on it. His hair was the same length, though pulled back as his father's had been in the other portrait. His face had the same smooth angles and planes. Apparently Ariel hadn't lied to me when she said Gabriel didn't age. Frowning, I looked up into the painted eyes. It was there that I saw it, this subtle yet crucial change. Something about my father's eyes was wrong in this painting, but for the life of me, I couldn't figure out what.

"Oh my." Gloria's voice nearly made me jump through the painting. She climbed the steps towards me alone. "I completely forgot to take that down. No wonder Gabe's in such a mood."

"Who is the woman he's getting married to?" I asked once my heart stopped trying to escape my ribs.

Gloria folded her hands in front of her where they all but disappeared into the folds of her white, linen dress. "If I tell you, you cannot discuss it with your father," she warned, a stern look on her face.

"Why not?" I asked, glancing up at the painting. They both looked so happy.

My grandmother sighed deeply and put a hand on my shoulder. It was delicate and warm. "A thousand reasons, sweetheart. Mostly because it makes him sad."

"Oh." My gaze darted between her and the painting, hoping she would go on.

Her eyes became distant and her face seemed almost wistful. "Her name was Olivia. She was your father's first wife. He loved her very much… more than I think he's ever loved anyone."

The sun had vanished below the horizon and the only light came from the one she'd turned on at the landing. It lit her smooth skin gently. Her crystal blue eyes darkened in the shadow. For the first time I thought she seemed older than my father.

"What happened to her?" I asked.

Gloria gave me an incredibly sad smile. I realized with a pang that she looked far more like my father with sorrow in her gaze.

"She was mortal," she murmured, stroking my hair absently. It had been a long time since I felt the reassuring touch of a motherly woman. I held perfectly still, enjoying the unexpectedly warm sensation of her touch. Even though I hardly knew her, there was something right and safe about Gloria's presence.

"You mean she wasn't Aware?" I asked when Gloria drifted off into silent remembering.

"No, she wasn't Aware," she replied, "and like all mortals, she eventually faded away." Something flashed through her expression—more than just sadness. Was it... guilt? Regret? I was too young and inexperienced to interpret it at the time and now the fog of memory obscures the details. Either way, I knew Gloria had feelings about this topic that she wasn't sharing with me.

After a long pause, she patted my shoulder and stepped towards the painting. Reaching up over her head, she took the frame in both hands and lifted it down gently. She looked down into the two happy, smiling faces for a moment. Then, without another word, she waved a hand over the painting and it vanished into thin air.

I'd seen my father do something similar enough times that I wasn't surprised. Most likely she'd teleported the painting to an attic or basement. My father had a habit of teleporting toys I'd left lying around the house directly into the center of my bed so that I had to put them away before I went to sleep. It was annoyingly effective at teaching me to pick up after myself.

"Come on, why don't I show you some pictures of your father when he was your age?" Gloria said, a happier glint in her eyes.

I glanced over my shoulder towards the stairs. She followed my gaze and smiled. "Don't worry, your dad and

D'nay went for a walk. They should be back before we go to sleep."

With that, I allowed her to lead me away from the darkened hallway.

CHAPTER 13

SECRETS

I spent the evening quietly with my grandmother pouring over old stills. She called them photographs, though I'd never heard that term before. Some of them were so old they were falling apart at the edges while others were carefully preserved in some kind of plex casing. These stills were of a much younger Gabriel, though Gloria and D'nay looked about the same. Gloria's hair length varied and occasionally she switched to a brunette look, but for the most part the adult Usuriels didn't change.

"Why don't Usuriels age?" I asked, staring down at a youthful photo of my grandparents with brown water stains over its lower half.

"Well, it depends upon the Usuriel you're discussing." Gloria continued flipping through the pages. It was a little odd to see a baby version of my father. He was a chubby child until he hit about two, then he slimmed down to a wiry little thing with huge blue eyes and dark brown hair. "Your grandfather's curse keeps him at the age he died. Your father and I, on the other hand, simply inherited immortality from our Anori ancestors."

"Grandfather is cursed?" I asked, trying to divide my attention between the pictures and my grandmother's fascinating conversation. We were passing through Dad's childhood years now, and there were a lot of pictures with him posing next to wheeled vehicles. That also dated the photographs. Bikes and scooters were occasionally used in the cities these days, but for long distances everyone used hovercraft, shuttles, or psi-gates. Of course, I'd never used a shuttle or a psi-gate, but I'd seen them on holo-programs.

Grandma Gloria laughed as if I'd said something funny. "Not with me around, I suppose." She cleared her throat. "Mortals call vampirism a curse, but in your grandfather's case I've always looked at it as a blessing. After all, I would never have met or married him if he'd died as some forgotten, mortal nobleman's son."

"So, D'nay is a vampire?"

"D'nay Usuriel is your grandfather," Grandma Gloria said with great finality. I decided it would be wiser to focus on the photos for a moment.

Once Dad reached his teen years, he started to appear next to shuttles. Pretty women started getting into the pictures, too, and that familiar arrogant tilt to his chin began showing itself.

"Ah, here we go." Grandma Gloria tapped a still of Dad and Grandpa D'nay covered in grease, taking apart what looked like a shuttle engine. "That's the shuttle your father nearly exploded in the test bay."

I grinned up at her and she began the first of several amusing stories about trouble Dad got himself into with groups of friends. Apparently he was a good pilot, but not too overly fond of following safety rules and regulations. She'd just finished telling me about the time he nearly wrecked one of D'nay's prototype shuttles on a dare when the man in question showed up in the doorway.

"D'nay had him running the supply drone for three weeks after that one," Gloria was telling me in a conspiratorial tone. "He hated those supply drones. I don't think they got much over fifty kilometers per hour. He used to say they were the slowest things he'd ever flown."

"They were," Gabriel said, knocking a bit belatedly on the open door. "Absolutely brain-drainingly dull."

Gloria smiled up at him. "How was your walk?"

He nodded absently as if he didn't really want to talk about it. "Telling Gracie all of my secrets?" he joked, sitting down on the bed next to us.

Gloria raised an eyebrow at him, her expression suddenly grim. He matched her look with a sharp one of his own. I had a strange feeling they were communicating silently over my head. For the first time I experienced the secluded frustration of a head blind mortal in the company of powerful telepaths. It would certainly not be the last.

Their silence stretched on a bit long and I squirmed. Finally, my father glanced down, meeting my gaze and forcing a smile. I nearly recoiled from the pain in his eyes. I suddenly understood what was different about him in that old painting.

"Go get a shower and change into your night clothes, Gracie," he said sternly.

Gabriel rarely took such a commanding tone with me. I paused, frowning up at him. "But I was enjoying the pictures with Gloria," I whined, giving him big, blue eyes. "I wanted to see Ariel when she was a little girl."

My father's voice dropped to a gravelly growl and his expression was one of pure fury. "Go get in that shower now," he snarled, "and don't make me repeat myself."

My heart clenched, anxiety rising from that deep fear of abandonment I hadn't felt since the group home. I quickly went to my suitcase and got out my nightdress. Holding the soft cotton to my chest, I dared a glance back up at the two adults.

My father wasn't even looking in my direction anymore. He had his arms crossed while glaring silently at my grandmother. She'd closed the still album and pressed it tightly to her chest, a flushed look of indignation on her face. Seeing me hesitating in the doorway, her expression softened and she got up to put a hand on my shoulder.

"You're scaring the child, Gabriel," she said, anger hotly riding her tone. "And keeping her in the dark is only going to do more damage than good. Mark my words."

My father's eyes were hard as he turned his gaze on me. A lick of blue flame flashed in his iris before sliding into a small thread of fire that flickered about his chest. His dark hair tossed about his shoulders and he glowed as if lit from within. Gabriel had never lost so much control at home. Startled, I shrank back against my grandmother.

I saw it the instant he realized how much he'd frightened me with his display of temper. The fire disappeared completely and instead was replaced with a blank expression that could have hidden a multitude of things. He closed his eyes and suddenly seemed very old to me. I found that almost as dreadful as his anger.

"Please go, Gracie." He sounded so tired. I no longer feared him, but a small thread of anxiety still squirmed in my stomach.

"Go on," Gloria echoed my father's request and I slowly left the room. I was beginning to realize that I was caught in the middle of an argument I didn't understand. It was a rather awful feeling.

In the shower, I tried to make sense of why my father would lose his temper at my grandmother so quickly. Little hints and clues nagged at me but no matter how I twisted and turned things in my head, none of it made any more sense. There had to be something big they weren't telling me. My mind drifted to my bag and the little blue book I'd hidden away inside one of my clean shirts. I had only ever seen Ariel outside of Angelus Quietum once, but perhaps if I wrote her a message, she might be willing to travel a bit.

By the time I left the bathroom, my teeth brushed and my nightgown neatly in place, I had a plan. When I walked into my little guest room, I wasn't surprised to find my father waiting for me alone. He sat, shoulders slumped, on the edge of the bed. He glanced up at me as I walked into the room.

"Hey, come have a seat," he said, patting the bed next to him. It was such a quiet, reassuringly familiar request. Obediently, I slunk over to the bed and sat down.

"I'm sorry if I scared you," he said, voice low. "You didn't do anything wrong. I'm just out of sorts, that's all."

I could hear that dreadful pain in his voice. It was his constant companion, but tonight it seemed especially raw. I thought about the painting and how happy he'd looked in it. My heart broke for him, and I tried to make it better in the only way I knew how. I wrapped my arms tightly around his waist and buried my face in his shoulder.

He made a startled noise, then wrapped his arms around me, holding me close. I closed my eyes and clung to his warm strength. I needed to believe that he was steady and solid, that he would protect me and take care of me. I needed him to be a parent, not a damaged, mysterious man who might lose his temper at any moment.

"I'm sorry," he repeated into my hair.

"Why were you angry with grandma?" I asked, even though I knew I shouldn't. What can I say? Insanely curious, remember?

"Because the world is an ugly place," he sighed, leaning back a bit so that we could look at each other. "I want to keep the bad parts away from you as long as I can. Do you understand?"

I nodded slowly. "What kind of bad parts?"

He shook his head and kissed the top of my head. "Someday, sweetie, I will tell you everything. I promise. But now it's time for bed. You smell nice and clean. Did you remember to wash your face?"

I grimaced at him. "Yes, Daddy."

"Good," he said, standing to pull back the covers. I dutifully climbed into bed. Gabriel switched on a night-light next to the door frame. He pulled Doggie Dog out of my suitcase and tucked him in next to me. Then Gabriel turned off the reading light by the bed and gave my cheek a last kiss. "Goodnight, Gracie."

"Goodnight," I replied, cuddling up against Doggie Dog's soft form. I wasn't even close to tired. But since I, unsurprisingly, wasn't getting any answers out of my father, I was eager for him to leave me alone.

He offered me a last sad smile before closing the door behind him.

CHAPTER 14

ASKING QUESTIONS

I waited for my father's footsteps to fade down the hallway before tossing off the covers and dashing over to the little blue suitcase. Unlatching it, I quickly pulled out the red shirt I'd tucked Ariel's journal into. The little book seemed unharmed from its trip. After rummaging about for a pencil, I took both prizes back to the bed.

Flipping the reading light back on, I curled up in the soft comforter and opened the journal. I'd had a few conversations with Ariel since our first one in the closet. They hadn't been about anything consequential, though. Mostly we'd talked about my birthday and shopping trips with Dad. She'd been quite amused by the little fashion show I put on for her benefit. I quickly flipped past the pages of those conversations and ran a hand over the next smooth, empty page. I'd never tried to summon Ariel or write in her book before, but I had a sneaking suspicion she'd be able to see it wherever she was. I spent a moment wondering where ghosts went when they weren't haunting people. Well, that was as good a question as any to ask.

"Ariel," I wrote carefully, trying to keep my writing neat and clean. I had only been writing in complete sentences for a year or two, though, so it was still a bit wobbly around the edges. I felt a touch bad about ruining a lovely page of my sister's journal, but I really needed to talk to her. "Where are you?"

A warm wind ruffled my hair and an intense smell of flowers and old books filled the room. I saw Ariel's red-yellow glow light up the walls and a huge sense of relief flooded me. I hadn't been sure writing to her would work.

"Right here, little sister." Her words were small, clean and neat next to mine. Even as I watched, her slim form materialized from thin air. She was seated at the foot of my bed, graceful white hands holding her version of the blue book in her lap.

"Where do you go when you're not talking to me?" I asked, tilting my head at her.

"Oh, here and there." She gave me a slightly cryptic smile. I glowered at her.

"Now you sound like Dad," I accused.

Her eyebrows went up. "What do you mean?"

"Every time I ask him an interesting question, he doesn't give me a real answer," I complained, folding my arms across my chest before glancing down at the book for her response.

"What is it that you want to know?"

The question made me pause for a moment. She was offering me the information I wanted, but suddenly I wasn't sure what information that was. My mind flew over the strange comments my father and grandparents had made.

"Gloria said my father was sick recently. What made him sick?"

Ariel shook her head. "I'm not sure. He wasn't at Angelus Quietum or Inspiration Landing for a very long time until recently. I really haven't seen much of him for the last fifty years."

My mind spun. First of all, I was shocked his daughter hadn't seen him in fifty years. That seemed like an incredibly long time to my seven short years. Of course, that implied that Ariel was older than fifty and she was Gabriel's daughter. Just how old was my father? Well, that was another good question.

"How old is my dad?"

"What year is it?"

I blinked at her blankly. "Three hundred and seventy-seven, I think," I said, remembering how Stella had me date my school papers.

"That makes him," Ariel paused a moment, a frown on her face, "Four hundred and six."

"Sweet Fate," I said, unintentionally echoing one of Gabriel's favorite clean curse phrases. "He was alive before they started counting years?"

"Our calendar started when the *Inspiration* left Earth," Ariel explained. "Gabriel was twenty-nine at that time. Stella did teach you about the Inspiration, right?"

"It was the generation ship that took the colonists from Earth to Cybele," I recited. Then I frowned. "Wait. So Dad was born on Earth?"

"Yes."

"Were you ever on Earth?"

"No, I was born on the *Inspiration*," she replied with a smile.

"Wow, that must have been amazing," I said. "Flying around the stars, fighting aliens! What was it like?"

"The *Inspiration*? Well, would you like to see it?"

I startled at her question. "What do you mean? The *Inspiration* was taken apart years ago."

Instead of answering, she leaned forward, one hand reaching out to touch mine. Unlike the last time we'd touched, I felt something. Her hand wrapped like warm air around my skin. Her green eyes burned into mine, beautiful and drowning in red flame. Then, with a sudden lunge, she dove at me. I gasped as her ethereal body slammed into mine, taking all of my breath away in a warm wall of liquid air. My eyes rolled shut as my body convulsed, a beautiful electricity flying up my spine as it bowed helplessly. I tried to cry out, but I couldn't draw air into my lungs.

"Call on your power, little sister," her mind murmured through mine. I suddenly understood what my father meant about speaking mind-to-mind. I could sense Ariel's vast knowledge, so sophisticated and grown compared to my childish mind. *"You have the strength to take us back. I have been waiting for someone like you for a very long time."*

I didn't understand. My lungs burned and the warm sensation flooding my body bordered on painful. I struggled against it and was rewarded by a flame of pure agony that tore up the core of my chest. My hands clawed blindly at the covers as my mind spun in panic.

"Pull on the fire! You know how to do this! Take the image from my mind, child, before it's too late!" An image resolved in the darkness behind my eyelids. A metallic room with large, clear windows looked out on endless stars. In the room were a large metal desk and several comfortable looking chairs. A broad-leaved green plant sat in one corner and a complex hologram hovered in the center of the room.

As this image resolved itself, the edges of my vision faded into little dots of color. My lungs screamed, begging for breath, my consciousness slowly evaporating. I fought against the force that held me rigid in its grasp. The room full of stars swam in my vision, ribbons of color bleeding in swirls of blurry mist. Fear and pain coalesced in my chest and I finally lashed out. The connection to my fire roared to life, flames ripping through my body, pouring out towards Ariel and the metallic room she'd pulled up in my mind.

Something stretched and tore, burning bright in my airless mind. I was compressed and then released as I spun with sickening speed.

Suddenly, the paralyzing force released me and I felt as if I'd been tossed from a great height. The sensation of falling lasted an eternity. I landed with a thud on a hard, smooth surface, gasping in pain and surprise. I dissolved into a fit of gulps and coughing, my oxygen starved lungs desperately sucking in air.

"Who are you?" A lovely, concerned voice said over my head. I glanced up, tears running down my face. I could feel my hair clinging to my damp cheeks.

Ariel was bending over me, her green eyes wide. I blinked dumbly up at her, completely stunned.

"What did you do?" I asked, pushing my soggy hair back from my face. I felt completely exhausted and wrung out.

"I haven't done anything," she replied. Her voice was even and clear. It took me a moment to realize I wasn't hearing her in my head as I had before. Nor was my sister glowing. In fact, she looked as solid and alive as I did.

I looked down at my hands. They were braced against a metal floor, its smooth, gray expanse cool and hard under my palms. I wasn't in my grandmother's guest room. Instead, the sterile metal room Ariel had projected into my mind was now a firm reality. I was sprawled beneath the holo-projector as names, dates and faces flashed through the air above my head.

"Where am I?" My voice cracked, much to my humiliation. I couldn't stop the hot tear rolling down my cheek. I'd never been so lost or afraid in my short life. "Ariel, why did you bring me here?"

My sister frowned at me, then got that slightly blank look on her face I'd learned to associate with silent communication. It was then that I noticed her outfit had also changed. She wore one of the colonial-era blue uniforms that I'd seen in my grandparents' portrait.

"What's your name, sweetheart?" she asked, offering me her hand.

"Gracie," I replied. With a sniff I reached up and took her slender hand in mine.

Blinding light exploded in my face; the floor dropped from under me again. I screamed as cold water splashed over me, leaving my body freezing.

"Gracie!" My father's face was inches from mine. I stared at him stupidly, my whole body rigid with fear and cold. He had both of my arms in a vice-like grip, holding me upright. Without his support, I would have collapsed back onto the bed. His face was as white as parchment paper.

"Gracie?" My grandmother's voice was gentler than my father's panicked shout. "Can you hear me, sweetheart?"

I nodded quickly, not trusting my voice. An uncontrollable shiver wracked me and I wrapped my arms tightly around myself, attempting to curl into a ball as best I could with Gabriel clinging to my shoulders.

"What's wrong with her?" my father snapped, turning sharply to his mother. The fear in his voice only made me shiver harder.

Gloria's warm hand touched my forehead. Her eyes were clouded with worry, but she seemed to be keeping calm more easily than my father. I was grateful for it.

"She's freezing," Gloria said, glancing at Gabriel with a strange look. "I think she's going into shock."

"How is that possible? I only left her alone for a minute!" I'd never heard my father sound so bewildered. I whimpered and shook.

"Give her here," Gloria murmured, moving closer to me and shooing my father out of the way. With gentle hands, she took me into her arms. I snuggled close to her shoulder, glad for her comforting, solid warmth. "You're going to be alright," she whispered into my hair. Then she lifted a hand to my forehead and an incredible heat flooded over me. My entire body relaxed into hers, the icy grip of my ghostly ordeal melting away with her gentle energy. With a small sigh, I tucked my head more firmly under her chin.

"There now," Gloria said soothingly under my ear. "She should be just fine."

My father's gentle hand touched my back and I glanced up at him with slow, sleepy eyes. I felt as if I'd climbed a dozen trees and ran around Angelus Quietum five times without stopping. Still, I wasn't cold anymore.

"Do you feel any better, sweetheart?" Gabriel asked softly. He was calmer now and I suddenly couldn't think of anything I wanted more than to curl up in his arms and fall asleep. With a whimper that was a bit more appropriate for a younger child, I reached for him.

With a grateful moan, he pulled me off of my grand-mother's lap and into his own. I clung to him tightly, still recovering from the fright Ariel had given me. The whole experience was such a blur.

"There now, my love, I'm sorry for yelling at you," he said, holding me tight, "You gave me a good scare, though."

"It was Ariel's fault!" I cried, "She ran into me and I couldn't breathe! Then she took me to a metal room and I was so scared. I didn't know what to do. Then she touched me and then I was back here and I was so cold."

Gabriel stroked my hair and frowned at my grand-mother. "This is what you get when you show children old photographs. They start having nightmares."

Gloria gave him a dark look, but said nothing. Instead, she peered into my face with a concerned expression. "Gracie, were you feeling sick earlier? Any kind of dizzi-ness?"

I shook my head and my finger slid unconsciously to my mouth. "No, I told you, it was Ariel's fault."

"Could it just have been a bad dream?" My father asked, glancing at his mother. I could see by his troubled expres-sion that he hoped this could explain away my strange be-havior.

Gloria narrowed her eyes and shook her head. "Not any bad dream I've ever seen," she muttered.

"Is the child alright?" D'nay poked his head in the door. He looked a bit out of breath.

"She's fine," Gloria called to him. She shot her husband a significant look and I wondered again what the telepaths were saying where I couldn't hear.

After a long, frustrating pause, my grandmother sighed. "I suppose you'll want me to pull a cot in here for tonight," she said, glancing up at my father.

He nodded. "If you don't mind. I really don't feel comfortable leaving her alone."

"Fair enough," Gloria replied, sliding off the bed. With a few simple gestures, the bedside table floated over to the corner and a neatly-made single mattress appeared in its place. Reaching into the air beside her, Gloria pulled out a pillow and tossed it on the bed.

"There now, I'll be asleep right beside you," Dad murmured, stroking a lock of my hair back in place. I had a feeling he hadn't heard a word I'd said about Ariel. Still, I didn't think my suddenly unfriendly ghost would come back to bother me with Gabriel sleeping on the floor next to me. With a sleepy smile, I let him tuck me gently back into bed.

CHAPTER 15

RUN

After that night, my father kept even more close-mouthed about his past than he had before. In fact, he seemed downright terrified that I would slip into some kind of fear-induced coma if he so much as breathed a word about it. Truth be told, Ariel well and truly scared some of the curiosity out of me. If sniffing around my father's secrets meant being nearly suffocated to death by a journal writing ghost, perhaps he was right and I should leave well enough alone.

The cause for secrecy was helped by the fact that Ariel didn't show up again for a very long while. I watched for her, of course, always half-afraid and half-excited that I might see her again. I had a serious bone to pick with that particular phantom. However, weeks and months dragged on without a sign of her and I pushed the memories aside. Perhaps they were nothing more than the visions of a terrified little girl in a new and overwhelming situation.

I might have convinced myself that it had all been a fever dream had it not been for what happened five years later.

I was twelve by this time and life had been settled for years. Stella gave me academic lessons, Gabriel taught me the ins and outs of using my pyrokinesis and Gloria stopped by with little snippets of news from the outside. D'nay was a less frequent visitor but a friendly one when he did drop in with his wife.

I rarely had playmates my own age. Looking back on it, I suppose most people would find my childhood rather lonely. It didn't bother me, though. If I wanted conversation, Gabriel and Stella were always willing to talk. If I wanted adventure, the wide open spaces of Angelus Quietum were ready and available for my exploration. My imagination was my playmate. Between reading books and charging about the meadow land on horseback, I rarely lacked for something fun or interesting to do.

It was a simple life compared to the city world so many of my peers lived in. However, I'd spent my early childhood so poor I hadn't gotten much of a taste for city conveniences. Certainly we didn't have them out here. I read about things such as shuttles and psi-gates certainly, but I didn't long to experience them just yet.

Those who don't believe me on how sheltered I was from my father's past, especially since I did have an implant put in around age eight, need to remember one thing: Stella herself was my constant companion in cyberspace. Whatever she and my father were to each other, she always did as he asked in my case. Which was to keep everything factual, simple, and as squeaky clean as possible. Honestly, I never even saw my father drink until James came along. But I'm getting ahead of myself—back to twelve-year-old me.

Five long years of running wild in the countryside left me long and lean. I wasn't early to womanhood, but I wasn't late either. Stella and Gloria made sure to explain the nuances of that transformation, so I wasn't shocked when my monthly blood started or I began growing curves. At twelve, the only thing that bothered me about adolescence so far was how awkward my once nimble body had become. It seemed as if I was growing too fast to keep up with my own shifting center of gravity.

Aside from my changing body, my world was quite perfect. That is, until the day Ariel showed up again.

It started like any other day. Dad was reading a memory pad and sipping tea as usual when I came to the kitchen for breakfast.

"Aubrie had her foal last night," he told me casually, glancing up mischievously over the edge of his memory pad.

"Really? Why didn't you wake me up?" I squealed, completely ignoring the bowl of rice he'd made for me and dashing straight out the back door. I thought I heard his chuckle as I all but flew out to the stables.

Aubrie was our beautiful bay mare. Her body was a deep chestnut and her mane and tail were black. Her face had a long, white blaze that covered most of her nose. She'd been bred to our neighbor, Carol's, gray stallion last spring and I couldn't wait to see what their foal would look like.

Dust kicked up under my feet as I ran down the path from the main house to the horse barn. The chickens looked up hopefully at me as I passed. They knew I usually fed them in the morning.

"Sorry, ladies," I panted as I dashed by. "I'll get to you in a minute, I promise!"

The door to the stable was tall, rough, and stuck like glue. I'd been telling my father to oil the hinges for years. I guess when you're as strong as any five men put together, you don't notice sticking hinges as much as the rest of us. I groaned as I hauled the door open and looked into the wan light of the stable row.

Old Hickory stuck his head over his stall door and nickered a greeting. I stroked his soft muzzle. "Hey, fella. I heard there was some excitement last night," I crooned to the elderly gelding. He pushed my shoulder with his nose and I smiled, slipping him one of the sugar cubes I kept my pockets stocked with.

Moving away from Hickory's stall, I held my breath as I came close to the loose box where Aubrie had been awaiting the arrival of her first foal. I couldn't see her dark flank from here so she must be lying down.

"Aubrie, sweetheart," I called to her, making her aware of my presence so I didn't startle the new mother. "I'm here to have a look at your baby."

A soft snuffling was the only response I got from the loose box, but I wasn't discouraged. Another step and I peered down into the darkened stall. Aubrie looked up at me with huge, midnight eyes. I beamed at her and the small form curled up at her side. The foal was gorgeous. His coat was dark and his little mane stood straight up. His ears looked far too large for his head.

"Oh, he's beautiful," I told the mare. She snorted as if to say she already knew that. I stifled a laugh at her motherly attitude and watched quietly as the baby slept. Watching a new foal wasn't something I got to do very often, so I leaned against the stall door for a long while, enjoying the unique sight.

A flutter of wings and raucous squawking brought me back to myself. Those hens were going to get rowdy if someone didn't feed them soon. I tapped my implant and muttered, "Time."

"Oh seven hundred forty," Stella's smooth voice replied, "and time for you to get moving." I sighed and tore myself away from the stall. Much as I could watch Aubrie's new foal all day, Stella was right. I had lessons and chores to attend to.

As I turned away from the darkened stall, a reddish glow caught my eye in the stable isle. Frowning, I turned towards it. The instant I realized who it was, I froze.

Ariel stood in the shadowy depths of the stable, her copper curls blowing in a familiar, intangible wind. Her eyes glittered like green gems in the darkness.

My heart thundered in my ears as I pressed my sweaty palms defensively against my waist. This couldn't be real. I was having another nightmare. I shook my head, trying to clear it. I'm not a child, I don't need imaginary friends anymore, I reminded myself. Still, my sister's glowing figure hadn't faded when I glanced back at the corner of the stable.

The incident five years ago came flooding back into my mind. What if she charged at me again? What if she tried to send me even farther away this time? Adrenaline made my hands shake and I reached out to steady myself against the stall door.

"What do you want?" I asked, willing my voice to be confident. It sounded thin and wavering even to my own ears.

Ariel's eyes burned into mine as she took a step forward. I stumbled back against the wooden stall door, my hands searching for something, anything I could use to fend her off. There was nothing in the stable aisle except for a halter and some hay. The phantom stepped into the aisle, blocking my escape towards the house. I backed up until I was literally in the corner between two wooden walls.

The wind picked up about the advancing ghost. It tugged at my hair. The smell of flowers flooded my senses. The only other time I'd felt the wind of Ariel's power had been the incident at my grandparents. Panic blossomed in my chest.

"No," I gasped, holding up a hand even though I knew it was useless. "Stay back!"

She ignored my cries completely. Holding my gaze steadily, she reached out for my face. I shrank back against the wall until the rough wood pricked splinters into my scalp. Her glowing white hands found the curve of my jaw anyway. A tiny, rational part of my screaming brain realized I wasn't much shorter than her anymore. Then, with a lightning fast lunge, Ariel threw herself into me just as she had before.

The blast of burning warmth was the same, but this time it didn't last very long. Instead, it dashed through my body in one breathless surge. As the heat flowed through my body, my sister's keen mind rubbed against mine. As before, she spoke to me, but this time it was a shout that reverberated in my head.

"Our father needs you. Now RUN!"

As suddenly as she'd appeared, Ariel's presence faded, leaving me cringing alone in the half dark of the stable. I clung to the wooden wall trying to get my trembling knees under control.

"Dad," I gasped and dashed towards the house.

For the second time that day, I ran through the yard as fast as my feet could take me. This time, though, fear made my eyes and chest burn. I careened around the corner of the house to the startled cries of chickens. I had no idea what could be so important that Ariel felt the need to seek me out, but I knew it had to be really, really bad.

"Dad!" I called as I came in shouting range of the back door. I paused a second to listen for a reply at the bottom of the steps. How ridiculous would I look if I charged back into the kitchen and he was calmly sipping his morning tea?

As I hesitated, one hand resting on the railing to the back steps, a loud crash made my already overworked heart leap into my throat. I didn't touch a single step as I flew through the back door.

Dad's mug lay in the shattered remains of a saucer on the floor. A small puddle of tea seeped underneath the shards. I glanced up from the jagged pieces of white porcelain to where my father stood leaning against the counter. Even with his back to me I could tell something was seriously wrong. Gabriel was not clumsy by anyone's definition. It was unusual for him to break something in the kitchen. It was even more unusual for him to just stand there with such a big mess on the floor.

"Dad?" I asked cautiously, stepping around the sharp ceramic. "Are you alright?"

"Gracie?" His voice sounded strained and I frowned as I came around him. Up close, I could see that his shoulders were tight and with another step I came into view of his face. It was deathly pale and twisted into a grimace. He'd unbuttoned the top of his shirt and one hand clenched hard on his chest.

"What happened?" I murmured, reaching out a hand to touch his shoulder. I didn't see any blood but I couldn't imagine my strong, youthful father getting sick. He must have been injured somehow.

"I..." He stopped and ground his teeth. One thing was clear. He was in a lot of pain. Common sense finally kicked in and I tapped my implant for Stella.

"Stella, get Grandma Gloria! Fast!"

"No, I'm alright," Gabriel protested, his voice as stubborn as ever. He was lying through his teeth. I could hear it in how out of breath he was. Still, it made me a little less afraid that he was well enough to protest.

"Maybe you should sit down?" I suggested timidly. My father had a sharp temper and, while he rarely turned it on me, I knew it had a habit of coming out when he was stressed. This counted as stress.

"I'll be fine in…" he cut himself off with a sharp cry. His fingertips pressed white on the counter top. I grabbed his elbow or he would have slid to the floor.

I cursed the accident of genetics that had given me my skill with fire rather than telekinesis. It would have been so much easier if I could bring a chair over with my mind. Even better yet, I could simply pick him up and put him to bed. Instead, I was a helpless twelve-year-old girl trying desperately to keep a grown man on his feet. It wasn't going to last long and I knew it.

"Stella, tell Gloria to hurry up!"

CHAPTER 16

LUCKY DAY

By the time my grandmother arrived, I'd lost the battle to keep Gabriel standing. It had been a slow sinking to the tile floor rather than a skull-splitting fall, however, so at least I'd accomplished that much.

"Gracie, what happened?" My grandmother arrived with a brief blast of stringent-scented air. She must have been at work in the University Hospital when she got Stella's message.

"I don't know!" My voice broke embarrassingly. Tears hadn't even threatened until Gloria showed up, but now I found them almost impossible to fight. I'd sunk to my knees next to my father, one arm pinned under his shoulders from my effort to slow his fall. His eyes were closed and he hadn't made a sound since his knees went out. I felt very small, vulnerable, and useless kneeling next to his prone form. "He was fine at breakfast."

"Gabriel?" Gloria bent down on one knee next to me and put a hand to his arm. She had to give him a good shake before he moaned in response. He was breathing hard, but apparently the pain wasn't keeping him conscious. Fear tore into my chest and I bit down on a terrified whimper.

My father was the only thing I had. What would happen to me if he died?

"Let me have him, sweetheart," my grandmother said firmly, slipping an arm alongside mine beneath his shoulders. She lifted his shoulders easily. I reclaimed my aching arm and scooted backwards to give her room. With a nod in my direction, Gloria gathered her son into her arms and stood, careful not to hit his head against the counter.

"Is he going to be alright?" I whispered, swallowing down panic. If I hadn't been so scared for Gabriel, it would have been comical to see my petite grandmother handle his weight as if it were nothing. As it was, I couldn't help noticing how dreadfully still and pale he lay in her arms.

With a grace only long practice could give, Gloria settled my father on the leather couch. I trailed behind her, hugging myself tightly. He gave a small whimper as she eased him down onto it. I cringed.

Gloria gestured and Dad's armchair slid over to her. She sat down delicately and laid a hand on Gabriel's chest. A gentle glow lit her hand with golden light and my father took a deeper breath. The iron bands of anxiety eased around my own chest as his eyelids flickered open.

"Liv?" he murmured, blue eyes searching the room. They looked dazed and unfocused. Then he caught sight of his mother and grimaced. "What did I do this time?" His voice sounded strange and thick.

Instead of answering her son, Gloria looked up at me. "Gracie, go pack yourself and your father enough clothes for a week. He's going to be fine, but he'll have to stay at the University for a while."

I nodded quickly and ran into the bedroom, relieved to have something productive to do. My bedroom was cool, quiet, and reassuring. I dashed to the closet where I still kept that old blue suitcase. I tossed it onto the bed and filled it with what I'd need for a few days away from Angelus Quietum.

My own clothes sorted away, I closed my suitcase before going into my father's room. I was more nervous to pack for him, but he'd taught me well. The first thing I needed was his black knapsack. I rummaged in his closet until I found it, then searched through drawers and hangers to find what he'd need for a week. I assumed he'd be on his feet sooner rather than later, so I packed everything from shoes to extra underwear.

As I was deciding which socks to tuck into his bag, I heard something that sounded suspiciously like his laughter. Relief and curiosity overrode my good manners and I crept closer to the door. I needed to hear his solid voice, to be reassured by listening in on normal adult banter between him and my grandmother. I strained my ears to hear their conversation in the living room.

"Oh, come on, Mom," Dad was saying, his voice a bit breathless but definitely amused. "You know it's funny in the most morbid sort of way."

"I don't find your self-destruction humorous, Gabriel," she snapped, sounding entirely put out.

"You have to admit, it's ironic." He made a strangled sound. They were silent for a moment, then his wry, breathless chuckle reached my ears. It somehow sounded more sad than tears. "Ten years on either side and today would have been my lucky day."

"Don't even joke about that," Gloria hissed. "A simple procedure and you'll be fine."

My father's laughter was a bit louder now and it had a hysterical edge that was almost frightening. "Oh yes, let's fix the damn thing. I've only been waiting for it to die and let me rest for two hundred and fifty years. But yes, let's replace it and make everything good as new." He cut off with a gasp that was clearly painful.

"Stop it, Gabriel," my grandmother sounded as if she'd be tempted to kill him if he wasn't already dying. "You're being selfish. Think about your child. Gracie's not even eighteen yet. She still needs her father."

"That's the best part," he groaned, the amusement turning to bitterness in his voice. "I'm going to lie back and let you do it because I still have five or six years of usefulness left. So what if I have another century or two of hell to live through afterwards."

"That's not fair and you know it." Gloria's voice was tired and for the first time I thought she sounded old. "That child is the best thing that's happened to you in the last hundred years. I've even heard you say as much. Don't you dare lie this at her feet, not even in your own head."

Gabriel sighed and there was a long silence again. When he finally spoke his voice was resigned. "Fine... but no morphine. I mean it."

"No narcotics," Gloria agreed. "I can respect that." Relief and a deep affection resonated in her voice. I shied away from it. For all that they called me their daughter and granddaughter, they had a very long history together that

I knew so very little about. This dark exchange only under-scored how much I didn't know about my own family. I hadn't felt this confused and alone since I was six.

"Where is she?" My father's voice caught and he made a small sound of pain. I belatedly realized I was keeping them waiting. I scurried back to my father's room to tuck a last few items in his pack before snagging both suitcases and rushing back out to the living room.

"I'm ready to go," I said, glancing between the two adults with more than a little trepidation. I didn't think they noticed me eavesdropping, but I couldn't be sure. They were telepaths after all.

"Good," was my grandmother's only response. With a wave of her hand, both packs disappeared. I assumed she'd sent them to her house which was much closer to the University. Then she got that distant look that told me she was communicating with someone mentally.

I glanced down at my father while we waited for Gloria to finish her conversation. He still looked pale but not quite as bad as before. He had his eyes closed and one hand rested across his chest. A surge of affection warmed my breast. He looked so fragile and for the first time it didn't scare me so much as make me feel protective. The sadness in his voice earlier made him more human somehow and I had that moment every child gets to at one point or another. I realized that my father was just a man; a fallible, vulnera-ble human being who was as subject to the whims of Fate as any of us.

It wasn't the last time I'd have that particular epiphany about Gabriel.

"Okay, I've talked to your neighbor, Carol," Gloria announced, blinking out of her distant stare, "She's going to watch the animals while you're gone."

I'd never known Carol was a telepath. Looking back on it now, it makes sense. Only one of our own would have lands that close to Angelus Quietum, or be willing to deal with Gabriel Usuriel and his reclusive daughter. Still, at the time it seemed like a shocking revelation.

"Let's do this, then," my father sighed, eyes flickering up at Gloria. With a nod, she took his hand in hers and offered her other one to me. I quickly stepped around the couch and accepted it.

Just as we began to fade from the room, I caught a glimpse of a golden glow with green eyes. I blinked, startled, but didn't let go of Gloria's hand. Then a University Hospital room came into focus and no strange phantoms seemed to have followed us.

I'd read about hospitals and seen a dozen or so holograms of them. I'd never actually been in one though, and I immediately felt out of place.

Remember what I said about city conveniences? Sure, Angelus Quietum had some technology, like Stella, memory pads, and a decent wheat thresher. This place was a whole different level of tech than I was used to.

Everything was clean and soft-edged. I don't think there was a single corner in the entire room. A great, curved window let in a flood of sunlight. The bed my grandmother had carefully materialized Gabriel onto was a long, oval shape. Gloria and I stood beside it, facing the bowed window. Curved cabinets reached up to a ten-foot ceiling, quite a bit higher than the eight-foot at home.

"Gloria?" A man's voice came from behind us. A tall stranger with white blond hair stood in the arched doorway. He wore a traditional green doctor's coat over tan slacks and brown shoes. He looked as if he was in his mid-thirties with a slim build and ice blue eyes. It had been a long while since I saw a man who looked over twenty-five outside of a holo-program. Even so, his features seemed strangely familiar. I couldn't quite place it, but I felt as if I'd seen him before. I gawked at him.

"Dax," my grandmother sighed and held out a hand to the man. He frowned, ignoring her hand while openly staring at my father and I. I dropped my gaze and shifted uncomfortably. Daring a glance back up at the stranger, I caught a look passing over his face that was half-fear and half-revulsion. Nervously, I shuffled towards my father's bedside.

"Is that who I think it is?" Dax asked. His voice was an attractive tenor, currently colored by disbelief.

My hand unconsciously found the edge of the hospital bed, wrapping my fingers in the fabric for comfort. Something about the way this man looked at us set off every alarm my head had.

"If you're asking if this is my son and granddaughter," Gloria's voice held a note of warning in it and I glanced up at her gratefully, "yes, it is. Now, why haven't you handed me a fresh intake chart?"

Dax blinked at her, then pulled a memory pad from the thin air over his left shoulder. He could teleport. I knew from Gabriel's lessons on Awareness that telekinesis, tele-portation, and healing by touch often went together. It made sense that a doctor would have such a talent.

With a slightly dazed expression, Doctor Dax handed my grandmother the memory pad. With a sniff, Gloria tapped a few things into the screen before sliding it into a port above the bed.

"You're actually admitting him?" Dax asked, leaning over Gloria's shoulder. "Is that wise?"

My grandmother rounded on the doctor. "Why shouldn't I? It's a simple enough procedure. I'll perform it myself if you have a problem with it."

"I…" Dax held up a hand and backed up, looking thoroughly bewildered. "No, it's fine. It's just… I mean … nothing. Never mind."

"You know, I'm right here." My father's voice was still breathless but his sarcastic tone was completely intact. Its familiar irreverence made some of the tension in my shoulders relax. "My heart is failing, not my ears. Speaking of which, it would be nice if someone did something about that little fact. I'm in a lot of pain here."

"An ungrateful bastard as always, Uncle Gabe," Dax snapped at my father. His ice blue eyes blazed threateningly and I suddenly understood where I'd seen his features before. For all their difference in coloring, Dax and Gabriel bore a striking resemblance to each other.

"Delightful language in front of your twelve-year-old cousin," Gabriel shot back. One hand had come up to his chest again and his teeth gritted in pain. Still, he'd propped himself up on one elbow and his blue eyes glittered with a dangerous amount of temper. If I'd been a touch older or bolder, I might have put a hand to his shoulder and pushed him back onto the bed. As it was, my timid gaze darted between my father, Dax, and Gloria. I hoped one of them would have the sense to stop the argument. Of course, we're discussing my father, so it was a pretty useless hope.

"Oh yes, because swearing in front of pre-teens is the most heinous of crimes," Dax hissed back. Apparently my fair-haired cousin had also inherited a decent amount of the Usuriel temper. "That's pretty damn ironic coming from you, Gabriel."

"Enough," Gloria spat, stepping between the two men. A bright, glowing wind had picked up around her, tossing her long hair about her head in a golden halo. She gave both of them a glare that could make fresh milk curdle. "Behave like you have a couple centuries of common sense between the two of you. Please."

"I'm sorry, Gloria." To my surprise, Dax backed down quickly. I sensed from the contrite look he gave my grandmother that he had much more respect for her than he did my father.

"It's alright, Dax," she said gently, the fire storm around her shrinking down to nothing. She reached out and gave his arm a squeeze in that reassuring way she had, "Will you go start prepping an OR for me?"

He nodded too quickly, eyes darting at Gabriel before he turned and left the room.

Gloria glanced down at my father. With a groan, he sank back on the bed. I wasn't sure if it was because of the chest pain or because of the look of profound disappointment my grandmother leveled in his direction. Either way, he looked exhausted and defeated with his eyes closed, hand still white knuckled on his chest.

"Promise me you'll be on your best behavior while you're here." Gloria's tone was almost threatening. "These people work very hard every day and the last thing they need is the business end of your temper." She tapped a few places in the air above the bed and a red light slid over my father's body. Numbers and images hovered in the air before her. She frowned at them before glancing back down at Gabriel's panting form.

He tilted his head back defiantly on the pillow. "He started it," Gabriel grumbled.

"I don't care," Gloria shot back, a frown tugging at the corners of her mouth as she studied the results of the scan. "You were a hundred and fifty by the time he was born. Promise me you will act like the bigger adult for once in your life."

I glanced down at the angry set of my father's jaw and knew this was a disaster in the making. I had firsthand experience with how he got with anyone who pushed his buttons. In this much pain, just about everything would set him off today.

Just when I thought he was going to shoot back a smart-mouthed retort, his body went rigid and a small cry escaped his throat before he could bite it back. When the spasm subsided, his shoulders slumped a bit dejectedly.

"You win, Mom," he murmured, much to my surprise. "I'll behave. You have my word." When he opened his eyes, they were a darker blue than usual. I could instantly see that his mood had changed. He held out a hand to me, his expression serious. "Gracie, sweetheart, come here a moment."

I trotted around the bed to take his hand. The grave set of his mouth frightened me. "You're going to be alright," I said quickly, squeezing his hand tightly in mine. "Grandma said so."

He gave me such a sad smile I had to look away. "I'm sure I will be," he said gently. "Even so, you know that I love you, right?"

I nodded too fast; my grip on his hand must have been uncomfortably tight. I trusted Gloria as completely as I'd ever trusted anyone. Still, I knew exactly what this was. He was saying goodbye in case things went badly. I tried to push the thought out of my head, but I wasn't a small child anymore. I didn't have the luxury of ignorance.

"I love you, too," I whispered. Then, before my adolescent awkwardness could stop me, I leaned down and laid a light kiss on his cheek.

"Be good for your grandparents," he told me, patting my hand before letting me go.

"I will be," I promised.

"Gracie." Gloria's voice was gentle but insistent. I glanced over at her and saw that someone else had stepped into the room.

This young woman was as red-haired as I was. Her eyes were as sky-blue as my grandmother's and her slim figure echoed the Usuriel matriarch's within inches. I wondered if Gloria and Gabriel knew anyone we weren't related to.

"Leesil, why don't you take Gracie down to the hospital cafeteria? Her father won't be out of surgery for several hours."

"'Lighted," Leesil agreed, a friendly smile on her face. I glanced back at my father. He gave me a weak smile and nodded.

"Go on. I'll see you tomorrow."

"Okay." My chest tightened at the thought of letting him out of my sight, but I knew my grandmother wouldn't be able to help him with me hovering about. So, with as confident a smile as I could muster, I followed Leesil out of the room.

CHAPTER 17

LEESIL

"So your name is Gracie, huh?" Leesil asked good-naturedly as we walked down the hospital corridor. Planters added natural beauty every few feet and green uniformed doctors and nurses moved briskly from room to room. I dodged out of their way, shrinking close to Leesil.

"Yes," I replied. My mind scrambled for appropriate small talk but came up pretty empty. I didn't have conversations with strangers very often. "You're Leesil, right?"

"You can call me Lee." Her smile was bright and her blue eyes danced infectiously. My shoulders relaxed in spite of myself. "I'm sure your dad will be fine," she said when it became clear that I didn't know what to say next. "Gloria's the best surgeon on Cybele."

I nodded. There wasn't anyone I trusted more than Gloria, except my father of course. Still, that didn't mean I wanted to talk about it. I searched for a new topic.

"Do you work here?" I asked as Lee palmed open a metallic door. With a whoosh it revealed the largest elevator I'd ever seen. It could easily fit twenty people. I followed Lee into it.

"Cafeteria," she said, tapping her implant. The door shut behind us and the lift took off sideways. I grabbed onto one of the waist-high metal handrails at the unexpected motion. I'd only ever experienced elevators that went up and down.

Lee tucked her wavy, flame red hair behind one ear and gave me a winning smile. "I'm more like a volunteer," she explained. I stared at her, then realized she was answering my earlier question. "The University offers us credits for good citizen hours."

"You're a University student?"

She nodded. "It's the only place you can get psi-gate certified."

"Oh." I had never thought about the fact that people had to run the psi-gates. In the holo-programs, characters would simply announce their destination and walk through the gate. The thought that someone was running the thing never crossed my mind.

"What do you want to do when you grow up?" Lee asked as the elevator door opened. We were in an almost identical hallway, except this one curved away to the right. My guide didn't miss a beat, stepping off the elevator and walking confidently down the hall.

"Um..." This wasn't something I'd really thought about before. I knew my grandmother was a medic. She talked about it frequently enough. My father had been a pilot at one point, at least from Gloria's stories. I'd never actually seen him fly anything. At the moment he ran the farm at Angelus Quietum. I had no idea what grandpa D'nay did, only that he worked long hours. None of them had ever seemed concerned about what I would do when I got older. "I don't know yet," I replied honestly.

"Well, you're a third-gen, aren't you?" Lee chirped, tilting her head at me.

"Third-gen?" I'd never heard the term before.

She made an elegant shrug and rolled up one of her green coat sleeves. "You know, third generation of Awareness."

I shook my head in confusion and glanced down at my own outfit. My fitted jacket and denim pants stuck out like a sore thumb in the sea of medical uniforms. The crowd got denser and I took a breath of relief when I caught a glimpse of some other people in street clothes making their way towards the food court.

"Here we go, the cafeteria," Lee announced, as if I couldn't see the throng of people forming lines at the food stations. "What do you like to eat?" she asked, pointing to a refrigerator on my right. "They have all kinds of things to drink in there. Pasta's at that station, meadow pie at that one, and over there is some kind of poultry today I think."

"I don't have any money." I nervously eyed the people moving from their chosen food station over to the checkout line.

"Are you serious?" My guide actually gave a short bark of laughter before catching my bewildered expression. "You really don't know, do you?"

My frown deepened. "Know what?"

It was Lee's turn to frown. "Come on, pick out something to eat. I think we need to have a chat, little cousin."

I hardly paid attention to what I put on my tray after that. I snagged the first thing that looked edible, which happened to be a pasta dish with red sauce. Once I'd waited my turn through the lunch line and Lee had put her hand print into the cashier's machine to pay for it, she led me by the elbow over to a secluded corner of the dining room.

"Okay." Lee settled herself daintily in the chair across from me, elbows resting heavily on the table while she leaned forward to watch me eat. "How is it that the first third-gen born in a century doesn't know the first thing about her own family?"

I poked at my pasta. My stomach growled, twisting into a tight knot of hunger and curiosity. "My dad doesn't like to talk about things that happened before I was born."

"Well, I guess that's understandable," Lee replied thoughtfully, settling her chin on one hand. "Still, you should really know about how the University system is set up so you'll be able to choose a career path. You don't even know about generations?"

I shook my head. "You're the first person I've heard mention them."

"Wow." She shook her head and several red strands tumbled loose, falling into her eyes. She tucked them back behind one ear with the absence of habit. "Okay, so that's the first thing I should explain." She took a deep breath, her eyes darting around the room as if searching for a place to start. "As you may have figured out, at least on the living side of things, Awareness is genetic. It's passed down from parent to child. Sometimes it skips generations, sometimes a child will be stronger than a parent, but those cases are rare. Mostly, the closer you are to the source, the stronger your gifts. There's only two sources of giftedness and the Terran side is unreliable. The only line that really breeds true is good old D'nay and Gloria. They're the first generation."

I took a long swallow of juice while she was talking. So far it made sense. Gloria and D'nay clearly had a large amount of Awareness and they'd passed it on to their son. "So if they're first generation, Gabriel is second generation?"

"You got it." Lee gave me a smile. "Which makes you a third. There aren't a whole lot of thirds left, especially on the Gabriellan side."

"There are other sides?"

"Only one. The Adoran side. Adora was Gabriel's younger sister. There are a couple of thirds left on that side. They tend to be longer lived."

I thought about that for a moment. "What happened to Adora? Why haven't I ever met her?"

Lee's mouth went thin and I could see her deciding what to tell me. The older I got the more I hated that look on adult faces.

"Adora died about sixty years ago."

I gave in to my hunger and took a bite of pasta. I wasn't sure if it tasted good because I was hungry or if the food was actually decent. Either way, it was hot. I took a sip of juice to wash it all down. "How did she die?"

"There's some disagreement on that point. Most accounts say she had some wires loose," Lee murmured, dropping her voice. "It was unpleasant business, either way. Makes some of us wonder how stable the rest of the Adorans are."

I let that information sink in while I swallowed another mouthful of pasta. "Who's us? How many descendants are there?"

My red-haired cousin shrugged. "I'm not sure about exact numbers but something well over fifty on the Gabriellan side. When you add the Adorans... who knows. There's enough to have twenty of us at the University at any given time, at least."

I had fifty relatives just from my father's previous children? My mind spun with the implications of Lee's revelation. I'd known Ariel was older than me, but the idea that she'd had children and her children then would have had children just never occurred to me. I stared at my older cousin. "So what generation are you?"

"Fifteenth," she said, twirling a lock of red hair around her finger. I quickly swallowed the bite of pasta I had in my mouth so that I wouldn't choke in surprise.

"Fifteenth?" I echoed.

She nodded. "There are lots of us in the tenth-gen and up. I think the first child of the eighteenth-gen was just born this year."

I shook my head in disbelief. "So, Awareness keeps being passed on down the generations?" I asked, clearing my mouth as quickly as I could without choking. There were so many questions I wanted to ask, but I didn't want to appear rude.

"To some degree or another. I'm pretty strong for a fifteenth Gabriellan. Plus I got lucky. My main skill is in teleportation, which means I'm perfect for a psi-gate."

"By Gabriellan, you mean you're descended from Gabriel, right?"

Lee's smile made her eyes sparkle, "Can't get anything past you, can we? That's right. I'm from Drexil's line."

"Okay, so there's Gabriel's side, the Adoran side, and the Terran side. Are those the only gifted lines there are?"

"Unless you're willing to be a corpse during the day, yes. That's all I know of, anyway," she admitted with a shrug.

"So what does any of this have to do with how I was going to pay for lunch?" I asked, pointing at the pasta with my fork.

Lee gave a small laugh. "Well, you're an elder child. You're eligible for the family trust."

"Family trust?" I was beginning to feel like a very clueless echo.

"Your father and grandparents were on the original *Inspiration* crew. As such, they were entitled to land grants when the colony was first settled. Most families opted for large swath land grants that have been divided and subdivided until they're just modest little homesteads," Lee explained.

"Right, Stella taught me about that in history class," I said, gratitude welling for the AI. At least she hadn't completely neglected my education. "That's why most cities are named after an original *Inspiration* family. They settled there and their descendants owned most of the land in that area."

Lee nodded. "The Usuriels were smarter than most colonists. They chose a few larger areas, such as Chronurea Valley and Angelus Quietum, and then spread smaller patches all over the map in strategic locations. Now they own incredibly valuable property in just about every major city on the continent. They then take all the money made by improving and renting the land and roll it into a trust fund. The University and its medical center both run off the Trust. Descendants up to gen five are given a percentage allowance every three years and descendants farther removed than that are given their share as free tuition to the University."

I considered that for a moment. "So I get an allowance every three years?"

"Yep. Well, right now Gabriel gets your share. Once you've graduated University, though, you'll be entitled to your own allowance." Lee chuckled. "So, yeah, you don't have to worry about lunch at the University. For all practical purposes, you own a share of this place."

We lapsed into silence while I ate. When my bites slowed, Lee cleared her throat and I glanced up at her. "What?" I asked.

"I know it's rude to ask, but I'm dying to know." She leaned in a touch closer. "What are your gifts? Are you a three-T?"

"Three-T?"

"Telepathy, telekinesis, teleportation," she rattled off, "at the University they're called the big three. Most people past the fifth generation don't have all three, but you're only a third. I'll bet you're really strong."

I shook my head. "Sorry to disappoint you. I'm a pyro-kinetic."

Lee's blue eyes got very round. "A third-gen firebird? Holy cow, no wonder Gabriel is keeping you in the middle of nowhere."

"What's that supposed to mean?" I hissed with a little more temper than I meant to. Lee blinked at my sudden waspishness and I cringed.

Fortunately, my cousin was apparently more good-natured than most of the Usuriel clan. She gave me a wry smile as she shook her head. "Sorry," she said quickly.

"That didn't come out right. It's just that pyros have a bit of a... well... reputation. Especially after Cara."

This was one story my father had told me. I suppose he figured I needed to know about the hazards of my own gift. Good to know he hadn't kept me completely in the dark. I gave Lee a mollified nod. "Yeah, I guess that makes sense," I allowed.

A look of relief passed over Lee's face. I didn't blame her. I wouldn't want to be the one to tell my younger cousin about the pyro who lost it and burned down a city block, either.

"Still, I would never hurt anyone," I felt the need to re-assure her. "I mean, I've never lost control and set something on fire by mistake."

"Of course not," Lee agreed with a cheerful smile. "After all, you have Gabriel Usuriel himself for a teacher. I'm sure you know exactly how to deal with your gift."

The mention of my father's name made a knot of worry cramp around the pasta in my stomach. The large, digital clock hanging over the cashier's station said it had only been an hour and a half since Ariel appeared in the stable. It seemed like an eternity. I wondered anxiously how the surgery was going.

Lee followed my gaze and her eyes softened. "I guess you're pretty worried about him, huh?"

"Yeah," I admitted, poking the last noodles with my fork.

"I'm sure he'll be fine," she said again, her smile the re-assuring fiction of someone who had never had anything truly bad happen to them.

"How old are you?" The question fell out of my mouth before I could stop it. I had the grace to look embarrassed, but Lee took it in stride.

"Twenty-two," she replied, unfazed by my breach of etiquette. "I'm in my last year of University so I've been looking for jobs. I've been thinking of the Stella Institute. I mean, Hal has fantastic beaches."

Hal was the large island not too far off the southern coast. Dad had taken me for a few day trips down to the palmstudded beaches there.

"Are there a lot of psi-gates there?" I asked.

"No, just two," she admitted, looking a little glum. "And competition is fierce. Still, I'm pretty strong for a fifteenth gen, like I said. I'm kind of hoping one of the sevens will retire in time for me to take his shift."

"Gracie?" A familiar voice called across the cafeteria. D'nay was striding towards us wearing a dark blue shirt and tan slacks that made him stand out from the crowd of green medical uniforms. It took all the self-control I had not to throw myself into his arms.

"Hello, Leesil," he said to Lee as he arrived at the table. Apparently he was more familiar with his descendants than I was. "Thank you for watching after Gracie."

"Anytime!" She offered me a hand. "I hope I'll get to see you again sometime."

"Yeah, I'd like that," I replied, flashing her a small smile. She'd been good company and a part of me was sorry to see her go. A larger part of me was ready to be back in familiar surroundings.

With a last wave, Leesil blended back into the crowd, off to whatever volunteer effort required her next.

"Ready to go?" my grandfather asked gently, straightening a few of my curls.

"Where are we going?" I asked, collecting the remnants of my meal on the tray.

"Back to my place," he replied easily. "Your grandmother already put your bag in the hover car, so we can leave whenever you're ready."

I took care of my dirty dishes and walked back to my grandfather. I tried to return his smile, but my cheeks refused to curve upwards.

"Don't worry," D'nay said with a pat on my shoulder. "Gabriel has pulled through far worse. He's too stubborn to let something like this keep him down."

I took a deeper breath and nodded before letting Grandfather lead me out of the cafeteria.

CHAPTER 18

THAT DAMN REPORTER

The aerodynamic curves of D'nay's sleek, gray hover car waited for us on the roof. He tapped his implant as we walked towards it.

"Stella, car doors," he muttered. The sides of the hover car obediently slid back to reveal a small but well-cushioned interior with my blue suitcase tucked into the back seat. Without a word, I flopped into the passenger side and fastened the safety straps.

D'nay spared a glance in my direction before folding himself into the driver's seat. With the tap of a button, the doors hissed closed and the interior lit up with a dozen controls.

"Just take us home, Stella," my grandfather sighed, running his fingers over the brightly lit display.

"Of course," the AI's smooth voice crooned through the car. I leaned my head back against the passenger's seat and closed my eyes as the vehicle lifted off the roof.

There was a short, companionable silence as we glided through a small town. I opened one eye as we passed a lovely, wooded collection of buildings. I wondered if that was the University. Then we were past it and climbing into the foothills.

"Can I see my dad later tonight?" I asked, fidgeting with the safety strap across my chest.

D'nay raised a tired eyebrow at me. "He won't be conscious until tomorrow," my grandfather said gently, tapping a few more controls on the car's display. Obediently, the hovercraft rose up and over a grove of trees.

"But he'll be out of surgery, won't he?" I pressed.

My grandfather ran a hand through his straight, dark hair. It was a familiar gesture. "Your grandmother knows how to take care of him, Gracie. Let her do her job. She's good at it."

"I know." I sounded petulant and I knew it. I just didn't care. "But I really want to see him tonight. Please? I just want to make sure he's okay."

D'nay shook his head, a small smile flirting with the corners of his lips. "I wonder if he knows just how lucky he is to have a kid like you."

I flushed and looked down at my hands. I had every evasive adult trick in the book memorized, however, and I wasn't about to let my grandfather flatter his way out of taking me back to the hospital.

"Please?"

"Fine." D'nay sounded half-annoyed and half-amused. "If it will make you feel better, we can go back as soon as your dad is out of surgery."

I nodded, still staring down at my folded hands. "Thank you," I murmured. Now that I'd gotten what I wanted, I felt a little lost. There was nothing else I could do except wait.

"So," D'nay said when the silence stretched a little long, "what did you and your great grand-niece have to talk about?"

"Grand-niece?"

My grandfather gave me a grin. "Leesil. She's actually about thirteen or fourteen greats, I think, but who's counting?"

"She called me her cousin."

"That's pretty standard slang among the Family, I think. They all just call each other cousin, even though the relationships are more complicated. It keeps things simpler, I guess."

"Oh." I supposed it made sense. "She was nice."

"I hear she's a top-rated teleporter," he said, something close to pride in his voice. His eyes were still on the landscape in front of us, but he wore a small smile. I wondered if he talked about me with that same proud little smirk. I hoped so.

"She said she wanted to move to Hal and work at one of the psi-gates there," I told him.

"I've heard that one before," my grandfather laughed. "Still, she should be able to find good work once she's T-gate certified. She's a sweet girl and a hard worker."

I nodded, my mind going back over the conversation I'd had with Leesil. "Grandpa, what do you do?"

"What do you mean?"

"Grandma's a medic; dad is… or… was a pilot. Now I guess he runs Angelus Quietum with me. What do you do?"

D'nay chuckled softly. In the distance Chronurea Valley loomed from the mist.

"I've done a lot of things over the years," he said, midnight blue eyes flickering in my direction. "Right now I teach a few classes at the Stella Institute. When I get the itch, I'll design a vehicle or two. It's nothing like the work I did on the *Inspiration*, though. Back then I was a full-time systems engineer."

"Oh," I replied, even though I wasn't sure what a systems engineer did. I decided to let it go as the large, white manor rose rapidly in front of us. The familiarity of the Usuriel homestead was an intense relief after the stressful morning I'd had.

"Why do you ask?" D'nay glanced at me as he finished setting the car down in the garage behind the house. Its door opened automatically once we got close and the hover car fit neatly into the shadowy space.

I unlatched my safety harness. "Leesil asked me what I wanted to do when I got older, and I hadn't thought about it before."

"A fair enough question," he admitted as he climbed out of the car. "Gabe's never talked to you about it?"

"Not really," I said, stepping out of the car and wondering how I was going to get the seat to come forward to grab my suitcase. My grandfather solved that problem for me by tapping a button. His seat instantly slid up and out of the way.

"Well, there are lots of things an intelligent young woman like you would be good at," he said, slinging the suitcase over his shoulder as if it weighed nothing.

"I'm not a telepath, telekinetic or teleporter," I pointed out. "What kind of jobs are there for pyrokinetics?"

D'nay inclined his head slightly to acknowledge my question as he led the way out of the garage. Once we were both clear of the doorway, he tapped his implant and said, "Stella, secure the garage, please."

Immediately, the car doors shut and the garage door came down with a great, final sounding thud. I jumped a touch, but D'nay didn't even react. I followed him quickly up to the back door of the house.

"Just because you're psychic doesn't mean that's all you have to offer," D'nay said as he pressed his hand to the palm plate on the back door. "I mean, you're really smart,

Gracie. Who says you have to use your pyrokinesis to make a living?"

I felt slightly stupid. Of course, why would Stella be giving me lessons on things like mathematics and reading if the only valuable skill I had was burning things?

"I guess that's true," I allowed, stepping through the doorway into the darkened kitchen.

I reached for my implant to ask Stella for lights, but a quick motion from my grandfather stopped me. His eyes glowed in the shadows as he shook his head and put a finger to his lips. I obediently froze.

"What is it?" I whispered, eyes darting about the kitchen. At this time of the day, the sun came in from the other side of the house so it was fairly dark in this room. Still, it was close to midday which meant I could see the usual island and stools sitting serenely in the center of the room.

"There's someone in the house," D'nay growled, setting down my suitcase silently.

Now, I always knew why people might find Gloria and Gabriel a touch scary. Between their effortless use of telekinesis and their habit of lighting up like a torch the instant their emotions got a little high, it was understandable. My grandfather, on the other hand, didn't have the same quicksilver temper as the rest of the family. That wasn't to say I'd ever thought of him as a pushover, but I never saw him as intimidating in the same way that his wife and son were.

That is, until that day in my grandparents' kitchen.

As I watched, the handsome, polite man I'd known most of my life suddenly became terrifying. With one movement he was across the room. It was so fast I barely registered it. I did a double take, but as he paused against the far wall I confirmed that his fingertips had lengthened into wickedly long claws. With another lightning fast movement, he disappeared out of my sight. I swallowed hard and shrank back against the counter. I didn't have long to wait before a low snarl and a crash sent me scurrying to the foot of the stairs.

D'nay had found the intruder and was holding the man pinned against the wall with one hand. Those long claws I'd gotten a glimpse of in the kitchen were digging into the dry wall on either side of his neck and the man's expression was complete terror. With another animal-like growl, my grandfather glared at the interloper from inches away. His teeth had lengthened to something quite unnatural and he looked as if he'd rather take a bite out of the guy than put him down.

"Please," the intruder begged, hands clawing uselessly at D'nay's wrist, "I didn't steal anything! I swear!"

"I don't take kindly to trespassers," my grandfather snarled. "Tell me what you were doing in my house before I decide having a live meal is worth replacing the rug."

The man's washed out gray eyes darted to me as he swallowed hard.

"You wouldn't kill a man in front of your granddaughter, would you?" the intruder whimpered.

D'nay froze for a moment, then sighed and glanced over his shoulder at me. I gave him wide, terrified eyes. With a groan, he turned back to the man in his grip.

"It's your lucky day," he grumbled, his fangs shrinking back into more human-looking incisors. Still, he didn't let the man go. "Gracie, come make sure this guy doesn't have any weapons on him."

I nodded quickly and ducked under his arm to check the intruder's pockets. I found a nice, new memory pad, but that was about it. I handed the pad to my grandfather who put it in his own pocket before gesturing for me to back away. I quickly obliged.

"No sudden movements," D'nay snarled, slowly withdrawing his hand from the man's neck.

"You got it." He held up his hands in submission.

"Now, give me one good reason not to call the watch and have you arrested," D'nay snapped, folding his arms across his chest. He'd allowed the claws to retreat back into his graceful fingers.

The intruder muttered something unintelligible and glanced between the two of us. I was closer to the door and, while I'm not a telepath, it wasn't hard to see the guy's line of thought.

"I wouldn't," I warned, putting out a hand and allowing a tongue of flame to flicker to life around it. The intruder turned another shade of white and I was pretty sure I caught a low chuckle from my grandfather's direction.

"Alright, alright," the man sighed, adjusting a battered set of spectacles on his nose and smoothing his shaggy straw-blond hair. "If you must know, I was doing some research."

D'nay groaned and put a hand to his forehead as if he'd just gotten a massive headache. "I knew I recognized you from somewhere," he rumbled. "You're that damn reporter from Skykyle City."

The man pulled his stained but expensive shirt a little straighter and lifted his chin. "Joe Blackmon, lead reporter for the celebrity news department."

"Right," D'nay muttered, pulling out the memory pad. He held it up in front of Joe who reluctantly put his hand to its surface, activating the screen. Grandfather tapped through a few settings and nodded. "Ah, good. You haven't uploaded anything to net storage today. Which means I really need to do this." With a quick gesture, he snapped the pad in half like a toy. Joe Blackmon made a choking noise but, after a withering glare from my grandfather, he didn't make a move. "Now," D'nay growled, "let's have the back-up disk."

Joe gave my grandfather huge, falsely innocent eyes. "What back-up disk?"

"The one in the side of your greasy neck," D'nay snarled. "No reporter worth his byline skimps on the latest archival technology. Let's have it."

With a groan and a grumble, Joe tapped the implant on the side of his neck. The flesh slowly opened to reveal a tiny slot. A servo whined as a chip the size of a fingernail poked its way out of the implant. The reporter rolled his eyes and handed the disk to my grandfather.

D'nay squinted at the disk and held it up to the light before tucking the offending plastic into his breast pocket. "Now, get out of my house."

"Before I go," Joe began, raising a pudgy finger. "You wouldn't want to make a statement about what landed your son in the hospital, would you? Is it drug related? Has he had a relapse?"

I seriously thought D'nay was going to flash fang on the guy again. Instead, he gave the reporter a glare that could have peeled paint. Joe shrank back and began sidling towards the door.

"Gabriel is in the hospital for a routine procedure," D'nay growled. "Aside from that, the Family has no comment."

"Right. Should have known," Joe said. As he oozed past me, the greasy reporter squeezed something small into my hand. "If you're ever interested in some quick cash, give me a call."

I glanced down into my palm and saw that he'd given me a little card with his name and a net address.

"Out!" D'nay barked. Without another word, Mr. Joe Blackmon ran out the door, slamming it shut behind him.

CHAPTER 19

A FAMILY SONG

I didn't get to see my father until the sun had been set for several hours. I watched it go down over the mountains in a blaze of red and gold while my insides twisted themselves into worried knots. By the time Gloria called I was beside myself with nerves. It was so dark outside I could barely see my hand in front of my face as we walked out to the hover car.

"Your grandmother says it went just fine," D'nay said for about the fifth time. His eyes flashed in the dark like a cat's, their glare the only indication he was beside me.

I chewed on a hangnail. It was a bad habit left over from my childhood that showed up even more when I was nervous. I never could keep my hands out of my mouth.

"Did she say anything else? Like what was wrong with him?" I chattered anxiously. I'd been holding down the growing sense of panic building in my stomach all day. Even though the wait was about to be over, I couldn't help squirming under its sickening pressure.

My grandfather glanced over at me, his eyes reflecting perfectly round yellow disks of light in my direction. It was a touch uncanny, especially after his display of temper earlier in the day.

"Gabe didn't tell you what was wrong?" D'nay sounded a little surprised.

I grunted. "He never tells me anything. I'm practically grown, and he acts like I'm still six."

It was too dark to see if my grandfather was hiding a smile or not, but I suspected he was. It sounded like it when he spoke again. "I guess your father just wants to protect you."

"From what?" I cried a bit more loudly than I intended to, "From his mystery illness? I mean, come on, what's it going to do? Come up and bite me?"

D'nay did chuckle at that comment, but he didn't reply. When the silence began to stretch, I decided it would be worth it to do a little fishing.

"Seriously, it's always stuff about him or the Family that he doesn't want to talk about. What could possibly hurt me from inside the Family?" I rolled my eyes in that adolescent way I was beginning to perfect. I figured my grandfather's night vision might be a bit better than mine, what with the eyes. Either way, the gesture was pretty new and I needed the practice.

"Well…" I could hear how reluctant D'nay was to broach the topic. I held my breath. "Some things are hard to talk about," he got out slowly. His shoulders tightened and he tapped a few lit buttons on the control panel.

The silence wore on. Perhaps I'd been aiming too high. He'd been almost ready to tell me what was wrong with Dad, which was definitely worthwhile information. Maybe if I just came out and asked…

"So," I paused, getting my thoughts in order. "What did the reporter mean when he asked if my dad had a relapse? Was he sick before?"

D'nay sighed and his shoulders dropped. Ahead of us, the hospital loomed. Its eight stories shone brightly from its curved rows of windows.

"Sort of," my grandfather muttered more to himself than to me. He ran a hand through his hair. "Your father has a heart condition. Or rather, he had one a long time ago."

"A heart condition?" I repeated. "What kind of a heart condition?"

"He was injured back on the *Inspiration*," D'nay explained. "He very nearly died. Thanks to your grandmother's talents he didn't. Still, the incident left some serious damage that only got worse with time. Eventually, things got bad enough that he had to have his heart replaced."

"Replaced?" I was starting to sound like a back-up chip, but I couldn't help it. I had heard of organ transplants before, of course. Usually it was related to someone who was in a horrible accident or had a really aggressive form of cancer. I had a hard time imagining my strong, confident father as fatally ill.

"It wasn't an easy time in our lives," my grandfather admitted. "If it hadn't been for Olivia, your father probably would have died."

"Why?" I interrupted, curiosity getting the better of me. It was the first time anyone had ever brought up Olivia in my presence since my grandmother forgot to take down the wedding portrait. I still caught glimpses of her from time to time around Angelus Quietum. She had a habit of watching my father when he fell asleep on the couch. Unlike Ariel, she never seemed to notice my presence. "What did she do?"

The hover car rose towards the roof of the hospital. Lights flashed over my grandfather's face, making his strong features even sharper. His eyes reflected bright flashes as he glanced in my direction. The expression on his face was a mixture of sadness and something else.

"She loved him," he said, voice soft.

I frowned. The answer didn't make logical sense, yet I felt satisfied with it. I mulled that conundrum over as my grandfather settled the hover car onto the roof.

With a low, whining hum, the engine died. My grandfather's eyes gazed into the dark distance and I wondered what he was seeing. I had a feeling whatever it was, it happened several centuries before I was born.

"Anyway," he said abruptly, pulling himself out of his daze. "That artificial heart has served your father well for the better part of three hundred years. Still, like anything that's in constant use, the parts sometimes wear out. I think your grandmother said he needed a valve and one of the internal processors for the pacemaker."

I blinked. "Internal processor… you mean he just needed a new computer chip?"

D'nay chuckled and undid his seat belt. "It's an important one. I would imagine it's hazardous if your heart forgets when to beat."

He had a point. I dutifully followed his lead and got out of the car. "Is that why he passed out? His heart forgot what it was supposed to be doing?"

"Something like that," D'nay said as I fell into step beside him. We walked companionably into the hospital. Even though I was nervous about making sure my dad was okay, I still held my head a little straighter. I didn't feel quite as lost or confused anymore. I decided I really liked knowing what was going on.

We made it down to the room without a bit of fuss. The doctors and nurses all knew my grandfather. Heck, judging by hair color and bone structure, half of them had to be his descendants. A friendly blonde nurse even seemed to be waiting for us when we arrived on the post-op floor. With a smile she led us directly to my father's room and told us to let her know if we needed anything. D'nay inclined his head to her and she drifted away down the hall.

"It's going to look worse than it is," Grandpa warned me. "Are you ready?"

I nodded, anxiety squeezing my stomach. I swallowed it down and followed him into the room.

The lights were lower this time and a curtain had been pulled most of the way around my father's bed. Wires, tubes, and slowly moving lights surrounded his still form. I'd never seen Gabriel so pale. His closed eyes were purple bruises in a paper-white face. The wall above his bed flashed with displays that showed everything from heart rate to brainwaves. Both seemed slow and steady when we walked into the room.

A woman's voice came from the other side of the curtain. Whoever she was, she had a lovely singing voice. I could hear her humming under her breath - something soft and melodious.

I peered around the curtain and caught myself before I jumped. I should have known Olivia would show up, what with my father so ill. Still, I'd never seen her outside of An-gelus Quietum where her presence could fill the room with light. Here, in the harshness of the hospital's technology, she hardly even glowed.

My father's first wife sat on the edge of the bed, eyes fixed on Gabriel's pale face. Her red hair fell in gentle waves around her face and she wore a simple white dress. I caught her whispered little melody again and she ran an affectionate finger along the edge of my father's face. Even unconscious, he relaxed under her touch.

I glanced quickly at my grandfather. Just like everyone else, his eyes passed right over the ghost sitting a few feet away. Instead, he glanced at the flickering displays before settling himself in a chair near the door.

I pulled up a small, alloy chair and sat down next to my father's bed. His chest rose and fell reassuringly. I took his hand in mine and rested my cheek against it. It was solid and warm as always. The simmering pit of dread bubbling in my guts finally settled. The awful part was over. My dad was going to be okay.

Olivia hadn't reacted when I touched Gabriel's hand, nor had she moved beyond stroking my father's dark hair. Her soft melody was calm and soothing. I watched my father's peaceful sleep and wondered if he heard her in his dreams.

"Hello, love." Gloria's voice was almost a whisper a few feet behind me. I heard the rustle of cloth and gentle brush of lips as she greeted her husband. "How is she coping?"

"As well as can be expected," D'nay murmured softly. "Though I think she'd like a little explanation. She's not a baby anymore. You might want to talk to her."

There was a long pause while I held myself still and pretended I hadn't overheard them. The truth was I didn't want to move from Gabriel and Olivia's comforting presence. There was something about the tenderness of Olivia's regard for my father and the fact that only I could see her that made me feel connected to their relationship. I knew he'd married again after her and she certainly wasn't my mother, but over the years I had begun to think of Olivia as the only real female counterpart to Gabriel. With her sitting there, humming her soothing nothings and my grandparents keeping watch behind us, I somehow felt as if my family was complete in a way it never had been before. I held on to that safe belonging and enjoyed the warm solidity of my father's hand in mine.

"Gracie?" Gloria's voice was a gentle intrusion but an intrusion nonetheless. I glanced up at her wearily. Little tendrils of warm contentment still clung to my awareness, making me feel half-asleep.

"He's going to be okay," I said. I knew it the same way I knew my name or that the sky was blue. As clearly as I could see Gloria standing there, I could see my father walking out the hospital door with his arm linked in mine. It was so startling and clear after my day of anxiety-ridden doubt, but there was no denying the vision. I met my grandmother's gentle blue gaze and smiled. "Thank you for helping him."

Gloria cocked her head at me, her eyes narrowing a touch as if she sensed something odd going on. She opened her mouth, then paused, reconsidering. "He's my son, Gracie," she said, finally. "I don't have to be thanked for looking out for him. I love him. Besides, it's my job."

I thought about Leesil and the extended family I'd never known about. I thought about the University and a certain persistent reporter. I thought about Olivia watching my father sleep hundreds of years after she died. For the first time, I wondered what my job was; what my responsibilities were to this exceptional family I found myself a part of.

"Are you alright?" My grandmother pulled me back from my reverie.

"Yes," I whispered. "I'm just fine."

CHAPTER 20

GABRIEL'S 'EXPLANATION'

Two days later my father came home just the way I'd envisioned. After having him collapse, senseless in my arms three days earlier, it was pretty incredible to see how easily he bounced back. His face wasn't nearly as pale and, if he didn't move quite as smoothly as usual, he was steady enough to teleport us back to Angelus Quietum without any fuss.

The next morning dawned with a clear sky and a gentle, warm breeze. A square patch of sunlight reflected off the mirror on my closet door and shone directly into my eyes. I tried to burrow under the covers to avoid it, but Stella's shrill voice quickly put an end to that plan.

"Gracie! Time to wake up!" She sang through my head. I put a hand to my ears even though I knew she was stimulating my auditory nerve through my implant. Covering my ears wouldn't help a bit. With a groan, I rolled out of the warm comforter.

"I'm up, I'm up." I tossed on a robe over my night shift and shuffled off to the bathroom. "Was Dad up in the night?"

"No, he slept quite soundly," Stella replied in my head. She didn't usually manifest visually unless I was in the main living area these days. I knew she could 'see' what went on throughout the house from the holo-cameras placed in every room, but it was nice not to have a silver-haired projection staring at me in the shower. The water felt fantastic as I soaped and shampooed. I waited to reply to the computer, knowing she would understand that I needed a moment to myself.

"Good." I stepped out of the bath. "Let him sleep himself out. I won't want him pushing himself too hard."

"I believe it is too late for that." Stella's tone was regret-ful. "He was up almost two hours ago."

With a groan, I rushed through brushing my teeth and tossed my robe back on to dash across the hall. Back in my room, I struggled into yesterday's denim pants and shoved on a clean shirt.

"What is he doing up this early?" I demanded of the computer. "Honestly! How hard is it for him to take it easy for a few days?"

"Don't forget to brush your hair," Stella scolded me as I reached for the door. With a grumble and a dark look at the camera, I snatched the comb on my dresser and pulled it through my wavy, wet locks. My fine, red hair tangled un-mercifully around the ridged teeth, but I savagely yanked through it anyway.

"There, happy?" I snapped and barged out the door, ready to tear into my father the moment I saw him. I'd learned by watching my grandmother that the only way to get Gabriel to take care of himself was to bully him into it. "Where is he?"

"In the back garden," I heard something akin to amused resignation in Stella's voice. I ignored it and charged through the living room, into the kitchen, and out the back door.

From the back porch, I could see the silhouette of my father against the crystal reflection of the lake. The gentle breeze sent dazzling reflections of the sun and mountains playing across the mirror-like surface. Against this backdrop, my father stood as a small, dark shape on the bank. The two, great willow trees on the shore framed him as he smoothly moved in what almost looked like a dance. The movements were so graceful and fluid I found myself pausing to watch, all thoughts of my hot-tempered lecture burning away in the calm energy flowing outwards from his confident limbs. His feet moved very little, but his arms and center of balance constantly shifted in a slow, gentle ripple that ebbed and flowed like the waves of the lake on the shore. It was hypnotizing to watch, his hands gliding through a steady yet elegant pattern, sculpting figures in the air about his slim form.

Just as my elbow found the edge of the porch railing, something ruined the smooth flow of my father's movements. I'm not sure if it was a gesture that pulled too tightly across his still-healing chest or if his blood pressure was still unstable enough to make him lightheaded. Either way, mid-step he stumbled. The beautiful stream of his dance suddenly became a jagged jumble and he sat down a bit hard.

A red-headed ghost and a shattered mug exploded in my memory. My breath caught, all air crushed out of my lungs. I dashed down the steps so fast I didn't touch a single one.

"Dad!" I called out, racing across the grassy backyard. By the time I got to his side, Gabriel was already back on his feet and brushing himself off, a frown of frustration on his face. "Are you alright?" I gasped, grabbing his arm more roughly than I'd meant to.

"Yes, yes, I'm fine," he insisted, rolling a shoulder as if stretching out a lingering pain.

"You should be in bed, not practicing martial arts," I scolded him, my heart rate still slowly settling back to normal. Aside from being pale, my father did seem perfectly fine. I felt a bit stupid for running across the yard.

"Tai chi is well known for being gentle," he insisted, his eyebrows coming down in a rebellious scowl. "Besides, your grandmother gave me a clean bill of health."

"That's why you're stumbling about like a new foal," I countered, putting a firm arm around his waist and taking a determined step towards the back door. "Now come inside and let me cook you a decent breakfast."

"Sweet Fate, Gracie." His voice had lost the half-amusement it held at first. After one step he planted his heels and I might as well have tried to push one of the willow trees towards the back door. His heart might still be recovering, but his mind was as strong as ever. "I'm old but I'm not doddering. For pity's sake, take it easy."

With a groan, I looked up at him with pleading eyes. "I promised Grandma I'd take care of you," I begged, knowing I was playing my last card. It was a good one, though, and I felt the chances of it working for me were at least fifty-

fifty so I leaned into it a little. "You're the only parent I have. What would I do without you?"

Gabriel took my face in his strong, warm hands. I looked up into his handsome, ageless face and let him see the fear in my eyes. It wasn't hard to put there. I genuinely loved him and, after this whole ordeal, his mortality seemed very real to me. I honestly was terrified of finding him on the floor again.

"Sweetheart," he murmured, "really, I'm perfectly healthy. Nothing is going to happen to me. I promise."

"You can't promise that," I whispered. "You know your heart is weak. Grandfather told me you had to have it replaced."

Gabriel raised an eyebrow and his lips pressed into a grim line. "Did he, now? Well, let me explain something, then. My heart is just fine. In fact, the artificial one in my chest is stronger than the natural one in yours. It will be beating along like a drum when yours has failed and turned to dust. Just because it threw a glitch doesn't mean I'm some kind of an invalid."

"Oh." I swallowed hard at the coldness that had crept into his tone. I pulled away from him and he let me go, the arrogant tilt of his chin warning me that pushing this issue wasn't going to get me very far. I somehow felt rejected, as if I'd put my vulnerable fears out where he could see them and he'd crushed them under his boot heel. I think he caught a glimpse of my wounded expression because he sighed.

"Wait," he groaned, running a hand through his hair in that absent way he had. "I'm sorry, I think that came out a bit wrong. Come on, let's sit down and talk about this."

"Can we sit down inside the house?" I asked, giving him wide, innocent eyes.

With a resigned chuckle, he wrapped an arm around my shoulders and set off towards the porch. Uncertain of how I'd won, but aware that I had, I kept my mouth shut and let him guide me up the stairs and into the kitchen. There, he gestured for me to sit down before pulling out the tea kettle and setting it to boil.

"Now," he sighed, turning to face me. He leaned his hip against the counter and folded his arms across his chest. I sat at the table and gave him my quiet, undivided attention. I knew how he was in this sort of a mood. I'd get the most out of him if I simply let him talk. "I'm sorry I snapped at you. I know you're just worried and I can understand that. It must have been very frightening for you to find me the way you did."

Slowly, I nodded but didn't say anything. Gabriel was one of those people who needed to be reassured of his emotional standing. If I didn't say anything, he'd try to justify himself until I gave him the response he was looking for. I hadn't been living with the man for the last six years without learning something about dragging information from between his tight lips.

"What I was trying to say, in my usual flippant way" — he ducked his head and hid behind his hair a moment at that statement—"is that you don't need to worry. My illness was a fluke, a once-in-a-century occurrence. I'm not fragile by any stretch of the imagination. And while I may not bounce back as fast as I once did, it still won't take me long."

I let some cool doubt fill my gaze. I knew he found it disconcerting being unable to read my mind the way he did everyone else's.

"You may not think I remember, but I do. Grandma Gloria used to fuss over you when we first went to visit her. You've been sick before and it was well within this century," I accused, keeping my eyes cold.

Gabriel's face went very blank. It wasn't the response I was expecting but I found it interesting nonetheless. I'd noticed that he and my grandparents had a habit of putting up that shield when they didn't want to discuss something or weren't sure how to react. Since I hadn't encountered many other adults, I assumed it was something everyone learned how to do at some point. I hadn't mastered shutting down my expression so completely yet, but I was practicing.

"That was… something else altogether," he said slowly. "Really, quite a different situation." It had been a while since he'd gotten so guarded. As usual, my natural curiosity kindled at his silence.

"Like what?" I demanded, leaning forward. "I've never seen you come down with as much as a sniffle. If it wasn't your heart, what was Gloria so flustered about?"

My father was silent for a long time. His eyes closed and I wasn't sure he was going to answer me at all. His jaw worked as if he were thinking hard about something difficult.

"Gracie, do you remember the day you asked me about your mother?"

I was taken aback by his question. It had been a long while since I thought about that day. Still, it was one of the defining conversations of my young life.

"How could I forget?"

He nodded, eyes cast down on his hands as he spoke. "Of course, silly of me to ask," he murmured. His blue eyes flickered up at me and I saw that ever-present pain in his gaze. "I explained how people sometimes get sick emotionally, not just physically, remember?"

I nodded, not dignifying his question with a spoken response.

"Your... mother wasn't..." He struggled with it for a moment, twisting his hands and running fingers through his hair. When he glanced back up at me, his eyes were a touch too bright, as if he were fighting back tears.

Five, almost six, years of living with the man and I'd never seen him cry. Never. Not once. A lump rose in my own throat as I watched him swallow hard.

Finally, he seemed to get his voice under control and met my eye. "Your mother wasn't the only one who struggled with that kind of illness. I have had bouts of it several times over my lifetime. It is an incredibly painful state and not one I would ever wish upon anyone."

Slowly, I nodded, sensing that this was a difficult admission for him to make.

"You said that was what killed my mother," I said slowly, my mind piecing together the facts I had. My eyes searched his and I could see that simmering pain that constantly hid in the back of his gaze rolling up to spill across the surface. "Were you ever that sick? Could you have died?"

Taking a steadying breath, he took my hand. "When your mother told me about you, I was in a very dark place. The darkest I've ever been, I think. But then you needed me. Learning of you was like having a light switched on in my head. I knew I had to pull myself together and take care of you. You gave me purpose again; a reason to get up in the morning. Honestly, I think you saved my life."

I swallowed hard but couldn't keep the tears from gathering in my eyes.

"I was just a baby," I whispered, brushing the tears away with one hand while I squeezed his hand with the other. "You were the one who saved me."

"We saved each other, then," he said gently, and opened his arms to me. Setting aside the awkwardness of early adolescence, I went around the table and let him pull me into his safe, warm embrace. I ducked my head against his shoulder and he buried his face in my hair. When his body shuddered with silent tears, I found it impossible to hold back the moisture in my own. We sat that way for a very long time.

When we'd both cried ourselves out a bit, he sat me on his knee the way he used to when I was small. I was getting too big for it at this point, but I was feeling vulnerable and didn't mind being treated a bit younger than I was.

"I am so lucky to have a daughter like you," he said with a bit more of a smile as I clung to his neck.

"You gave me everything," I whispered, leaning back to see his face. "You and Stella and all of Angelus Quietum... even Grandma and Grandpa... I would never have had any of it if you hadn't come for me. You're the best dad on all of Cybele!"

He laughed and hugged me tight again. I breathed in the mint and tobacco smell of his hair and relaxed into that familiar safety of home that can only be found in your parents' arms.

"I'll always save you, Daddy," I whispered into his warm neck.

He swallowed hard and I knew he was fighting back tears again. "I know you will, sweetheart," he murmured, kissing the top of my head. "I know you will."

CHAPTER 21

GROWING UP

Several years passed in my quiet and content childhood.

I trained Aubrie's foal, whom we dubbed Charcoal for his dusky coat, and looking back I daresay that the process trained me as much as the young horse. I learned patience and tenacity even as my father imparted the ways of motivating others to do your will.

"Kindness and trust are more powerful than the harshest whip," he'd say when I stomped into the kitchen covered in mud. "Did you remember to praise him when he did things right, or did you only strike him when he erred?"

I began to see the same patterns that my father encouraged me to use with Charcoal in the ways that he approached training me in Awareness.

"Almost, Gracie," he'd say when my focus slipped and the fireball I was lobbing towards the lake turned into a graceless gout of flame. "Keep the image pictured in your mind. You can do it, you've done it before. You just have to have confidence."

I grumbled and muttered about being treated like a yearling colt, but I had more success the next time. My father's faith in me never wavered and because of it, my faith in myself didn't either. At my core I always think of myself as intelligent and capable and I truly believe it is because of that confidence my father fostered in every lesson he ever gave me. That is probably one of the biggest gifts he imparted and I don't think I appreciated it at the time. How can one fully comprehend that kind of a psychological service? Only time and hindsight allow us to truly see the shape of our parent's legacy.

Around the age of sixteen I had yet to appreciate these lessons. Instead, I began to chafe under the isolation of Angelus Quietum.

Stella always kept me in plenty of reading material and I'd begun to explore more adult fare at that point. I imagine my father loosened the parental controls on Stella's selections for me around the age of thirteen, but it wasn't until a year or two later that I was interested in the racier novels. Once I discovered them I couldn't get enough of the romance and sensuality that steamed through the memory pad's screen.

Still, between lessons, chores, and training Charcoal, I was kept quite busy and I think that is why I didn't start pining for a male presence outside of my father's until I was solidly into my teens. I had no experience with such interactions outside of fiction, of course, but after reading a dozen accounts of every flavor of romance, I thought myself quite the expert.

The descriptions of the fair maidens in the stories were slowly beginning to align themselves with what I saw in the mirror as well. Long, lean, and supple was my youthful body, with high, perky breasts that needed the support of a bra when I rode now.

Grandma Gloria took me to Skykyle City's upscale district to purchase some acceptable undergarments when I was thirteen. By sixteen, she made a yearly point of taking a day trip to update my wardrobe. We'd go to the pricey little shops with their falsely-friendly sales girls and pick out the latest fashions. My grandmother never mentioned the price of what she bought me, though I was always careful not to ask for something if her eyebrows raised at the tag. They rarely did.

After gaining a collection of bags and boxes, Gloria and I would sit in a little café and sip exotic fruit drinks while we watched the mass of humanity float by. I began to envy the gaggles of girls and boys my own age who appeared to be without chaperons at all. They wandered through the shops giggling and flirting. I'd carefully spy on the couples holding hands, their young eyes mooning up at each other as if the only thing in the world was the beautiful companion at their side. A ringing hollowness rose in my chest and, feeling exposed, I'd quickly look away.

That hollowness haunted me more persistently than any ghost ever had. I tried to shake the feeling by throwing myself into my usual pastimes but that primitive, private yearning had taken hold of my youthful flesh and there was no escape. It nagged at me as I sent Charcoal through his paces, singing through his movements under my tender thighs. It teased me at lessons as I learned about the great couples of literature: Romeo and Juliet, Anthony and Cleopatra, Elizabeth and Darcy, Lessa and F'lar.

There were even several risqué poems in my English textbook regarding my father and his first wife. Usually Stella glossed over the particulars when it came to my immediate family but this one was right in the middle of the literature book's discussion of traditional sonnets, so the computer hadn't been able to censor it. Afterwards I found my unrequited desire suddenly cast in a new light.

Did my father have these urges? Intellectually, I knew he was ancient, but his physique was still that of a young man in his prime. Surely he had physical needs, otherwise how could I have been born? Yet in all the time we'd lived here at Angelus Quietum he had never once brought around any female visitors. It puzzled me because I knew he was handsome. Even the sonnets described him in glowing terms, with eyes blue as the ocean and limbs supple as young wheat stalks. Why did he stay alone out here in the wilderness?

If he noticed my discomfort, my father said nothing. He did comment on how lovely the new clothes Gloria and I selected looked on me, as well as the progress I made on Charcoal's training. He also made a point of picking up feminine products for me when he went to the store and placing them where they were easy to find under my bathroom sink. Other than that, I might as well still be ten for all the notice he gave my budding maturity.

Then, something unexpected happened and in less than twenty-four hours everything changed.

CHAPTER 22

FLYING LESSONS

"The sky is finally clear today," Gabriel said, glancing over his memory pad at breakfast to peer out the window. I nibbled on a scrambled egg while reading over a review of yesterday's history lesson. Stella was a big fan of pop quizzes and I wasn't completely confident in my knowledge of Hal's political structure.

"Huh? Oh, yeah," I agreed, tapping through the notes I'd taken. "Dad, do you know if Hal is a providence or a protectorate?"

"It was established as a protectorate but petitioned to come into the Continental Government... oh... one hundred and twenty years ago? Something like that. It's been a providence for over a century."

"Thanks," I muttered, making another note on the pad.

"Sweet Fate, how hard is Stella working you?" Gabriel grumbled, grabbing my mostly-empty plate and rinsing it in the sink. "Come on, you've earned a day off. What do you say I give you a different kind of lesson?"

I raised an eyebrow and set down the memory pad. "Extra Awareness practice?" I asked, tired just thinking about a whole day of using my pyrokinetic skills. With Dad's help, I could sustain a small flame without fuel for several hours now. Though it wasn't useful for much other than a night-light and afterwards I wasn't useful for much other than a nap.

"Nah, you'll never be a telepath, but your pyro skills are as good as many adult firebirds I've known. Not that staying in practice isn't important, but no. I thought I might teach you how to fly," he said, a mischievous smile lighting his face. "Does that sound like fun?"

"Fly?" I asked, confused. "I'm not a telekinetic any more than I'm a telepath."

He laughed, a rich, open sound that filled the kitchen with his happy energy. "No, no, of course you aren't. Not with your mind. I'm talking about a shuttle."

"Oh!" My eyes got very wide. "Really!? But I've never even driven a hover car. I know the theory, of course, but I've never actually done it. Oh my, is it even legal?"

He shrugged. "I'm the most qualified instructor you can find, except perhaps my father. And who wants to drive a silly hover car when you can see the stars? As for legality, we're in Angelus Quietum, which is just another way of saying 'nowhere.' Who's going to stop us?"

With a happy yelp, I threw my arms around his neck and he laughed again, giving me a quick squeeze before setting me on my feet. He'd become more aware of our physical interaction lately and was quicker to pull away than he used to be. It was his only nod to my blossoming sensuality and, even though I knew it was proper, it hurt my pride somewhat to be put off by the one and only man in my life.

"What kind of shuttle are we taking?" I asked, glancing outside at the stable yard. "I don't think I've ever seen one in person."

"Oh, I've always kept one around for emergencies," he said brightly, palming open the back door so we could step out onto the back porch. "I prefer teleportation or my own two feet when it comes to planetary travel, but one never knows when one might need to get off world in a hurry. I suppose that's the colonist in me talking, but I've always felt safer knowing the *Hawk* was around."

Striding purposefully, Gabriel led the way down the back stairs and over to the side of the barn. There, he tapped one of the slats of siding with his knuckles three times. To my amazement, the slat slid back to reveal a touch screen. Laying his hand against it, my father treated me to a wicked grin. My mouth fell open in wonder.

"How long has that been there?" I demanded, feeling as if the stable yard were an alien place I'd never been before

"Oh, much longer than you've been here, my dear," he said gently, pulling me closer to his side as he let the siding fall back into place over the hand plate. The ground beneath our feet roared and shook. I clung to his arm with trepidation.

Not twenty feet from where we stood, a huge seam opened in the dirt. Gears ground to life after a long sleep, their protests roaring up from the widening pit. Our frightened chickens scattered away from the dreadful noise while Aubrie and Charcoal stomped anxiously in their stalls. I covered my mouth with one hand as dust from the yard rose with the thunderous vibrations, squinting my eyes to avoid clogging them with grit. Then, as if it had materialized from another time, an ancient shuttle rose from the ground on a metal pedestal.

The shuttle was rounded and nearly completely see-through. Ribbons of alloy threaded through the organic curves of the plex-glass before becoming a more solid piece that swept back into huge twin engines balanced like spread wings on the rear end of the vehicle. I gawked at the pristine antique.

"Come on!" There was a fiery gleam of life in Dad's eyes as he trotted towards the shuttle. His excitement caught in my chest as I followed him up to the beautiful vessel.

"Sweet Fate," I breathed as Gabriel pressed a hand to the side of the shuttle and a plex-glass panel slid back to allow us entrance.

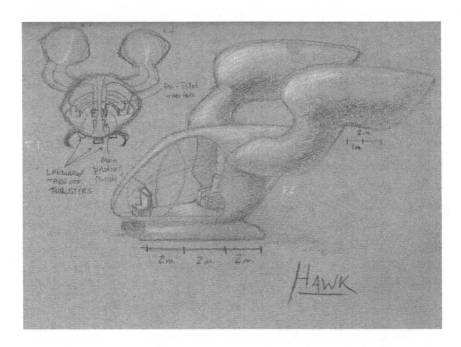

Perhaps five people could have stood in the shuttle, but six would have felt crowded. In the center of the room, a raised chair sat covered in twisting wires and tubes. Behind it curved a bench with cushions so worn I had no idea what color they had been when new. At the front of the plex-glass dome was another chair, this one close enough to the glass that the person sitting in it would have been able to touch the clear surface.

"Can this thing still fly?" I asked, glancing at the configuration of the wires and circuits. I wasn't an engineering student by any stretch of the imagination, but I'd seen schematics of modern shuttles. This thing belonged in a museum.

"Are you kidding?" Dad laughed and ran a possessive hand over the back of the raised chair. "This was the first shuttle to achieve accelerated drive. There were only two psi-pilots back then, and it wasn't the safest job in the world. Nearly fried myself on this thing the first time I used it."

He smiled to himself and lapsed into silence, his gaze going distant. I cleared my throat.

"You didn't answer my question."

With one hand he dismissed my question and his lively features grimaced to offer his opinion of my doubts. "Of course she works," he grumbled. "The *Hawk* was designed by your grandfather himself."

Unsure such a fact was as reassuring as my father thought it was, I resigned myself to the knowledge that criticism of D'nay's work was most likely a mistake. With a shrug, I slid into the front-most seat.

"Okay, so how do I fly it?"

"Well, it's a team effort in this case," he said, tossing his work-a-day shirt onto the alloy floor and perching himself on the raised center seat. "It takes two to fly the *Hawk* properly. Don't look so worried. I'll guide you through the whole thing."

Feeling more skeptical by the moment, I watched my father settle himself into the psi-pilot's chair. It wasn't anything like the modern psi-pilot's stations I'd read about with Stella. Those were plex-glass tubes full of neuro-conductor that the pilot entered naked. I was glad my father got to keep his pants on for this model, even if it meant the ship we were about to send into orbit was dangerously out of date.

"Tap your implant to sync it to the piloting computer." Dad's voice wasn't loud but it carried across the cabin easily. Obediently, I tapped my implant. Instantly a display popped up on the plex-glass in front of me. Glowing boxes and a 3D holo-model of the ship flooded me with an overwhelming amount of information.

"Where do I even start?" I whined, running a finger over the edge of the holo. The image of the shuttle obediently turned with my touch and I breathed a sigh of relief that some of the controls behaved in a familiar way.

"First you need to spin up the engines," Gabriel coached, "and then use the red set of coordinate settings to plot an orbital course."

Stella taught me enough about coordinates in class to achieve orbit. With that basic knowledge, I was able to tap my way through a series of pre-programmed screens with

little trouble. Dad still had to give me a few exact coordinates, since he knew the velocity equations better than I did,
but overall everything went smoothly for a first time.

"Okay, it accepted that set," I told him. The engines had
warmed up to a nice, singing hum by that point and it was
harder to hear him over their whine.

"Good. Take her through the launching protocol, then."

I tapped through the green set of icons that set the shuttle's lift and acceleration. With an unsettling lurch, the
Hawk lifted off of the platform. I swallowed hard with apprehension, but before I really started sweating, the little
shuttle settled down and responded to my commands.
Within a few moments, we were skimming above the lake's
glittering surface.

"Follow the ascension path," Dad reminded me, though
I'd already figured that part out on my own. I'd used flight
simulators enough times to know what to do with an ascension path after all!

We glided over tree tops and the snow-covered mountains that dominated our little valley. My head swiveled in
every direction at once, watching the gray, weather-
cracked rock disappear below us. Up here, the peaks
looked like children's toys.

"Hold her steady!" Dad hissed at me. "Watch your wind
shear!"

The shuttle trembled and dropped a few dozen feet before the auto-stabilizers caught us. I let out a thrilled and
terrified laugh even as I heard my father's indulgent groan.
My fingers flew over the control panel, correcting for the
higher wind velocities in the upper atmosphere. The *Hawk*

shuddered to a smoother ascent as we pulled above the worst of the turbulence.

"Better?" I called over my shoulder. The options for the accelerated drive lit up in the top corner of my display.

"Better," Gabriel agreed. "Now it's my turn. Would you please activate the psi-drive?"

"Coming online now," I said, spinning up the engines to an even higher peak and enabling the organic relays that allowed Dad to tap into their strength. The low rumble of the engines rose to a thundering crescendo as my father's powerful mind entered the merge.

There was a low chuckle from the seat behind me and I glanced over my shoulder to see my father cloaked in a screen of bright, ever-moving light. He was barely visible behind the constantly shifting array of data, but the engines picked up a low bass thrum that vibrated deeply in my chest. Then the force of his acceleration slammed into me and I clung to the ragged cloth of my seat.

Through the plex-glass walls the clouds sailed past at incredible speed. My gaze lifted and, despite the daylight, the sky ahead of us darkening and filling in with stars. I sucked in a delighted breath at the thrill of speed and flight.

"Gracie! Pay attention!" Dad snapped at me. Quickly turning my attention back to the console, I corrected the angle of our thrust by a few degrees and tapped on the artificial gravity. The sky continued to darken while I watched the readings. The options for the autopilot lit up and I switched the shuttle into stable orbit mode.

"Ta da!" I sang, springing up and out of the pilot's chair. With a spin of long, curly red hair, I danced about the edges of the shuttle as I admired the endless fields of stars around us. A huge smile spread across my face as I turned to my father. He pulled his shirt back over his shoulders and gave me an answering grin. "I did it! Can you believe it?"

His rich laugh made me squirm with proud delight. "You did. Good job," he said, taking a few steps to look at the front console I'd just abandoned. "Ah, here we are."

Under our feet, the shuttle tilted and the great curve of Cybele rose below us. I gasped at the beauty of the sunlit globe of blue and white that swam below us. A swirl of pale, gossamer silk shifted to reveal the rich green and white expanse of the continent. Chasing after the mainland's rich shore was the sharp emerald of Hal's volcanic island.

"Sweet Fate," I breathed as Dad came over and put an arm around my shoulders. "It's so beautiful."

"Yes," he murmured, "it is." A brightness shone in his eyes as he watched our magnificent home. When he looked down at me, however, the melancholy folded away behind his usual mischievous smile. With an affectionate hand, he straightened a few of the curly locks between my shoulder blades. "For a first flight, that went quite smoothly. No surprise there. After all, you *are* my daughter."

I beamed under his praise. He wandered back over to the manual pilot's station.

"What's wrong? Did I make a mistake?" I asked as he sat in the chair I'd just occupied.

"No, no, you were fine," he reassured me, his long fingers sliding through coordinate menus so fast I could barely follow them. "Where we're landing is a little... tricky. That's all. And we won't need me as psi-pilot coming down from orbit. You just relax and enjoy the ride. I'll have us down in time for tea."

With a slightly hurt shrug, I went to sit on the back bench while Dad initiated the descent protocol.

My irritation was short lived as I watched the stars. For the first time I experienced them without the cloak of atmosphere between me and their shimmering depths. Their beauty was beyond anything I can put into words; a shining, bejeweled expanse that sang through me like a plucked string. I watched them fade away as Cybele's life-giving veil of oxygen wrapped its fingers around us once more. My eyes slid shut when the clouds thickened and we were enveloped in a world of white.

"Gracie."

My father's voice brought my attention back to the here and now. My eyes widened as a huge city loomed up from the rocky crags below us. This wasn't the curved, elegant lines of Skykyle's urban sprawl. The spires of this metropolis were thin and iridescent as they reached for the under belly of the shuttle. I'd never seen such angular and aggressive architecture, even in holo's.

"Where are we?" I leaned forward on the bench eagerly. It had been years since I went anywhere that Dad and I hadn't discussed and researched thoroughly before arrival. This day was just full of surprises!

"New Terra," my father rumbled. A thrill went down my spine.

"We've left the Provinces?" I whispered as the shuttle wove smoothly between the towering crystalline structures.

Through their gleaming, transparent surfaces, strange faces peered out at us.

"We have," Gabriel agreed, landing the shuttle so smoothly that the only indication of our meeting with the rocky ground was a delicate spiral of snowflakes that momentarily obscured the quiet clearing we'd settled in. However, once the white powder cleared, two still figures waited for us at the edge of a pine grove.

"Who are they?" I asked my father.

He didn't reply immediately, focusing his attention on powering down the shuttle's systems. Once the little ship was silent, he turned to me with an intense expression on his sharp features.

"We are a long way from home, Gracie," he said, standing in one graceful movement. "I need you to stay quiet and follow my lead."

I nodded, anxiety building in my chest. Gabriel rarely used such a stern tone with me and I took him seriously when he did.

"Are we in danger?" I asked, my heart rate picking up.

"No, no," he gave me a small, reassuring smile and offered me a hand. "Nothing like that. We're just in a different culture which means we need to be cautious. That's all."

I took his hand and allowed him to pull me to my feet. The excitement of exploring an exotic city and meeting new people began to win over apprehension. I fell in behind him as he jumped down through the shuttle's automatic door. I shivered and wrapped my leather jacket tighter around myself as my shoes crunched in the thin coating of snow.

"Eva Andronikov greets you, Gabriel the Undying."

CHAPTER 23

EVA

I watched the Terran woman warily from behind my father's broad shoulders. There was something odd about her skin; its flawless expanse was so white she nearly blended in with the snow. She wore a thick, full dress and a woolen overcoat with a fur-lined hood that left very little bare to the chill air.

"Greetings, Eva," my father said, inclining his torso to her. She smiled and put out a gloved hand to touch his elbow.

"The pleasure is mine," she murmured, then tilted her head if just noticing me. "Who is this?"

Gabriel gestured in my direction and a bit of what I hoped was pride slid through his expression. "My daughter, Gracie. She's helping me pilot the *Hawk.*"

"I see," Eva raised an eyebrow as she glanced over the antiquated shuttle. "There are vehicles that a psi-pilot of your abilities could manage alone. Perhaps that would have been the wiser course of action?"

My father looked nonplussed. "Gracie may be young, but she is trustworthy and discreet, not to mention strongly Aware."

The woman met my gaze and I was startled by the color of her eyes. Rings of brown and orange swirled in an unusual pattern and I found myself openly staring before I tore myself away. My grandmother taught me better manners than that.

"Young and inexperienced," she sighed, "but I suppose we all come onto Cybele that way. Who am I to question an Usuriel? Perhaps it is better that you have an assistant for today's task."

"I'm here for a task? I was unaware." My father's voice was parched. "You haven't introduced your companion."

"Ah, how rude of me!" she exclaimed, turning to the young man at her side. "This is James Galling, one of our most promising Scholars."

"James," my father echoed, sounding a bit taken aback. The youth ignored Gabriel's strange reaction and offered his hand in greeting.

"Welcome, Eternal Flesh," he said, his voice more deeply accented than Eva's. His clothing was more colorful than his companion's, though equally heavy, with swirls of red and black twisting about a well-tailored torso. It covered less of his skin and where it gaped, his flesh was so pale as to be translucent in places. Unless it was my imagination, tiny rivers of blue light flashed beneath the surface.

"Very good then, all introductions are made," Eva said. "Let us go inside. I doubt the temperature is comfortable for you or your daughter here."

Dad gestured to her and she lead us away from the clearing. The glistening towers of glass loomed larger now that we were on the ground. I stared up at them so hard my neck hurt. Fortunately, my spine didn't have long to contort it-self because Eva turned and entered one of the first build-ings we encountered. The door must have had a motion sensor because it slid open easily to admit the four of us.

I took a deep breath of warm air as we entered the foyer. Large-leafed plants and lush carpets greeted us in the high-ceilinged, narrow-walled space. There were a few individ-uals in the room, most of them behind the counter on the right hand side. They were not as elaborately dressed as our hosts and their sidelong glances at Eva made me think they were not used to having someone of her status here.

"Everson Nodvech representing Gostinaya Soyedinen-naya greets you, honored guests."

Eva inclined her head to the rather plain individual who had just introduced themself. Their face was too smooth to be real with a shine that reminded me of plex-glass. An AI like Stella, perhaps? Large, green eyes gazed at me, intelli-gent yet discreet, as they sketched a formal bow.

"Thank you, Everson," Eva said dismissively, waltzing past the counter and into a narrow hall. Gabriel followed on her heels while James politely gestured for me to go in front of him.

"You... you're taking... them... down there?" The recep-tionist sounded as if they were struggling between the fear of giving offense and the nervousness of an employee wit-nessing an infraction.

"Are you questioning me?" Eva's voice held enough warning to make me flinch.

"No. Of course not, but... they are not Terran."

"I am the Council's Speaker. I have full access to the Hall of Hearts. This discussion is terminated."

"Discussion terminated," Everson echoed. I wasn't sure if they sounded nervous or relieved.

Without another word, Eva turned and led us down the narrow hall.

The four of us silently walked on. I stared at my father's back as we moved deeper into the crystalline building and found myself extremely thankful for my family's special abilities. At least if things got too strange, Dad could have us back at the shuttle in the blink of an eye.

The tiny corridor snaked right, then left, passing several doors before ending abruptly in a small, metal room. To fit into it, we had to stand so close to each other I could feel the heat coming off of my father's skin. Oddly, there was no similar heat from James standing directly in front of me.

Once we'd arranged ourselves, a slim, alloy door hummed closed and the floor of the room slowly dropped. It reminded me of the University Hospital transport and I spared a quick glance in my father's direction. He looked as strong and steady as always. For a moment I wished I was a telepath like the rest of the Family so that I could ask him what he thought of Eva and James. Wishing was about as helpful as a paperweight in zero gravity, so I wracked my brain trying to think of every reference to Terrans I could remember from Stella's lessons while I waited for the elevator to settle on a floor.

My musings weren't very helpful; what I knew might fill a single text file page. New Terra was a sovereign country located on a landmass to the North of the Provinces. Stella often prattled on about treaties and trade agreements with them, but I'd never cared enough to pay attention. I did remember that the Terrans started out as a separate wave of space colonization, also from Earth just like the *Inspiration*. Due to some kind of flaw in the Terran interstellar technologies, they'd ended up joining the *Inspiration* crew but I couldn't remember what that flaw was. I was still trying to recall those details when the floor trembled to a halt. Then the smooth, alloy door fell away to reveal one of the most incredible sights I'd ever witnessed.

"What is this place?" I whispered as we stepped out of the lift.

Weak, blue light carved Gabriel's face out of black shadows. I followed his gaze to our two companions. The tiny flickering lights dancing inside James' skin—so faint in the sunlight—were now radiant blue sparks. Then Eva turned to us and her eyes did more than just reflect the light; they glowed with an electric orange fire.

"Welcome to our most sacred space. The Hall of Hearts is where we keep our most precious and vulnerable treasures safe from the world's dangers," Eva explained to my wide eyed gaze. With one pale, gloved hand she gestured out into the immense blue-dotted darkness. "Few visitors have the opportunity to see our inner sanctum. You should feel privileged, child."

My eyes adjusted to the dim lighting and row upon row of tall, incandescently lit cylinders resolved themselves into hard-edged objects rather than a field of indecipherable dots of light and shadow. The closest ones to us were only ten feet away, their inner glow broken up by lines of electrodes and metal plates. However, it wasn't the vastness of the chamber or the incalculable number of cylinders that made my breath catch. Rather, it was the naked human forms floating silently in their depths that made me take a step closer to my father's side.

"I apologize for being so short with you earlier, Father Gabriel, but I'm afraid this is the only place near the city where we can be sure there is no one listening," Eva said in a more conversational tone.

"I suspected as much," Gabriel replied, his voice even and collected. I found his calm profoundly comforting. "Now, why don't you start explaining why you found it necessary to send me such an urgent summons."

Eva didn't turn to respond, but rather spoke over her shoulder as she walked around the edge of the cavernous room. Much to my relief, her path did not take us any closer to the glowing cylinders.

"We have a… delicate situation. You have been an advocate for us since the beginning. I knew you wouldn't ignore such a plea."

"Still rather arrogant, don't you think," my father warned, though I detected a touch of amusement in his voice. His lithe figure fell into a rolling stride that easily kept up with our host. James and I fell in less gracefully at the rear.

"I apologize if it seemed that way." Eva didn't sound sorry. "We did not mean to offend. However, as you will quickly see, I was acting out of need. It was not my intention to abuse our privilege as Family members."

I was a bit taken aback by Eva's claim of kinship. James seemed neither shaken by our surroundings nor overly intrigued by the adults' conversation. Alone in my bewilderment, I strained my neck around James' shoulders to get a better look at the people floating in their strange cylinders. Were they alive or dead?

"You have my interest," Gabriel conceded as we approached a small doorway on our right. The sealed passage hissed open the moment Eva stepped in front of it. Without breaking stride, the four of us moved through the portal and into a more normal sized room. It was mostly bare with a few simple, plastic chairs against the far wall.

"I hope I will have more than your interest by the end of the day," Eva replied. I was young and inexperienced in the social realm, but I recognized how carefully she and my father were choosing their words.

We passed through another doorway into a second, smaller room. One of the large cylinders built into the left hand wall dominated the room. A slim young man floated serenely in the electric blue effervescence that cast the room in shifting circles of light. Directly in front of him, an open pool of strange liquid slowly bubbled. My nose twitched at a sharply antiseptic scent.

"I'm assuming you are aware of Dalton's death," Eva murmured, stepping next to the vertical tank to give my father, James, and I space to move into the room without falling into the open vat.

"I was sorry to hear of it." My father inclined his head as he prowled to the foot of the pool. It placed him across the room from Eva, yet he didn't plant himself. Rather, he paced around the small space, intelligent eyes flickering from our hosts to the various surfaces and devices in the room. "It was quite the unfortunate accident."

"You wouldn't have any information on who might have been involved in that little… accident," Eva asked quite pointedly.

Gabriel raised an eyebrow before gesturing to me. "It has been a very long time since I involved myself in those kinds of politics. I've been rather busy with my own business."

"Indeed," Eva said, giving me another appraising look with those electric eyes. "So I'd heard. Of course, if Parliament would just loosen their rules about avatars…"

"And let you install a receiver on Providence land? We're more likely to discover a new habitable moon lurking over the horizon."

James had stationed himself next to Eva during the discussion. The two of them exchanged a meaningful look at my father's pronouncement. She nodded and I watched James' head drop. His shoulders were tense and his spine bowed as he quietly settled himself upon a small chair in the far left corner. It was built into the same wall as the cylinder and, as he leaned back, the very substance of that wall melted around his shoulders.

"That's what I thought you'd say," Eva murmured, sounding unhappily resigned. "This, of course, means that we no longer have an ambassador in Skykyle City to represent our interests. I hope you understand how grave a situation this is for us."

Gabriel nodded as if he'd expected this to come up. "I do understand why it is unfortunate. However, I think it is more of a long term problem than an urgent one. None of the Providence farm holds are about to stop selling their produce to such a consistent and appreciative clientele just because there's no one in Parliament holding their hand."

"For now, that may be true," Eva agreed. "However, we both know old prejudices run deep. The current arrangements that Dalton set up for us are both competitive and, for the moment, solid. Such agreements have an expiration date, however, and we must be able to adjust to the ever changing economy should there be cause."

I was still listening to the adults, but my eyes had long since strayed away from Eva's carefully controlled face in favor of watching James slowly disappear into the pliable gray substance of the wall. I tucked my hands firmly in my pockets and gave the walls a wide berth, lest I become the room's next unhappy victim.

"You mean you still want to get in on the O'Harre accounts," Father grumbled.

The look Eva gave him was dryly amused. "I thought you weren't involved in such politics these days."

Gabriel shrugged, his face carefully neutral. If I knew him, however, he was pleased that he still held some cards Eva was unaware of.

"Of course. You *are* Gabriel Usuriel after all. Well, then, I think you may know what I'm about to ask you."

"I can't possibly imagine," my father murmured.

With one hand she gestured to the young man floating in the blue liquid. "You have met James' avatar. He is an intelligent and gifted young man, though inexperienced. He was being groomed by Dalton to be our next assistant diplomat. However, he hadn't taken him to the Provinces yet."

Gabriel raised an eyebrow. "Wait... you mean to tell me..."

"He's never been in the flesh. Yes, that's correct."

My father is a pale man to begin with so when he lost a shade or two of color, he looked downright sick.

"I'm neither a nursemaid nor a healer," my father protested. "Do you have any idea what that boy is about to go through?"

"Better than you," Eva replied evenly. "I realize I am asking a lot of a man who prefers his privacy, but look at it from my perspective. I need someone who is completely comfortable in the flesh that is also discreet and trustworthy. With Dalton dead, that narrows down my options considerably."

Gabriel scowled, those midnight eyes narrowing down to dangerous slits. "Surely there are some better options. In fact, several of them come to my mind immediately."

Eva tilted her head at him. "I assure you, I have looked at this situation from every angle. You really are the best situation for him."

When my father got that expression, I usually took the better part of valor and lived to fight another day. My eyes darted rapidly from his angry face to the shallow indentation where the wall had completely swallowed up James' defeated figure. Whatever was going on, I was getting more confused and nervous by the minute.

"My mother is a much better fit," Gabriel pointed out. "She and Dad have a larger home, to start with. They're closer to the University, which I'm assuming he'll be attending in a year or two. Not to mention the fact that she's a healer who will know what to do with a twenty-five-year-old infant!"

"He's seventeen, actually," Eva replied evenly. "Which is another reason for him to stay with you. While our society recognizes emotional and intellectual maturity at whatever age it occurs, yours still has archaic ideas of chronological majority. James has six months before he is eligible for the University and he requires training during that time in a variety of areas, some of which he can only gain through access to a man of Awareness such as yourself."

Dad wasn't having it. "My mother is fully capable of training him in Awareness. Male and female doesn't matter in those kinds of things. I should know; she was my teacher."

"No, Gloria is off the table," she shook her head vigorously, her arms now crossed firmly across her chest. "Your parents are simply too visible in Landing. James is young and completely inexperienced in the flesh. He's bound to make mistakes. If he's ever going to be an ambassador, he can't afford that kind of first impression. He would always be bargaining from a position of weakness."

"Are you sure it wouldn't be better for him to stay here for a little while? Get his feet under himself so to speak…"

"We don't have the facilities here." Eva's voice held a note of pleading. "From food production to waste management, we're not set up for more than short visits from individuals in the flesh. Even our medical professionals have minimal experience with an active metabolism. Please, if you have any compassion for this young man, you will do us this service."

Though I read some nervousness in Eva's expression, she met my father's eyes unflinchingly. Gabriel, for his part, seemed to be genuinely considering her words.

Finally, he glanced over his shoulder at me. For the thousandth time, I wished I was the telepath he'd first thought me to be. His expression communicated his conflicted emotions effectively enough, though, even if I wasn't sure why he had them.

"When you put it that way I suppose I have little choice," my father sighed. "I would not deny you in a time of need. Yes, I'll take the boy. If you truly feel we have the best place for him, Gracie and I will make him welcome."

Eva's shoulders lost some tension and the smile she gave us showed her perfect teeth. "Thank you for trusting my judgment," she said.

Gabriel shrugged and gestured to the tank on the wall. I was startled to see that it was now empty. "I'm guessing it was a bit late for me to say no a while ago."

Our host ignored that remark. Instead, she leaned over the open pool of bubbling liquid and pressed a small button on the inside wall. Almost instantly, a shadowy shape emerged from its depths.

"James is a remarkable young man. You will be impressed with how quickly he learns everything you have to offer," she said evenly.

"I'm sure it will be a learning experience for all of us," my father muttered under his breath. I'd tuned both of them out by this point, however. All of my attention was completely riveted on the naked youth slowly rising from the blue ooze. A platform of the same gray material as the walls lifted his body until it was even with the sides of the vat. Did I mention he was completely nude? I couldn't help but stare.

It didn't hurt that James was an attractive young man. His body was thin but not skeletal, wiry muscles swelling under his pale skin. He was completely hairless; his flesh a flawless ivory expanse that revealed his humanity only in the small, flushed areas where blood brushed close to the surface.

I was there when he took his first breath.

A rasping gasp of air lifted his bony chest. I was standing only a few feet away as he opened his eyes and saw the world for the first time without a computer interface. They were faded blue, a few shades lighter than Dad's and my own.

Almost immediately, James began to shiver violently, and that initial breath turned into rapid, frightened gulps of air as his eyes darted about the room.

"It's alright, James," Dad said, stepping closer to the platform and putting a hand on the boy's shoulder. He'd opened his mouth in Eva's direction, but the instant their skin touched, my father cried out and sank to his knees.

"Dad!" One moment I was across the room, the next I'd pulled my father away from the platform and had both arms around his shoulders as he got his feet back under himself.

"It's fine, really. Gracie, I'm alright," he insisted, though I could feel him shaking. He had one arm over my shoulders while the other clung fiercely to my sleeve. Still, he recovered quickly, his breathing and expression rapidly getting back under skillful control. He pinned Eva with a steely glare.

"Why didn't you tell me he was a high level telepath?" Gabriel growled. Giving my shoulder a squeeze, he took a step back and stood under his own power again. Seeing that he'd been more surprised than hurt, I didn't resist his move. However, I stayed close by his side.

"He's well trained," Eva protested. She'd produced a glass of thick, dark liquid that she held gingerly in one hand. "He hasn't had trouble shielding for years."

"Not with skin-to-skin contact," my father growled. "Physical contact makes every gift stronger, especially telepathy."

Eva stared at him as if at a complete loss. She glanced down at James who was shivering so hard I could hear his teeth chattering from across the room. With one hand, she reached down to touch his shoulder.

"Don't!" my father snapped, taking a step forward and halting her hand with his own. "Even an avatar's touch is going to be too much for him to block right now," Gabriel explained.

"He needs to drink this protein compound," she protested, "and I do not think he can sit up on his own yet."

Dad met my eye with a reluctant yet knowing look. "I assume you have a blanket and some clothing for him in the other room?"

"Yes, of course, but he needs nourishment first," Eva insisted, beginning to look distressed.

"Give me the drink. You go get that blanket," Gabriel instructed firmly.

Her mechanical eyes whirling that oddly neon orange, Eva reluctantly handed my father the glass and left the room.

"Come help me with him, Gracie," my father said once we were alone.

I gave him a quick nod before moving to the young man's side. Once he mentioned James' telepathy, I suspected this was coming. After all, it didn't matter if the boy could shield or not. If my grandmother couldn't find a crack in my mental walls there was no way this Terran youth could even scratch them. I wasn't sure how I felt about touching the naked stranger in front of me, but I would have had to be physically blind as well as head blind to ignore his suffering.

By now, James had curled his arms tightly to his chest in an instinctive attempt to keep warm. Cold bumps covered his exposed flesh. All of the blue ooze from earlier had evaporated or soaked into his skin somehow because he was dry to the touch when I laid a hand on his arm.

He turned his head quickly and flashed wide, frightened blue eyes in my direction. I gave him what I hoped was a reassuring smile. "I'm not going to hurt you," I said quietly.

"Anything?" Dad asked, peering around my shoulder. He was careful not to let any of his skin brush against James.

I couldn't help a touch of disappointment as I shook my head.

"I thought as much." My father gave me a smile that I had trouble reading. "Well, that iron shield of yours had to come in handy one of these days. See if you can help him sit up."

"Okay," I replied, though I had little idea how I was going to do such a thing. James was thin, but I had a feeling he was going to be taller than me once we got him standing. How was I going to lift this guy by myself? "You're going to have to help me some here," I informed James.

"Slide your arm under his shoulders," my father suggested.

I'd been trying to avoid pressing my breasts against his bare skin, but there really wasn't another choice. Swallowing hard, I got a firm grip on his upper arm and began working my other hand under James' back. His flesh was extremely cold.

"Can you lift your head?" I asked, hoping fervently that the answer was yes.

It took a moment, as if he was still sorting things out, but slowly he did as I asked. That little shift in angle allowed me to get my arm the rest of the way around his shoulders and, as gently as I could, I successfully levered him into a sitting position.

Eva came back into the room with a pile of silvery linens in her arms. She gave me a sharp look as she came around to stand at the foot of the platform.

"I thought his shield wasn't strong enough to be comfortable at the moment," she said, scowling at my father as he lifted the glass of dark liquid to James' mouth. He was still being careful not to brush his own skin against James' exposed flesh.

"It's not," Gabriel replied, not taking his eyes off of the delicate task at hand. "But Gracie is a special case. She's past head blind; almost head mute if you will. Even my mother can't read her and believe me, she's tried."

Eva raised an eyebrow at me. It was a strange expression on her oddly-smooth face. "I thought you said she was Aware."

Dad met my gaze and the corner of his mouth lifted into that mischievous smirk. "Gracie?"

"It's not that kind of Awareness," I said. James was adapting to his own flesh well enough to drink Eva's compound without choking. He still leaned heavily against my right arm, but he seemed steady enough for me to spare my left. Lifting it carefully away from his body, I called a small spiral of flame into my palm.

"Oh, I see," she murmured.

"W-why am I... s-shaking?"

James' voice was lower than his avatar's. It surprised me. It also startled Eva into handing me the blanket. I quickly wrapped it around his freezing shoulders.

"You're cold," I explained. "There, this should help you warm up a bit."

"Thank you," he chattered, his voice a little more steady on the second attempt. I gave him a genuine smile and rubbed his arm through the silvery material.

"You're welcome," my father said in that steady, gentle voice he usually reserved for nervous colts and me. "Now, finish getting the rest of this down. Your body will need its strength."

Obediently, James finished the contents of the cup in several long swallows. He coughed a bit at the end and looked a little more green than ivory, but he'd stopped shaking in my arms.

"Clothing?" Gabriel snapped over his shoulder. Eva quickly supplied him with a pair of drawstring pants and a basic short-sleeved shirt. Dad looked over the outfit with a critical eye as he traded them for the empty cup. "We're past the permafrost line up here," he pointed out. "He'll freeze in this."

"You can take the blanket as well," Eva replied evenly. She treated Gabriel to a dark glare.

My father shrugged off any other objections and knelt to my side. "I can support him through the blanket," he said. "You need to help him into the clothes."

Trying not to think about what I was about to touch, I nodded and took the folded items from his hand. "Okay, let's get you into these," I said. I remember meeting James' eyes as I held open the first pant leg for him. His expression was so open and thankful that my standard-issue smile turned into something more genuine.

Getting him into the clothes was every bit as physically awkward as I'd feared, but with James' gentle, polite personality it seemed a little less so emotionally. When we were done, my father wrapped the blanket tightly around the youth before swinging him lightly into his arms.

"Is there any reason I shouldn't teleport directly to the *Hawk*?" my father asked Eva pointedly. Clearly he was unimpressed with the way this was being handled.

"I had hoped to see him onto your ship..." Our hostess shifted her weight uncomfortably.

My father had been inconvenienced enough by this woman, however. I could see it in the impatient expression on his face. I quickly suppressed a teenage smirk at what I was pretty sure was coming next. Sure enough, Gabriel had already decided to disregard Eva's anxiety. Before I could chuckle, he'd teleported the four of us into the snowy clearing next to our antique shuttle.

Eva gasped and stared around the pine grove as if it were an alien planet.

"Gracie, the door," my father rumbled, his arms still full with James' weight. Obediently, I trotted over to the shuttle door and put my hand to the plate. With a quiet hiss, the plex-glass curve slid open.

My father nodded his thanks before carrying the young man into the shuttle. Not wanting to be left alone with Eva's shock and awe, I quickly followed them into the *Hawk*'s shaded interior.

"Gracie," Gabriel rumbled, "come see to the boy. It'll take a little longer, but I can pilot this bird by myself."

I opened my mouth to protest, but a quick glance at my father's expression made me shut it again. I didn't need telepathy to understand that his concern was for the pale, shaking young man slumped in the seat in front of him, not my piloting ability. I swallowed my disappointment at losing my turn at the helm and obediently sat on the bench next to James.

"Very well." Eva was recovering her composure. She raised a hand to us, her shoulders straightening and the haughty tilt of her head returning. "He's yours, then, Eternal Flesh. Please let us know if you need anything for his upkeep. We will do right by him and you."

My father merely inclined his head to her and sat in the psi-pilot's chair. "I expected as much. I have no quarrel with Terran honor." He raised a bushy eyebrow.

Eva apparently understood his meaning because she nodded almost obediently and stepped out of the shuttle.

"Good luck," she murmured in James' direction before the door hissed shut behind her.

The floor vibrated as the twin engines roared to life under my father's expert direction.

"Keep him conscious," Gabriel called back to me. Then all of his attention was taken with piloting the *Hawk* and I was left to deal with a strange man-child by myself.

CHAPTER 24

JAMES

James sat quietly the whole shuttle ride back to Angelus Quietum. So quietly, I had to shake him a few times to make sure he was still awake. I didn't want to disappoint my father when he'd specifically said to keep the boy conscious. Each time, James gave me a soft-eyed smile and I'd flush. He was the first boy I'd ever seen naked and he wasn't ugly. I wasn't completely sure what to think of him yet, but I knew there was something different about the pit of my stomach when I put a hand on his shoulder.

Eventually the frozen tundras floating below us gave way to the rolling ocean. It had taken us a blink of an eye to travel over it on the way here, but then my father had taken us up much farther and engaged the psi-pilot. Using the *Hawk*'s regular engines, it took almost an hour before the green edge of the continent came into view and another two hours before we were spiraling down over Angel's Rest.

"You live here?" James asked, his voice barely audible above the roar of the engines. We leaned against the curved plex-glass wall together and I pointed out the house as we descended.

"It's so green," James murmured, almost more to himself than to me, as the *Hawk* settled on its pad in the barnyard.

As the hum of the engines wound down, a slim blonde figure stepped onto the back porch from the kitchen door. She shaded her eyes from the sun in our direction, then waved and trotted towards us.

Dad got up from the pilot's chair and opened the door to let our visitor in.

"Well, hello there!" Grandma Gloria said, beaming at the three of us as she climbed into the shuttle. She gave my father a peck on the cheek and my shoulder a warm squeeze before turning to the pale young man staring at her with wide eyes. "You must be James," she said gently. "My name is Gloria and I'm a medic here on the mainland. Would you mind if I gave you a quick examination?"

"Gloria... Usuriel?" James sounded rather faint.

My grandmother gave him a gentle smile that wasn't intimidating in the least. "I'm guessing you've been briefed on mainland politics."

"Uh, I... I've always liked history," he stammered.

Her musical laugh filled the cockpit with sunny warmth. "I understand. I'm afraid longevity does get you into a few history books. Come on, let me teleport you into the house and we can have a nice chat while I take a look at you."

She'd left no way for him to decline politely so with a trembling hand he took her dainty fingers in his. As quick as breathing, the two of them faded from the *Hawk*, presumably to reappear in the house's modest guest bedroom.

"You warned her we were bringing him, didn't you," I accused Dad as the two of us hopped down from the *Hawk*.

Gabriel shrugged. "I told Eva my mother was more suited to look after him at first," he replied as we strolled back to the exposed hand-plate in the wall of the barn. With a touch, the *Hawk* descended back into the depths underneath the stable yard. "I'll have to show you how to clean and re-fuel her later," Dad said with a smile as the shuttle disappeared underground.

"Sure," I agreed, even though that sounded boring. "So... what is the Terran's deal? I mean, what the heck was with all the floating bodies back there?" I had a guess, but I wanted to hear Dad's evaluation of it.

"That's how they keep themselves safe—by cocooning their mortal flesh in stasis pods. It does extend their lifetimes. They probably live twice as long as the average mortal."

"And those people we saw besides James... they were... androids? Some kind of robot they inhabit?"

Gabriel's long stride was taking us close to the house faster than I wanted to go inside. I wanted to digest some of our adventure before I faced James again. My father glanced over at me. "Hasn't Stella gone over Terran history with you?"

I shook my head. "She mentioned the colonial-era Terrans during our study of the *Inspiration,* but we haven't discussed post-landing politics for them. I think it's on next semester's syllabus."

"What did she say about the colonial Terrans?"

It had been a while since that unit and all I remembered about it was a bunch of empty names and dates. Even though she lived through it, Stella's habit of omitting the personal details bled any interest from a story.

"They were a different wave of space colonization that eventually joined with the *Inspiration*." I hung back on the step while he stood on the porch. "I guess they were more technologically advanced; something about human and machine interfaces. Were they the ones who came up with psi-pilots?"

"Fates, no." Gabriel snorted and peered in the kitchen door's window. "They actually got that idea from us. Much to my chagrin at the time, I can tell you. My first experiences with heart ships and psi-pilots were not exactly positive."

I glanced over my shoulder at the empty patch of dirt the *Hawk* had disappeared into. "You made it look easy today."

"Oh, your grandfather and his team worked the bugs out of the psi-pilot merges long before we made landing." He smiled and tapped his chest where I knew that thin white scar was hidden by his shirt. "Also, the new ticker. It helps. Though I never have been nor ever will be strong enough to run a heart ship. That's Mom and Adora's domain. Well... it was..."

I had so rarely heard him mention Adora that my attention snapped to his face. The pain there was sharp as knife's edge before he ducked his head and that long, wavy hair obscured his expression. He palmed open the door to the kitchen and bustled inside.

"Terrans, though. We were talking about them," he called to me through the open door as I cautiously followed. His hands filled the tea pot while his telekinesis pulled open the cabinets and set the table with our usual cups and saucers. My stomach reminded me we hadn't had lunch.

"Yeah," I said, opening up the cooling unit to get out last night's leftover chicken.

"It was the radiation from their accelerated drives that originally forced them to figure out how to replace organic organs with mechanical ones. It's a useful technology," he explained, moving on to the canister where he kept the loose leaf tea. "At least, I have found it useful."

"They replaced your heart?" A small shock made me pause. I'd always assumed Gloria and D'nay came up with and installed that creative solution to their son's illness.

"Yep," he agreed. "A gift that keeps on giving, let me tell you. Only thrown one glitch in three hundred years. That's pretty impressive if I do say so myself."

"So that's why Eva seemed so sure you would help them," I mused aloud.

"Don't forget to pour water," Dad said. "Not everyone wants tea with lunch."

"Right." I got out the water pitcher and filled it from the sink. Dad settled himself at the table, pulled out the bread, and was making himself a sandwich by the time I came back to pour the water. "But I'm right, aren't I? They think you owe them a favor."

He ran a knuckle along the center of his chest as if the scar was bothering him. I knew the pain was psychological rather than physical. "By most accounts, I do."

"What about your account? Do you think you owe them a favor?"

He narrowed those deep blue eyes at me. "You are entirely too insightful for such a young child."

"I'm sixteen," I said with some indignation.

"And I'm four hundred and sixteen," he said with just enough of the same mocking arrogance that we both smiled. "Sorry, sweet pea, but you'll always be a child to me."

I supplied him with an adolescent glare and sat down to make my own sandwich. "Okay, you've dodged it twice now. Let's have an answer. Do you feel like you owe one to the Terrans or not? And if so, is that why Naked Boy is in the back with Grandma right now?"

Gabriel actually chuckled at that one. "You have always been good at cutting to the chase," he muttered, taking a sip of tea. He waved a hand at my stern look. "Yes, yes, I'm answering the question." Swallowing another bite of sandwich, he eyed me with less attitude and more honesty. "I suppose, from time to time, I am grateful the Terrans kept me on this side of the mortal coil. Though I probably would have taken their trainee out of political savviness, even if I didn't owe them a thing. One doesn't make it past a century without realizing that connections in government are usually a good thing."

I nodded, finally done making my sandwich. We ate together in companionable silence.

"So what about modern Terrans and all the floating bodies?" I asked when my mouth was free again. "Are they... somehow hooked up to those android-type things?"

My father nodded. "Avatars. They call the machines they use to interact with the world avatars. And they vary with wealth and social status just as much as clothes do in Skykyle city."

"Why can't James bring his avatar to the mainland?"

"Because the relays that would allow his mind to connect to the avatar are outlawed here," Grandmother Gloria said as she ushered our guest back into the room. She'd obviously raided my father's closet because James was wearing a white button down and black slacks that looked suspiciously familiar. His shoulders weren't quite as broad or muscular as Gabriel's. The loose fabric made him look incredibly frail and thin. Apparently he was strong enough to walk the twenty feet it took to get from the bedroom to the kitchen, but Gloria had to help him pull out the heavy wooden chair at the table.

"Why are they outlawed?" I asked and quickly bit my tongue. I was nervous about being so forward around a stranger, but all of this was so curious.

James kept his eyes downcast as he sat down. "The Provinces don't approve of our avatars. Some people think they make us dangerous somehow."

I raised an eyebrow. "Dangerous? Why would you be dangerous?"

"An avatar is fifty times stronger than an average mortal," James replied evenly. He wasn't boasting; simply stating fact.

"Well, so is Dad, but they haven't outlawed him," I pointed out.

James quickly looked up at my father, but it wasn't fear in his eyes. It was something else. Knowledge? Anxiety? I wasn't sure, but when I glanced over at Gabriel, he didn't meet my gaze.

Gloria cleared her throat. Even she looked a little uncomfortable. For the Usuriel blank face to crack so badly I must have said something off, but I had no idea what it could be. The Usuriel matriarch recovered her composure first, and gave me a small smile. "No, they haven't outlawed us," she said. "Good point, Gracie. But I think there is something... unnerving about knowing the person you are talking to isn't really there in the same room."

"I do not understand that," James said, shaking his head. "If he'd been allowed to bring his avatar, Dalton would not have been killed in the accident. There would have been no need for me to come here."

"I think that is part of the issue." My grandmother sounded reluctant. She spread her hands towards James. "Cut me and I still bleed. I may be able to defend myself better than the average mortal, but I am still vulnerable. The avatars make you completely immune to attack which some find uncomfortable. And the whole virtual reality thing only makes it worse."

I raised an eyebrow at James and he quickly looked at the table. "Virtual reality thing?"

Gabriel groaned. "I wasn't going to bring that up."

"She'll find out sooner or later anyway," my grandmother went on in a matter-of-fact tone. "I don't completely understand it myself since I've never been plugged into an avatar. But from what I have heard, the avatars can be set to whatever stimulation level the user desires. That means that the avatar could step into a blast furnace and the user would not feel a thing. In fact, they can view reality through any filter they prefer."

"They could even set up the avatar so that a simple hand shake would be... extremely provocative," my father supplied.

I'd read enough adult fiction to understand their innuendo. "Sweet Fate." My face burned. I stole another glance at James. He looked like he wanted to disappear into the floor.

"And since they have total control over the reactions of the avatar, they could be in extreme pain or ecstasy, and you would never be able to see it on their face," Gabriel sounded neutral about the idea but I knew from experience that his dry tone meant he didn't want to discuss this.

"The *Inspiration* crew was always very open minded compared to their Earth-dwelling peers," Gloria said, "but even modern Province culture has a hard time dealing with people who can use a stranger's facial features for any fantasy scenario they might dream up — and could even be living it out while pretending to have a calm conversation."

"Such practice is frowned upon in Terra Nova, as well," James said quietly, "but it does happen."

"Does happen," my father snorted. "A diplomat already! Please. Let's be honest, at least here among telepaths. There are coders who are paid to fine tune the virtual reality programs your avatars use. They might be the equivalent to hookers on the street corner of Skykyle city, but they're a lot higher paid. And they aren't illegal in your country, either."

James shook his head at my father, the look on his face somewhere between horror and awe. "I see why Eva sent me to you. I had no idea there were any foreigners who knew about that."

Gabriel grunted and took a long drink of water.

"Well, we know." Gloria said, "and I'm pretty sure the senators know, too. There won't be any relays any time soon."

"Which means you're stuck here, kid," Gabriel said, softening his statement with a mischievous smile.

All this talk of 'fantasies' made me wonder exactly how the Terrans made babies. If they were stuck in those tubes I didn't think they went about it the old fashioned way. But James had already turned five shades of red and I wasn't sure Dad and Grandma Gloria were the people I wanted to discuss it with, even if I loved them both dearly. I filed that question away for a different day.

"You should probably eat something a little more solid than whatever they gave you right out of the tank," Gloria suggested to James, gesturing to the bowl of fruit and sandwiches on the table. "A banana would be a good place to start. Easy on the stomach and highly nutritious."

"Okay," he sounded nervous as he eyed the yellow fruit doubtfully.

"You peel it first," I explained when he made no move to do so. He turned to me with a look that showed a little too much white around the eyes. With a reassuring smile, I took the banana from the bowl, peeled it, and broke it into thirds. I placed two-thirds on his plate and took a bite from the last one in my hand. "See," I said between bites, "you barely even have to chew it. Bananas are basically baby food."

Carefully, he mimicked me, picking up one of the banana thirds and making two bites out of it. The expression on his face when he first tasted the savory fruit was somewhere between surprise and delight.

"This is... taste?" he asked, mouth full of banana.

I giggled. Dad cleared his throat. "Yes. One of the many perks of living life first hand. Though we usually discourage talking with your mouth full."

James frowned at him a moment, then glanced between me and Grandma Gloria. "Mouth full?" he asked, swallowing his first bite of banana.

"When you're chewing your food it's polite to keep your mouth closed," Gloria explained.

"Oh." He looked quite chastened. "There are rules about chewing? This eating thing is very complicated."

"Well, yes, I suppose it is a bit," Gloria agreed. "But when you spend a lot of time doing something, especially something as social as eating, there are bound to be a lot of cultural rules that spring up around it."

James frowned harder. "How much time do you spend eating?"

I thought about that. "Well, we usually eat three meals a day. Sometimes more if we have snacks."

"I'd say most people eat every two to four hours," my grandmother said thoughtfully. "Obviously we eat bigger meals if we have gone longer in between them. And we go a long time at night without eating because our metabolism slows down. But at the beginning every two hours is a good idea for you."

"Every two hours?" James sounded shocked. "And how long do I have to do this?"

"The rest of your life," Gabriel chuckled. "Don't look so horrified. Most people use meals as an opportunity to be social. As a diplomat, you can use that to your advantage. Someone doesn't want to talk to you? Invite them to dinner. Have a drink. Have two. Suddenly, discussions become much more relaxed and natural."

James considered this with a frown. "Interesting," he said. "This is a technique they did not discuss in my training."

"Like you said, Eva sent you to me for a reason," Dad replied, popping the rest of his sandwich in his mouth. He chewed quickly, then pointed to James' plate. "Now, finish your banana."

***

After lunch we gave James the grand tour of Angelus Quietum, but it was clear that just walking around the main house was a bit much for him. Once he'd seen how it was laid out, and we'd gotten his things settled in the guest room we let him retire for a nap.

Dad sent me to catch up on my abbreviated lessons for the day while he and Grandma Gloria went for a trail ride. I knew they wanted to discuss James outside of the young telepath's mental ear shot (and away from my careful scrutiny of facial expressions). I'd already gotten out of four hours of classwork that day so I wasn't going to complain.

Even so, Stella had to keep bringing my attention back to my work. My thoughts kept drifting back to floating Terrans in their strange tubes of goo. I tried not to dwell on one Terran in particular, but it was kind of hard not to think about James' naked form and the possibilities of his stay with us. I might be a sheltered teenage girl, but I was still a teenage girl. I wanted a taste of romance so badly I'd give my eyeteeth for it, and this whole situation felt like a script from a holo. At that point, I'm not sure if I was more enamored of James or the racy novel about us I was writing in my head.

By the time Grandma Gloria and Dad got back from riding, smelling like horse and the outdoors, my initial nervousness about having a stranger in our house had dissolved into a fever pitch of excitement. I almost broke every plate in the house in my eagerness to help Dad set up for dinner. He and Gloria gave me that gentle smile adults get when they know what's on your mind but don't want to bruise your ego by saying it aloud. For once I didn't care. Nothing could ruin my mood with this exciting guest in the house.

To my great disappointment, James was almost silent through dinner. During his nap I'd had the time to build him up to be some kind of dazzling romantic lead in my head and the reality of a pale, sickly stranger who looked like he'd rather be anywhere other than my father's dinner table, was a bit of a letdown. Even so, I gave him as many smiles as I could manage and made inane chatter about all the different kinds of food we were having.

"Wait." James stopped me mid-lecture of Dad's best fishing techniques. He pointed his fork at the pale flesh of the fish he'd been nibbling at. "You mean to tell me this is a fish? Like, the kind that swims and has a tail?"

"Of course," I replied cheerfully. "Dad caught it two days ago right off of our pier."

The shade of green he turned was quite spectacular.

"Whoops," Gloria said, and in a flash she and James disappeared. I glanced up at my father, a startled look on my face. He swallowed an amused grin as the sound of retching echoed from the bathroom.

I didn't see James again that evening. I'd neglected a few chores besides my lessons that morning and I spent the time after dinner catching up around the farm. Once the long shadows merged into true dark, I wandered along the lake side, unsure how I felt about going back to the house. Dad had come out earlier and showed me how to clean and refuel the *Hawk* before going back to the house. I guessed that he and James were already discussing diplomacy and politics. Despite my curiosity about their conversations, I was too embarrassed about the dinner fiasco to relish facing our guest again.

Eventually the cool chill of evening chased me inside. I arrived to find my father sitting alone watching a log burn in the living room fireplace. He had a pipe in his mouth though it wasn't lit. I think it was just something to keep his hands and mouth occupied while he thought.

I was about to open my mouth to say something when I saw a flickering light that didn't belong to the crackling fireplace. My body froze, the pit of my stomach clenching tight.

Olivia's red curls tossed in a wind that didn't touch my skin. She watched my father with sad, quiet eyes as she stepped close to his side. As usual she ignored me and some tension drained from the muscles in my back. I could deal with Olivia. It was her daughter I'd rather avoid.

"Dad," I said gently, knowing that he would be in a fragile mood if Olivia felt the need to be present. I was never sure if the ghost was the cause of his melancholy or if she was somehow summoned by his darkest thoughts. Either way, I'd figured out the connection early in my stay here.

"Mmmm," Gabriel hardly acknowledged me, just a slight tilt of his head and flick of a fingertip.

"I'm going to bed," I said. "Do you need anything?"

There was a long pause, but I knew better than to think he hadn't heard me. Sometimes it took a while for him to process when he was in this kind of mood.

"What do you think of James?"

The question was unexpected, as was the sharp expression on my father's face as he turned towards me.

"I... well..." A few racy thoughts from earlier today chased themselves through my mind and for once I was sincerely grateful for my mysterious mental boundaries. "I'm not sure. I mean, we've just met."

Dad cocked an eyebrow at me and I knew he wasn't letting me off the hook with such a paltry excuse. I squirmed.

"He seems polite enough," I allowed, perching on the arm of the couch. My legs were tired, but I really didn't want to get any closer to Olivia than I needed to. Sitting on the sofa cushions would bring me nearer to her glowing aura than I preferred. "And it's hard to say what he'll look like with his hair grown in, but his features are regular enough."

My father watched me closely, the chiseled planes of his face reflecting the fire light like a flickering statue. I studied his perfect face more carefully than usual. Truthfully, compared to my father and grandmother, James looked rough and unfinished. Even my youthful glow never quite matched their level of painful beauty. And James... he was mortal and it showed around the edges. Perhaps one eye was a touch higher than the other or one ear had a bit of a tilt. Maybe his chin was a little rounded and didn't quite square off his jaw in such an appealing way. There were a dozen little flaws I could sit and pick out if I wanted to. My father had no such flaws.

Pushing the unfair comparison out of my mind, I thought on James' personality. "I think he wants to do his job well. And he seems a little overwhelmed by losing his avatar. Certainly he'll have to work on the food thing." I shrugged. "What do you think of him?"

Gabriel blinked at me slowly, then shook his head. "I'm too old," he sighed and ran a hand through his hair, pushing the long, dark strands away from his face. "I don't trust first impressions anymore. Not my own, anyway. Too many memories. Too many paths I know it could take." He rattled the pipe against his teeth and leaned forward to stare into the fire.

He was silent again for a long while and my attention drifted between him and Olivia. The ghost stood perfectly still, her eyes on Gabriel's back as if he were the center of the universe itself.

"I'm kind of tired," I said finally, rising from the couch arm. "Will you be okay if I go to bed?"

"Hmmm? Me? Oh, of course, sweetie," he replied, reaching out a hand to me. I dutifully took it and leaned in to kiss his cheek. He gave me a one armed hug and a quick kiss on the top of my head. "Don't worry about this brooding old man. You get a good night's sleep, and I'll see you for lessons first thing in the morning. I love you."

"Goodnight, Daddy. I love you, too."

CHAPTER 25

ADORA

The instant I walked into my bedroom, I knew my relief had been premature. Apparently Olivia hadn't been traveling alone tonight.

Ariel met my eye as she gently glowed on my bed. She held her blue diary to her chest as if she were too nervous to set it on her lap. She didn't react when I closed the door firmly behind me.

I had expected to be terrified the next time I ran into Ariel. After all, really bad or scary things seemed to happen every time she was around. But seeing her here in my own room, glaring at me as if I were overdue for an appointment, all I could feel was irritation.

"What do you want? And don't pretend you can't hear me because you had no trouble shouting at me last time you showed up," I snapped.

Ariel's eyebrows knit together in a scowl. Then I noticed that she'd laid out an outfit for me on my bed. I had never seen her manipulate physical objects besides her journal before. She gestured sharply to the short, black skirt, rainbow top, knee-high rainbow socks and arm-length gloves. Where she'd found a tiny mini-skirt or the satin-looking black gloves I had no idea. The other items were from my own collection.

"Am I supposed to put these on?" I asked, nearly tripping on the boots she'd apparently placed at the foot of the bed to complete the outfit.

She inclined her head at me, those immortal features anachronistic with the wisdom and experience in her eyes. It didn't seem odd to me at the time, of course, simply familiar. After all, I spent most of my time with Gabriel and his parents who had a corner on the whole beautiful but ancient thing.

"Tell me what you're planning because I already don't like it," I informed her, crossing my arms and glaring at her. I hoped I looked more intimidating than a sulky sixteen-year-old.

With a heavy but inaudible sigh, Ariel waved a hand at the last object on the bed. It was my old copy of her journal. She gave me a fierce look and waggled her version at me just to make sure her point was crystal clear.

With an eye roll, I gave in and picked up the journal. It only took me a moment to flip to the end of our old conversations. Ariel had apparently started writing before I arrived because her first few statements were already waiting for me.

"I apologize for the inconvenience and discomfort of our last two interactions. But if you will remember, I did help you save our father's life last time. So will you do me a favor, and at least hear me out tonight?" Her handwriting was neat and flowing, just as it had been before.

"Inconvenience and discomfort... that's one way to put it," I grumbled, glancing up at her. She no longer looked irritated, though. She had a gentle expression on her face, green eyes wide and brows arched. "Fine, I suppose I'm not getting rid of you until I at least listen to what you want. But I'm not agreeing to anything until you tell me exactly what's going on."

"Fair enough," scrawled her reply in my book. "You're old enough to understand things better anyway."

I nodded my agreement with that assessment. "So what's with the clothes?"

"There are a few people I'd like you to meet tonight," she wrote. "Most specifically, me."

"Ummm…" I was at a loss. "What? I have met you. More often than I care for, honestly."

"You've met... this version of me. You don't know the me who was your age once-upon-a-time. I really think you should meet her."

An intriguing possibility, if the last time I'd tried to time travel hadn't gone so completely horrible. "Yeah, not so sure about the whole time jump thing. I mean, last time nearly froze me to death and Grandma Gloria was right there."

"Gloria is as close as an implant tap away," Ariel pointed out. "But I don't think you'll need her now. I wasn't quite sure what I was doing, and you were only seven. It was foolish of me to push you so soon, I just had to know if it was possible. And it is! So, now you're older, and you've been training with Dad which means you're far more in control of your psi-powers than you were as a small child.

Also, I have a better idea of how it works now and can guide you more effectively."

She was right about getting better with my other psi-powers. Or should I say, psi-power? I only had the one, unless you counted that one brutal trip back in time. But I had grown a considerable amount in my ability to control the flames. And what had been terrifying as a seven-year-old no longer seemed so horrible if it meant I would be able to actually look around the *Inspiration* at its peak. Have I mentioned the terminal curiosity streak I have?

"If I were to consider it," I said slowly, "what do you want me to do?"

***

Half an hour later I found myself dressed in possibly the most ridiculous and provocative outfit I'd ever tried on.

"Are you sure this is what you would have worn to a party on the *Inspiration*?" I asked, giving my left glove a last few tugs to get my fingers firmly in place.

"At sixteen? Absolutely," she wrote and gave me a self-deprecating smirk. "Though I added the gloves so you're less likely to touch anyone. That's what sent you back last time—skin to skin contact. I'm not sure what that's about yet, but I didn't want to chance it."

"Right," I said, rubbing my gloved hands together. They fit perfectly, but the silky material made my hands feel odd. "So now what? You said you could guide me better this time."

"Here's what I've been able to figure out," she wrote quickly, her handwriting becoming a little more loopy and tilted in her excitement. "Your ability to time travel is pretty much a variation on the standard teleportation skill. Only, your usual ability lies in calling up the element of fire. Something about the flames' interaction with that tele-portation engine triggers a time shift."

I frowned as I considered this. "Why? That doesn't make any sense. What does fire have to do with teleportation or time travel? And what do either of those things have to do with seeing you?"

Ariel looked at me as if I'd just dunked her in the lake. Then she began to scribble furiously in the journal. "Wait... what do you mean, have to do with seeing us? Do you think that being able to see me in this state has something to do with your psi-abilities?"

"Well, it must, right? I mean, no one else can see you. So either I'm going completely mad." I glanced down at the outfit I'd just put on. That was a distinct possibility. "Or the way I can see you and Olivia has something to do with my time traveling ability. I haven't heard of either one of those areas of Awareness and Stella finally let me do a research project on them last semester so I should know."

"I hadn't thought about that," Ariel responded, her handwriting as neat and thoughtful as her face. "But you're right. Your ability to see me and the others is what prompted me to try the shift with you in the first place." She frowned at me and squinted, as if she were trying to see something small or confusing.

"What?" I asked, running fingers through my hair and glancing in the mirror. According to it, Ariel was just a faint glow hovering over the bed. But it also said my hair looked fine.

"It might... still be your connection to the flames," she wrote slowly. "Almost a background effect—the door being open a crack all the time. Like the fire is always eating little holes in time for you to peer through. That's what Olivia and I are in essence; echoes from another time. And really, that's what your time travel ability is, too: burning a bigger hole in the fabric of time—one that's large enough for you to step through."

When she put it that way everything made more sense. It was the quasi-logic all of our awareness abilities seemed to follow, so I shrugged and accepted it. I did know from experience that having such a concrete way of envisioning the transition would help me when it came time to attempt the time leap. Perhaps I wouldn't have to page my grandmother for medical help after this experience after all.

"Okay, let's go with this burning theory," I said. "Why would touching you bring me back to my own time?"

"I'm still not sure. Perhaps because I was the one who reached through the smaller hole you'd burned to pull you in the rest of the way. Maybe it made some kind of connection, like a circuit being completed?" She sighed. "Look, I'm not an expert in these things. I'm a geneticist and amateur historian, not a psiologist. Lillian could tell you a lot more, but even she wouldn't have all the answers. Psi is just not easy to understand. Sometimes it acts like electricity, like when Dad or Grandma use it in the psi-pilot to boost an engine's power. Other times it acts like a knife, cutting through space to bring two points together. Yours is the first case I've seen where it acts exclusively like fire, but who is to say there haven't been other examples back on Earth? Certainly Adora used psi in unusual and unexpected ways from time to time."

"Okay," I said, stifling a yawn. "I think I get the concept enough to try this."

Ariel nodded and tilted her head at me. I took a deep breath and opened my arms to her. She came floating towards me as a beautiful, glowing ball of light. As she melted into my skin I heard her voice whisper in my head.

"Remember what we talked about. Don't talk to Dad or Mom unless you have to, and try to keep the spoilers to a minimum."

The image of a small, metal room with a circular window full of stars filled my mind even as the thick, syrupy warmth of her presence settled over my body. There was more control this time, just as she'd promised. It wasn't uncomfortable in the least, and since I knew she wanted me to draw on my fire I had no problem pulling it up and out towards the image of that tiny bedroom. My own training and skill kicked in now and I smoothly transitioned to step from my bedroom on Cybele into Ariel's on the *Inspiration*. It wasn't just a step of thousands of miles, it was also a step of over three hundred years. The weight of those years pressed heavy around me, much the way my father's energy could fill a room when he was angry. Yet I felt no emotion aside from excitement as I emerged from the warm embrace of the time jump.

There were two sharp gasps as I stepped into the cool recycled air of the *Inspiration*. One was mine and the other belonged to another young, freckled redhead who happened to be sitting on her bed.

"Who the hell..." Ariel breathed, staring at me in open wonder. "Who the hell are you, and where did you come from?"

"Ummmm..." I said, looking around at the tiny bedroom. It was cluttered with the same things as my bedroom—memory pads, dirty clothes, jewelry. Of course, the style of everything was different from the shape of the memory pad (hers was smaller and boxier than the one I used at home) to the jewelry (mine tended to feature naturally tumbled stones while hers were shiny, cut crystals), but the functions were the same. Three centuries didn't change life as a teenage girl as much as I might have guessed. "You aren't going to believe me if I tell you."

Ariel stood and stalked around me, green eyes flickering over my hair and outfit. I evaluated her in much the same way. I wasn't sure what kind of fabric she was wearing, but it had a different texture from my own—more smooth and stretchy from the way it sat on her figure. She wore her hair back in a complex twist of smaller braids that fed into one much larger one while still leaving some curls free around her face. The cut of her outfit wasn't too outlandishly different from what her ghost had chosen for me in my own time, but there were clear differences in the angles of our skirts and tops.

Aside from these cosmetic details, we looked disturbingly alike. I found myself staring openly at her face. My father's high cheekbones and arched brow were softened by large, emotive green eyes and a smaller, more feminine chin. It was a combination I was intimately familiar with in the mirror, even though my own eyes were blue rather than green. The scattering of freckles across her cheeks were pale and hardly visible whereas mine were darker and cascaded across my neck and shoulders. Besides that we could have been twins.

"You look like... me," Ariel said warily. She squinted her eyes at my figure. "But you're not. Your eyes are blue and you have," she grabbed her own small breasts to indicate my own slightly curvier set. "Are you me from the future?"

"Actually, you're not that far off," I admitted. "I am from the future, but I'm not you. I'm your sister. Well, half-sister, really."

One eyebrow raised, but she accepted this concept much more rapidly than I'd expected. Just a slow, sensible nod greeted my outrageous claim. "How far in the future?" she asked. "How old are you?"

"I'm sixteen. Same age as you, I think. And I've just traveled about three hundred years back in time... about... I think..."

"That's a big jump to be imprecise about." Ariel seemed skeptical. "What kind of technology did you use? Is it more like a psi-pilot or a heart ship?"

"Actually, it's a part of my Awareness," I said, pointing to my head. When she looked at me blankly I tried to elaborate. "You know, like teleporting only through time instead of space."

Her eyes widened. "You mean you can psychically jump from one time to another?"

"Well, yeah," I agreed, suddenly realizing it was true. I had made the jump with my own psi power. The ghost version of Ariel had provided the clear memory of her old room, but I was the one who opened and stepped through the doorway to get here. I wasn't sure if discussing her future ghost was a 'spoiler' as ghost-Ariel had put it, so I decided to take credit for the whole thing. It was easier and mostly true.

"Wow." Ariel did another circuit around me, looking even closer at my clothes until she apparently gave in to the temptation of fingering the material of my skirt. I braced myself to be sucked back into the present, but it didn't happen. My half-sister just shook her head and gave me a smile. "What is your skirt made of? I've never seen fabric like this before."

"Ummm... I'm not sure," I said honestly. "Most of our clothes are cotton or an alpaca wool blend."

"Alpaca? No wonder it's so soft," she said, shaking her head. "Most natural fiber cloth besides hemp is long gone here. We use mostly synthetic blends that can be melted down and recycled."

"You recycle your clothes?"

Her laugh was musical and echoed my father's like a genetic fingerprint. "If you don't, then I'm guessing you made it to Cybele! No, wait. Don't tell me. I'm sure there's some kind of paradox loop to that kind of major information."

I stared at her in open astonishment. "You're taking this time travel thing way more calmly than I thought you would."

She shrugged, an impish smile on her face. "I live on a generation ship in the middle of deep space. My father is a mixed immortal mutt. I have a brother from another mother whose parents are cybernetic and my grandmother frequently doubles as the accelerated drive for this entire ship. Ask me how often crazy things happen around here."

When she put it like that, my life was pretty unusual, too. But that didn't keep it from being pretty darn boring. Then I caught sight of her impatient expression and realized she was still waiting for me to ask the rhetorical question. "How often do crazy things happen around here?" I finally obliged.

"Not often enough!" She dissolved into genuine laughter. I found myself giggling along. "Seriously, though, I can only imagine how crazy my life would sound to someone from the future. I know what it's like to be the unbelievable one. Besides, you are clearly family, but I don't know you, which means wherever you came from is crazy far away. If you say it's three hundred years in the future, I believe you."

Her reasoning was amazingly calm and rational. "Thanks," I said, feeling relieved.

"Sweet Fate, I have to tell Dad about you," she breathed, eyes lighting up with excitement.

"No!" I said quickly. "I know Gabriel in my own time. I'm pretty sure he didn't know about me before I was born so it would probably be a bad idea to introduce us." I clapped a hand over my own mouth. "Whoops, that was spoilers, wasn't it?"

"Nah, Mom won't be around having kids in three hundred years and besides, Dad's the one who passes on psi talent. I knew you were his kid which means you most likely knew him." She shrugged. "But if you don't want to meet him, is there anyone else you want to avoid?"

"Probably Olivia," I said, thinking about the advice ghost-Ariel had given me. "And... maybe D'nay and Gloria.

But other than that, no. I don't think it would be dangerous to meet anyone else."

Ariel raised an eyebrow but didn't say anything about adding her mother and grandparents to the avoid list. "Well, I'd say you can come to the party, then."

***

The party was actually a gathering of about fifteen teenage to young twenty-somethings in a lush garden Ariel teleported us neatly to. Though I wanted to see more of the ship, I understood her caution since Dad and Olivia were asleep a few doors down from her tiny bedroom. It just made more sense to teleport than to risk trying to sneak out of the POD (their word for a ship-board apartment) the old fashioned way. I'd been slightly afraid her psi powers would trigger my own and send me back to my own time, but we appeared with a quick rush of cool energy in the leafy twilight of the garden.

"Where are we?" I asked, looking around at the plump foliage. We'd arrived near a metal wall with a large double door. The room was a tangle of branches, grass, and flowers. I could even hear the rustle of birds in this artificial forest. I couldn't believe they had such a place on board a starship. It seemed just as alive as the fields of Angelus Quietum.

"This is the 'Ponics orchard," Ariel said, gesturing to the citrus trees that filled the air with a sweet tang. "We grow apples, oranges, and pears here."

"Wow," I said, fingering an orange leaf. Sure enough, the round globes of fruit clung to the branch farther up.

They looked blue in the low light. I wondered how they got enough sun here on the *Inspiration*.

"Come on, the others are waiting for us," Ariel said, pushing between some branches to my right. I fell in behind her and the rows of fruit trees gave way to a pretty little clearing surrounded by large strawberry bushes. Several of the light, metal chairs, similar to the one I'd seen in Ariel's room, had been pulled in a circle, and several young adults were gathered around them. No one looked older than twenty-five or younger than fifteen.

"Ariel!" A blond boy who might have been a little older than us, or perhaps just taller, waved as we walked up.

"James!" She called back and gave him a casual hug. Clearly they were comfortable with each other. "Gracie, this is my brother from another mother," she said with a smile, turning to present him to me.

James. The name ran a chill down my spine. I looked up into his face and discovered that this James was also blond and blue eyed. Unlike the young diplomat in my time, however, this boy was clearly comfortable in his own skin. He was taller than future James and considerably more muscled. His broad shoulders and regular features were pleasing in the imperfect way mortals often are. But when he smiled at me I could see that his personality made him genuinely handsome.

"Gracie?" he asked, eyes darting between me and Ariel. "Did you sprout a twin without telling me?" His expression faltered, and I was reminded that we were on a spaceship. He would know everyone on board and instantly realize I didn't belong.

"Nope. Half-sister. From the future. The fucking future!" Ariel crowed with an infectious laugh. "I knew it was possible! I told you time travel was within the scope of psi-talent! Here's the proof!"

James blinked as if completely thrown. "Wow... just... holy cow. Let me shake your hand," he said to me, holding out a large palm. Obediently, I gave his hand a firm grip. "Dang, she is your sister. That's Gabe's handshake and no mistake."

Ariel rolled her eyes. "As if the Usuriel nose isn't proof enough. Handshakes. Men. Whatever. Where's Adora?"

"The party has arrived!"

I turned at the exclamation behind me. It wasn't yelled so much as confidently announced by a voice that was simultaneously too melodic to be masculine and too low to be feminine. When I caught sight of the person it belonged to, I didn't find myself any less confused.

This person was an Usuriel. That much was blatantly obvious. The cheekbones, the fiercely beautiful features, these things screamed out our shared heritage. However, that was the only thing I was sure about. The chiseled jaw, which seemed broad and masculine on my father, was narrower and pointed suggesting a feminine identity. Yet the excruciatingly high cheekbones and rail thin, angular figure could have gone either gender. To further confuse things, their hair was cut in a sharp bob that fell into their face and obscured the features just enough to make them hard to identify. Up swept, pointed ears were pierced at least six times all the way down their edge. And to top it all off, this person wasn't just pale—they were white. Skin, hair, even the clothes they had picked out all seemed to be shades of silver and white. That is, except for a huge pair of clunky, black boots that looked as if they had seen better days.

The other teens who had been covertly observing my introduction to James now mobbed the newcomer. They laughed and jostled while the slim, white figure handed out bottles and tiny little glasses. These objects appeared from thin air so I was guessing this new Usuriel was a three-T just like Ariel and my father. The other party guests seemed thrilled with them and began to pass around the small glasses.

"Who is that?" I asked Ariel quietly. She and James had not made a move to join the rest of the crowd, but they were watching the scene with interest.

"That"—her smile was something between smug and amused—"is Adora."

Once the crowd died down, Adora sauntered in our direction. There's no other word for the way she moved. It was smoother than smooth; even more graceful than my father on a good day. Yet she did it so casually that it was obviously habit, not an affectation.

As she came closer, she reached into the thin air by her head and pulled out a slim, white stick. She put it to her lips and a tiny blue flame kindled on the end before flickering out and leaving it smoldering. With a deep breath, she closed her eyes, then pulled the stick from her mouth with two fingers before exhaling a long plume of blue smoke. When she opened her eyes again, she was directly in front of me.

"Hello, Gracie," she said evenly and pulled another small, white stick from nothingness. "Cigarette?"

I stared at her openly. "You can... read my mind?"

"Nope," she said evenly, as if admitting her failure caused her no discomfort at all, "but I can read Ariel loud and clear. Three hundred years in the future, huh? Am I empress of Cybele yet?"

Ariel, James, and I obligingly chuckled. I decided that interpreting her question as humor was a better idea than letting on that she was almost a century dead in my time. She gave us a cool smile, then lit the second cigarette she'd offered me and extended it in my direction.

"Thanks," I said, accepting it and holding it in two fingers as I'd seen Adora do. I'd never seen tobacco smoked in anything but my father's pipe and even that was rare. The scent of burning filled my nostrils and I almost balked, but something about Adora's fierce, pale gaze made me finish the movement, taking a deep gulp of the smoke.

I instantly regretted it. My lungs and throat were on fire. I coughed and sputtered while Ariel patted me on the back.

Adora's laugh wasn't malicious, but it wasn't kind either. "First smoke? I bet this will be your first drink, too. Oh, we'll have a good time tonight."

I recovered enough to glance up at her face. Her unusual eyes were half-lidded as she caught my gaze. I flushed.

"So, wait, you can't read her, either?" James asked. "I thought it was just me."

Ariel shook her head. "I can't read her either, but I thought it was just because I wasn't strong enough. If Adora can't, I bet Dad can't either. That has to be handy."

"No, it's not just you. Grandma Gloria says I'm past head blind. Not sure what that means, but I've never met anyone who can use telepathy on me," I explained. Then I turned with a frown to James. "Did you say you tried to read me? I thought the Usuriels were the only psychic family on board."

James gave a small shrug and didn't ask how I knew he wasn't part of the Family. A glance was enough to identify

D'nay and Gloria's genetic stamp. "Terran genetic tamper-ing. It's banned on the *Inspiration* now, but things were faster and looser back before we joined this crew. I guess some of the other experiments didn't turn out as pretty, but a little telepathy has helped me keep up with this crowd well enough." He gave Ariel a wink. She smiled fondly at him.

"Boring!" Adora declared and pulled another bottle out of the air. With a flourish, she produced four of the tiny glasses and poured a measure of liquid into each one. "We're not here to talk! We're here to party!"

Each of us took a glass and Adora quickly raised hers. Ariel, James, and I followed suit.

"To Benson! May his taste in liquor be better than his taste in women!" my pale aunt declared and downed her glass in one gulp.

Seeing that Ariel and James were following her lead, I quickly drank whatever was in the glass. It was a strange green color, and I tried to swallow whatever it was fast enough that I didn't have to taste it. Unlike the cigarette, this time the burn was slow and seemed to warm me from the inside out. This was a lot less unpleasant I decided.

"Smooth," Adora commented, smacking her lips a bit and looking down at the bottle in her hand. "I prefer some-thing a little more aged, but this isn't bad."

"Did you really get this from Benson's private stash?" Ariel asked, coughing slightly. The face she was making said that she hadn't liked her drink quite as much as Adora had.

Adora chuckled. "Plausible deniability, my dear niece. Plausible deniability."

"There are only so many people who can teleport tilque out of a liquor cabinet," James pointed out. "Lack of evidence can be evidence in and of itself."

Adora rolled her eyes. "I hear a certain brother of mine has a decent reputation for teleporting substances he's not supposed to."

Ariel bristled. "Dad hasn't had that reputation since before I was born. That's unfair and you know it."

"Tell me about it," Adora sighed, rolling the bottle of tilque in her hands absently. "I don't think he's had more than a beer with dinner since I was two. Reputation as the best party animal on the ship and he won't even have a drink with his own sister."

James and Ariel shared a dark look while Adora poured herself another glass of the tilque. She downed it almost absently, then shrugged. "Okay. Let's get this party started," she said with a snap of her fingers.

Instantly, music began to play and the other party guests looked up from their drinking and socializing. A cheer went up as a fast, steady beat began to vibrate the floor. With a laugh, Ariel and James both held out their glasses to Adora for a refill. This time, I decided not to follow their lead. They didn't seem to notice.

Young men and women began to get up and dance, which from what I understood of these gatherings was not unusual. But the look on their faces was intense and almost glassy as they flung themselves up and into a tiny patch of grass that seemed to be the designated dance floor.

I turned to James and Ariel to find that they also had strange expressions on their faces. I put a hand to Ariel's shoulder and she turned to me slowly, her eyes unfocused and a wide smile on her face.

"Come on," she breathed. "Let's dance!" She grabbed my hand and pulled me towards the others. I didn't resist and quickly found myself surrounded by crew members. None of them paid a bit of attention to me. Their focus seemed inward as they jumped and shook to the beat of the music.

Then, I felt it. Like a combination of the wind of my father's teleportation and the pressure of my own time jump, I could sense psi power filling the room. It raised the hair on the back of my neck and sent shivers down my spine. Startled, I looked around to see if someone was teleporting in. Instead, I looked up directly into Adora's pale eyes.

She stood on the edge of the crowd, a bottle of liquor in one hand and a fresh cigarette in the other. She held my focus unblinkingly as she took a long drink. With a casual gesture she tossed the empty bottle into the shadows of the orchards. Taking a long drag from the cigarette, a smile spread across her face that sent ice into my veins. There was just something quite mad about the glee in her eyes as she joined the gyrating mass of humanity on the dance floor.

I danced a bit longer, but it was quite clear to me that the others were in the grip of some kind of psychic spell I was unaffected by. They writhed and shuddered against each other in ecstasy while I tried not to get pinned in between anyone.

"You are so beautiful," James breathed in my ear and I startled, eyes darting up into his face. He was flushed and his pupils hugely dilated, but he offered me a smile that didn't seem crazy or threatening. I smiled back and let myself enjoy the way our bodies moved together. Had I been a little less afraid of letting our bare skin touch each other, I think I would have liked it quite a bit more. As it was, his attention quickly slid back to Ariel after a few minutes.

Once James left me alone, I slipped away to the edge of the clearing and watched in bewilderment as my new acquaintances lost themselves in the growing frenzy of bodies and limbs. In the low light it was hard to pick anyone out, but I could see Adora's white hair like a beacon.

I'm not sure how long I watched before another psychic wind raised the hairs on my arms and the music abruptly stopped.

"Okay, kids, the party's over."

I'd know my father's voice anywhere. I thought about calling on my flames and making a jump back to my own time before he got to the clearing, but I kind of wanted to see how this ended. After the disturbing trance-like state the others were in, I wanted to be sure Ariel and James came out of it okay. There is also something to be said for the safety of the familiar and watching my father's tall, strong figure emerge from the trees was strangely comforting after all the new and unusual things that had happened tonight.

When I first saw him, I didn't think my father had changed much in the last three hundred years. The angle of his shoulders, the wavy length of his dark hair, the smooth efficiency of his stride were all identical to the Gabriel I knew. But when I caught sight of his face, it was as if all air had been crushed from my lungs.

I'm not sure I can describe the difference yet it sliced into me instantly. It wasn't exactly tangible. Even at the time I remember trying to put my finger on why he looked so different to me and failing utterly. His features were the same—no scars or huge fluctuations in weight disguised him—and there was never any denying the sharpness of the Usuriel profile. Yet something about his face looked so much younger and... I wasn't sure what it was but it made me look away to keep burning tears from blurring my vision.

Adora extricating herself from the dancing crowd with a small, happy cry. I cleared my eyes in time to see her fling herself around her brother's neck.

"Ah, finally decided to join us!" she purred, eyes bright and a little wild. With one hand she pulled his head down to hers and tried for what looked like a very passionate kiss.

Gabriel twisted his head away from her and scooped her up into his arms as if she were a small child.

"Come on, Adora. You've had enough. Time for bed," he said gruffly.

"Mmmmm...." She ran a hand over his shoulders. "Come on, one drink with your sister. Just one. You never do."

"It's never just one drink with me," he replied evenly, body completely unyielding to her caresses. "Alright, kids. Party's over. Ariel, if I have to talk to your mother about this you will be extremely sorry."

With that, his powerful mind cut through the strange spell that was filling the room. The drunken revelers swayed on their feet and looked around in surprise. There were several curse words as they realized who had discovered them.

"Home with you," Gabriel snapped as several of the party goers made a dash for the door. It started a mad exodus and pretty soon James and Ariel were some of the only people left in the room. Gabriel shook a finger at them. "Home. Now."

Ariel bowed her head and reached a hand out to James. He took it and the two of them dissolved into sparkling, golden motes.

"Where'd Gracie go?" Adora whined in Gabe's arms. Her voice sounded thick without the music to disguise it. I had never seen anyone drunk, but I suspected she'd had a bit too much tilque.

"Who?" Dad asked as he turned away from the clearing and carried her towards the door.

With a deep breath, I closed my eyes and envisioned my room at Angelus Quietum. I could see it as clearly as standing there. I opened my mind to my flames, and they surged into the space between me and the safety of my bedroom. With a sigh of wind, I was standing there in reality and not just memory. A cold chill let me know the shift had cost a decent amount of energy, but I had no trouble staying on my feet.

A slightly older-looking Ariel raised her glowing head from where she was sitting on my bed. She smiled and handed me her journal. In it, I found a detailed description of the night's events from her point of view. I read over it quickly and was flattered by the glowing tone she used to describe her "sister from the fucking future!"

"Well, that was quite a night," her entry concluded. I glanced up at her and saw an echo of the smart, carefree girl she used to be on her mature face. I found myself warming up to her in spite of myself.

"Yes, yes it was," I agreed, shedding the silken gloves that were now sticky with sweat before sitting down on the bed next to Ariel to untie my boots. To my surprise, she didn't fade away or try to engage me in any more conversation while I undressed. When I had pulled on a night shirt and tossed the dirty clothes in the hamper, the two of us sat quietly on the bed together for a long while.

"How long was I gone?" I asked finally.

"You weren't," Ariel wrote me in the journal. At my questioning look, she elaborated. "When you were younger, I think the same amount of time elapsed here and in the past. It left your body unattended for a while which is what I think caused your bad reaction. This time, you obviously had more control because you only stood there a moment before you returned to your body."

"Wait... so my body doesn't go with me? That doesn't make sense. How was I interacting with things in the past, then? I should have been a ghost."

Ariel gave a fluid shrug. "I told you, I don't exactly know how these things work. Sometimes they just do. Either way, you definitely do 'leave' your body in the present and it seems like the more controlled your return is, the closer you can get to coming back at the exact same time you left."

I considered this facet of the time shift in silence before climbing into bed. Even though it had been an extremely long day and my body was exhausted, my mind still felt on edge. I squirmed in the pillows, trying to get comfortable.

"Ariel?" I said, after a while. Her glow had faded several minutes earlier, but I suspected she might still be around if I wanted to talk to her. I looked down at the journal I'd tucked next to my pillow.

"Yes, little sister?" she wrote. I glanced up and found her sitting in the chair by my closet door. She didn't seem to notice the pile of dirty clothes clearly visible through her waist.

"Why did you send me back to that time? I mean, you obviously lived longer than sixteen years. Why that night?"

There was something thoughtful in her gaze as she looked around the room. Finally, she met my eye again before bending to write her reply.

"What did you think of Adora?"

"Well..." I considered her question. "I'm not really sure what to think. She seemed a little..."

"Crazy?" My sister supplied.

"Something," I agreed.

We were quiet for a few moments before she wrote me another question.

"Did you see Dad?"

I swallowed the lump that rose in my throat. This, I suspected, was the real reason I was having trouble falling asleep. I didn't look at her when I nodded. It took me a long moment before I glanced down at her next message.

"What did you think?" she wrote.

I sighed. She wasn't going to let me shy away from it, but I didn't want to admit how painful it had been to see him in the past.

"He looked... different."

"Yeah," she agreed, "he did."

I glanced up at her and I could see my own heartache written in her gaze. "He wasn't always as broken as he is now," she wrote. "There was a time when Gabriel was truly alive and happy."

Before tonight I would have argued with her. I would have told her that my father was alive and happy here at Angelus Quietum. I would have protested her use of the word 'broken' and insisted that he had a good life here with me. After what I'd just seen, though, I was pretty sure Ariel was right.

Ariel laid a glowing hand on mine. It was the first time she'd ever touched me for comfort rather than a purpose.

"I feel like I should be able to help him," I said slowly. "Like it's my fault he's not as happy now as he was on the *Inspiration*."

"No, it's not your fault," Ariel reassured me quickly. "But, I do think there may be something you can do to help him."

I scowled at her. She slipped a hand into her pocket and when she removed it, a small, empty syringe was in her palm.

"I've been working on something that just might help. I'm not quite there, yet," she wrote, "but I have some hope that if I can work with blood samples from all of Dad's children it might come together. I have samples from all of them... except one."

I blinked at her. "You want a blood sample? From me?"

"You said you wanted to help," she replied, her face a picture of innocence. I was too familiar with Gabriel to completely believe her act. But the image of my father back on the *Inspiration* was fresh in my mind. He'd looked so... alive.

"You really think it might help him?" I asked, feeling doubtful about what good a blood sample would be in improving my father's mood.

"I wouldn't ask if I didn't think so," Ariel assured me.

With a careful breath, I offered her my bare arm. "Okay, I guess so."

"Look at your cork board," Ariel suggested. Obediently, I turned my head so that it was facing away from my arm.

I felt the warmth of her ghostly hand on my arm, then a sharp pain. I whimpered but held still. The cold alloy of the needle pressed into my flesh. When it was gone, I glanced up at Ariel. She was removing a vial of my blood from the back of the syringe.

"Did you get what you needed?" I asked.

"We'll find out soon," she wrote with a smile. Then she laid a ghostly kiss on my forehead and I shivered at the electric tingle her lips left on my skin. "Thank you, Gracie."

"Sure," I replied, a yawn creeping in to take over my face. "Anything to help Dad."

"You're a good daughter. Dad is lucky to have you. Now go to sleep."

I nodded, cuddling closer to the pillows. Sleep had finally found me and this time I was powerless to protest. Behind my closed eyelids, Ariel's glow faded away to darkness.

CHAPTER 26

DIPLOMATIC DINNERS

Life with James and my father began to fall into a new rhythm.

After chores, mornings were spent at lessons with Stella and James. I hadn't had a classmate since the group home, but James turned out to be quite intelligent and he added a new, unique perspective to Stella's often dry lessons. I was suddenly more engaged in my school work than I had been in years.

Grandma Gloria left some resistance bands for James to do special physical therapy exercises with, so after lunch while I fed and worked with the horses, he did his workout. Then Dad would take us to the lake shore and have James practice telepathy with him while I went through my martial arts routines and pyrokinesis techniques. That meant Dad and James just sat there staring at each other while I went through yoga poses and sustained carefully designed pillars of flames. Afterwards, Dad would check my forms before walking back to the house to make dinner. Then, after a subdued meal, we would have a little time to ourselves before bed. I usually found a book and read or spent some time soaking in the tub.

For the first few weeks, James had trouble keeping up. By the time he and Gabriel were done with their psi practice he was often pale and shaking.

One day, after what must have been a particularly difficult session, James looked almost green as he watched my father's retreating back. He made no move to get up from his seat on a fallen log.

"You okay?" I asked him. We were friendly at lessons and meals, but outside of those formal situations we rarely talked.

James glanced up at me, his expression surprised. I usually ignored him on my way into the house, or at least pretended to. I'd half-abandoned the wild fantasies I'd had about him that first day we met. The reality of doing lessons together every day made James less exotically alluring. However, with his hair growing in and his strength slowly gaining, I still found myself awkward around him.

"You really can't hear a thing," James said after a long silence. "Telepathically, I mean. I thought it was just a really strong shield, but you don't have any control over it, do you?"

"Nope, not a bit," I agreed with a laugh. "According to Dad, I'm the most mentally silent person to ever live on Cybele."

James blinked at me, then offered a tired smile. "Well, living with Usuriels, that has to be a bit of an advantage. At least you don't have to worry about them peeking in when you'd rather keep a thought to yourself."

"That's true enough." I screwed up my nerve and offered James a hand to help him up off the log. "Though it also means I get left out of a lot of conversations. There's nothing more frustrating than knowing the people around you are talking and you can't hear a word."

James took my hand and a quiver of excitement radiated from the warmth of his palm. I pulled him to his feet with relative ease though he leaned heavily into my arm. I wasn't sure, but even without telekinesis I suspected I was stronger than the average sixteen-year-old girl. Of course, working around the farm and riding horses everyday didn't hurt.

I returned James' smile with a bit of color in my cheeks. He only stood a few inches taller than I did and had gained a bit of weight from his now-regular meals, but his petite frame still looked boyish and unfinished in my father's shirts. He had a charming habit of rolling up the sleeves and leaving the top few buttons undone. I was disappointed when he dropped my hand to walk in for dinner.

"So what are your lessons with Gabriel like?" I asked. "I've never had a telepathy lesson. I can't even listen in on one, what with being beyond head blind."

"I'm not sure how to explain it if you haven't experienced it," he said. We walked quietly towards the house a ways before he continued. "He's trying to teach me how to keep others out of my mind. So he shows me how to build... well, walls are the best analogy. But psychic walls can have a lot of different properties and, depending on the situation and what part of your mind you are working with... well it gets complicated."

"I never thought about levels of shielding before. Either you can hear someone's thoughts or you can't."

"Think of it like having a conversation," James explained. "When you are with your dad, you can be kind of blunt and honest in ways you wouldn't be with a stranger. You don't try to hide the emotions on your face or the body language you are using from someone who is closer to you. Same thing with a telepath—especially among other telepaths. The closer you are to someone the more transparent you are with them. Of course, there is a limit to how much you want to share at once or even how deep into your thoughts you want someone to go."

"So does that mean you need multiple walls?" I asked, climbing the steps to the back porch.

"Well, most houses need more than one wall, right?" He gestured toward our home. "Think of it as owning a whole farm like Angelus Quietum. You have a front yard with a picket fence that most people can see into but know to stay out of unless they have a legitimate reason to enter. Then you have a house with solid walls in the center. Those walls have windows and doors so that people close to you can come in but only with an invitation. And within those walls you have more public rooms, like a living room, and more private ones, like a bedroom."

"Wow, that is kind of complicated," I said, opening the door to the kitchen. I could hear my father clattering cookware and knew I'd get a scowl from him if I didn't set the table quickly. Dutifully I went to the cabinet and pulled out plates and glasses. I kept having to remind myself to count out three places rather than two.

"I had no idea shielding was so involved," I said as I laid out the settings on the kitchen table. To my surprise, James had grabbed the silverware and was laying them down beside each plate. Normally he sat and watched Dad and I deliver dinner. He must be slowly acclimating to life without an avatar if he still had the energy to move around this late in the day.

"It isn't for you, my little fortress," Dad said, popping a casserole into the oven. He gave James and I a smile as he surveyed the complete table setting. "Good, now that you're done with that, come help me cut up some pears and apples for the fruit salad."

***

I'm not sure how long after that day Gabriel decided to teach James about diplomatic dinners—perhaps a month or two—but I do remember the fiasco it turned into.

It didn't start out so badly. Dad announced that we would get out of our morning lessons for the day so that we could finish our chores early. He told us he wanted the whole afternoon and evening for a special lesson.

Obediently, I took care of the horses and chickens for the day while James did his exercises. Afterwards, Gabriel assembled us in the kitchen and went over an elaborate menu we were going to prepare.

"Formal dinners in the Senate are not the same as the casual ones we have here," Dad explained. "There is a minimum of four courses: a soup, a salad, a main dish, and a dessert. I had Stella find one of the more recently used menus so you'll be able to see some of the types of food you can expect."

I looked over the recipes with dismay. "We don't have half of these ingredients," I protested, "and if these baking times are right, we'll be cooking all afternoon!"

"Well, I asked your grandmother if she would be willing to make a little shopping trip for us," Dad said with a smirk and opened the cooling unit to reveal a much better stocked larder than usual.

"Guess we're cooking all afternoon," James chuckled.

So that's what we did. And to be quite honest, that part was a lot of fun. Dad told Stella to put on some of our favorite songs and the three of us sang and danced through the esoteric recipes. Dad and I laughed at certain food combinations while James stared at us uncomprehendingly. He didn't have enough experience with food to know what went together and what didn't.

This was James' first time attempting to cook. Despite this, he was quite good at following the directions and always open to letting Gabriel or I step in if he felt overwhelmed. So when the flour settled and the three of us sat down to our four course meal, it turned out quite well.

"I had no idea you could dip bread in egg and make something so delicious," I said, enjoying the crispy bread sticks we'd created to go with the sweet-but-savory soup course.

"It's an old Earth trick," Dad said. "They used to call it French toast and serve it in syrup."

"Syrup?" James asked, nibbling his bread stick.

"We have something like it here, but the good kind was made from a special tree sap on Earth," Gabriel explained, smiling at the incredulous expressions James and I gave him.

"Okay, it's not just you, James. I've eaten a lot of things over the years, but tree sap?" I asked.

Dad chuckled. "You would be amazed at what people will eat. And Earth had a few more centuries to get creative with food than our cultures. We're just beginning to scrape the surface of what there is to eat here on Cybele."

"Trust you to think two hundred and eighty-odd years is 'scraping the surface,'" I said with an eye roll. Gabriel stuck out his tongue at me and I doubled the exasperation in my expression. "Honestly, act your age!"

"Well, according to my mother's people I'm not even marriageable yet," he said with a sly smile. "They'd still call me a teenager!"

I put my hands on my hips and scowled at him. We'd had this little spat before an uncountable number of times but it was fun and comfortable.

"Well, according to MY mother's people you should be a great-grandfather!"

"In that case, I am acting my age," he shot back with a wink, "because I've been a great-grandfather for several centuries now."

"I don't think great-grandfathers stick their tongues out," I accused.

"This one does," he laughed. "Okay, who is ready for steamed salmon?"

He gestured for James and me to get the plates of salmon we'd prepared that were currently being kept warm in the oven. As we came back to the table, setting the hot plates down onto cloth settings so as not to harm the wooden table, I saw that my father had just produced a bottle of some kind. I watched with interest as he pulled thin, transparent glasses from the air and set them in front of himself before uncorking the bottle. The liquid inside was a pale yellow that glowed golden in the waning sunset light streaming in the kitchen window.

"What you drink at a meal like this is almost as important as what you eat," Gabriel explained, pouring half a glass of the honey colored liquid into each of the three glasses. The glasses were unlike anything I'd ever seen before with long stems that lifted the cup up off of the table. My father set aside the bottle, nodded his thanks to me as I set his plate of salmon in front of him, then placed a glass of the pale liquid at each of our plates. "Perhaps, in some ways, it is even more important."

I settled myself in my seat and eagerly awaited the next phase of the lesson.

"We are eating fish, which means the proper pairing is usually a white wine. Because we've selected salmon, which is a full-flavored fish, we want a wine with a bit more body to stand up to it. A pale red or blush wine would pair well with it, too, but I've selected a stronger white," my father said, picking up the bottle of wine again and passing it to James. He studied the label before passing it to me. In bold letters it advertised "Landing Vineyards" with large pictures of grapes and vines twirling about the edges. Underneath the brand was the text "P'rigio."

"We've never had wine before," I said, setting the bottle down.

My father inclined his head. "While Cybele doesn't have drinking laws, on Earth where I grew up the drinking age was twenty-one. I typically don't serve anything alcoholic to anyone underage. However, I doubt the University or Senate body will have such reservations, so James needs to have some knowledge of what to expect. I thought it would be safer for him to have his first experience with strong drink here rather than in front of a diplomatic assembly."

Now he had my interest. I watched him closely as he took a bite of the salmon, then picked up his wine glass and swirled the contents, inhaling deeply.

"The bouquet, or smell of the wine, is something you should pause to enjoy first," Gabriel instructed. "Then, a small sip with your food to pair the tastes together."

Exchanging a glance with James, I eagerly cut into my salmon. He looked more nervous than I felt was necessary, but he was only just getting the hang of the whole food thing. I guess adding drinks on top of it might be overwhelming. I decided to focus on my own experiment. First I sampled the fish. The flesh of the salmon was moist and succulent. Copying my father, I picked up my glass and inhaled deeply. The warmth of a grape field greeted my nose. With a smile I took a sip of the wine. The corners of my lip curled as the acidic taste of alcohol sapped the moisture out of my mouth. I hastily swallowed and took a large gulp of water.

"What do you think?" my father asked. Half of his fish was gone and he was already pouring himself another glass of the wine. This time, he filled the cup.

"It's... different," I said, trying to hide my disappointment. It smelled so wonderful but the taste was dreadful. I decided to try again. When my second mouthful was just as disgusting as the first, I abandoned the wine and focused my attention on the fish. At least it tasted good.

"What about you?" Gabriel asked James between bites.

"I find it very enjoyable," James said with a reserved smile. He seemed hesitant, but when my father offered him a refill he didn't refuse. In fact, the two of them kept sipping at their glasses throughout our dessert course and into the political discussion afterwards.

"No, I don't think the Riland legislature will ever let an undead delegation speak, let alone hold a vote on their issues," Dad was saying with a shake of his head. He'd leaned back in his chair and appeared more relaxed than he usually was around James, but otherwise he didn't seem affected by consuming half a bottle of wine. James, on the other hand, had pink in his cheeks and he was speaking louder than I think he realized.

"I know there's some lasting stigma there, but I haven't heard of any violence in over twenty years. Certainly it's time to open discussions on basic human rights," James insisted as I gathered up our empty dessert plates and loaded them in the groaning dishwasher. I might as well run it tonight even though we'd just run it yesterday.

"Vampires aren't human, as Garret Stafford would happily point out," Gabriel sighed, "so why do they need human rights?"

"I wouldn't let Grandpa D'nay hear you say that," I called over my shoulder from the kitchen. After I piled the rest of the dishes into the sink to await my father in the morning, I rejoined the table.

"I didn't say I agreed with the sentiment," Dad pointed out as I settled myself in the chair to his right. "Obviously I think my father is a worthwhile individual. However, we were discussing the political climate of Riland, and that's not a place that is exactly friendly to the Aware population. Or Terrans for that matter."

"They have a problem with Usuriels, too?" James asked.

"Stella said that Landing and Skykyle are the most welcoming cities for all Aware individuals," I said, glad to have some kind of knowledge to add to the conversation.

"True. And Riland is probably the least friendly to anyone who isn't strictly mortal," Gabriel said, picking up the empty bottle of wine before tossing it in the recycling bin. I could tell from the tone of his voice that he wanted to change the subject. "But enough of politics for now. I'd say it's time to discuss after dinner drinks."

Without further ado, an assortment of bottles with a variety of shapes and sizes appeared on the table along with several low, wide glasses, and a bin of ice.

"After dinner, it is common to enjoy mixed drinks," my father explained. "But here is where you need to be careful. Liquor is much stronger than wine so you want to watch how much you have in a short period of time. You'll see what I mean."

And with that he began mixing cocktails. He must have had us sample half a dozen. Well, he and James sampled half a dozen. After the first two burned like fire and tasted like paint thinner, I declined to try any others. But this did not deter Gabriel. He was calm and matter-of-fact, keeping up a constant commentary while mixing each set of ingredients with deft, steady hands. It quickly became apparent that he was extremely knowledgeable about this topic and was relishing the chance to share it with us. It was fun to see how he combined the colorful liquids in interesting and often beautiful ways. I also enjoyed watching James' expressions as he sampled various concoctions.

"I'm gonna use the bathroom," James said after a particularly strong cocktail that even made my father wince. James' voice held that same thickness I'd heard in Adora's a few weeks earlier. The young diplomat staggered as he got up and very nearly toppled over before finding the wall.

Gabriel chuckled and leaned back in his chair, setting down the glass he'd been sipping from. "Grace, I think you might need to help our guest."

"Ummm... maybe you should help him?" I suggested, feeling color rise in my face. I watched as James slowly made a wobbly line out the door towards the bathroom.

"Nope." My father shook his head and got out of his chair. He wasn't quite as graceful as usual, but he seemed steady enough as he walked into the living room after James. "I'm going to sit in my chair, finish this drink, and go to bed."

"Okay," I replied, trailing after the men feeling unsure what to do with his pronouncement. "What should I do?"

"Probably should check on James," Gabriel suggested, settling into his armchair with an exaggerated sigh. I scowled into the dark room, feeling like I was missing something. "You still there, Gracie?"

"Yeah, Dad, I'm still here," I said.

"Will you light the fireplace?"

"Sure." I sent a spare thought over to the dry logs stacked in the grate. It took little energy to set them alight.

"Thanks," he murmured and I heard the clink of ice in his glass as he took another sip of whatever they'd last poured themselves. "Hmmm...probably better you don't care for the taste of alcohol. Might keep you out of trouble." He regarded me quietly as the flames began to brighten and light up our faces in a soft yellow glow. "You'd better go check on James."

With a shrug I dutifully, if reluctantly, headed towards the bathroom.

I didn't have to knock awkwardly the way I'd feared. Rather, the door had been left wide open and I found James leaning heavily against the sink trying to figure out the button to his slacks.

"Need some help?" I asked, stifling a laugh. I didn't even feel dizzy from the few sips I'd had, but clearly James was drunk. I'd read about such a state, but aside from my little trip to the *Inspiration*, I'd never been around someone intoxicated. It was both funny and a little scary. James looked about to fall over just unzipping his pants.

"'Dunno why they make these so complicated," he muttered as his fingers fumbled over the clasp.

I'd already seen him naked once, but it didn't make undoing his pants for him any less embarrassing. However, James took it in stride and his look of relief as he emptied his bladder into the toilet made me blush a bit as I turned my back to give him some privacy.

"Your dad's really som'thin'," James slurred as he finished and began trying to manage the sink. I quickly adjusted the water pressure so that he didn't soak the whole bathroom. "N'ver knew eatin' and drinkin' could be so much fun."

"He was in rare form today," I allowed. "I've never seen him talk about this stuff before."

"Never?"

"Nope," I said. "In fact, I don't think I've ever seen Gabriel drink alcohol before."

He mulled that over while he fumbled with the hand towel.

"Why do you call 'im that?" James asked as he pushed away from the sink. He immediately wobbled so badly that I put an arm around his waist. My pulse picked up as our bodies pressed together and the flush in my cheeks returned. I was grateful to Stella for turning off the bright bathroom light since the dimmer hallway illumination revealed less of my reaction.

"What do you mean?" I asked, steadying James as he wove down the hallway. He supported himself with one hand on the wall and the other around my waist. Despite his regular meals here at Angelus Quietum he still only outweighed me by five kilos. As wobbling, unsteady weight, however, he was difficult to keep on his feet. I decided Dad was right about heading to bed.

"'Gabriel. 'E's your dad s'you should prob'ly call 'im that," James slurred as we reached the bedroom. "But 'alf the time you call 'im Gabriel. Seems odd."

"Oh," I said, easing James onto the bed. His speech was getting more garbled and he seemed practically boneless as I helped him lie down. Even so, it felt safer to continue the conversation than to comment on the diplomat-in-training's impaired state. "I guess I don't think about it. He introduced himself as Gabriel when I met him so it's kind of... I don't know... interchangeable."

James frowned up at me, eyes half-lidded. "Introduced?"

"Yeah, when he picked me up from the orphanage." I waved a hand to dismiss the oddness of that answer. My young childhood was a bit too much to explain to him at the moment. "Never mind, it's a long story."

"You're... adopted?"

I shook my head. "Do I look adopted to you? No, I'll tell you tomorrow when you can see straight again. It's actually a semi-interesting story."

"M'Kay..." For a moment I thought he might be drifting off, and I started to quietly back out of the room. Before I could get far, however, his hand caught clumsily at mine.

"What's wrong, James?"

"I don't feel... so good." He sounded green even in the mostly dark room. "I'm afraid. Please... I don't wanna be alone."

I'd never been sick in my life, so I wasn't exactly sure what to do. But he sounded really pathetic and that weird piece of my brain that couldn't decide how it felt about him urged compassion over avoiding awkwardness. After all, I did know what it felt like to be alone and afraid in the dark.

"I guess I can stay a few minutes. Just until you fall asleep."

I glanced around our little guest bedroom. The bed, a night stand, a closet, and a small writing desk rounded out the tidy space. James hadn't brought much with him in the way of clothes or personal items so the room didn't seem much different than usual. The hallway light illuminated everything in a soft, warm glow from the cracked doorway while the rest of the room was a deep, blue twilight. I didn't have much trouble finding the desk chair and pulling it up to the bedside.

James moaned as I sat down. His face was extremely pale in the shadows.

"What's it like?" I asked quietly. "Being drunk, I mean?"

"Awful," he groaned and belched sickly. "Think... I'm dying..."

I thought back to Adora and Ariel's party. No one seemed this sick afterwards, at least not that I'd seen. Concern squirmed in my stomach and I decided it might be a good idea to check in with my father. Even if he hadn't been in a talking mood, maybe he would be willing to come make sure James was okay. I didn't really want to call Grandma Gloria unless it was an actual emergency.

"Wait here. I'm going to go get my dad," I told James with a pat on the shoulder and trotted quickly back to the living room.

"Dad?" I called into the flickering firelight. I could just make out his crossed knees silhouetted against the burning logs.

I didn't get a response. For a moment I thought he might have fallen asleep in his chair. Then I heard the tinkle of ice in his glass and realized he was still drinking. It seemed like a long while to still be nursing that same cocktail from earlier.

"Dad," I said again, coming closer. "I'm kind of worried about James."

Gabriel didn't say a word. As I rounded the edge of his chair I could see he was staring into the fire, his face extremely blank. A bottle of one of the stronger spirits sat next to the chair and the glass in his hand was about half empty.

"Dad," I tried again. "Dad, I wouldn't bother you if I wasn't really worried."

My father's eyes slid closed and for a moment I thought he was deliberately ignoring me. After a pause, though, his eyes opened and he shook his head.

"No need to be concerned, Gracie. I wouldn't let the child give himself alcohol poisoning. Just let him get sick enough to know what his limits are." Dad's voice didn't wobble or slur the way James' did, but I could hear the drink in it. I didn't like it.

"You knew he would make himself sick?" I asked. "What about me? Were you going to let me drink myself sick, too?"

My father's fluid shrug was more of an answer than I cared for. "It would take almost twice as much to make you ill. Usuriel metabolism. But if you'd wanted to try... well... we all have to learn sometime," he replied evenly, then took a long drought of the liquor in his glass. He didn't even react to what I knew was its potent burn.

Thoroughly disgusted with my father, I put my hands on my hips and scowled at him. "Okay, great. Well, now what? How long will James be sick?"

"Probably a few hours. Like a bad stomach flu, no worse."

"A what?"

Gabriel blinked and finally glanced at me before chuckling. "Right. You're an Usuriel—you don't get stomach bugs." I gestured for him to continue. "He'll probably bring up most of what we drank tonight. Once he's empty, he'll fall asleep. He'll feel like death in the morning and probably a bit into the afternoon, too, but he's young. He'll be fine."

"And what exactly am I supposed to do with him?"

"If you feel like being kind and don't want to make him clean up in the morning, I suggest you find something for him to heave into," my father said. "Otherwise, there's not much you can do."

"Great," I grumbled and went off in search of a trash can.

***

James was miserably sick. I mean, throwing up, moaning, and sobbing for over an hour. I'd never seen anyone be physically ill before and I decided it wasn't something that I enjoyed. If James hadn't been utterly pathetic and slurring

his gratitude for my company every two minutes, I probably would have retreated to my bedroom. Instead, I sat in
the semi-dark and let him cling to my hand while his body
purged the poison my father had cheerfully poured down
his throat.

I think that was the first time I questioned whether or not
Gabriel was a good person.

"I'm so sorry," James slurred for the twentieth time. I
patted his shoulder and wondered if I would actually get
any sleep tonight. "You've been so nice t' me. I'm sorry you
'ave to see me..." Another heave and he demonstrated what
he was apologizing for. I cringed and made sure he was
reaching the trash can. I had no desire to clean him up, but
I also didn't think I'd have the heart to let him sleep in his
own sick. The trash can was a good compromise. He could
clean that thing out tomorrow.

"It's okay," I told him.

He recovered a bit from his bout of retching and laid
back on the pillow. I took the can from his shaking hand
and set it a few feet away where the smell would be less
offensive.

"Feeling any better?" I asked quietly, a part of me hoping
he had fallen asleep and wouldn't answer.

"No," he moaned softly.

We were both silent for a long moment. I was just about
to start sneaking for the door again when James made a
small noise of pain. Feeling guilty for trying to abandon
him, I laid a hand on his arm.

"I'm still here," I told him. "Is there anything I can do to
make you more comfortable? Would you like another blanket?"

"No," his voice was so faint I could hardly hear him. "Will you talk t' me?" he whispered. "I like the sound of your voice."

Again, I was glad the dark hid my startled expression. "Oh. Okay. What do you want me to talk about?"

"Anything," he whimpered. "Jus' talk."

"Well..." I cast about for something to chat about. "You were asking about when my dad and I met. I guess I could tell you about it."

"Mmmmhmmm."

"Let's see..." I said and fiddled with the edge of the blanket. "My mother didn't let my father know about me until I was older. I guess they weren't in a relationship, though my dad has never said one way or the other. Anyway, my mom lost custody of me to the Providence when I was about five."

"Why?"

I was surprised he had the presence of mind to ask a question at this point. But I shrugged and answered it the best I could. "I'm not completely sure, but she was gone a lot at night. Looking back, I think she may have been involved in something illegal."

"So... what 'appened to you?"

"I went into a 'group home' for unwanted children." I thought back to that rickety, wooden house full to the brim with heartache. "I spent a year there."

"That's so sad," James slurred. I caught sight of his face in the soft hall light and shied away from the drunken sympathy in his eyes. "You were all alone?"

"Yeah, it was pretty awful. But things turned out okay in the end," I reassured him. "When I was six, I guess my mom or someone else let Dad know about me. He came and took me away. It was actually pretty amazing. Gabriel did-n't have any patience for the bureaucracy—just came in, handed them the paperwork, and told them they couldn't stop him from taking me. I guess he was right."

"'E really loves you," James sighed.

"Yeah, I guess he does. I mean... yeah. I know he does."

"You've been through a lot," he said slowly. "But you're still so kind. I'm a stranger 'ere, but you've made me feel real at 'ome. And keepin' me company like this... I don' think my friends back at 'ome would 'ave stayed with me... while I was sick. You might be the nicest person I know. You're def'nately the prettiest."

I chuckled. "Thanks, James."

"Nah... really... you are." He was fading down into sleep. I could hear it in his voice.

"Get this into him before he's completely out."

I nearly jumped out of my skin at my father's voice. Ei-ther he'd teleported into the room or he wasn't drunk enough to lose all of his cat-like grace. I frowned at the glass of clear liquid he handed me. An experimental sniff and subsequent sip told me it was water.

"Trust me, his head will thank you in the morning." Ga-briel's voice trailed off down the hall. "Oh, and lay him on his side. Just in case he's sick in his sleep."

I wasn't sure if I was more pissed at my father for getting James puking drunk or for ditching me with him. Either way I felt like torching the whole collection of alcohol bottles he'd shown off tonight. I decided then I was not a fan of drinking or its effect on my father.

"Here, Dad says you'll feel better if you have some of this," I said, shaking James' shoulder. His eyes opened enough to let me know he was still awake. "Don't worry, it's just water."

He opened his mouth but clearly couldn't lift his head. After a few attempts that nearly left him soaked, I ended up crawling into the bed and half-cradling his head in my lap just to get a good angle for him to drink. A few long gulps later he was back to hanging over the bed, stomach heaving up the last of its contents into the trash can. I'd been caught unprepared and was trapped under the weight of his shoulders as he was violently ill. I patted his back awkwardly and could feel the sweat bleeding through the thin cloth of his shirt.

"Get all of that mess out," I said. "You'll feel better for it, I think."

At last, empty, he collapsed into my lap. He spent the reprieve catching his breath while I wondered how the Sweet Fate I was going to get out from under him if he passed out.

"I'm n'ver touching alcohol again," he moaned slowly. To my utter surprise, his fingers found mine and laced themselves so gently and thoroughly through them that I felt a rush of... something... all the way through my core. "Thank you... for taking care of me," James whispered, his cheek nuzzling into my thigh and his hand pulling mine around to rest on his chest.

A bemused smile played around the corner of my lips and I found the fingertips of my other hand coming up to explore the growing fuzz that covered the top of his head.

"You're welcome," I whispered. Then, I remembered what Dad had said about the glass of water. Even if he just brought it all back up, it was probably good for him. Either he'd be less dehydrated or have less alcohol souring his stomach. "Here, let's try some water again. Smaller sips this time, I think."

James all but climbed into my arms for this round. I blushed furiously, but awkwardness aside I had to admit it was easier to get the water into him that way. We stuck to slow, small sips and this time he managed to keep it down. He really wasn't lucid enough at that point to do much but ask for more water and thank me for keeping him company. Sometime well past midnight the two of us fell asleep in his bed; his head resting on my shoulder while my arms wrapped around his slowly rising and falling chest.

CHAPTER 27

CHANGES

The next day I woke up early enough that James was still passed out. I gingerly disentangled us, then carefully positioned some pillows to keep him on his side as my father had suggested. The young diplomat didn't so much as stir in his sleep. Feeling a bit maternal, I pulled the blanket up from the foot of the bed and laid it over him before heading into the bathroom for a much-needed shower.

Neither James nor my father showed their faces until around noon and then they didn't look exactly like the picture of health. Gabriel wasn't suffering for the night of hard drinking nearly as much as his young apprentice, but I knew him well enough to see how carefully he was moving, as if he had a headache he was trying not to set off. James, on the other hand, periodically dashed off to the bathroom to be sick and looked as if he'd managed to lose a few kilos between dinner last night and this morning.

Other than a chuckle and an admonition to drink his orange juice, Dad didn't comment on James' obvious discomfort. For his own part, Dad just seemed to assume we would go about business as usual.

So that's what happened. Lessons, chores, exercise, dinner, free time, bed. There was so little comment on the incident or how badly the night had gone that it almost felt unremarkable.

Except for two things.

The first was James and I.

There is a certain level of intimacy you have with someone once you've fallen asleep in their arms. Where before we'd been cordial strangers slowly getting to know each other, now we were actual friends.

That first day after the fiasco, I checked on him a few times and even through the pain of his hangover, James managed a bashful apology. I waved it off with a laugh and, when he finally felt well enough to join us at the evening meal, he brushed my elbow with his. I looked up, startled, and met his gentle smile. For once I didn't blush, but instead experienced a delightful sense of connection I'd never had before. I'd been there for him when he needed someone. Outside of my father, I'd never really helped anyone with something big or scary before. It felt good.

After that, James started coming out to the barns to watch me ride when he got done with his exercises. He'd lean against the fence post, the sun catching in his lengthening blond hair as he watched me put Charcoal through his paces.

For my part, I made sure to stop and chat with the young diplomat after our afternoon lessons. Soon, we were even spending our after dinner free time together. Sometimes it was as simple as sitting in the same room to read for homework or pleasure. Other evenings it was spirited conversation or a card game that my father would occasionally join us for.

Also, starting with that little nudge of elbows at the dinner table, James and I slowly pushed the boundaries of personal space around each other. During morning lessons we no longer put such a large space between us at the kitchen table. Each week our chairs drew a little closer. After our afternoon lessons with Dad we would walk slowly back to the house, shoulders and fingertips brushing against each other in electrifying little connections.

One random day, James sat on the couch reading after dinner and I settled into the seat next to him. I could feel his warmth from inches away and I caught him glancing down the length of the sofa to see if someone had left a pile of books or memory pads that forced me to sit closer than strictly necessary. There was nothing on the other end of the couch but an empty cushion. Ignoring the flush that crept into his cheeks, I kept my attention on my book.

He didn't move away. In fact, as I was finishing my chapter, his bare arm brushed gently against my own. My heart beat picking up, I cautiously leaned into that subtle touch. James leaned back. Suddenly, I found his arm around my shoulders and the long line of our bodies pressed against each other from shoulder to hip. I glanced up at him, a small smile touching my lips. He returned it and sent heat blossoming in the pit of my stomach. We stayed reading like that for over an hour, until it was time for bed and I reluctantly peeled myself away to find a cold shower.

The next day, as we walked back to the house from our afternoon lesson, I slid my hand into James'. When he didn't pull away, I glanced up at him. Those lovely, faded-blue eyes met mine with gentle desire. Then his fingers laced between mine and he gave my hand a squeeze. It took every ounce of control I had not to squeal like a lovesick teenage girl. Though, that is exactly what I was.

The second change was Gabriel.

It started subtly. I almost didn't notice at first. But as the weeks wore on, the years gathered around my father like a dark cloud that followed him around Angelus Quietum.

It wasn't that his face gained more lines. There was not an ounce less muscle in his shoulders or a lessening of the fierce line of his waist and hips. He was no less perfect and powerful as the day I saw him stride up those group home steps.

But the change was undeniable. It was in the catch of his step. It was in the hovering shadows in the hollows of his eyes; an inescapable sorrow that lingered in the set of his mouth and the angle of his brow. The sadness I'd always seen in his eyes, even as a young child, was no longer easily dispelled by a mischievous smile. Instead it rode his gaze no matter what mood he attempted to convey.

More and more nights were spent by the fireplace. It became a common sight: the silhouette of my father's lean body curled into the armchair, a glass of something stronger than wine at his elbow. When I think back to those evenings spent learning the gentle language of attraction with James, I can still hear the tinkle of ice in my father's cocktail glass in the background.

Not that Gabriel seemed to notice what was happening between James and I. Looking back, it's ridiculous to think he didn't know. He was a high level empath and telepath with the best training of anyone on the planet, save perhaps one. James' inexperienced mind must have been screaming adolescent lust like a constant roar in the background of his thoughts. I imagine for the first time, my father was glad I was as head blind as a stone.

But Gabriel never lectured or shook a finger at us. He just smiled and turned an indulgently blind eye to our growing attraction. It was the kindest thing he could have done.

***

"Does that mean you don't have sex at all?" I asked, glancing at James sidelong as we walked through Angelus Quietum's sprawling woodland. He'd progressed enough in his physical therapy to allow him to go riding instead of using his stretch bands. Thus, the two of us spent many blissful hours riding through the sprawling grounds on Charcoal and Aubrie. We had to be careful not to run late on Gabriel's lessons, but for an hour or two each day we were able to ride, walk, and talk about everything under the sun.

Today, he'd been explaining Terran reproduction. Apparently, all Terrans were created in a lab using their parent's reproductive cells and an artificial womb. Then they had simple, child avatars that were delivered to their biological parents once they were old enough to control one. But that left me wondering what James thought of our blossoming romantic relationship.

"Of course we have sex," he said with a laugh. "An avatar can do anything a person can do. Usually, better."

His pride in his people's tradition was clear in his voice. My face heated up. I decided to steer the conversation in a more innocuous direction.

"Except, apparently, eat," I teased. "Or taste things for that matter."

He gave a shrug followed by an easy smile. "Nothing is perfect," he allowed. "But they are a lot easier to interface with than these implants."

I fingered the small lump on the left side of my neck. "Mine's never given me a problem."

"A problem? No, of course not. But they give you access to such limited information, only visual and audio files. Through an avatar interface, I can experience an event exactly as it was in full tactile detail. It makes history much more... immersive."

"That does sound more interesting than Stella's version of the colonization era," I admitted.

We passed from the edge of the forest into a grove of blossoming fruit trees on the banks of Lake Angelus.

"So what was it like growing up in Terra Nova? Do you have any family back home?"

"Of course," he said. "I'm the eldest of three boys."

A few gentle questions and the rest of his family history poured out. His parents were government officials of some obscure branch of Terran bureaucracy. They were proud of his training and had been sending him letters via the net each week since he arrived. Apparently they were storing his avatar for him so that it would be ready if and when he wanted to visit.

"Do you miss them?" I asked.

"Of course," he said, ducking under a branch, "but I am learning so much here. Most days, I don't think about it until I go to bed. Then, I sometimes find it hard to sleep."

"Really?" I said, pulling Charcoal's head away from a lush tuft of grass.

"The avatar has a shutdown mode. It stimulates the sleep part of our brains and we pretty much just fall asleep instantly. I've never really had to go to sleep myself until now."

"Wow," I murmured. "That sounds awfully handy."

He leaned against a tree trunk, playing with Aubrie's lead in his hands. "Yes... and no. I find myself thinking about things at night. Working things out, making connections. I think it can be a useful time as long as it doesn't last all night."

I frowned at him. "You've stayed up all night before?"

"A few times. At the beginning," he admitted. "The first week here was very hard."

"Really? You didn't seem upset," I said. "Quiet, maybe, but not sad."

"No, no, I wasn't sad. Nervous. And sick. My stomach didn't really know what to do with food at first."

"Yeah, I bet that was pretty hard," I agreed.

CHAPTER 28

THUNDER

Not long after that conversation, Gabriel decided to go on a business trip.

"I've tried to delay it, but I can't any longer," my father sighed, running a hand through his dark hair. He was less pristine lately, a hint of scruffy beard dirtying his face.

"Why can't we come along, again?" I asked, rather put out that he was gallivanting off to Skykyle City without us. As if I wanted to stay at Angelus Quietum any more than I had to. Plus the idea of touring fancy restaurants and boutique stores in the big city with James sounded like a great time.

Gabriel squeezed my shoulder in apology. "No, this is politics and the two of you would just be bored. I can't be chaperoning you in the city while I'm trying to meet with Senators."

"What is it you are meeting about?" James narrowed his eyes.

"Nope, sorry. I actually can't talk about it," Dad said with a rueful shake of his head. "But trust me when I say, I'd much rather be here."

James scowled up at my father, his slim arms folded across his chest. I think he meant to look serious and intimating, but the two inch height difference and his extremely obvious youth made it ineffective.

"Give me your word this meeting doesn't impact Terran interests," James demanded.

Gabriel raised an eyebrow, but he answered the diplomat with more patience than I would have. "No, no, it has nothing to do with... well... perhaps a little. It's complicated. Look, you have my word that Terran interests will not be harmed by this meeting. Okay? Can we leave it at that?"

James mulled this over, eyes still narrowed in suspicion. "That's the best I'm going to get, isn't it?"

"Yep." My father attempted his usual impish grin but just ended up looking sad. "So you might as well take it."

"Okay," James nodded. "How long will you be gone?"

"Two days. Three at the longest. I've told Carol to keep her ear open to you just in case you need anything or there's an emergency," Dad said, laying a kiss on my forehead.

"Stella and Grandma Gloria are only an implant tap away," I reminded him, giving him my best reassuring smile. I hadn't really wanted to admit his deterioration to myself until recently. Now, guilt was squirming in my stomach. I'd been so preoccupied with James lately, I really hadn't paid attention to my father.

So, the next day, Gabriel cleaned himself up better than he had in weeks, packed a bag and teleported off to Skykyle City. James and I said goodbye to him in the living room. After he'd faded from the room, we turned to each other.

"Any ideas on how to use the next sixty hours?" I asked, raising an eyebrow at James.

"It's been really warm lately. Maybe a swim?"

I smiled in agreement and the two of us set off to find swimsuits. We played and splashed and shrieked in the lake just like any typical teenagers, I imagine. I remember the sun baking my skin and the water being deliciously cool. James seemed stronger and much more tan than he had been when he first came to us. He'd been learning the basics of swimming lately and I happily demonstrated a few new strokes for him before we retired to sunbathe between the willow trees.

"Your chores will not do themselves," Stella reminded me sternly after we'd been laying about for a while.

"Fine," I grumbled, tapping my implant to shut off her annoying alarm. "Come on," I said to James. "Our babysitter says fun time is over. We've got to feed the chickens and horses."

Dutifully, the two of us headed inside to find fresh clothes.

Once the chores were done, we both realized we hadn't eaten anything since breakfast and went hunting for some food. Discovering leftovers in the cold box, we made a neat meal before settling into the living room to read and do homework. James was forever making lists and charts of political influence, as if committing all the relationships to memory would somehow make him immune to their machinations once he was making the rounds of the Senate. I, on the other hand, had a book review to write for my language course. I was mostly through the novel I selected and it wasn't half bad. Of course, without my father there, we cuddled up on the couch. I leaned back against James' slim chest while he used my shoulder as a rest for his memory pad. I was so comfortable that, when I found myself dozing off, I decided a nap wasn't a half-bad idea.

"Gracie?" I woke from a dead sleep to a dark house and the sound of my name being whispered with urgency into my ear. "Gracie, wake up."

"Sorry," I muttered, leaning forward to let James slide out from under me. I assumed he had to use the restroom or relieve pressure on a pinned limb.

"You didn't hear that?" he hissed, pulling me back against him. His grip held enough anxious tension to rouse me from the last of my sleep fog.

"Hear what?" I whispered back, eyes darting around the room. It was utterly dark; the kind that settles in without notice when no one is awake to turn on the lights. Wan, green light illuminated the far wall by the front door, but otherwise everything was silent and the color of pitch.

With a sudden flash, the room lit up as bright as day. Following on its heels, the violent cymbal crash of thunder rattled the house. James jumped and let out a little yelp, his body shaking under mine as he clung to my shoulders in terror.

"Relax." I turned so I could see his face. The odd green light of the storm outside cast his rounded, mortal features in stark contrast. "It's just thunder. We're safe enough inside the house."

"Thunder," he echoed, his wide-eyed expression beginning to ease at my calm reassurance, "you mean, like an electrical storm? I didn't think we were close enough to the equator to have them here."

"We get one from time to time. Down on Hal, they happen almost every evening. But at Angelus Quietum it's more like once or twice a year."

My explanation concluded aptly with another peal of thunder. We both startled and James' arms wrapped around me a little more tightly, but this time he didn't cry out. I chuckled softly and pressed my cheek to the center of his chest. I could hear his heart beating rapidly and slid my arms around his waist to give him a reassuring squeeze.

"I've read about electric storms, of course," he said, his voice a little calmer. "But I never realized just how loud they really were. That last one shook the whole farm."

"It was pretty good," I agreed. At almost that exact moment, the clouds gave way and the distinctive, all-encompassing rush of heavy rain surrounded the house.

James glanced around the room, blue eyes washed a muddy green in the storm's light. "What's that?" he asked softly.

"Come on." I rolled to my feet and offered him a hand. "I'll show you."

With an apprehensive expression, he took my hand and let me pull him to his feet. I offered him a smile as I led him to the front door and put my hand to the door plate. It slid open to a wave of warm, wet air and the distinctive song of rain on grass and gutter. James took a deep breath of the fresh, wet-soil scented air and let his eyes fall shut.

"Of course, it's rain," he murmured, leaning against the doorway. "It's beautiful."

I joined him, looking over the front lawn, with its carefully cut grass and winding stone walk out to the fence's tidy white gate. The trees bowed their leafy crowns to the weight of the water, fat droplets rolling downward towards the stream that divided our farm from Carol's.

"Yeah, it is," I agreed, tucking an arm around James' waist. He glanced down at me, his expression somewhere between cautious and affectionate. Then, as if he'd come to a decision, his smile deepened and he lifted his arm, allowing me to rest the length of my body against his. We weren't that far off in height, my shoulder tucking neatly under his. His hand came to rest warmly against the curve of my hip.

Every part of me felt alive in that moment. Listening to the wind swell about the house and toss sheets of driving rain against its walls, while James and I stayed sheltered in each other's arms, was safe and companionable in a way I'd never experienced before. I pressed my cheek to his shoulder and smelled the warm rain mixing with the scent of his body as we rested in the doorway.

"I've never smelled rain before," he said softly. I wasn't sure what emotion was in his expression as he looked out into the storm, but I wanted to press my lips to his so badly it was almost a physical pain. "I guess it was always too cold up in Terra Nova. But here, it smells like green, growing things."

My free hand strayed up to the swell of his chest, drawing his attention back to me. His faded blue eyes met my saturated ones and his gaze tingled all the way down my spine.

"Come on," I whispered. I could hardly speak past the eager and unfamiliar emotions building in my chest. "I know the best place to watch a storm."

James raised a playful eyebrow and my face split with an idiotic grin. My heart hammering in my chest, I grabbed his hand again and all but dragged him behind me as I charged through the house. Barely pausing to press my hand to the back door plate, I dashed out onto the rain-soaked porch. James made a noise that was half distress and half amusement, lifting a hand to protect his head. The two of us dashed through the pelting wet, our feet dodging puddles in the hard-packed dirt of the chicken yard. A few breathless moments and we were in the horse-tinged shelter of the barn.

"Come on," I said again, leading the way to the loft ladder.

"Where are we going?" The grin on his face said he didn't mind our little adventure.

With a fierce, mischievous laugh, I finished climbing the ladder and turned back to offer him a hand up.

The sound of the rain on the solar-paneled roof echoed loudly up here. It filled the space with a dull roar that made the low-ceilinged hay loft cozy and warm.

James took my hand and I had little trouble pulling him up the last few steps. Still holding his hand, I led the way across the tiny space and pushed open the round window at the end of the loft. Instantly, the storm's damp wind rushed over me, pushing my red curls back from my face like silken flames.

"Here," I sighed, relinquishing James' hand to lean in the curved window ledge. "This is my favorite spot when the rains come."

The young diplomat glanced around the little loft, a look of relaxed curiosity on his face. His hair was now long enough to fall across his forehead, softening his looks and making him less "other."

"It is cozy," he agreed, settling himself next to me in the window. Usually I was the one who pushed the boundaries of our physical space. This time, he'd come closer of his own volition and he'd left so little room between us that I could feel his body heat adding to the thunderstorm's muggy atmosphere.

As if on cue, a flash and peal of thunder made the rafters tremble. Suddenly, there wasn't any room between us at all as James startled and leaned into me, his shoulder pressing against mine.

"It's just hot air and cold air having an argument," I told him, quoting my grandfather's favorite explanation of severe weather. "Nothing to worry about."

James took a deep breath and gave me a sidelong glance. "You're really not afraid of much, are you?"

"Nope. I'm Gabriel Usuriel's daughter and a third-gen firebird. What do I have to be scared of?"

James' narrowed eyes were softened by the bemused smile on his lips. "There must be something. I mean, everyone has that one thing that keeps them up at night." He nudged my shoulders with his.

"Hmmmm," I murmured as I leaned in the window frame and considered his question a little more seriously. "Well..."

"Well, what?"

I caught myself gnawing on my finger. I quickly took it out of my mouth and folded my hands firmly on the window sill in front of me.

"There are a few things," I admitted finally, my voice just loud enough to be heard over the murmuring rush of the rain. "Mostly, I'm afraid I'll never get a chance to leave and live my own life; that I'll be trapped here under my father's thumb for the rest of my existence."

James considered that, his face lifted to the gentle breeze still flowing in from the storm. "That's not quite what I meant. What you're talking about is what my father calls *libertas libidine*."

"*Libertas libidine?*"

"It's something all teenagers go through. A desire to travel, see the world. You know, escape from their family and start their adult life."

"Oh," I said, feeling a little stupid. "Did you feel that way about your family before you left?"

"Of course," James replied with a laugh. The smile he gave me lit up his lopsided, mortal features into something genuinely handsome. I found myself returning it despite my gaff. There was something about James that simultaneously made me awkward and yet strangely at ease in his presence. "I mean, not as bad as some people get. I was never angry or defiant with my parents the way my friend Dario was. But," he spread his hands and indicated Angelus Quietum with an expansive gesture, "obviously, I wanted to see more of the world than just Terra Nova!"

"You're so lucky," I groaned, leaning my chin on my palm as I turned back to the rain. "Getting to take off halfway across the globe without your parents. And you'll go to University soon, too."

"Well, you could go to University in a year or two, right?" he said, tilting his head at me.

"I guess," I said slowly. "Dad and I have never really talked about it. I'm pretty sure he thinks I'm still six."

James chuckled. "He is pretty protective of you," he agreed. With that statement, he leaned away from me and

I had a sinking feeling this conversation might not head in the direction I wanted it to if I didn't say something now.

"Dad doesn't have to know about... anything that happens between us." I laid a gentle hand on his arm. "I mean, I won't tell if you won't."

James glanced up at me again, nervousness in his faded blue eyes. "He's in my head for lessons, Gracie. I can keep some things from him, but... strong emotions are the hardest to shield."

I swallowed hard and took my courage in both hands. "Does that mean you have some strong emotions for me?"

We'd turned to face each other now. My hand hadn't moved from his arm, but I could feel the rapid rise and fall of his chest as if he were having a hard time catching his breath. My own heart was pounding like the rain outside.

"Do you really have to ask that question, Gracie?" He said it so softly I hardly heard him. Then, he reached up and brushed the slightly damp curls from where they clung to my cheek. His fingertips were warm and I felt them all the way into the pit of my stomach. He gazed into my eyes, a small frown creasing his face.

"You're so head blind. It's almost a shame. Anyone else, I would be able to share this feeling with, but you... you really will never know just how incredible it feels just to do this." His thumb traced the edge of my jaw before brushing gently down the skin of my neck. Heat rose in my cheeks and I knew they'd be as flaming as my hair soon. For once, I didn't care.

"I think I might have a tiny idea," I breathed. "Telepathy be damned, I know it makes me really want to do this."

Without giving him a chance to react, I took his face in both my hands and closed the space between us in a rush.

I'd never kissed anyone before. Not in a romantic way, anyway. It was quick and artless, but even so it sent a rush of warmth through my whole body that begged for more. When I pulled away, James just stared at me a moment with wide, blue eyes. Then, a tiny smile tilted up the corner of his mouth and his hands slid over mine.

"Well, he can't be too angry if you started it, right?" There was still a note of nervousness in his voice, but when I figured out what he was referring to, I actually laughed.

"You mean Dad?" I chuckled. "Oh, come on. He won't care. I swear I don't know how I was ever born because the man acts like sex doesn't even exist."

"Yeah, well... you're his daughter. You're supposed to think that," James said, a knowing gleam in his eye. Then his expression became serious again and he leaned his forehead against mine. "But I do think, if he knows you wanted this, he won't be too angry. He'd give you the world wrapped up with a bow if you asked for it."

"I'll be content with another kiss."

That is what James gave me. And another. And quite a few more beyond that. By the time we came up for air, the topic of my father had completely left both of our minds and been replaced by the soft magic that is exploring a new partner for the first time.

I think it was me that unbuttoned his shirt first. Soon we were both stripped to the waist and curled up in a nest of soft, dry hay that smelled of sunlight and fresh, growing things. James himself reminded me of a warm day—his hair the soft yellow rays of morning sun and his eyes the color of a midday sky. His hands slid over my skin like a gentle breeze before tangling in my hair, his lips raining kisses that I soaked up like the dusty soil. Over our heads, the storm raged on, but in James' arms I was safe and warm.

The sun set and we eventually retreated back to the house in search of food. After a simple meal of sandwiches, I lit the fireplace and we curled up together in its soft glow. We fell asleep in each other's arms, drifting off into dreams that couldn't hope to match the perfection of that day.

CHAPTER 29

AN UNSETTLING DREAM

I rarely remember my dreams but, like the night I dreamed of my mother's death, this one stuck with me.

My father stood in a large, semi-dark room. There were stains on the wall despite the grandeur of the architecture. Gabriel was dressed neatly in a white shirt and black slacks. Despite his Usuriel blank face, there was bone-deep pain in his deep, blue eyes.

"Adora," he said, her name a caress.

"You came," she whispered, her face bleeding out of the dark. "I was afraid they would set you against me."

Adora wasn't the carefree, young, twenty-something I'd met with Ariel. Like her brother, she hadn't aged physically past the twenty-five mark. Her angular face and figure remained borderline androgynous, but something in the hollows of her cheeks now held that timeless quality I was beginning to identify as the youthfully ancient. While she'd seemed a little unbalanced when I first met her, there was now something wild and terrible in her gaze. It only took a glance and, as you know things in dreams, I knew she'd gone truly mad.

"Me? Against you? My love, how can you think it?" My father's tongue was as smooth as ever. He walked closer to her and my dream perspective shifted with him. She was half-crouched over something, perhaps a bed of some sort. There was something disturbing about the way she hovered over it and something even more disturbing about the figure that lay upon it. My eyes didn't want to grasp what lay in filth and shadow. Instead, my dream sense told me it was too dreadful to look upon and—despite being unable to identify why—the bed filled me with horror.

"Come, sit with me," Gabriel said. "I've brought you a gift."

"A gift?"

He nodded and offered her a gentle smile that actually reached his eyes. It made his perfect features approachable. "Yes, little sister, a gift. Come sit with me."

Slowly, Adora unwound herself from her unnatural position and came to join Gabriel at a small table. She walked with the beyond-smooth Usuriel grace, her head held high even though her long, white dress was stained in dark splatters. She'd adopted a strange hairstyle—shaved on one side and a pointed, shoulder-length cut on the other. It made her perfect features seem lopsided and, when combined with her pure white coloring and unusual build, it reinforced my impression of madness.

"Do you remember when you used to complain that I wouldn't have a drink with you?" My father chuckled. It sounded so natural and yet to my ears it seemed sadder than a sob. He'd produced a bottle of red wine and two long stemmed glasses which he was filling.

"We have remedied that over the years," Adora said with a bit of satisfaction in her voice. "Though I will always gladly share a drink with my brother."

"I thought you might," Gabriel replied and handed her a glass. With a smile, she took it and waited while he picked up his own.

"To us," she said, lifting the glass, "the most perfect sibling pair Cybele shall ever see."

"To us," my father echoed and raised his own glass.

There was the slightest of pauses as Adora regarded him through half-lidded eyes. Gabriel shrugged and took a healthy sip from his glass. His face lit in a smile and he raised an eyebrow.

"It's not as good as Earth vintages yet, but not bad. I've come to enjoy the Landing vineyards."

Adora's face also brightened and she downed her glass in two large gulps. My father watched her with sad eyes before finishing his own glass and setting it down next to the bottle.

"I knew you'd see things clearly eventually," Adora said. "I'm sure Darius will welcome your help in the cause." She gestured to the shadowy bed and that same horror crawled up my spine.

Gabriel's face had returned to careful blankness, but I thought I saw a flicker of his own disgust.

The shatter of glass drew my attention back to Adora. One pale hand had gone to her stomach while the other wrapped around her long, slender neck. Her pale, blue eyes searched my father's face.

"What have you done?" she gasped.

Gabriel shut his eyes and swayed before steadying himself against the table. Then, in two quick steps, he closed the gap between them and caught his sister deftly before she hit the ground.

"It's time, Adora," he whispered to her. "We've been here a long time. Too long."

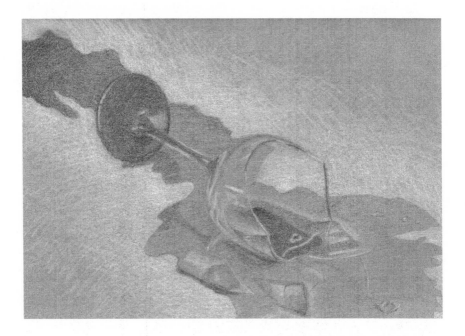

The madness rose in her eyes and the blue susurrus of her power sang through the room. I heard the rattle of furnishings as her energy passed over them.

"Darius!" There was a wet pop as something on the bed reacted to her mind's searching. I waited for the abomination to rise but nothing came to her aid.

Then, as if her waning strength also bled the madness from her mind, something much more lucid flooded her gaze. Her fingers shook as she reached up to touch the edge of Gabriel's face.

"Yes," she whispered. "Too long. Especially for you... or perhaps especially for me." Her voice was getting thick, her breathing uneven. "It... yes... I think... it is time."

Slowly, Gabriel lowered her to the floor. My heart clenched as I watched his strong shoulders slump and his breathing began to take on the same erratic quality of his sister's.

"Kiss me," Adora whispered as if she could barely move the air past her lips. "One... last time."

Gabriel obeyed her, pressing his lips to her forehead as she clutched at his shoulders. For a moment they looked rather beautiful together, his black waves mingling with her straight, white strands. Then he pulled away from her and looked down into her still face.

A sob escaped him then. It shook his whole frame and he was grief—bent and broken over his sister's lifeless body. The sound of his sorrow echoed in the huge, ruined hall as he gently closed Adora's sightless eyes. Then the poison overtook him and he sank to the floor, limbs twined with Adora's as he went still.

"Daddy!"

My shout was involuntary. It sprang from the core of my being where I was still that timid, abandoned six-year-old girl. It bubbled up from another nightmare with a woman in a white dress who never came back. It came from that very center where my flames rested, waiting for me to loosen my grip and let them flow outwards, along my skin...

And then...

I had form. I was no longer just a disembodied spectator. I was myself, from my curly red hair to my battered running shoes, I was there.

The stench of the ruined hall flooded me with a mixture of blood, decay, and sewer. I suppressed a gag reflex as I ran to the fallen pair.

My father had slumped onto his side next to Adora, dark hair covering his face. I pulled him onto his back and searched his neck for a pulse. It was there, slow and steady as the clockwork heart in his chest that just didn't know how to die. When I pushed his hair away from his face, however, it was a dreadful shade of gray and his lips were beginning to turn blue. If he didn't take a breath soon...

"Come on, you ornery son of a bitch," I cursed at him. "Sorry, Grandma Gloria."

I tilted his head back and tried to remember his own lessons in rescue breathing. Finally, I gave up trying to remember and figured that any air was better than none. I covered his mouth with my own and watched his chest rise with my exhalation. Buoyed by my success, I paused, then gave him another. I dared a glance at his face. The gray had eased into something merely pale and his lips were once again a touch more pink than his skin tone. However, even as I watched, the progress began to reverse itself and his chest showed no signs of rising on its own.

"Stay with me, Dad," I murmured and bent to the task of keeping him alive long enough for the poison to run its course. How long it took, I'm not sure. What can be certain in dreams? But it seemed like a long time that I paced his breathing against mine. Finally, he gasped and a shudder went through his whole body. I rolled him onto his side just in time for him to bring up the wine, like a puddle of blood that spread about Adora's head.

I leaned back on my heels and watched as color crept into his cheeks. His chest rose and fell gently on its own.

"Liv," he whispered in his sleep. "Liv... forgive me..."

The room began to fade around me in streaks of color. Ribbons of red and orange flame flickered past my gaze, obscuring the filth and ruin of my father and his sister. Their patterns shifted, flickering and popping before coalescing into a face—a face that was both intimately familiar and yet also incredibly unsettling.

"Gracie," Ariel murmured my name through lips that danced like fire. "Come back to the present. Our father needs you."

I tried to take a breath to protest that I'd just finished saving him, but my lungs burned with suddenly intense heat. My skin felt raw and painful, as if it were blistering. Ariel's smoldering green eyes expanded, larger and larger, until they were huge emerald pits into which I fell helplessly, my fingers grasping at thin air in a vain attempt to prevent the inevitable.

Icy chill.

I plunged down, deep, into the dark. The fires quenched. I drifted in stunned relief.

Thick wet.

The weight of water surrounding my limbs was suddenly crushing. I opened my mouth to draw breath and there was only cold, unforgiving liquid flooding past my lips. Fear shot through my gut and I closed my mouth again, knowing the price of pulling water into my burning lungs.

Trying hard not to panic, I cast about for a glimpse of light that might give me a hint of the surface's direction. Nothing but murky brown water met my gaze. Choking, I'd almost given up when a small bubble of air escaped my lips. Gently it floated away towards my left arm. Turning, I tracked its path and made out a tiny glimpse of green-tinted light. Hope swelled in my breast and I kicked with all my might in that direction.

My head broke the surface and I gulped in air. The air was even colder and there was no relief from the wet. Raindrops pelted my skin, causing the surface of the water to splash and ripple around me. Coughing, I pushed my sodden curls away from my face. I looked around, trying to get a sense of where I might be.

"Dad?" I called out, craning my neck to get a glimpse of the shore. The water—still as bathwater when I first arrived—now traveled with a current that was getting swifter by the moment. I was borne downstream at a frightful pace, tree limbs and odd bits of unidentifiable debris drifting past me too rapidly for my searching fingers to grab hold.

"James? Dad!" I called again. There was still no answer.

Without warning, I slammed into a wall. With a shriek I tried to cling to the solid object that blocked my way, yet it had no substantial form. I got an impression of warmth and a faintly blue glow before I was sucked back under the water by the thwarted current.

The water spun me ruthlessly, dislocating any sense of time or direction. Hard, sharp objects tore at my face and arms. I thrashed about, trying to protect my head while also fighting my way back to the surface.

Just as I thought the water was going to have its way with me, I surfaced again with a spluttering gasp. The current still pulled me forward, but this time I could see the barrier before I hit it. Despite my sodden state, the hair on the back of my neck rose and I knew the wall for what it was.

"Psi," I panted, using all of my strength to fight the undertow. I was a good swimmer, having spent many a warm day playing in Lake Angelus. Briefly my swift strokes kept me a short distance from the barrier but the current was relentless. I wasn't going to last long.

Shouts drifted up to me and I blinked through the spray. It sounded like men working—nothing panicked but instead steady, careful directions. Pausing my doomed efforts, I craned my neck over my shoulder to peer over the edge of the mostly-transparent wall.

"Dad?" I murmured. It was so brief I almost doubted my senses. Yet Gabriel was the one person I knew better than I knew my own reflection. The angle of his shoulders, the fall of his dark waves, the exacting grace of his steps—it could be no one else.

I also knew his voice.

"We can't hold this forever!"

"We need more time for the evacuations!" The impatient answer sounded thin compared to my father's rich tenor. "There are only so many teleporters available and the whole city will be underwater if the dam goes!"

"Get some shuttles out here then!" I could hear the strain in Dad's voice. "The Family can only do so much! What's the point of having tech if you only rely on our psi?"

That was the last I saw or heard, however. With a last little gasp of fear, I lost my fight with the swift waters. They pulled me down, deep into the churning depths.

But this time I wasn't alone.

Ariel's face bloomed from the dark like a fiery phantom. Exhausted and light-headed from lack of oxygen, I had little room for fear as she rushed towards me. Instead, I welcomed the warmth that pulsed through my breast when her glowing skin met mine.

"Pull on the fire, little sister. Time to go home. You know what to do," she murmured in my mind.

Too tired to protest, I obeyed.

CHAPTER 30

WARNINGS

"Gracie?"

The voice wasn't my father's, but it was familiar. I blinked, my eyelids gritty as if full of sand.

"James?" I muttered, his face coming into focus. My young diplomat-in-training offered me a lopsided smile and squeezed my arm.

"You were having a nightmare," he said, lending me the steady weight of his shoulder to pull myself into a sitting position.

"A nightmare," I echoed, feeling breathless and disoriented. I was still sitting on the rug by the fire where James and I had fallen asleep last night. That gentle contentedness seemed like a lifetime ago. I turned back to James. His hair was damp and he'd changed into a fresh outfit. "What time is it?"

"Oh eight hundred," James replied cheerfully. "I woke up early, but figured you probably wanted to sleep in. I was about to make some breakfast. Can I get you anything?"

While James was talking, my gaze drifted to the hall doorway. There, a softly glowing woman stood with her arms crossed. Scowling, Ariel tilted her head at me as if asking what I was still hanging about on the floor for.

The end of the dream came flooding back to me and I jumped to my feet.

"No time! Dad needs our help!"

"What?" James blinked at me as if I'd lost my mind. "Gabriel? He's not supposed to be back for another two days..."

I cut him off with a snarl and a finger to my lips. "Shhhh! Stella? Stella!"

"Yes, Gracie?" The AI's elegant form materialized in the center of the room.

"Link up to the Net. Tell me if there are any flood watches or warnings in effect," I said.

Stella gave one of her famous pauses, her entire body freezing in a look of inquisitive concern. Then, with a flourish of one hand, she pulled a map from thin air and projected it on the back wall.

"Unusually heavy rainfall has occurred for the past week in the section indicated in orange," she said. "As a result, there is currently a flood warning for Landing and the general University area. That area is indicated in red."

I stepped closer to the map. I wasn't surprised to see Angelus Quietum in the orange area. The lake was probably over its banks after the storms last night. I knew Lake Angelus drained towards Landing, however, and so did several of the other waterways in that orange patch.

James cleared his throat. "Your dad is in Skykyle, all the way up here," he said, pointing to the map. "That's North—upstream and in a completely different river system—from the University. He's perfectly safe."

I shook my head. "That doesn't matter. If there's an emergency in the Provinces, who do you think they'll call? The mortal watch? What are they going to do about a flood?"

James shrugged. "Evacuate the area?"

"That won't save a dam from bursting," I muttered, running a finger along a blue vein of the Drexil River. The Landing Reservoir was just a little way down the river from Lake Angelus. It was fed by both the larger lake and the runoff from the western side of the Galloway Mountains which were also currently in the orange zone. The dam in my dream was likely the little dot labeled the Mystra Galloway Hydroelectric Plant on Stella's map. It was right on the edge of the darkest red patch.

"A dam?" James seemed to finally follow my logic. His face paled a shade as he looked at where my fingertip had come to rest. "Fates, you think the Galloway Dam might fail? That thing is huge. Have you ever seen holos of it? All of Landing and the University would be flooded."

I nodded grimly. "Exactly. Which is why Dad will be there when it starts to fail."

"I... wait... stop. Stella, has there been any flooding reported yet, or is this just a warning still?" James asked the AI.

"Minor reports at the University have been received," she replied, cocking her head as if listening to something we couldn't hear. "However, no one has observed any major structural damage."

"There," James said with great finality as if this settled the matter. "See? You're getting all worked up over something that hasn't happened." One gentle hand found my shoulder. "Is this about your nightmare?"

I took a steadying breath. Maybe I was overreacting. I glanced over my shoulder at where Ariel had been standing. Sure enough, her bright green eyes were still boring into mine.

"I... I think it was more than a nightmare," I said softly.

James frowned, a little crease of concern forming over his blond eyebrows. "What do you mean?"

I shook my head slowly, unsure what I wanted to tell him. I'd been keeping Ariel and my time travel a secret for so long it felt almost impossible to put any of it into words.

"Sometimes," I said slowly, after a long, pregnant pause, "sometimes I have... visions. It's like I can see things from other times or places. I know it... it probably sounds crazy but..."

"No," James said, rubbing my shoulder. "It doesn't. You're an Usuriel—Gabriel Usuriel's daughter at that. It would actually surprise me more if you didn't have a few undiscovered talents floating around."

I took a deep breath and felt strangely lighter, as if the weight of my secret had been wrapped tightly around my chest for years. Oddly enough, speaking it aloud seemed to loosen its constrictive grip.

"Thanks," I murmured. James raised a questioning eyebrow. I smiled. "For believing me."

"Of course," he replied with a shrug. "Does Gabriel know about your visions?"

"Ummm... a bit," I said thoughtfully. "He knows I've had at least one. I don't know if he realizes that I still have them from time to time."

James nodded. "Okay. So what about this one? What makes you think this dream was a vision?"

I glanced guiltily at Ariel. She lifted an eyebrow as if daring me to say her name. I swallowed hard.

"Ahhhh... it was really vivid. And it had to do with my flames. I called on them, which is usually a sign that I'm dealing with some kind of psi."

The ghost shook her head at me. Then, with one finger she pointed to the little implant on the side of her neck. I got her hint. We were running out of time.

"That makes sense," James allowed. "So what happened in the dream? You said there was a flood?"

There were also Adora, poison, and strange rotting corpses, my subconscious filled in. I decided the first part of my dream wasn't really relevant, not to mention way more disturbing than I felt able to deal with at the moment. Perhaps it hadn't even been literal—more of a way that my subconscious could tell me that my father was in mortal danger. Unsure if this was a comforting idea or not, it nonetheless made me feel steadier.

"At first it was just dark, murky water," I said, "but then it started moving really fast and there were trees and stuff floating in it."

"That is an accurate description of flood waters," Stella's voice was even and grounding. I gave her a grateful smile.

"Then I ran into some kind of psi-wall. I think it was Dad's because I could hear him way down below me talking to some mortals, telling them to hurry up with evacuations because he wouldn't be able to hold the water too much longer."

James looked thoughtful as he met my gaze. "Did you see anything else?"

"No. I got sucked under the water and..." I forced myself not to look in Ariel's direction. "Then the dream ended."

James took a deep breath, his eyes troubled and distant. "Okay. So, you're convinced this was a premonition. Which means there currently is—or will be—a dangerous flood that causes damage to a dam. Gabriel will be called in to help while the mortals evacuate. That all makes sense," he gestured to the map with its bright orange and red patches. "But how does that affect us? I mean, neither of us is a telekinetic or a teleporter. So how can we do anything but get in the way?"

"I... I'm not sure." I stammered, partly because I wasn't sure how to answer and partly because Ariel had chosen that moment to swoop in my direction. Her expression told me she found this whole conversation pointless and she wasn't going to put up with us wasting any more time. With one glowing hand, she waved demandingly in front of my face before pointing sharply out the back door.

"But I think I have an idea. Come on," I called to James as I followed Ariel's now-charging transparent figure out into the chicken yard.

"Wait! Gracie? What kind of idea?" James asked, obviously thrown by my rapid change of direction. He followed after us, which hopefully meant he didn't think I was completely crazy.

We trotted through the yard and over to the side of the stable where James and I had our tryst just hours earlier. The mood was completely different from the playful sensuality of last evening's adventure, however. Though it was no longer raining, thunder rumbled in the distance and I felt the hum of electricity along my skin. The storm had quieted, but it wasn't over.

I followed Ariel's glowing figure to the wall, where she pointed meaningfully at a barely visible panel in the siding.

"The *Hawk*," I murmured, comprehension dawning. Without Gabriel's teleportation, I usually thought of myself as stranded at Angelus Quietum, but there were methods of travel that didn't require psi. I quickly followed my sister's advice and pressed my hand to the hidden sensor. Instantly, a deep rumble shook the ground beneath our feet as the ancient shuttle rose up from its subterranean bunker.

"The shuttle?" James asked, a bit out of breath and looking more confused than ever.

"If we move quickly, we can warn them," I said. "Let people at Landing know that a flood is coming and they have to get out of the way!"

James blinked at me and I could almost see him composing a diplomatic answer in his head. "So, your plan is to fly down to Landing and start shoving people into an antique shuttle we've stolen from your father?"

Well, when he put it that way...

"And what are you going to tell them, exactly?" he continued, his eyes kind despite the slight smirk that was threatening to take over his mouth. "You had a dream and it told you there was going to be a catastrophic flood? I know you're an Usuriel, Gracie, so psi is normal to you. But most mortals aren't used to taking their dreams quite this seriously."

"I know!" I snapped, my flames rising up to flicker about my shoulders. For a moment it was all I could do to keep them from exploding into the space between us. "Why do you think I usually keep them to myself!"

James' expression fell and he raised a cautious hand. "I'm... I'm sorry. I think that came out wrong..."

"No," I snarled, turning and walking towards the *Hawk*'s translucent side through the now-settling dust of its arrival. "I understood you perfectly."

I pressed a hand to the door plate and heard the satisfying hiss of pressurized air releasing. I glanced over my shoulder at James, still hesitating by the barn door.

"No one said you had to come!" I raised my voice over another ominous rumble of thunder. "If you think I'm crazy, you can just wait here!"

I didn't stay to see what his response would be. The door to the shuttle was open now and I wasted no time climbing up into the cockpit. I flung myself into the pilot's seat so violently that its aged springs creaked in protest. With a single tap, I synced my implant to the shuttle's computer. My fingers flew over the console, initiating the navigation system and warming up the engines.

On the edge of my vision, a blond figure came to stand at my shoulder. James cleared his throat, but I ignored him as I laid in a flight path. Finally, the engines making every-thing vibrate with a mechanistic hum, I turned my head the tiniest bit in his direction.

"Probably want to go have a seat," I all but shouted over the whine. "She might be old, but her engines still have a kick."

I almost startled as his hand found my shoulder and gave it a squeeze. Without another word, he settled himself on the bench behind the empty psi-pilot's chair. I took it for what it was—a wordless apology for his tactless comment. A small smile tilted up the corner of my lips and my flames settled back down into my chest with a little flutter.

"Okay," I breathed, more to myself and the shuttle than James. "Let's see if I remember how to do this."

My fingers slid over the accelerator, caressing the glow-ing strip that controlled the engine's pitch. As I'd predicted, the *Hawk* was eager for liftoff. Within moments, the little shuttle had cleared the barnyard and we were skimming smoothly over Lake Angelus.

Behind me, James let out a whoop of high spirits and I couldn't help but echo his enthusiasm with a nervous gig-gle. Then the mountains came rushing at us and all of my attention was taken with adjusting for the altitude and wind shear.

It got a little bumpy, I will admit. It was only my second time flying the *Hawk*, the first without my father's steady-ing hand. I felt this acutely as I pulled up a map of the con-tinent and began plugging in coordinates for Landing. As my thoughts turned to Gabriel, my high spirits faded and the deep pit of fear from my dream reached up from my empty chest.

A wine glass fell from limp, pale fingers.

Swirling, churning waters sucked me under their icy, irresistible waves.

"Hurry up! I can only hold the water for so long!"

I could hear his voice as clearly as if he were in the cabin with me.

"I'm coming, Dad," I murmured and put the engines to max.

CHAPTER 31

FLIGHT

Despite its easy beginning, our flight to Landing was anything but smooth. Compared to this, my flight with Dad looked absolutely flawless. First off, without the psi-interface engaged, the shuttle was slower and the computer more exacting in its need for explicit direction.

Then, there was the little factor of the weather.

Wind and rain were violent pieces of the landscape. This storm was no afternoon squall. No, it was a massive system that stretched across the whole southern half of the continent. Fortunately we were in a calm when we made our ascent at Angelus Quietum. As James and I approached Landing, that rapidly changed.

"Hang on!" I called to James as the *Hawk* plummeted a dozen meters, caught in a powerful downdraft that rocked the shuttle's alloy frame. The crash of thunder echoed a brilliant flash of lightning that left floating lines behind to obscure my vision.

"Gracie!" His voice cracked on my name as the shuttle bucked and rocked violently despite my efforts to adjust for wind shear.

"I'm doing my best!" I snapped, though I doubt he heard me over the storm's anger. I fought to read the altitude and speed displays as the console jumped and vibrated. A particularly savage jolt and my hand came down on the wrong sensor, causing us to pitch dangerously to the left. With a little shriek, I scrambled to fix my mistake.

"Take it easy." James' voice was surprisingly calm in my ear. I took a ragged breath to tell him I didn't have time to calm down. Then I realized that he'd knelt down at my side and was rapidly tapping through screens. To my shock and awe, the little shuttle stabilized.

"Thanks," I murmured, my heart beating a little less frantically against my ribs. Maybe I wasn't going to get both of us killed after all.

"No problem." James was much easier to hear when the whole shuttle wasn't trying to rattle itself apart. Not to mention the closer proximity. He glanced up at me from a few inches away and my face heated up. "Pay attention to our heading," he told me with a nudge of one elbow. "I'm just making sure the stabilizers stay ahead of the wind. You're actually telling this thing where to go."

"Right," I said, quickly turning back to the controls. There will be time for you later, I told my libido firmly. "Let's get to Landing."

The *Hawk* was much easier to control between the two of us. There were a few more scary moments, but the rest of our trip went somewhat smoothly.

"Down there!" James called, pointing through the plexglass front of the shuttle. "There's the dam!"

James hadn't been kidding when he said the dam was huge. Below us, the swollen reservoir and rolling foothills of the Galloway Mountains dropped away and the massive, gray concrete wall of the Mystra Blackmon Hydroelectric Plant filled our field of vision. The change in air currents made the *Hawk* shudder and drop before James found the proper angles for the stabilizing thrusters.

True to Stella's sources, the dam seemed to be holding for the moment. Large openings mid-way down its side spilled huge amounts of water into the swollen river below, but I didn't see any cracks in the broad expanse of concrete above them so I assumed they were normal functions of the hydro-electric plant.

"Maybe it will hold after all," I murmured aloud, adjusting course to send the *Hawk* in a loop over the huge structure. I was still having a hard time wrapping my mind around the scale of the dam. It was easily over two hundred meters tall with a paved walkway across its top wide enough to land the shuttle. Several covered observation stations perched like spikes upon the top edge of the structure, giving it a crown-like appearance. A figure dressed in dark clothes hurried out from one station. They hunched against the flood water's spray, but the driving rain had paused so I could see them fairly clearly.

"Is there... someone standing on the dam?" James sounded incredulous as he leaned around my shoulder.

"I think so." I tapped in a course that would bring us around for another pass.

"They must be spore tripping," he muttered in my ear as we swung around the dam in a wide arc. "That catwalk has to be slippery as ice. They're dead if they fall in those flood waters."

I nodded my agreement, too focused on keeping the shuttle on course to answer him. Finally, I got the *Hawk* around to the reservoir side of the structure and began a second approach.

"I'll see if I can get us a little closer," I said.

That was when we heard it—deep, low, and booming. At first I thought it was another rumble of thunder. However, the skies were less intense now, with patches of sunlight beginning to dapple through the greenish clouds. Also, the sound seemed to come from below and with a certain aquatic quality, as if the churning waters themselves were rippling with the acoustic vibration.

"Sweet Fate," James whispered and all breath left my lungs in a huff of terror.

A crack fissured upwards through the concrete of the wall. Compared to its incredible size, they were just tiny spider webs, but I knew up close they would be as long as my body. They were concentrated in one small area just to the left of the structure's center. The crack widened, sending off dangerous fingers directly below the tiny figure on the crosswalk.

"That whole section is about to collapse." James' voice was barely a whisper. "He's as good as dead."

That last statement seemed to trip a switch in my head. A surge of fire licked up in my chest and I readjusted the shuttle's trajectory.

"Hang on."

"Huh?" James barely had time for the startled exclamation before the *Hawk* swerved, taking us to the edge of the walkway. The tiny figure was now scrambling back towards the observation station. A two-meter section of the lip began to buckle directly behind them. Unless they developed telekinesis in a hurry, they were about to plunge into the churning flood below. The memory of icy water closing over my head momentarily felt so real, my breath stopped.

With a gasp, I came back to the present moment. "Stabilize us!" I shouted to James as I frantically reprogrammed coordinates. The ancient shuttle whined in protest, pulling alongside the observation station.

James flashed me panicked eyes before leaping to do as I said, engaging the thrusters that allowed the *Hawk* to hover mid-air.

"What are you doing?" he demanded as I put the engines in idle. I didn't respond as I dashed across the small space between the flight controls and the transparent door. The door plate warmed my hand and there was hiss of pressurized air. The plex-glass lifted away and the wind's warm breath blew my hair back from my face in a tangle of red curls. Another ominous crack echoed from the failing structure below me as I leaned out the opening.

"Grab my hand!" I called to the running figure, now only a few meters from the ship. My left hand extended out towards the crumbling walkway while I wrapped my right arm around a safety bar bolted to the door frame. I tried not to look down into the meter-wide gap between the shuttle and the edge of the dam.

The person running towards me, balancing precariously on the crumbling concrete, was a man. Rounded shoulders and a plump middle covered by a clinging, navy-blue rain slicker were about all the impression I got before his slimy hand found mine. His substantial weight barreled into me and the two of us landed with a wet thump on the *Hawk*'s alloy floor.

"Oof," I grunted involuntarily, my head just barely avoiding a painful impact with the metal. My back and buttocks sure felt the fall, however.

"Thank Fate," muttered the individual on top of me. His breath was disgustingly sweet, as if he ate nothing but candied peppermints. With a grunt and a groan he peeled his sopping wet bulk from atop me. Unsure if I should feel relief at my hair-brained plan's success or disgusted at my now-soaked clothing, I rolled to my feet before I even noticed our guest offering me his pudgy hand.

"I'm okay," I muttered, brushing myself off ineffectually.

"Gracie, we've got to move!" James shouted from the control panel. The engines began spinning back up at the same moment that the dam gave another boom.

A huge concrete chunk of the observation tower came loose. It teetered a moment before sliding past the *Hawk*'s tail so closely I could have touched its rough surface. It hit the flood waters half a dozen meters below us, casting water across the whole side of the shuttle.

I didn't wait to watch more. I didn't want to know how much danger my little rescue had truly put us in. Trying not to envision another house-sized section of concrete plunging towards our roof, I scrambled to the control panel. In addition to making careful, constant adjustments of the stabilizers, James already had the engines ready and waiting. Fingers clumsy with haste, I had to type in the coordinates twice before getting them right. I released a huge sigh of relief when the ancient shuttle obediently streaked away from the dam's side. Once we had some distance from the failing structure, we turned and resumed course towards Landing.

A great roar made me glance over my shoulder. Far below us, the flood waters tumbled through a gap where the observation tower used to be. Compared to the dam as a whole, the failed section wasn't large but I could see long cracks radiating out into other sections. That didn't bode well for how long the rest of the structure was going to hold.

The volume of water already pouring through the failed section was uprooting huge trees below and tossing them aside like so much kindling.

"Well now, that's a view!"

I almost startled at our guest's voice. I hadn't even noticed him standing at the plex-glass side of the shuttle. He'd closed the door and was leaning against the clear wall beside it. His soaked hood was pushed back to reveal a balding head and battered, black-rimmed spectacles. In one hand, he held a small device that glowed with artificial blue light. Slowly, he turned his head and saw me staring at him. His smile broadened and he lifted the device in my direction.

"Smile, Gracie Usuriel," he said, his middle-aged face creasing into a greasy grin. "You're a hero."

CHAPTER 32

GIVE US YOUR GOOD SIDE

"Is that a holo-recorder?" James asked. I was grateful for his steadying hand on my shoulder as he came to stand beside me.

"Ah yes, you have a handsome accomplice." The older gentleman prattled on as if he hadn't heard James' question at all. "What's your name, young man? The net is eager to hear who helped Gracie Usuriel rescue Joe Blackmon, everyone's favorite reporter for Skykyle News." His greasy smile widened and my revulsion grew. "Give us your good side. We're live."

That name jogged my memory. It wasn't a pleasant one. One eyebrow lowering, I opened my mouth to mention the time this idiot broke into my grandparents' house. I never got the chance to even begin the thought, however, because a different kind of wind picked up in the tiny cabin of the shuttle.

This wind wasn't related to the flooding disaster outside. No, its hair-raising, blue-tinged psi was incredibly familiar. Tears threatened as Gabriel materialized in a flash not unlike the lightning outside.

"Daddy," I gasped. All the horror and anguish of my dream seemed to squeeze in on my chest like a fist. It was everything I could do not to burst into sobs. My father took two powerful strides across the shuttle and snatched the little recording device from the reporter's hand.

"I'll take that," Dad snapped, "and I'll thank you not to film on my shuttle without permission."

"Wait, I'm an agent of the free press!" Reporter Joe protested hopelessly as my father closed his fist around the tiny alloy-and-plex recorder. It gave a muffled squeak and a weak spark of protest before being reduced to slightly smoking ruin.

"Write whatever you want," Gabriel growled, "but keep my daughter's face off of your filthy billboards."

My father handed the twisted wreckage of the holo-recorder back to the reporter. Joe looked as if he'd taken a big bite of something sour.

I bit down on a whimper. With Dad standing only a meter away, all I could think about was his face turning gray as I tried desperately to force air between his lips. It was just a dream, I told myself. It was no use. Those images felt as real as the *Hawk*'s alloy under my feet.

The world was swimming with tears as my father turned to James and I. If I'd been able to think past that dream I probably would have cowered in fear at the tiny, blue sparks catching in his eyes and the grim, thin-lipped set to his mouth. But I was too happy to see him alive to be particularly afraid of what he'd think of me stealing his shuttle.

"Daddy, you have to come home with us! This whole place is about to be underwater!" The words tumbled over each other as I grabbed Gabriel's forearms.

"Yes, I've noticed the failing dam, Gracie." Dad's voice sounded more controlled than it had earlier. With a precise turn, he disentangled himself from me and began typing commands into the piloting console. "Which is why you need to go home and I need to stay and keep people safe."

"No, Dad, you don't understand! You're not safe here!"

Gabriel raised a thick, dark eyebrow in my direction. A lump rose in my throat and I wanted to tell him every-thing—even the most disturbing parts of my dream. If I could shock him, maybe he would listen to me and teleport us all home.

Reporter Joe sniffed and my eyes darted in his direction. It was one thing to tell James and Dad about my dreams, but I wasn't so sure about saying something in front of strangers, let alone a reporter for the free press. I tried to come up with something from the dream that would con-vince Gabriel this was too dangerous. But I hadn't even seen anything that might suggest how or why things went badly with the flood. All I knew was that Dad would be here and that I needed to be, too.

Dad must have seen the desperate, conflicted expression on my face, because he gave my arm a squeeze. "I don't know why you're so upset, but we'll talk about it later, okay? Right now, the people of Landing need me to protect them."

"I know, but what about you? Have you seen the size of that dam? If it collapses, you'll die!"

Gabriel's expression turned stern. "Lots of situations are dangerous, Gracie. That doesn't mean we run from them. We're Aware, which means we have an extra responsibility to our community to keep it safe. Which I'm not fulfilling very well at the moment because I'm dealing with you and my shuttle." His anger shone through on that last bit and I could hear the accusation despite the fact that he hadn't said the word 'stealing.'

My face burned and I dropped his gaze. He had a point. If I hadn't shown up, he could have been spending this time preventing further damage to the dam. Maybe I'd interpreted Ariel's warnings wrong and I was just making things worse. The shuttle blurred with a fresh wave of confused tears.

"Gabriel... it wasn't all Gracie..." James' timid voice piped up from the other side of my father's lithe frame. Dad turned to the blond diplomat-in-training as if he'd completely forgotten James was even there. Before James could say anything else, Dad cleared his throat and went on.

"No, James, I appreciate you trying to take some responsibility, but I know my daughter." I didn't have the backbone to look at Gabriel when he said that. "When she gets an idea in her head, there's no way diplomacy is going to stop her. So I don't blame you. However, once I have this shuttle landed safely, you will both be going straight back to Angelus Quietum."

"Ahhhh, I was wondering about that." Joe's slimy voice was much too close to my other elbow for comfort. I tried not to squirm as the reporter leaned against the edge of the piloting console, effectively trapping me between him and Gabriel. "Out for a little joy ride without permission? In this storm? How reckless! What could you have been thinking, young lady?" At the horror on my face, the balding mortal gave a barking laugh. "Looks like you're officially a member of the Family now, Gracie Usuriel! After all, you can't be Gabriel's kid without tying some rules into knots!"

I ground my teeth and was formulating a cutting response to Joe's insinuations, but I never got the chance to open my mouth. With another blast of psi wind—this one a bit paler blue than Gabriel's—another figure appeared just behind the piloting console.

"Gabriel! What the hell are you doing here?"

The woman who demanded this of my father couldn't have stood taller than my shoulder. Her mane of black-and-white-streaked hair framed a face so small and petite it seemed doll-like. The black eye patch, complete with radiating scars, combined with a deathly serious scowl and aggressive hands on her hips, undermined any description as 'cute.' She was wearing a blue uniform that fit her tiny, trim figure the way only a tailored garment could. At the moment, it was spattered with dark splotches. Her hands were covered in mud almost up to her elbows.

"I'll just be a moment, Vanessa," Dad replied, looking back down at the displays in front of him.

"A moment? Gabe, listen, I'm grateful for the help. I am. But we don't have a moment. Seriously! If we want a chance of saving Landing from being completely submerged, I need you to come with me now." Vanessa's voice was higher pitched than mine, but not by as much as her diminutive size would suggest. She also spoke with the unconscious authority of someone who was used to being obeyed—quick, loud, and to the point.

"We're almost to the hospital," Dad replied evenly. "I can land the shuttle there and then we can teleport to the dam."

Vanessa glanced between our shoulders, her whole body craning as she compensated for her bad eye. "No, you're not," she said sharply, turning back to Dad. "Look, I know you're protective of your kid. It's admirable and I'm not complaining or anything. But let's face it, she just flew all the way out here from Angelus Quietum. Not to mention executing an incredibly daring and intricate piece of flying to pluck that spore-wit off the dam in one piece." She jerked a thumb in Joe's direction without a glance at him. When my father didn't respond, she jabbed his shoulder with one finger. "Are you listening to me Gabriel? If these two kids can pull off a rescue like that, they can land the shuttle on a designated landing pad."

Dad's eyes flickered in Vanessa's direction, but his head didn't move. If he'd looked at me like that, I would have burst into tears again.

"Vanessa," he growled her name in a tone so low it blended with the hum of the engines. I could feel his irritation as a buzz of low-level psi filling the air with a rapidly mounting pressure.

The wild-haired woman didn't back down. She matched him glare for glare and I got the distinct impression that they had switched to telepathic communication rather than continue their fight with an audience. To my surprise, Gabriel was the one who looked away first.

"Dad," Gabriel muttered, tapping his implant. Instantly, a new comm window pulled up on the plex-glass in front of us. D'nay's sharp features appeared, framed by a slightly green glowing square. From the background, I suspected he was at the hospital.

"Gabe? How bad is the dam?" my grandfather asked, concern in his deep blue eyes. "I have camera drones in route, but they're at least twenty minutes out."

"I haven't had a chance to assess it yet. I'll let you know when I do. Vanessa and I are about to teleport over. But first I want to be sure you'll have a welcoming party waiting for the *Hawk* when it arrives at the hospital," Dad said. I could hear the hard control in his voice and tried not to think about what kind of a talk we were going to have when we all got back to Angelus Quietum.

D'nay nodded. "We'll take care of Gracie and James, don't worry," D'nay told us with a smile. "You go prop up that dam before the dormitories are completely under water."

"No, Dad, please." My hand found his arm. It was warm and solid under my fingers. I tried not to think about his cold, clammy flesh in my dream.

Dad put a hand over mine, but he didn't turn to me. Instead, he addressed D'nay with a look of resigned determination. "Okay. I'll see you back at the Homestead when we're done."

D'nay nodded and the display of his face winked out in a little flash of light.

My stomach sank as Gabriel turned to me. I knew that look in his eye and it meant any arguments would fall on deaf ears.

"Gracie, I know you're worried and just trying to help, but you're actually making things a lot more dangerous," Gabriel said, meeting my gaze intensely. "When you get to the hospital, listen to your grandfather. Do exactly as he says."

The lump in my throat prevented me from speaking, but I managed a reluctant head nod.

"We will," James murmured from behind Dad's shoulder.

Dad glanced at him and gave a curt nod before extracting himself from my grasp and turning to Vanessa.

"About time," the petite woman muttered. Then the two of them dissolved into a shower of blue motes.

CHAPTER 33

VOLUNTEERS

"Well, you got lucky, didn't you?" Reporter Joe chuckled into the sucking silence of Dad and Vanessa's departure. "If 'Nessa hadn't shown up, you were about to be on the receiving end of the original Usuriel temper."

I wanted to grab that man's tongue and pull it right out of his mouth.

"Gabe's sensible enough when it comes to Gracie," James said, stepping forward to tap at the displays on the piloting console. With the autopilot on, there probably wasn't a whole lot left for us to do. "He's only angry because she put herself in danger."

"As any parent would be," Joe acknowledged, though his mouth twisted as if he weren't too happy with that statement.

Fortunately, the conversation was interrupted by our arrival at University Hospital. With a swooping grace that only my father could have programmed into an auto-pilot, the *Hawk* settled itself on top of the landing platform. As promised, Grandpa D'nay was standing just outside the roof-access door, his straight, dark hair whipping about in the wind of our arrival.

"Alright, there Gracie?" Grandfather asked as the three of us emerged from the Hawk's plex-glass door. I could barely hear his voice over the buzzing whine of the still-settling engines.

I nodded in response to his question, but ducked away from his gentle, familiar gaze. I wasn't sure I trusted myself to speak without bursting into tears. A feeling of impending doom had settled in the pit of my stomach ever since Dad teleported off with Vanessa. Why hadn't I just been honest and told him about my dream? Fates, who cared if some mortals on the net thought I was a lunatic? Wasn't that worth Gabriel's life? My throat was rapidly closing and my thoughts spiraling into bitter self-recrimination when James' hand on my arm jolted me out of my anxious self-pity.

"Gabriel told us to go home," James said to D'nay, his mouth so close he was practically shouting in my ear. I'd missed part of the conversation. The engines were quieting now, but the storm winds were still loud enough to make normal speaking voices hard to hear. I focused on Grandfather's lips so I'd be able to understand what he was saying.

"Come inside and we'll discuss what needs to happen next," D'nay said, gesturing for us to move towards the roof-access door. Reporter Joe was already walking through said entrance, his balding figure comical in the soaking rain slicker.

Obediently, James and I trailed after the adults. We went down several flights of stairs into a large, open atrium.

The first thing I noticed was the huge number of people everywhere.

Some were wet and wrapped in blankets, shivering as they sat in the waiting room chairs off to our right. An elderly woman and two teenage boys were distributing hot drinks and additional blankets from a cart.

A young woman with light, blonde hair materialized out of thin air near the cart. She was holding the hands of a woman and a child, both of whom were completely soaked. The elderly woman quickly took charge of the shivering pair, wrapping them in blankets and pouring out steaming mugs. Once they seemed settled, the blonde woman disappeared into a cloud of golden motes, presumably off to find others who needed help.

Men and women in green medical uniforms dashed about, all of them acting like they had important places to be. Some of them wove among the shivering survivors, checking vitals and escorting the more seriously injured to an elevator on the far wall. More than one looked like they had Usuriel blood from the smoothness of their gait and the tell-tale angles of their features. None of them took any notice of the four of us as we strode into their midst.

We approached a group of three individuals talking in a tight knot. They looked nervous, their heads close together and their hands gesturing as they spoke. All three fell silent as we drew closer, their eyes flicking between my grandfather and the rest of our motley assemblage.

All three of them had Usuriel blood, that much was obvious. However, none of them had that 'youthfully ancient' look I'd come to associate with individuals who had lived beyond an average mortal lifespan. In fact, I knew one of them was only a few years older than me.

"Hi, Leesil," I said, more flatly than I meant to.

My great-grandniece's tired face split into a sunny smile. "Hey! Gracie! Wow, you've grown!" She stepped closer for a hug. The dread in the pit of my stomach didn't fade, but some of the tension in my shoulders eased. "Have you met my friends?"

I shook my head, taking in the tall, dark-haired young man and brown, middle-aged woman beside her.

Leesil's smile was as easy and friendly as always. She gestured to her companions with a wave of one pale, freckled hand.

"Gracie, this is Liam and Jillian."

I nodded to them in turn and found myself openly staring. It just wasn't often that I met strangers.

Liam also wasn't much older than me, perhaps somewhere around eighteen or nineteen. He had my father's coloring with the dark hair and blue eyes, but he wore his hair in a short, modern cut rather than long like D'nay and Gabriel. He also had my father's cheekbones, but his face was longer and narrower, much like the rest of his body. He easily stood half-a-head over D'nay, who was the next tallest one there. He gave me an easy smile.

Like Liam, Jillian seemed friendly and relaxed, especially considering the situation. Her dark complexion and rounded face weren't as Usuriel as Liam's, but I would have recognized the shape of her eyes and nose in a mirror. She was wearing a blue uniform with a pleated breast, like the one I'd seen on Vanessa earlier.

"Hi, I'm James!"

I realized belatedly that I probably should have said something. I glanced at James as he shook hands with everyone. He seemed much more comfortable in his own skin than he used to be.

"Telepath?" Liam raised a puzzled eyebrow as he shook James' hand.

"Yes. I'm a Terran ambassador. Well, one that's in training anyway."

"I didn't know there were non-Family telepaths," Liam said, a frown creasing his long face.

Jillian gave Liam a jab with one elbow. "The Peace Child was a telepath," she pointed out in an almost scolding tone. "Don't you pay attention in history class?"

Liam flushed and looked down but James laughed. "It's okay, Liam. We're pretty rare. The trait tends to skip more than one generation and I don't think there was a living Terran 'path in at least three decades before I came along."

Liam visibly relaxed and the smile he aimed at James made his Family features quite handsome.

"Jillian?" Grandfather cleared his throat and gestured to Reporter Joe with one elegant hand. "Will you escort this gentleman somewhere he can get a fresh change of clothes?"

Jillian's eyebrows went up, but the smile never left her face. "Sure, Grandfather," she said, inclining her head to D'nay respectfully before stepping towards the dripping reporter. "This way please..." she paused as if waiting for him to fill in his name.

Joe looked rebellious but a glance at my grandfather's face forestalled any protests. With a grumble, he fell in behind Jillian.

"Joe, you can just call me Joe," he said, his mouth forming a grim line. Despite his disappointment, his beady eyes flicked around the room, taking in every detail.

"Come with me, Joe," Jillian said with a smile, one hand coming to rest on his round shoulder. How she stood touching him was beyond me. "We'll get you warm and dry in a nano."

Grandpa D'nay watched the two of them leave, his expression alert and serious until the pair rounded a corner. Once they were out of earshot, his shoulders visibly relaxed and he cleared his throat.

"Well, that's taken care of," he muttered, more to himself than us. Liam gave a little relieved huff that James echoed. Grandfather cleared his throat and our attention returned to him. "Okay, let's see where we need the four of you most."

I exchanged a glance with James. "Gabriel was pretty clear about us going back to Angelus Quietum," James said slowly.

D'nay waved away his statement with one long-fingered hand. "Gabriel means well but he can be an overprotective mother hen. I'm not wasting time and energy sending two fully capable individuals of Awareness back to the middle of nowhere when they can be useful right here and now." His saturated blue eyes flicked up at us over the edge of his memory pad. "Unless you don't want to volunteer with the relief effort."

James blinked, clearly torn between following what he'd been told and the ethical decision of helping in an emergency.

Before he could reply, however, a crisp, clear voice called to Grandpa D'nay from across the large room.

"There you are, Grandfather." A woman came to stand next to Liam, her head held high. For a split second, I thought she was Adora. Between the white-blonde hair, snow-white skin, and commanding demeanor, if someone had told me this was my long-dead aunt back from the dead I would have believed them. "Where do you need me?"

"Ah, Lillian." Grandfather took the specter's arrival in stride. I found myself staring between them, my eyes practically bugging out of my head. If they noticed my reaction, neither of them gave any indication. "I'm glad you're here. We were just discussing where we needed people."

My Grandfather's words finally penetrated the shock in my brain. Lillian... had I heard that name before? I felt like I had at some point, but I couldn't place where. Now that I was observing this woman more closely, there was a softness to Lillian's curves that spoke more of my father than his sister and I'd never seen Adora with her white hair long enough to pull back into a utilitarian ponytail. Lillian glanced in my direction and I saw that her eyes were a more gentle shade of blue than Adora's ice.

"That is, assuming you two are willing volunteers?" Grandpa raised one black, bushy eyebrow in our direction.

"Just tell us what to do," I said, giving James' shoulder a squeeze to forestall any protests.

To my relief, my blond diplomat-in-training simply gave me a long look before nodding his agreement. "Gabriel told us to do exactly what you said," James said, a tiny smile tilting up the corner of his mortal lips.

"Good," Grandfather said curtly, then flicked a finger at the memory pad. "Sync your implants to this display." Some of the nervous tension drained from my shoulders as we all obediently tapped the base of our necks. Instantly, a map of Landing sprang to life in front of us. I could see where we were located by a glowing yellow "X." It seemed to be pretty well into the flood zone which was outlined in different shades of blue. Perhaps those indicated water depth? A small yellow circle surrounded the hospital and I assumed that was the three-T's keeping the hospital safe.

"Where's Gloria?" Lillian asked.

"Tending wounded upstairs," D'nay said absently.

"How's the dam?" I blurted, unable to resist checking in on Gabriel while I had the chance. The churning pit of my stomach had calmed somewhat at the idea of staying with the relief effort. At least I would be close by if anything happened to Dad.

"Well, it's not completely given way as of yet." Another flick of Grandfather's fingers zoomed in to a point directly north of Landing. The dam came into view and live video streaming from the location filled a bubble-like sub-display. I was relieved to see the majority of the structure still standing, though its distress was obvious. Water was still pouring through several cracks, making it look more like a decorative fountain than a functional dam. However, the large chunk that had given way earlier looked like it had been lifted back into place. The large, orange vehicles of the mortal repair crews lined the stable parts of the dam's top edge.

Even from the camera drone's distance, I could see the familiar blue-tinged psi of Dad and Vanessa's energy fields surrounding several sections of the damaged dam.

"Gabe and Vanessa are shifting the weight of the water back, away from the damaged sections of the dam so that the repair crews can reinforce its structure here and here," D'nay explained, pointing to the largest two cracks. "If the whole thing goes, the hospital will likely be the only thing that survives in a ten mile radius. Outside of Gloria, you're probably the only telekinetic strong enough to help them, Lilly."

If Lillian looked arrogant at first approach, it was nothing to the expression on her face now. Her head was high, blue eyes wide, and sculpted nostrils flared as if Grandfather had just suggested she take off her uniform and parade naked in front of the whole crowd.

"I know it wouldn't be your... first choice," Grandfather's voice struck just the right tone between cajoling and firm. "I wouldn't ask this of you if it weren't an emergency."

Lillian's eyes closed and her mouth formed a grim line across her delicate, thoroughly Usuriel features. I couldn't hazard a guess as to her age though I was willing to bet it was over a hundred. The stillness she achieved in that moment of frustrated disgust just wasn't something you saw from mortals.

"Very well," she breathed after a long pause. Her voice was so low, I doubt James even picked it up. "But I'm not merging with him."

D'nay inclined his head to her. "That is your prerogative, though you may have a time convincing him of that."

With a clipped grunt, Lillian gave our grandfather an elegant bow before disappearing in a swirl of pale blue motes.

Grandpa let out a sigh and I realized we had all been holding our breaths. "Good, glad that's settled," D'nay adjusted his blue tunic with one hand as if trying to release some tension from his shoulders. "Now, that should take care of the dam. As for you lot, I think you'll be of more use at the University."

I glanced at Leesil as she leaned closer to my ear. "Grandma Gloria and the other three-T's can ensure the safety of the hospital," she said under her breath, "but that's probably about the limit of their abilities."

"Evacuations are already under way. However, we need more teams to sweep the campus buildings to make sure no one's ignored the evacuation orders or gotten trapped somehow," Grandpa D'nay explained. "I'm assigning the four of you to sweep the dormitories and the research center."

He tapped the display once more. The close up of the dam faded away and was replaced by two half-submerged buildings. They weren't far from the hospital, but I wasn't sure how we'd reach them without a boat.

"I'm a three-T," Liam protested. "I thought you needed all the strength here at the hospital that you could get. If you don't need me for the dam, I'll just stay here."

D'nay shook his head. "We have ten telekinetics outside, plus your Grandmother and Dax inside if things go badly. That's plenty for now. Later we'll need you to start rotating into their shift, but at this point evacuation is more important."

"I'll work with Gracie," James volunteered quickly.

"Nope," D'nay shook his head. "Each team needs a tele-path and a teleporter. Since Liam is both, he can take Gracie. Leesil is a top notch teleporter, so you can complete her team."

James looked slightly disappointed but he nodded duti-fully.

I frowned up at my grandfather. "I'm not a telepath or teleporter. I'd probably just get in the way. Why doesn't Liam go on his own? I can stay here and help with the sur-vivors."

"No, no one goes alone," D'nay shook his head. "Even a three-T needs someone to watch their back. You have an implant, that's plenty if you need to call for help. Call me or your grandmother if you get into trouble."

"Okay," I agreed, trying to settle the anxious knot in my chest as I glanced over at Liam. He gave me a shrug and a resigned grin that I took to mean he didn't mind me tagging along. I managed to smile back, glad for his easy-going at-titude.

"Take the coordinates from my mind," D'nay said, mak-ing eye contact with Liam and Leesil in turn. Both paused, clearly getting the image for the teleport, then nodded that they understood.

D'nay tapped his implant and the diagram spun to zoom in on a new section of Landing. "Looks like the team in the market district has hit a snag," he said and made a shooing motion with his hands. "I think you know what to do from here. Keep in close contact and let me know if you need anything. I'll route whatever personnel and supplies I can muster in your direction."

"Ready?" Liam asked me. I glanced over at James. He was already moving closer to Leesil. With a deep breath to get my nerves under control, I took Liam's offered hand.

"Good luck," Grandpa's voice drifted after me as the hospital lobby bled away in streams of color. Unlike my father's teleport, the energy seemed to press down and against my skin almost painfully and we spent several breathless moments compressed in an airless void before we emerged in a darkened room.

"Phew!" I stumbled back from the disorienting shift and nearly toppled over a metal shelf full of test tubes. They rattled and sang as the glass vials swung in their holders. I gave Liam a startled look.

"Sorry, I'm probably not as comfortable a ride as Gabriel," he said with a rueful smile. "But I get where I'm going, don't worry."

"I guess you do have a little less practice," I said, swallowing a cutting remark and brushing myself off. Then, seeing his hurt look, I managed to return an echo of his grin. Something about Liam put me at ease. I turned my attention to our surroundings and found myself gaping at dozens of shelves just like the one I'd nearly toppled. "Where are we?"

"I think this is the genetics lab," Liam said, looking around at the dimly lit space. I heard a rumble of thunder and realized that the noise of the crowd at the hospital had been drowning out the continuing storm outside. It was extremely quiet here. I found it oddly comforting. "We should be in the Ariel Science Wing of the research center."

A loud curse echoed from down the rows of vials. Liam and I exchanged a glance before heading in that direction.

"Ariel... like Gabriel's daughter?" I echoed quietly as we wove between the rows of test tubes. Some were empty while others were full of various colored liquids. Then I came to a wall that had no windows. Built into it was a large, thick door with a huge handle.

"Yeah, Gabriel's oldest," Liam said, trailing behind me. "She ran this lab for years."

Another angry epithet came from our left. Peering around the last shelf, we found a tiny matchstick of a woman in a white lab coat several sizes too large. Her hair was red streaked with gray and piled into a tight bun atop her head. She glared down at several vials as she quickly selected one, put it in the box at her feet, and then placed the rest back on the shelf. Swiftly, she moved on to the next shelf of vials and began the process of selecting and cursing all over again.

"Ummm... madam?" Liam said quickly. When she didn't look up from her work, I cleared my throat.

"Yes, yes, I know," she snapped, not pausing in her work. "The evacuation order. I know. I'm coming."

"It's serious," Liam said. "The dam could go at any minute."

"I said, I know!" she hissed, redoubling her speed. I was surprised she didn't break the vials in her haste, but each one found a safe place in her box. I peered down into the container. She'd laid packing material thickly around all three sides. In the center was a lattice of cardboard tubes that each vial easily slid into. It was obviously made for such a purpose and I was impressed with its cleverness.

"I need to teleport you somewhere safe, outside the flood zone," Liam said. "Now, if you don't mind..."

She flapped a hand at him. "You're next to me, now. Give me five minutes and I'll be done. You can teleport us all out at the first sign of trouble if it happens before then."

Liam sighed and glanced over at me. I shrugged and wandered a little way back down the row of shelves. I honestly didn't mind having a moment to breathe and look around.

"Fine," my cousin grumbled, "five minutes."

I found myself drawn back to that large, heavy door in the wall. Something about it sparked my interest. Without thinking, my hand found the large, metal handle of the door. It felt smooth and somehow right. With a strong tug, I pulled the door open.

Cold air hissed out of the chamber. A familiar glow flooded out to meet me. The instant Liam had said her name, however, I knew she would show up. I wasn't surprised when I saw Ariel waiting for me in the depths of the walk-in cooling unit. She motioned urgently for me to come closer.

"Ummm... Gracie? What are you doing? I'm pretty sure there aren't any stray researchers in there. We're supposed to be evacuating the building, not rifling through their stuff." Liam's voice echoed as he peered into the cold box after me.

I didn't have my journal with me, so I couldn't communicate with Ariel directly. Nor did I think writing in a notebook in the middle of a rescue mission would boost my cousin's opinion of me. But Ariel had been the one to start me on this little adventure and if I knew her, this was exactly where she'd intended for me to end up. That pit of dread in my gut warmed and chill bumps rose on my neck and arms. I shivered.

"I'll be just a second," I called back to Liam.

"And we wonder how Usuriels get a reputation for being crazy," Liam muttered, but he moved off to babysit our stubborn researcher.

"What is it?" I hissed as quietly as I could to Ariel. I'd walked the rest of the way into the cooling unit and my short sleeved shirt was not standing up to its chill. Even so, I glanced around with interest. The whole place was lined with shelves full to bursting with rows of little vials. In each carefully labeled vial was a few ounces of a dark red liquid. I was fairly certain I'd found Ariel's stash of Family blood samples.

The ghost herself was waiting for me at the very back of the cold box. The shelf there held something different than the others. Several small bottles and jars had different labels, though they all were written in Ariel's familiar, looping handwriting. The whole shelf was covered in a thick layer of dust. I could see several smudges in the dust, as if a few of them had recently been removed. My sister was fervently motioning to a small, stoppered bottle with a little loop of twine about its neck. Dutifully, I picked up the bottle.

"TT126 - G," I read aloud. I glanced back up at Ariel. "What does this mean?"

My sister looked at me impassively. After how effectively she had communicated earlier, I found her lack of response unnerving.

"Now you don't want to talk to me? Oh, come on!"

"Hey, Gracie?" Liam sounded oddly muffled from outside the cold box. "I think we'd better move."

"Why?" I took a step towards the door and made a small splashing noise. There was now about an inch of water on the formerly dry floor. With a gasp, I looked back at Ariel. She met my eye, then nodded once and faded gently away. The cold box instantly plunged into an almost perfect darkness, cut only by the sliver of light from the open door. "Okay, I'm coming!"

CHAPTER 34

LIAM AND THE BOAT

I couldn't get out of that cooling unit fast enough. With a quick push, I closed the door behind me. The locking mechanism clicked shut, and I dashed down the rows of shelves looking for my cousin. It didn't take me long to spot Liam's tall figure. A flash of lightning cast his dark hair in shades of blue as he stood by a large wall of windows. On his right were several bulky pieces of equipment I didn't recognize, their screens and tubes silent and dark. To his left was a glass door leading out to the hallway. He had his hand on the door plate and it was sliding open as I came up at a run.

"Sorry," I said, skidding to a stop next to him. The water was already creeping over the toes of my boots. "Where did the researcher go?"

"I teleported her to D'nay and Gloria's. That's where the rest of the Family is reorganizing. It's just outside the flood zone." Liam looked half-amused, half-annoyed. "What were you looking for in there?"

I shrugged and shoved my hand in my pocket. The little bottle fit easily. I didn't know how to explain why I needed to steal a vial from the genetics lab. I didn't feel bad about it, I just didn't want to discuss it with my cousin.

"I've never seen a cold box you can walk into before," I lied easily. I met his doubtful gaze with a small, amused smile hovering over my lips. It was a good approximation of my father's blank face when he was trying to pretend it wasn't blank.

"You are past head blind, aren't you?" Liam said after a minute. He ducked through the doorway and started down the hall. I followed behind him, grateful he didn't seem inclined to pause and quibble over my strange behavior any longer. The water seeped into the hems of my pants, making them heavy and awkward.

"That's what my dad tells me," I replied as we sloshed down the hallway.

"But you're a third-gen." Liam sounded almost offended by my lack. "You should be a three-T at the least!"

I shook my head. "Nope. Fire. That's the only thing that's ever worked for me."

"Fire," Liam echoed. His dark brows lifted. "Wait... you're the new firebird?"

"Ummm, I guess," I said, mimicking him as he poked his head into office doors and empty classrooms.

We left the rooms we'd searched open so we would know where we'd been. It didn't take long to clear the floor and find the stairs. I was grateful to leave the ankle-deep water behind as we climbed upwards. Even so, my neck was painfully tight.

"We didn't search down there very thoroughly," I pointed out. "I mean, someone could have been hiding in a closet or something."

"Nah, I would have heard them," Liam said with a shake of his head. "Even unconscious, I can hear someone's mind if they're within twenty feet."

"Oh, well, that's handy," I replied, beginning to feel out of breath from the stairs. The building creaked and groaned under the weight of the water and I clutched the handrail a little tighter. "It would be handier still if you could sweep the entire floor without going room to room."

"Your father could, or Grandma Gloria," Liam said, confirming what I'd already been thinking but didn't want to say aloud. I'd already compared him unfavorably to my father once this trip. He'd laughed it off with good grace, but I didn't want to make a habit of telling him how much he didn't measure up to Gabriel. I was sheltered but I knew when I was being rude. "Hell, Lillian and Vanessa probably could, too," Liam was continuing good-naturedly. "That's why they got tapped for dam duty."

That made sense, but I decided not to comment on it. "So you're a three-T. What generation are you?"

"Seventeenth," he said. "Which is why I got sent on evacuation duty."

"You're awfully strong for a seventeenth-gen, I would think," I offered as we stepped onto the next floor.

"Only three-T of my generation, as far as I know." Liam gave me that little smile again and I saw an echo of my father in his face. Seventeen generations and those genes still shone through.

I shook my head and began opening doors on the new hallway. This level had a lot of empty hospital-type rooms and large pieces of strange equipment I didn't understand. There were so many doors. It took us a while to finish, even though we didn't see anyone except that lone researcher in Ariel's lab.

"So are you actually Gabriel's daughter or are you a Family member he just kind of adopted?" Liam asked as we cleared a large lecture room. So far the water hadn't reached this level yet, but I was keeping a sharp eye on the floor as we searched.

"I'm his daughter," I said, then paused because I wasn't completely sure. How did I know Gabriel hadn't just taken me in out of pity and a sense of Family obligation? After all, I looked like an Usuriel, but my talents weren't what a third generation was expected to be. Perhaps I was just a random tenth or fifteenth generation Usuriel child that my father adopted. It was the best theory I'd heard so far for why I wasn't a three-T.

Then I thought about Leesil and Liam, the only later generation Usuriels I knew. While they both resembled D'nay and Gloria, their features had a blurred look to them as if their mortal sides were trying to erase the perfection of their exceptional ancestors. While I wasn't quite as painfully beautiful as my father or grandmother, I was a lot closer than Leesil or Liam. If I wasn't third-gen, I also wasn't fifteenth.

"Wow, a third-gen firebird," Liam mused as we made our way to the stairwell again. I glanced down the winding steps. The water had made it halfway up the floor with Ariel's lab in it. "I bet you could do a lot of damage if you wanted to."

I glanced over at him, surprised at his reaction. "Yeah, I guess I could," I allowed.

"What's the biggest thing you've ever blown up?" Liam asked, mischief in his midnight-blue eyes.

I laughed and was about to answer when a crash from outside made both of our heads snap around.

"What was that?" I asked Liam as we bolted through the first door on the third floor.

"I think someone's trying to break in," he replied breathlessly as we dashed to the window of a small, cluttered classroom.

Peering out of the window, the scope of the flood became immediately clear. Muddy-brown currents swirled around the large, stone-faced buildings of the University. Trees, branches and other debris collected against walls and tangled in larger thickets. I couldn't see the hospital from this side of the research center, but off in the distance the curve of foothills and clumps of trees parted to give a glimpse of the dam.

"What the hell does he think he's doing?" Liam asked, forcing the window open to hang over the sill. I followed my cousin's lead and leaned out the window. "Hey!" Liam called down as I caught sight of a small boat idling at one of the windows below us. There was a man sitting in the boat, his hand on the tiny, outboard solar engine. I caught a flash of movement as a second figure slipped into the broken window the boat's prow was bumping against. "There's a mandatory evacuation in effect for the whole University area! The waters are rising and the dam isn't stable! It could go at any moment! You need to get out of here!"

The man ignored him and continued to idle the boat. Liam narrowed his eyes and flared his nostrils.

"Well, now what?" I asked.

"Stupid," he muttered. "Honestly, mortals complain about our response when things go wrong, but half the time it's their own stupidity that gets people killed."

I raised an eyebrow at his angry outburst. "Isn't one of your parents a mortal?"

"Actually, both of my parents are Usuriels," he replied, his chin lifting. "Probably why I'm a three-T."

"Ummm... okay..."

He chuckled. "Nah, it's not as weird as it sounds. My mom is an Adoran and my dad's a Gabriellan. They're fifteen generations removed from each other. That's way over the Five-Gen-Rule."

Stella covered the Five-Gen-Rule during government class. In order to apply for a marriage license in the Provinces, you had to prove that you were five generations removed from your prospective spouse on all sides. Exceptions were made for orphans and wards of the state who didn't have access to genealogy records, but otherwise the Five-Gen-Rule was pretty strictly enforced. It made sense with the small genetic pool of colonists who came to Cybele. Inbreeding could happen very quickly if pairing wasn't closely monitored.

"Well, I don't think they're listening to you," I said, looking down at the man in the boat.

"Gah..." Liam ran a hand down his face, distorting his long features into something even longer. "This is why I wanted to work on the dam."

Then, before I could say another word, he'd grabbed my elbow and teleported both of us back to Ariel's lab.

I gasped as we alighted on a table top. Liam had been correct. The broken window was only feet away. A hooded figure emerged from the cold box I had been so drawn to. I put a hand to the tiny vial in my pocket. Its small, reassuring lump was still there.

"There's a mandatory evacuation order in effect for this area," Liam said to the man.

"No problem, no problem at all." Joe the Reporter waded through hip deep water while holding a very nice memory pad over his head. He gave my cousin that greasy smile as he adjusted battered spectacles on his nose. "We'll just be a moment."

I narrowed my eyes at him. I wasn't sure how he'd slipped away from Jillian, but I had a feeling it wasn't her fault. I was beginning to have a sincere dislike of this particular mortal.

"Didn't you learn a damn thing earlier today?" I snapped. "If James and I hadn't shown up with the *Hawk*, you would have died. This area isn't any less dangerous. You need to get in your boat and leave now."

"Ah, well," the reporter's gray eyes held an ingratiating gleam. "Last I checked the Provinces had a free press." With a quick motion, he brought his memory pad up and tapped it. A flash painted the world in blurry spots of color. "What shall I put down for the caption? 'Militant Usuriel thugs try to cover up University experiments'? Or perhaps 'young heroes rescue reporting crew.' Honestly, it's your choice."

Liam groaned. "Great. Only thing worse than a haughty mortal is one that's affiliated with the press."

"I didn't know the press also specialized in breaking and entering," I blurted before my brain could catch up to my mouth. "Today isn't the first time I've caught you trespassing."

Liam titled his head at me. I ignored him, folding my arms and glaring at Joe. The reporter took the jab in stride, however.

"So you do remember me!" he cried with a laugh. "I was beginning to think I hadn't left an impression!"

I stared at him, frozen in disgust. This, of course, gave him the perfect opportunity to snap another picture of me.

"Dad will not be pleased if those get published," I growled at the reporter.

Joe merely shrugged and gave me a wicked smile. "Good thing you're considered a public figure and unless I publish something blatantly untrue, he can't sue me for libel."

"Okay, you've gotten your pictures and your story. Now let's get out of here before we have to swim out," Liam grumbled.

"Fair enough," the reporter said with an easy shrug. "Lead the way."

He'd made the mistake of getting close enough for Liam to touch his shoulder. I was glad for two reasons. First because this whole exchange was an unqualified disaster and second because the water was beginning to work its way up my calves despite standing on the table. I grabbed Liam's other hand and in the space it took to cough we were balancing in the tiny boat. The rain had subsided enough that it was only a fine mist but, I still found myself squinting into the precipitation.

"Okay," Liam said gruffly, shoving the reporter onto one of the boat's wooden benches. "Now get out of here. It's way too dangerous for anyone who isn't Aware."

"So, you want to let me in on what was discussed after I left?" Joe prattled on. I would give the guy one thing: he was determined and seemed good at his job. "No, let me guess. If Gracie's here, the old man is still out dealing with the dam. He wouldn't let you so far off the leash, but

D'nay's a practical sort about his descendants. He wouldn't say no to a few more volunteers."

I exchanged a look with Liam. Neither of us said a word, though I assumed by "old man" he meant my father. I officially hated this guy.

"Even ol' Gabe needs some back up on something that big," the man standing by the engine chimed in. He was a completely typical, middle-aged mortal. In the stormy light it was hard to tell what color his eyes were and a large, floppy rain hat hid any hair he might have. He seemed a little thicker in the middle than Joe, but otherwise he couldn't have been more ordinary. "Didn't you say 'Nessa was already up there with him?"

My least favorite reporter nodded in agreement. "Yeah, you're right, Abrum. Vanessa's with him, but I don't think the two of them could handle it alone. The Matriarch is probably too busy protecting her castle. She doesn't like anything messing with her precious hospital. So it'll fall to the thirds. I'm betting D'nay sent Lilly out to 'Nessa and Gabe."

I carefully kept my face blank. It was slightly disturbing to watch these two outsiders accurately predict exactly what the Family's response would be to this disaster. Especially since I hadn't had any idea who or what to expect before I got here. How was it that these reporters knew more about my own family than I did? I was going to convince Stella to let me see a Family genealogy chart as soon as I got home.

"What does it matter?" Liam was getting louder. "We have a building to clear and you need to get out of the flash flood zone!"

The two reporters kept right on speculating as if Liam hadn't spoken.

"You really think Lilly will do it?" Abrum asked. "I mean, it would make sense. She's probably the next strongest after Glory, Gabe, and Vanessa. But..."

"She'll do it. She won't like working with her father," Joe shrugged, his gray eyes glinting with shrewd intelligence behind those glasses. "I don't think she's talked to Gabe in... over fifty years? Sixty? It's been at least that since they were seen at the same event together, that I know of. But Lilly's still wearing the OW Blue, which means she'll do whatever they tell her, especially in an emergency."

A chill went down my spine. Lillian was Gabriel's daughter. How I hadn't put it together before I wasn't sure. She'd been mentioned a number of times as someone who was nearly as strong as my father. Even Grandma Gloria had talked about how Lillian had stopped aging. It made sense that she would be a third-gen. With her coloring, I assumed she was Adoran. The fact that I'd just met a living half-sister made my heart jump into my throat.

"You wouldn't care to make a statement on the status of your father's relationship with Lillian? I'm sure you have more insight than I do," Joe said. I wanted nothing more than to set him alight.

"No," I managed to mutter. "No comment."

"Come on," Liam said, grabbing my hand. "We don't have time for this." I glanced up at him gratefully. "I want to see the back of this boat heading away from the dam every time I look up for the next hour. If I don't, I will personally teleport your sorry asses to the hospital where you can explain why you're still here to D'nay himself. Are we clear?"

Joe and Abrum's smiles took on a strained edge and I realized that Liam finally had the upper hand. "Of course," Joe said smoothly. "We were just on our way out anyway."

"Perfect," Liam replied and with another wrenching leap, the two of us were once again standing in the research center. This time we were in the third floor stairwell.

"Whoa, take it easy," I said, almost catching Liam as he staggered against me. "Are you okay?"

"Yeah, sorry," he panted, and sat down heavily on a step. "I'm not used to making this many jumps in a day, especially carrying other people."

I decided it wasn't a half-bad idea to take a little break. I peered out the stairway window to make sure that the reporters had begun to make their way out of the flood zone first.

"There's some rations in my bag." Liam sounded faint. I caught sight of the reporter's little boat heading away from the dam. Good, they were gone. Turning my attention to Liam, I unzipped the small backpack he was wearing and dug out some food.

"Here," I said, handing Liam half of the sandwich and a bottle of water.

"Thanks," he accepted the sandwich and fell upon it ravenously. I perched next to him on the step and ate my own lunch with more decorum.

I kept thinking about Lillian and how much she looked like Adora. It was uncanny how much she favored our aunt. It made me wonder who her mother had been. If Lilly stopped aging the way my father had, did that mean there was a chance I might also? It seemed unlikely, considering my lack of powerful psi-abilities. Still...

"Liam, do you know much about Lillian?" I asked, glancing at him.

He took a long drink of water to chase the sandwich. "I've met the professor a few times. She's serious and likes her privacy, but otherwise she's a nice sort. Gracie... don't let those reporters rattle you. I swear, half the Family feuds were started by wild net press rumors."

I raised an eyebrow at him. "Feuds?"

Liam nearly choked on his water. "They weren't joking about Gabe's leash, were they?" he said when he recovered. I curled my lip at him. "Sorry, sorry," he said, holding up his hands. "That was unfair. But, does he let you on the net at all?"

"He set Stella's filter so that I can only get to peer reviewed sites," I said, "and even those she'll refuse to access sometimes."

"That's... almost scary." Liam scratched his head. "No. No, that's actually scary. I mean, I know he's gotten some bad press over the years but keeping you completely in the dark about the entire Family? That just seems foolish. I mean, you're bound to read all of it eventually."

I swallowed down a wave of anxiety. Fate knew what my father would have to say when he found out James and I stayed for the rescue effort. One problem at a time, I told myself. And all the more reason to pump Liam for all the information he would give me since my father would be grounding me within an inch of my life as soon as we got home.

"He and Grandma Gloria fight about it every once in a while. They didn't talk for a month last time. So far, all I get is a glimpse here and there when we run into Family members, which isn't often."

"Well, that part isn't surprising," Liam said, getting to his feet. "Gabriel isn't easy to get along with and a lot of the Family would just rather avoid him."

I zipped Liam's knapsack and stood. "That's something I've never gotten. I mean, I know he has a temper and a sarcastic streak. But honestly, he's not a monster. Every time we're around the Family, someone treats him like he's contagious."

Liam groaned as he started clearing the third hallway. "I'm not sure how much is for me to say," he sounded cautious. "But let's just say your dad has a reputation. I don't know him personally, so I have no idea what rumor is true and what's complete fantasy. There does seem to be enough legend that springs up around those of us who have Awareness. Multiply that by a couple of centuries and I guess it's impossible to avoid being the subject of some crazy fiction."

"D'nay and Gloria don't seem to suffer from that problem," I grumbled, opening the door of yet another silent room. The third floor was as empty as the second.

"They're too public to be shrouded in rumor. I mean, they go to Landing market once a week. They bake cookies and muffins for any distant relation who shows up at the door. Plus they're adorable and head over heels in love with each other. You do know that particular back story, right?"

"Generally. Grandma Gloria's family disapproved of their marriage so they helped design and fund the *Inspiration* project to get away from them."

"Yeah..." Liam agreed as we got back to the stairs, "but why exactly did they disapprove?"

"Because Anori aren't supposed to consort with the undead?"

"Not back on Earth, they didn't anyway. Not sure why it was so taboo. We manage it here on Cybele just fine," Liam laughed as he opened the door to the roof. Gray clouds and the damp of rain greeted us. "Though, I doubt even her family had any idea what effect her blood would have on him."

"Oh!"

The two of us turned at the exclamation. A pair of University students huddled under a make-shift awning a few hundred feet away. It looked like they had been attempting to save a small, tidy garden from being completely swamped. From the grins on their faces, they were the first people at the research center who were actually happy to see us.

"Thank goodness." The boy spoke first. He had a long, thin neck and a pronounced nose. He rubbed his arms and nudged closer to the plump, blonde girl beside him. "I thought we were going to have to try shoving all these plants into that tiny boat down there. Then they sailed off and left us and we were convinced they'd stranded us! But you're Usuriels, aren't you? You can just teleport us out of this mess."

Liam's tired eyes moved over the collection of tubs, tins, and soil. "All of this has to go?"

"I can't do all of this research again!" the girl cried suddenly, tears welling. "This is four years of agricultural advancement! We're integrating native Cybele photosynthetic cells into the wheat and corn genome in ways even Ariel herself wished after! You can't just let it all drown!"

"Okay, okay," my cousin raised his hands in defeat and I patted his shoulder.

"Do you want me to call D'nay for help?" I suggested. "We could probably fit this in the Hawk."

"No, they're probably using the shuttle for evacuations," Liam sighed. "I'll take care of it."

***

Less than an hour later, I was sitting on my grandparents' couch with a very pale, exhausted Liam. After delivering the last blue tub of genetically enhanced crops into Gloria and D'nay's backyard, my cousin looked so pathetic I practically dragged him into the living room.

"Ah, here's the hero of the hour," said Jessie, handing each of us a hot cup of tea. "I heard you saved the future of Cybele's agricultural sector." Her gentle green eyes sparkled in the soft creases of her face while her pure gray hair tried to curl out of the bun atop her head.

I had never seen an elderly Usuriel before, but Jessie was almost exactly what I'd expected Gloria to look like the first time I'd heard the term "grandmother." Her features still held an echo of the Family's good looks but they were weathered and wrinkled with time. Even so, the years didn't ride her the way they did my father. If anything, her eyes struck me as playful and friendly. She was having no trouble organizing and provisioning the refugees that had begun to gather at the Usuriel estate.

"Drink up, child," she told Liam kindly. "You'll feel better after a meal and a good night's rest."

"Thanks," Liam said, sipping at the tea. He seemed too tired to talk much and I didn't want to further exhaust him. The researchers, including the one we'd teleported out of Ariel's lab and the pair from the rooftop, had formed a tight knot at the dining room table and were commiserating about the damage to their laboratories. There were a few other University students wrapped up in blankets warming themselves by the fire I'd coaxed to life in the fireplace, but they seemed just as content as Liam to sit quietly and recover.

"Is there anything I can help with in the kitchen?" I asked Jessie.

"Oh, well, I'm sure I could use some help somewhere," she said with a broad wink. "Come on, I'll put you to work."

I trailed her aproned form into the kitchen and was instantly assaulted by a mass of young Usuriels. None of them could have been over twelve and there were quite a few under five. The older ones were distributing snacks and drinks to the younger ones while the middle children engaged in a game of tag that involved more teleporting than the games I'd seen at the group home.

"Drex! Don't knock over the plant stand!" Jessie called to a freckled boy with bright, red hair as he teleported a little too close to the window box full of ferns.

"Sorry!" he shouted, quite unrepentant as he dashed off to the other side of the kitchen. A small dark-skinned boy giggled and disappeared in a cloud of blue motes, only to reappear inches away from his cousin.

"Gotcha!"

"Angie, take the little ones up to the playroom. I don't mind if they take their cookies with them. We'll just have to clean up the crumbs later," Jessie told a strawberry blonde girl of perhaps twelve. "I've got to get meals ready for the rescue teams as they get back, so keep the children out of the way."

"Okay, Grandma." Angie scooped up a set of blond twins who couldn't be more than two before turning to a black-haired girl around nine. "Did you hear Grandma? We've got to take the kids upstairs."

"Drex, Camry," the nine-year-old called to the boys racing about the perimeter, "come on, we need you to help us teleport the littles up to the playroom."

With a grumble and an eye roll, the boys came over and followed the girls' lead in picking up the smaller children. The whole lot of them disappeared in a swirl of gold and blue motes. I shook my head and wondered exactly how many generations it took to exhaust the Awareness in our Family genes.

"I haven't seen you at any Family gatherings," Jessie said to me as she wiped down the crumb filled counters.

I hadn't said more than a few words to her and had only picked up her name because she'd introduced herself to all of us as a group when we arrived. I flushed when I realized she might not be as friendly when she figured out exactly who I was.

"Sorry," I said. "I don't have much practice meeting people. My name is Gracie."

Her eyes widened a touch, but then her gentle face split into such a welcoming smile that I couldn't help but echo it. "Why, you must be Gabriel's youngest! So glad to meet you! I'm a Gabriellan myself, so we're from the same branch of the old Family tree, so to speak."

I returned her firm handshake and accepted the towel she offered me to dry off the counters she'd just cleaned.

"What gen are you?" I asked. "If you don't mind me asking."

"No, no, of course you can ask me anything," she said cheerfully, rummaging around in D'nay's pantry and pulling out ingredients. "I'm an eighth generation Gabriellan. From Ariel's line, if you want to get specific."

I tried to do the math on how old she might be but kept getting stuck on the fact that Usuriels didn't age the same way mortals do. Who was to say that an Usuriel couldn't have a child at age two hundred and fifty? My father had been four hundred when I was born. It was impossible to calculate, so I shrugged it off and finished drying our work surface.

"Are you a three-T?" I asked.

"Heavens, no," she laughed, pulling out bread and a huge amount of pasta. "I certainly wouldn't be here if I was! No, I'm an empath for the most part. I can do some minor physical healing, but emotional healing is my strong suit." I could think of a few Family members who might be in need of her services, but I kept my mouth shut as I watched her go through the cooling unit and pull out a package of ground meat. "And you're a pyrokinetic, aren't you?" she asked as she laid out the ingredients for a huge amount of pasta in meat sauce.

"Yes," I admitted. "Not what anyone expects from a third-gen, but it's what I've got."

"Work with what you have," Jessie said with a smile. "That's all any of us can do."

With that, we began making enough spaghetti to feed a small army and I decided I liked Jessie a lot.

CHAPTER 35

BACK AT THE HOMESTEAD

James and Leesil came back first, hauling a load of scared and soaked University students who had fled to the roof of their dormitory. Leesil looked as tired as Liam as she slumped onto the couch next to him. He put a brotherly arm around her while I fetched a cup of tea from the kitchen. After Leesil was settled, James found an unoccupied wall where he could see all three downstairs rooms and watch the growing crowd with silent, observant eyes.

Then, Dad, Vanessa, and Lillian arrived, dripping wet and already fighting.

"We would have been done in half the time if we'd just merged!" Gabriel snapped as they burst into existence next to the kitchen table. The strength of my father's teleport was clear in the swift and efficient wind that rose sharply and then dissipated as if it had never existed. It made Liam and Leesil's efforts look tremulous at best. "The construction crew wouldn't have had to drag their equipment from one safe zone to another..."

"Let it go, Gabe," Vanessa sighed, massaging the temple next to her bad eye as if she were trying to stave off a headache. Her hair looked even wilder than it had this morning.

"No, I'm sick of this crap. She needs to give me a straight answer. What is your problem, Lilly? Why are you treating me like..."

"Like what?" Lillian hissed, eyes blazing as she rounded on our father. "Like you're a criminal? Well, there are some varying opinions on that, aren't there?"

Gabriel opened his mouth to reply, but Vanessa beat him to it.

"Finally! Yes, let's get to the heart of this! I've been listening to the two of you all damn day and I'm tired of dancing around the issues!" Her one good eye blazed with blue fire and the tips of her black-and-white hair began to spark. "You," she pointed an accusing finger at Lillian, "are not a majority of the Overwatch council! You don't get to mete out justice or declare someone guilty just because you don't approve of their lifestyle. I don't care if he's your father. Unless you have some solid evidence to make a complaint, keep your prejudices and wounded pride to yourself! And making sly little nasty comments in front of mortals of all stripes only makes your dirty laundry more public and I don't think that's what either of you wants."

My father crossed his arms and gave Lillian a superior glare. James sidled up next to me at the counter, his warm shoulder reassuring as we watched the fireworks between the older three-T's.

"And you"—Vanessa's finger landed on Gabriel this time—"need to grow up and realize that your actions have consequences. Sometimes, sorry isn't enough and it's never going to be. So, good for you that you've owned a few mistakes and made some changes. Don't expect that it magically erases the emotional damage you've done to the people around you. Some things are past fixing and you're just going to have to live with it."

Dad's face shut down. "Is that true?" he asked quietly, trying to make eye contact with Lillian. She was looking anywhere but in his direction. "Have you decided that I'm past apologies? Have I really betrayed you so badly that you can't even be civil anymore?"

I saw just the smallest crack in her icy expression and her shoulders dropped a touch. "I don't know, Dad," she said finally, sounding more tired than angry. "Maybe... and maybe not. But for now, sorry isn't going to fix it and I do know that I don't trust you enough to merge. I just can't have you in my head right now. But... you know... let me live with it for a century. Time heals a lot of things and Fate knows, we have enough of it."

Gabriel looked like all those years his youthful face usually hid had caught up with him, but he managed some dignity in his nod. "Wouldn't it have been easier to say so this morning?" he muttered, and turned to Jessie. "Sorry to cause such a commotion. Thank you for looking after the Homestead and making food for everyone."

"Oh, you're welcome, Gabe," Jessie said warmly, putting a gentle hand on his shoulder. He gave her such a grateful smile that she quickly linked her arm through his and drew him closer to the steaming spread of food on the counter. "Come on, why don't we all sit down for a bowl of pasta? I'm sure Gloria and D'nay will be with us shortly."

James and I found ourselves pressed into service dishing out bowls of spaghetti and sauce. I was okay with that since it gave me an excuse to avoid my father's eye. He didn't seem especially angry to find James and me here instead of back at Angelus Quietum. I had my fingers crossed that Grandpa D'nay had managed some kind of conversation with him earlier. As it was, I hoped that staying busy and looking useful might assuage a tiny bit of his temper when it finally came down on me.

It wasn't hard to look busy. There were over a dozen mortal refugees and eight adult Usuriels plus the gaggle of Usuriel children in Jessie's care. It took almost a half hour to get everyone served, including ourselves. When James and I finally had our plates put together, the only spaces open were beside my father at the dining room table. I swallowed down a curse as I pulled out my chair.

"So, it sounds like you did manage to save the dam," James said to Dad, breaking the uncomfortable silence at the table.

"Yes, we did," Gabriel agreed, dragging some crusty bread around the edge of his second bowl of pasta. "Inefficiently," he added, just a touch of irritation in his voice as he glanced over at the living room where Lillian and Vanessa were eating from the coffee table. "But yes, the repairs went smoothly once we got there."

I let out a small breath of relief that his anger seemed squarely focused in a different direction at the moment. I knew he wouldn't forget about the shuttle, but hopefully he'd decide to wait until we were back at home before dismantling my self-esteem on that count.

"Do you think it will hold?" asked the young blonde University student we'd rescued from the roof of the research center. She seemed aware of the somber mood at the table, but was thankfully tactful enough to ease it.

"What does it matter?" grumbled the older, wiry researcher who had saved the box of vials from Ariel's genetics lab. "The DNA bank in the basement is ruined if the seals failed. If so, this is a loss on the magnitude of the Library of Alexandria."

"Be more dramatic," said Liam with an eye roll. He sat on the other side of my father looking like a pale reflection of Gabriel's ethereal features. It was distinctly odd to see the two of them sitting side by side: one fresh-faced and vital with the rough imperfections of mortality blurring the sharpness of his good looks into easy approachability, the other painfully perfect in every angle and line yet ancient and haunted in the recesses of his eyes.

"She's actually not exaggerating," Gloria said as she materialized with a gentle swirl of golden light. She made the teleport look completely casual—like breathing. Even my father's show of strength hadn't felt so effortless. "The vault is where we keep the original DNA samples from Earth. While we have many samples in other research facilities, it would be difficult to replace everything in the vault." She gave the researcher a small smile. "However, I doubt the seal has been breached by a little water. It survived the voyage on the *Inspiration* and was designed to deal with anything from the vacuum of space to a high-velocity plunge from orbit into an unfamiliar landscape. Besides, D'nay services it on a pretty regular basis to make sure the sealing mechanisms are in working order. Last I checked, our little ark was perfectly impenetrable."

"I'm glad to hear it," the dainty woman said, sounding slightly mollified. Ducking her head, she went back to the kitchen to put her dishes in the sink. The other two researchers followed her lead, leaving the far side of the table vacant.

Gloria sighed and claimed one of their empty seats. Jessie came over, balancing a large bowl of pasta and a tall glass of the sweet fruit juice my grandmother preferred.

"Where's Grandfather?" Jessie asked as she laid the plate down.

"D'nay's still dealing with the rescue teams sweeping the residential districts." Gloria rubbed one eye with the heel of her hand. "I'm heading back to the hospital after a short break, myself."

"Well, make sure you bring him some food." Jessie gave Gloria's shoulder a motherly pat.

"Come, sit." Gloria turned to Jessie and put a hand over hers. "You've been moving all day, too, I'm sure. The nurturers are always the ones who forget to care for themselves. Believe me, I should know!"

With a small laugh, Jessie took the seat next to Gloria and accepted another glass of fruit juice that her ancestress teleported onto the table for her.

"Thank you," Jessie said, taking a long drink. "Ah, yes. That does set one back to rights, doesn't it?"

"Eat something with it, or you'll just sugar crash again in an hour or two," Gloria advised, gesturing to a plate of steaming food that had appeared out of thin air right in front of Jessie. Once the empath seemed satisfactorily engrossed in her meal, Gloria turned to Gabriel. "So what is this I hear about you and Lillian having another public spat?"

Dad shrugged and finished the last of his bread. "I was just trying to get everything accomplished in a timely manner. Lilly was the one who refused to merge and slowed everything to a crawl."

Gloria groaned. "And you had to let her know how annoying and asinine she was being all day, didn't you." It was more of a statement than a question.

"I wasn't rude." Gabriel's quiet voice maintained an excellent air of mild offense. "I simply stated the facts."

"Over and over again ad nauseam, I'm sure." Gloria's expression was thin lipped. "Honestly, this is why you have a reputation for being hard to work with, you know."

"It wasn't my fault," Dad insisted, standing and picking up his plate. "I just wanted to do things quickly and efficiently. Not that there was any reason to hurry. No swamped dwellings or ruined buildings or children of mine putting themselves in danger when they should have been at home."

I focused on my plate of pasta, but I could feel his glare heating my face up to a brilliant red anyway. When no one rose to his barbed remark, my father concluded his rant.

"Nah, no reason for me to want things done fast and safe," he growled. "No reason at all."

With a little more energy than he really needed, my father set his dishes in the sink and came back to his chair. I was still avoiding his eye, but the sound of his movements remained fierce and defiant when he sat back down.

"Gabe," Gloria said, looking as if she was developing a headache. "Gracie and James were only trying to help. And from what D'nay said earlier, they have been quite useful to the evacuation efforts today."

Out of the corner of my eye, I saw Dad lean in across the table. "If I had pulled that stunt at her age, you would have had me running supply drones for a month!"

Gloria spread her hands. "I'm not saying there shouldn't be consequences for taking the *Hawk* without permission. You have every right to discipline them when you get back to Angelus Quietum. But before you do, may I also point out that at her age, we would have told you to teleport over to help us in an emergency, not expected you to hide at home when you could be saving lives."

I dared a glance at my father's face. His cheeks had little patches of red in the center of them and I could almost see the blue flames licking in his eyes. I ducked away.

"Oh, so what you're saying is it's my fault for wanting to keep my daughter safe," Dad's voice was softer but no less angry. Bad sign.

"I didn't say that," Gloria sounded frustrated too, but Gabriel cut her off.

"You didn't have to! Everything is my goddamn fault!" His fist hit the table. James and I jumped. "That's been the theme of the last ten years! And you know that the worst part is? I've sat around and taken it because I figured I deserved it. For a whole decade, I bowed and I scraped. I let people get away with more than I ought to appease tempers and I minded my own business instead of getting involved in politics. I've done everything you've asked and more, but it doesn't make a lick of difference. No one listens to what I have to say, even when I'm trying to save their own precious University!"

I could feel the strength of his mind pulling little currents of air around the corners of the room. All conversation in the living and dining rooms had stopped and there were about twenty pairs of eyes staring in his direction. I had a bad feeling about where this was heading.

"Okay, I get your point." Gloria sounded smooth and re-assuring. I wondered if she was projecting calm in his di-rection, too. If I was an empath, I would have been. "We've all had a long and frustrating day. Why don't you go home, get some rest, and worry about the blame in the morning? After all, everyone will have lots of time to discuss it while we rebuild Landing."

Gabriel opened his mouth to add something heated, but a quick glance at the near-silent rooms made him pause. He took a deliberate breath, cleared his throat, and took a sip of water from his glass.

"Yes, well, I suppose we're all tired," he agreed more calmly.

"I'm almost done," James said, seeming chastened that he wasn't finished eating yet. He was still figuring out the whole spoon-and-fork combination for the spaghetti and it was taking him longer than the rest of us.

"Take your time," Dad said, waving a hand and planting his elbows on the table. "Mom is just reminding me that I have an audience. As she should," he inclined his head to her. Then he caught my eye and his expression softened. "And you're not completely wrong about the kids. I know they were only trying to help. And I suppose it's a possibil-ity that my daughter isn't six anymore."

"Oh my, you finally noticed." Grandma Gloria chuckled and gave us a smile that made her look far older than I was used to. For a moment, I could even believe she was older than my world-weary father. Then the look passed and she leaned over her meal with a good appetite.

The quiet murmur of voices began to come up around us again as interrupted conversations restarted. I discovered that the muscles between my shoulders had developed a tight knot. I deliberately relaxed them as I stood and took my own dishes to the sink. As I came back to my seat, Dad reached up and touched my arm. I glanced down at him and saw a small smile on his face. My neck and shoulders relaxed the rest of the way as I returned his affectionate expression.

"So where are all these people going to sleep?" Gabriel asked as I sat down.

"Here, I suppose," Gloria sighed, looking even more tired. "Though, I have to be back to the hospital soon."

"I don't mind supervising," Jessie offered, finishing up her plate of pasta. "Really. I enjoy being in the center of things. You know that."

"You're an absolute wonder," my grandmother told her. "Gracie, have you met Jessie before?"

I shook my head. "No, but she's been amazing today. I have no idea where she got so many blankets or tea mugs."

"The Usuriel clan is never without disaster supplies. Fate knows we need them often enough." Jessie stood with a small laugh and a cheeky wink at my father.

Gabriel groaned but even he couldn't resist a smile at her gentle teasing. "At least I'm not the disaster this time," he chuckled, "nor did I end up in the hospital for a week. So that's probably a good sign."

"Thank Fate," Gloria raised her water glass as if to toast his good health. "Let's keep it that way for another decade!"

"I will do my best," Dad offered a little mock bow in her direction. That playful gleam in his eye said he was getting over his attack of wounded pride.

"I think that's what she's worried about," Jessie said over her shoulder as she cleared away her dishes. I was unsurprised when she didn't come back, instead supervising the clean-up at the children's table.

"I don't remember her being that sassy as a child," Gabriel mused as he watched Jessie collect plates and begin herding young Usuriels back up to the playroom.

"She was," Gloria murmured, resting her chin on her hand. "You just weren't paying much attention to the little ones at that point. She was born right around..." Her voice trailed off and she caught herself, her expression closing down as if she'd almost said something too painful to put into words.

"Ah... yes... I suppose she was," my father agreed, the years slamming down on his head again. My hope of the night not ending in another empty liquor bottle went up in smoke.

"Do the two of you ever finish a sentence?" I asked, the relief of not getting the full brunt of my father's temper loosening my tongue. "Or talk about things that the rest of us can understand? I mean, honestly, you've spent the last half hour alluding to incidents that happened before James and I were born. I doubt etiquette writers put together the rules of conversation with immortals in mind, but if they had I think they would consider the two of you incredibly rude."

Gloria and Gabriel turned to look at me as if I'd sprouted another head. Then they burst out laughing. It was a good, healthy, wholesome sound and for all my irritation, I couldn't be mad in the face of their genuine mirth.

"Oh, sweetheart," Dad said, wiping away a tear as he gave me a one-armed hug. "No, I suppose none of our discussions make much sense to you, do they? I'm sorry. You're right. We get so bogged down in things that happened long ago... what do they really matter? Right here, right now, we're together. We've shared a meal and some good company and all we can do is lick old wounds."

"So true," Gloria said cheerfully. "The curse of a long life is that we're always dwelling on the pain of yesterday when we should be counting today's blessings. I, for one, would say that if we must have a natural disaster, this one appears to be less damaging than most. We only have two or three serious injuries in the hospital. Everything else is superficial. I'm sure the clean-up will be expensive but I'd rather pay in money than lives."

"And even if it was inefficient, Lillian and I did manage to work together without killing each other," my father allowed, giving my shoulders a squeeze. "And you and James did some good work with the *Hawk* without wrecking it or getting yourselves killed. You're absolutely right. I need to think about the here and now, not keep dwelling on the past. That's why I need you around, kiddo. You keep me grounded."

EPILOGUE

SHALL WE DANCE?

The next two weeks were spent helping with the clean-up effort in Landing. I found myself impressed with my father's seemingly-inexhaustible mental strength. He alone did more heavy lifting than all the three-T's over five-gens combined. Lillian and Vanessa did their fair share, I'm sure, but I didn't see as much of them since I typically was assigned to whatever reconstruction team my father was leading.

The example that always comes to mind for me is the day we found a house that had been swept by the flood waters right off of its foundation. It had been tossed like so much kindling into another structure a few hundred yards away. The two hover cars, once sheltered in its garage, were lodged ten feet off the ground in the tangled branches of several large trees.

It took Liam, Oli, and Camphor—the younger three-T's that were with us—over an hour to disentangle and bring down the hover cars. In that same space of time, my father lifted the house back onto its foundation, albeit in pieces, and pushed the leaning frame of the other building back into its moorings. All the mortal crew had to do for the second structure was reinforce its frame and patch the hole in its side. I remember watching my sweating, exhausted cousins finally land the second hover car in the grass while Dad casually picked up a hammer to help the mortal crew do the framing. He hadn't even broken stride to catch his breath after doing six times the work of his descendants.

Dad, of course, enjoyed every minute of it. The shadows of his centuries seemed to lift from him and leave him as young and exuberant as a true twenty-five-year-old. When I say inexhaustible, I mean it. He worked hard from sun up to sun down and never once complained of an ache or pulled muscle. The rest of us were limping by day two but Gabriel had a spring in his step that defied all physical weariness. Looking back, I'd say he was in his element. His particular brand of strength was needed and appreciated. Even members of the Family who had given him a wide berth when we first joined the clean-up effort were smiling at him and patting him on the back after a long day's work. After watching him spend an entire morning hauling logs that had to weigh metric tons off of a farm house before raising the new frame for the building with nothing but his bare hands and force of will, I found myself thinking he might have earned that arrogant tilt his chin so often liked to adopt.

For my part, I was always willing to lend a hand where and when I could. I could wield a hammer as well as the next teenager. I could also provide light and warmth if such was needed on the work site. I was actually pleasantly surprised at the number of times my pyrokinetic skills seemed to come in handy. James also proved himself to be useful with the mortal crew, lending his young back and telepathic communication skills wherever they were requested.

I'd never been around so many people. The mortal crew was a bit shy around us at first, but James and I struck up conversations with each other and slowly they began to chime in. They were quite curious about life at Angelus Quietum and Terra Nova. I was the first to tell them Angelus Quietum was just another farm, which meant James got the majority of the questions. I was just fine with that. He seemed happy to enlighten our curious audience about the daily lives of Terrans.

As for me, no one was ever rude or unwelcoming. If anything, a few of them seemed to pity my lack of three-T status. Or perhaps it was my father's overwhelming shadow that made them give me sympathetic glances. Not being a telepath, it was impossible for me to know. But I did appreciate getting to spend more time with Liam, Leesil, Jessie, and the other Family members actively a part of the clean-up effort.

What James and I didn't get anymore was any kind of privacy. The first day, after spending ten hours hauling debris and hammering house frames, Dad teleported the three of us back to the shores of Lake Angelus. As James and I began staggering towards the house, Dad stopped us.

"Oh no, your day's not done." With a sharp gesture, he teleported a pitchfork and shovel into his hands and shoved them in our direction.

"Really?" I groaned, glaring at him with half-lidded eyes. "I just mucked out Aubrey and Charcoal's stalls this morning."

"And you'll do it again tonight," Dad said. "Along with all the other stalls."

"But..."

"Think about this the next time you decide to take a joyride in my shuttle."

I shut my mouth and took the pitchfork. James shouldered the shovel and followed me towards the stables.

That was Dad's final word on the matter and we didn't argue. Each day, after long hours of clearing, cleaning, and rebuilding, Dad would teleport us back to Angelus Quietum to take care of the chores. I quickly taught James how to care for the chickens and help me with the horses. We still rode Charcoal and Aubrie for an hour or so in the evening, but we were both so exhausted at that point that our focus was usually staying on the horses rather than making conversation. Every time we found a moment of quiet together, Dad would show up with a new chore one of us had to complete right then. By the time we had a chance to follow up on the interesting direction our relationship had taken the night before the flood, we were both too awkward to broach the subject.

Then, once the dust settled and downtown Landing was looking more like a market rather than a disaster zone again, the University held a big celebratory dinner at one of their newly-refurbished ballrooms. All the Family members and mortal construction crews came out to eat, dance, and enjoy the new friendships we'd made.

Before the dance, we gathered in Angelus Quietum's kitchen to await my father's teleport. James dressed up so nicely I had a hard time not staring at him. The young diplomat's hair had grown in a bit more and its straight, blond silk was beginning to fall into his eyes. He wasn't heavily muscled, but the last few weeks working outdoors had given his slim frame some well-earned definition. Despite being on the small side for a man, the modern cut of his tunic followed the compact lines of his torso in a way that made me blush. Where he'd gotten the new clothes I had no idea, but he saw my reaction and gave me a winning smile.

"I love your tunic," I told him.

"Your dress is lovely, too," he said, meeting my eye in a way that would have set my cheeks flaming if they hadn't already been pink.

I glanced down at my emerald green party dress. It came off of my shoulders to show off my collar bone—something I really liked about my looks despite the freckles that dotted them.

"Thanks," I said, giving the skirt a little twirl. I hoped it would give him the idea that dancing might be fun.

"Ready, you two?" Dad called from the doorway. I glanced up and the breath caught in my throat.

To say that Gabriel cleaned up nicely is to say that a diamond is a pretty rock. I knew, of course, that my father was extremely handsome; perhaps even one of the most handsome men on Cybele. There is a difference between knowing and understanding, however. Seeing him in a contemporary dress tunic the color of his eyes, his hair brushed loose and clean around his face, that perfect grace as he leaned against the doorway—I suddenly understood why women wrote sonnets about him. I glanced between him and James and realized once again what an unfair comparison it was. It might have been in that moment that I realized no man would ever live up to the standard of beauty I'd been raised with.

I made eye contact with my father and felt the pull of his perfect features. Then, deliberately and unflinchingly, I took James' hand. My chin lifted up into that arrogant tilt it had learned so naturally as I dared him to comment on it.

Gabriel didn't even blink. "You both look nice," was all he said as he stepped to our side and put a hand on each of our shoulders. Then, with a quick tuck and fold, we were at the dinner.

James and I held hands openly and no one commented when we were one of the first couples to dance after dinner.

"I've never done this in the flesh," James said shyly as he twirled me about the dance floor. I smiled at him and found myself much more focused on the way his youthful shoulders felt under my hand than any fancy dance moves.

"That's okay. It's not like I have much practice, either," I replied. "The closest I've come is probably martial arts with you and Dad."

"Really?" James seemed surprised. His hand tightened on the small of my back, pulling me closer against him. The feeling of our bodies pressed together tightened things in the pit of my stomach. "You're very good at it!"

I flushed. "Thanks," I said, looking away from him so that he wouldn't see my reaction. I caught a glimpse of Leesil and Liam cutting a fine figure across the other side of the dance floor. Clearly they had more practice than we did. Liam caught my eye and flashed me a cheeky wink. I smiled at him and leaned into James' shoulder. He was warm and slender and I couldn't think of a single place I'd rather be than in his arms.

As the night wore on, the atmosphere continued to be lighthearted and celebratory. Even Lillian and Dad managed to sit near each other at the table without quarreling. I tried to approach my sister once or twice but each time I would get close it seemed as if she were surrounded by other people. I was having too much fun dancing and flirting with James to care all that much, so I gave up without too much frustration.

"Come on, Gabe." Gloria was on her feet, a smile on her pixie face. "You can't sit there all night! Let's show these children what a real dance looks like!"

James and I were catching our breath nearby so we got a front row seat as Gloria led her slightly reluctant son onto the dance floor.

"It's been years," Dad protested, tucking an errant lock of wavy, dark hair behind one ear. Even so, he took his mother in his arms as naturally as breathing.

"Oh, I think you remember," she chided him. There was something sad in her eyes as she looked up into his face, yet something joyful, too. It was such an intense look that I found myself shying away from it, feeling as though I'd somehow intruded into her privacy just by witnessing it.

She was right, though. Dad remembered how to dance.

The two of them on the dance floor is not something I can easily describe. The other members of the Family made dancing into a graceful exercise. Certainly some of them were extremely good at it and could do very intricate moves. Gabriel and Gloria made them look clumsy by comparison. Where he moved, she followed as if drifting on an invisible cloud. Every movement was perfectly efficient and timed precisely to the beat of the music. I'd never seen my father dance before but I did know he used to teach it aboard the *Inspiration*. Finally, I understood why.

The rest of the guests paused what they were doing to gather around and watch. It wasn't a complicated dance; a few spins and dips but nothing acrobatic in the least. Still, it was so beyond graceful, so incredibly fluid and vital, that the two of them were absolutely hypnotic to watch.

"May I?" I glanced to my left in surprise and realized my grandfather was giving me a courtly bow and offering a graceful hand.

"Who, me?" I squeaked, taking another look at my father and grandmother. There was plenty of room on the dance floor, but they were the only couple on it. Everyone else had formed a circle to watch their elegant dance.

D'nay's handsome face split into an amused smile. "I promise to make it easy for you," he said. "I have some experience taking the lead."

I exchanged a half-terrified, half-excited look with James who gave me a helpless shrug. "Very well," I agreed against my better judgment.

I shouldn't have been nervous. My father had to learn to dance from someone and after allowing my grandfather to pull me onto the dance floor, I seriously suspected it was D'nay. He moved with confidence and easy grace. I quickly found the less I thought about what I was doing the more easily we glided across the floor.

Grandfather smiled down at me. "Well, you're not half bad at this," he teased gently.

I laughed and let myself relax a little bit more. Following the movement of his arms and shoulders was so instinctive it felt completely natural. Before I knew it, the two of us were gliding next to my father and Gloria.

My father's musical laugh slid over us and I saw his midnight eyes flash in our direction. Then, with an easy turn and twist that felt as if it had been practiced a thousand times, I found myself handed from one dark and handsome Usuriel man to another.

"Gracie!" Dad smiled down at me as my hand found his shoulder. His lead was no less effortless than his father's and I found myself grinning up at him.

The music slid seamlessly into a new song, this one with a little more of a defined tempo. Gabriel moved so smoothly from one rhythm to the next that I hardly noticed.

"I think Grandpa just wanted to steal Grandma back," I observed, glancing back at D'nay and Gloria as the sound of my grandmother's laughter rose above the music. She'd wrapped her arms around her husband's neck as he put her into an elegant dip. Then, as smoothly as if it were choreographed, she slid up from the dip, back into his arms and into an unashamedly passionate kiss. A few cheers and good-natured cat calls came from the audience as he lifted her into his arms and she wrapped both legs around his waist.

"Get a room!" Dad called over his shoulder at his parents, but there was a giddy smile on his face. I realized I hadn't seen him this happy in years; maybe ever. Perhaps whatever Ariel was planning wouldn't be necessary after all.

***

The night ended as blissfully as it had begun. After a song or two, Dad expertly landed me next to James who wisely did not try to follow the Usuriel men's performance but rather led me outside to sit on the step and get some air.

"Hard to believe I'll be living here in another week," James said, looking around at the elegant stone buildings of the University. I could still see where some of the flood waters had damaged and dirtied their facades. But fresh landscaping and the efforts of over two dozen Family and mortal workers had really brought the campus back to a sense of dignified academia.

"Has it been six months already?" I asked, feeling a sudden rush of panic. We'd been so busy with the repairs, I hadn't had the time to appreciate how close James' departure date was getting.

The wind ruffled James' hair and the soft purple of twilight painted his features with forgiving shadows. At that moment, I thought he was more handsome than my father on his best day.

"I'll miss you," he said softly, glancing in my direction. My chest tightened at the thought of him being farther away than the next bedroom over.

"Yeah." I could barely even get that much past the lump in my throat.

"The last six months have been..." he stalled out, hand squeezing mine as if he wanted to say more but didn't want it to be the wrong thing.

I wanted to ask him what would happen to us once he left. I wanted to ask how he felt about me. I wanted to beg him to stay and at the same time I wanted to beg him to take me with him. But all of those words seemed stuck like a physical presence behind my breast bone and, no matter how I tried, there was no way to dislodge them.

"It's been pretty great getting to know you," I said lamely.

"Yeah," he said with a smile. "I've been really lucky to have you and your dad to show me... you know... how things are done here in the Provinces."

"It was fun." I returned his smile because I couldn't help it. James always made me feel such a mixture of awkwardness and familiarity. It would have been infuriatingly contradictory if it hadn't been so pleasant. "Well, most of it was, anyway."

"There were a few rough moments," he admitted, leaning his shoulder against mine and giving me a gentle nudge. "But you got me through them. I don't think I would have survived your dad's lessons without you."

"Nah, I just watched mostly," I protested, nudging him back and making both of us laugh the way that lovesick idiots do. "But I am glad you came to stay with us."

"Me too," he said quietly.

We sat there, watching the stars slowly appear in the night sky while the sounds of the party spilled out from the ballroom behind us. We didn't move or talk for a long time, just clinging to each other's hands as if we were each afraid that the other would disappear if we let go.

ABOUT THE AUTHOR

 Abigail Silver grew up in Pennsylvania and currently lives near Charlotte, NC with her husband, son, and fur children. When she's not reading, writing, or drawing (which is rare), she enjoys blasting music with the windows down on long road trips.

ACKNOWLEDGMENTS

There is no witty or amusing way to say "thank you" a thousand times. And yet that is precisely what I must do here because I owe a thousand thank yous to the incredible people who have made this work possible.

First and always to my family, especially my parents and brother for being my first audience. You inspired my love of reading with countless hours of family read-alouds and book chats that lasted late into the night. My mother for her love of libraries and willingness to listen to long, rambling imaginings. My father for allowing me to destroy his comic collection and dog-ear the covers of his sci-fi novels. My brother for enlisting me in his burning passion for Harry Potter. Infinite thank yous for all of this and so much more.

And of course to my new family - the one I have built with my endlessly-patient husband and our beautiful little boy. Both of you have sacrificed time and affection to fictional characters. Our shared love of stories is one of the many things I cherish. I cannot thank you enough for the love and support you show me on a daily basis.

Then there is the family of writing. This is formed not by blood but by a shared bond with the written word. The first on this list must always be my editor, Harlow Kelly. She was one of the first readers of my work all the way back in our college years and she continues to be a constant source of inspiration and support. I am forever in her debt and incredibly grateful to call her friend.

The other betas and critique partners on this journey were no less critical. I could not have made this journey without them. J.A. Waters, Jordie Nichols, Jessica Ritchey, Jessica Blasko, Rachel Greene-Phillips, Theresa Gonzalez, Ann Darlington, George Beckman, Marisa S, Paula Braley, Rebecca Amiss, Ernie Fink, CD Storiz, and so many others. For those who were with me for one novel or many, for those of you who chatted about plot lines and characters in person or over the phone or in text messages, for those who only made it a little way into a piece before giving me critical feedback about why you chose not to go on, please know that all of you contributed to a better piece of writing. I owe you tremendous debts of gratitude.

To the teachers who have inspired my love of art and writing, I cannot be more grateful. Yours is a labor of love rarely repaid. This story and its illustrations wouldn't have been possible without all the hard work you poured into me all those years. I wish I had expressed more gratitude then. Know that it is absolutely felt, both then and now.

I would also like to acknowledge the source imagery for some of my illustrations. I started with very specific visions of many of these characters and scenes, but every good artist needs reference material to help that vision stay true to life. So thank you to Missy and Callie Wright, Tessa Davis (our child guest-artist for Chapter 5), Lee Davis (the typsetting miracle worker), Joe Garland (layout guru) and the following photographers on UnSplash.com: CHUTTERSNAP, The National Cancer Institute, Susan

Holt Simpson, Hristina Satalova, and Jonas Vaitkevicius. Also a posthumous thank you to Dante Gabriel Rossetti, whose work inspired both the cover art and the title of Book 3 in this trilogy.

And finally, to all the readers who have chosen to pick up this book and go on this crazy ride with Gracie, thank you. It is not money nor fame that makes a story great. It is the sharing between the author and the reader—a dream of places distant and magical that only exists because we will it to be.

With eternal gratitude,

Abigail Silver

Made in the USA
Columbia, SC
26 July 2021